ALSO BY OLIVIA DRAKE

THE UNLIKELY DUCHESSES
The Duke I Once Knew

THE CINDERELLA SISTERHOOD
The Scandalous Flirt
His Wicked Wish
Bella and the Beast
Abducted by a Prince
Stroke of Midnight
If the Slipper Fits

HEIRESS IN LONDON SERIES
Scandal of the Year
Never Trust a Rogue
Seducing the Heiress

FOREVER

My Duke

OLIVIA DRAKE

St. Martin's Paperbacks

This is a work of fiction. All of the characters, organizations, and events portrayed in this novel are either products of the author's imagination or are used fictitiously.

First published in the United States by St. Martin's Paperbacks, an imprint of St. Martin's Publishing Group.

FOREVER MY DUKE

Copyright © 2020 by Barbara Dawson Smith.

All rights reserved.

For information, address St. Martin's Publishing Group, 120 Broadway, New York, NY 10271.

www.stmartins.com

ISBN: 978-1-250-17439-0

Our books may be purchased in bulk for promotional, educational, or business use. Please contact your local bookseller or the Macmillan Corporate and Premium Sales Department at 1-800-221-7945, ext. 5442, or by email at MacmillanSpecialMarkets@macmillan.com.

Printed in the United States of America

St. Martin's Paperbacks edition / January 2020

10 9 8 7 6 5 4 3 2 1

Chapter 1

Hadrian Ames, the eighth Duke of Clayton, shut the door against the noise of the taproom. With a jaundiced eye, he surveyed the cramped confines of the private parlor. This delay had wreaked havoc with his schedule. He'd departed London at dawn in order to arrive in time to take dinner with the family of his prospective bride.

Instead, an ice storm had slowed his progress and forced him to stop overnight at this ramshackle inn. It would have been foolhardy to attempt the last dozen miles over the slippery hills of southern Warwickshire, drenching his postilions and outriders. Especially since the day had already been long with numerous changes of horses. The ping of freezing rain on the darkened windows of the parlor confirmed the necessity of the halt.

Hadrian stripped off his wet greatcoat and slung it onto a wall hook. Awaiting his supper, he sat down in a creaky, ladderback chair by the hearth. The air smelled musty and smoky. He stretched out his booted feet in hopes the meager blaze would thaw his chilly limbs.

To pass the time, he picked up a discarded newspaper from a table. The local journal was several weeks out-dated, but even old news interested him since he'd spent his boyhood in these parts. He was perusing a report on the previous year's corn yields when a knock sounded.

Before he could say *enter*, the door swung open. A prune-faced man garbed in funereal black stepped into the parlor, his sparse white hair combed over a balding skull. On one palm, he balanced a tray that held several covered dishes.

Hadrian peered over the newspaper. "Ah, Chumley. I trust you've brought my coffee."

"There is none to be had in this inferior establishment, Your Grace. So, I took it upon myself to substitute a pitcher of hot mulled wine. It was prepared by my own hands, for the kitchen here is shockingly inadequate."

"Don't tell me you ruined one of the bottles of burgundy that I brought from my cellar."

"It was necessary for medicinal purposes," the valet said as he set down the tray. "Your Grace mustn't risk catching cold in such foul weather. It only goes to prove one ought never to venture north before Eastertide."

The peevish tone rolled off Hadrian's back. Chumley had been in a snit ever since learning the purpose of this journey. In fact, Hadrian had a wry suspicion that the servant had doctored the wine in protest. But he made allowances for the man, who had been with the family since before Hadrian was born, having first served his sire, then Hadrian himself when he'd ascended to the dukedom as a lad of five. The old retainer wasn't likely to change his fussbudget nature at this late date.

He accepted a goblet of mulled wine and gamely endured the herbal taste. "It's the second week of March. No one could have predicted an ice storm."

Chumley sniffed in lieu of a reply. He unfolded a length of white linen and draped it over the scarred wood table. The valet always packed items for unforeseen stops like this one, though apparently he'd neglected to bring coffee. With finicky precision, he laid out serviette and silver utensils, then uncovered several dishes, arranging them atop the tablecloth.

"Appalling!" he muttered.

"What is it now?" Hadrian said, looking up from his paper.

"The innkeeper's wife had nary a roasted chicken nor even a beefsteak to offer. In all my years, I've never had to serve the Duke of Clayton slops fit for a pig's trough."

Allured by a delectable aroma, Hadrian arose to take his seat at the table. He glanced down at the bowl containing chunks of potatoes and meat in thick brown gravy. The fragrant wisps of steam made his stomach growl. "They must be pampered pigs," he jested.

"Bah, this is hardly the sort of inn suitable to one of Your Grace's stature. The servants here are slipshod, and the other guests might charitably be described as riffraff. Had you seen fit to heed the duchess's wishes and remain in London—"

"My mother had no say in the matter."

"One cannot dispute Your Grace's authority as head of the family. Yet if I may be permitted to point out, the duchess only desires what is best for you."

Sampling the tasty mutton stew, Hadrian reflected that his mother's idea of *best* was derived from the silly romantic novels that she liked to read. She had reacted to the news of his marriage plans with pouting and pleading, accusing him of scorning love, of being cold-blooded like his father, and had even lapsed into a bout of weeping. The tears had almost been his undoing. He'd disliked having to wound her tender heart. But it had been necessary to speak firmly in order to convince her that his decision to wed Lady Ellen was final.

Now, though, it seemed she had gone behind his back to recruit Chumley as her advocate.

The hot savory meal put Hadrian into a mellower mood. Eyeing the valet's puckered brow, he said, "Speak up, man. Vent your spleen and be done with it. I won't have you suffering a bout of dyspepsia on my account."

Chumley huffed out a breath. "It is merely that I find myself in agreement with the duchess. She believes Your Grace needn't feel bound by that long-ago contract between your father and his cousin, Lord Godwin. Dynastic marriages may have once been common practice, but they are not in vogue in these modern times."

"They are far more practical, though. It saves a man the trouble of wading through a sea of matchmaking mamas and their simpering daughters."

The old retainer dolefully shook his head as he set out a plate of bread and cheese. "Be that as it may, the betrothal plan was agreed upon when you and Lord Godwin's eldest daughter were mere babes in arms. When Lady Audrey eloped with that preacher a decade ago and fled the country, it nullified any obligation on your part."

Hadrian had suffered no regrets over the loss of a marriage to his second cousin, Audrey. Though pretty, she'd been sober-minded, her nose either in a prayer book or in his face, scolding him for his lack of spiritual pursuits. At least she'd never known of the discreet liaisons that had occupied his time when he wasn't studying at Oxford. At eighteen, he had not been ready to don the leg shackle.

Now was another matter. He had sown his wild oats and had gained the maturity to settle down.

Hadrian tore off a hunk of bread and buttered it. "One would think you'd be pleased that I would honor my father's wishes. Anyway, it's time I set up my nursery, and Lady Ellen will suffice to be my wife as much as any other well-bred girl."

"Then there was no need for this long journey," Chumley said mulishly. "Lord and Lady Godwin will be bringing their daughter to London for the season. There will be time aplenty to court her."

"Ah, but it's better for the courtship to take place away from the prying eyes of gossips. Having never been in society, Lady Ellen may feel nervous—especially as we've not seen one another since she was twelve."

The valet refilled Hadrian's goblet. "Your mother fears the girl still has chalk dust from the schoolroom on her fingers. She can hardly be prepared to step straight into the role of duchess."

"Mama wed at eighteen, the same age as Lady Ellen."

"Dare I suggest that is precisely why she would counsel Your Grace against the marriage . . . among other considerations?"

Wiping his mouth with the serviette, Hadrian aimed a shrewd glance up at the valet, who stood rigidly at attention before the table. "Ah, we arrive at the crux of the matter. Mama objects not to the age of my bride, but to Lady Ellen's father. She still harbors a grudge against Cousin Godwin."

"Can you blame Her Grace? She lost not only her husband but you, as well. At the tender age of five, you were torn from her loving embrace and given over to the guardianship of Lord Godwin. You spent your childhood exiled halfway across the country."

"Ninety-four miles is hardly the ends of the earth. And I did visit her twice a year."

For a week at Easter and one in August, Lord Godwin had permitted Chumley to escort Hadrian to London to see his mother. His fond memories of those times included many childish delights: outings to the circus, boat rides on the Thames, visits to the menagerie of lions and bears at the Tower. She had lavished toys and books and other gifts on him, too, so many that upon his return, Hadrian was allowed to keep only one item. The rest was donated to charity, for Godwin believed in the virtues of austerity and thrift.

Hadrian often had chafed against that strictness, though now he could appreciate the value of his stern upbringing. While other noblemen were losing fortunes at cards or fighting duels, he had acquired a reputation for cool deliberation. Accruing wealth meant more to him than frittering it away.

"Had I remained in my mother's care," Hadrian went on, "she would have coddled me, as she did Lady Elizabeth. I'd have grown up to be an indolent fribble, lacking any knowledge of how to manage my estates. Now, don't look daggers at me, Chumley. You know as well as I that my sister is just as much a rattlebrain as my mother."

"Rather, it seems that Your Grace would do well to heed the voice of experience. The duchess knows the difficulties of being a naïve young lady forced into a marriage arranged by her father."

"You are mistaken to presume that Lord Godwin has *forced* his daughter," Hadrian said rather testily. "I grew up in his household. Lady Ellen may have been ten years my junior, but she knows I'm no villain."

"Nearly a dozen years, and she was only a child when you reached your majority and moved away."

"Yes, well, I've seen her a time or two since then. Enough to assure me she possesses all of the qualities that I require."

The valet fixed him with a doubtful stare. "*All*, Your Grace? Dare I say the duchess would prefer that love be your primary criterion. She believes that a strong bond of affection is vital for marital happiness—"

"Enough! It isn't my mother's choice to make—nor is

it yours." Having had his fill of the pointless conversation, Hadrian frowned up at the servant. "In time, she'll see this is for the best. As will you. Now, I'm sure you've duties to attend to."

"Yes, Your Grace."

Chumley pursed his withered lips and bowed, then took Hadrian's greatcoat from the wall hook. As the man shuffled out of the parlor, the door closing behind him, he didn't appear so much peeved as troubled.

That look of concern on the servant's face irked Hadrian. Why the devil did Chumley and the duchess think he would be swayed by their arguments? Marriage for a man of his stature was a grand alliance, not a fantasy out of the pages of a lady's novel.

Love! What balderdash!

He assuaged his irritation by listing his standards for the ideal wife. She must be attractive, of course, and a blueblood of impeccable background. A modest young lady who wasn't overly chatty. He had no intention of wedding a sharp-tongued shrew.

Lady Ellen appeared to perfectly suit his requirements. This journey would enable him to confirm that presumption before the start of the season. He was glad Lord Godwin had written to him and suggested the visit.

Hadrian finished his dinner, content to be alone with the snapping of the fire and the hissing of sleet against the window. He was looking forward to his nuptials. For years, he had been hunted as society's biggest matrimonial prize. At balls and routs and parties, he was pursued by flocks of females who thought to win his heart with their inane coquetry. It had become tiresome to ward off all the eager debutantes who hoped to become the Duchess of Clayton.

Although he relished the sort of flirtation that would gain him entry to a beautiful woman's bedchamber, he found society ladies in general to be shallow creatures who could speak only of fashion and gossip. That was why he had made up his mind to marry and be done with it. There was no point in holding out for a paragon who didn't exist. Then, once the ring was on his finger, he would be free of the ambitious mamas who steered their insipid daughters into his path.

Satisfied with the plan, Hadrian returned his attention to the newspaper. He was deep into a piece about the training of the local militia when the rattling of the doorknob disturbed his concentration.

"Back so soon, Chumley? I'm in no humor for—"

He glanced up and stopped in mid-sentence. A young boy of perhaps five or six years darted into the room and shut the door. Garbed in homespun shirt and trousers, he had a thatch of messy, straw-colored hair and a smudge of dirt on one freckled cheek. A slingshot dangled from the pocket of his pants.

His blue eyes fastened on Hadrian at the table. "Hallo, mister."

Hadrian cocked an eyebrow. Judging by the rough quality of the clothing, the lad appeared to belong to one of the servants. "You aren't allowed in here," he said, not ungently. "This is a private parlor."

"Aw, I won't bother you, promise I won't! I only need somewhere to hide."

Without invitation, the lad commenced to prowling around the small room, looking for a suitable spot. The sparse furnishings offered no convenient draperies to slip behind or chest in which to conceal himself. He made a complete circuit and then ended up by the table, eyeing it speculatively.

All of a sudden, he flashed a triumphant grin and ducked underneath the cloth to crouch at Hadrian's feet.

"Ahoy, mate!" came his muffled voice. "This is the best spot ever!"

What the devil—?

Flummoxed, Hadrian dropped his newspaper. He was accustomed to being obeyed. Instead, the urchin was huddled against his leg, no doubt leaving dirty pawprints on his polished Hessian boots.

He snatched up the edge of the cloth to frown at the boy. It was tight quarters under the small table, and the long drape of linen formed a tent that reached almost to the floor. From out of nowhere, a snippet of memory flitted through his mind of himself at that age hiding from his nurse.

An unexpected twist of humor stirred in Hadrian. But it wouldn't do to chuckle when he needed to maintain authority. Summoning a stern tone, he stated, "You cannot be playing games in here. Now, run along."

That freckled face held a look of tragic entreaty. "But it's hide-and-seek. She'll never find me here."

"Who? I won't have a throng of children dashing hither and yon."

"That won't happen, mister, I promise you!" He sketched an *X* over his scrawny chest. "Cross my heart and hope to die!"

"Don't be absurd." Though amused by the boy's earnestness, Hadrian spoke firmly. "Now, this is my final warning. If you don't leave of your own accord, I'll be forced to—"

A tapping sounded on the door. Hadrian glanced up at the disturbance, then looked back down at the brat. His eyes had widened and his sturdy form quivered. He scrunched himself up into the smallest possible ball.

"Please, you mustn't give me away! It's only for a minute. Now, *shh*."

Reaching up, the boy tugged the tablecloth back down to conceal himself. Hadrian was tempted to haul him out by his ear and frog-march him out of the room. But it was too late, for the door was already opening. A woman stepped into the parlor.

His heart rocked in his chest. The world faded as he stared at the vision standing before him.

Pretty seemed too tame a word to describe her. Appearing to be in her mid-twenties, she had a frank gaze and an aura of distinction that set her apart from the ladies of his acquaintance. She was tall and willowy, her chin held high, as if to take pride in her height. In the glow of the firelight, several curls of dark sable hair had escaped her chignon to frame her face with its pert nose and rosy lips. Her skin had a healthy glow as if she'd spent a good deal of time outdoors without a parasol. The cinnamon-hued gown with its long sleeves and plain scoop neckline would be considered pitifully drab by London standards, yet it skimmed her feminine curves in a way that lent her a natural flair.

Hadrian tried to put his finger on precisely why she fascinated him. He had seen plenty of other lovely women over the years, but none of those others had affected him on quite such a visceral level. Perhaps it was her eyes. They were a deep, vibrant green that lit up like sunlight on emeralds when she smiled.

As she did now. "Pardon me for intruding, sir. I'm looking for a little boy."

Her melodious voice held a faintly foreign flavor which he tried to place. Not Welsh or Irish or Scottish or even Cornish. It was as mysterious and appealing as the woman herself.

As she gazed inquiringly at him, Hadrian realized he was still sitting and gawking like a dolt. He shot to his feet. If that scruffy imp belonged to her, he could not imagine she was one of the upper ten thousand, yet he felt compelled to show her the respect afforded a lady.

He bowed. "Ma'am."

She gave him a distracted look and then ventured closer, gazing around the small parlor. "Leo? I know you're in here. I saw you go through this door when I was coming down the stairs."

Hadrian held an inward debate. As much as he admired this splendid creature, he had a gentleman's distaste for tattling. It was an unwritten rule that males did not betray one another's secrets. Especially not to the female of the species.

Or did that honor exclude disobedient cubs like Leo?

Fortunately the dilemma was resolved without any duplicity on his part. With a small cry, she sprang forward and lifted the edge of the tablecloth to peer underneath it.

"There you are, you naughty child!" she said on a trill of laughter. "That's quite the clever hiding spot."

"It wasn't very clever since you found me," Leo griped.

"Well, come out of there at once," she said, watching as he scrambled to his feet. "And next time, mind that your toes don't stick out. Now, pray make your apologies to the gentleman for disturbing his dinner."

"Sorry, mister."

"There's no harm done," Hadrian said, forgetting that he'd chastised the lad for that very thing only moments ago.

"Sometimes Leo doesn't stop to think about his actions," the woman said ruefully. "It is a trait we are working on modifying. In the meantime, I must thank you, sir, for being so understanding."

Her mouth curved in that appealing smile, she leaned over the table and extended her hand to Hadrian.

Startled, he realized that she meant for him to shake

it as a gentleman would do to his equal. Not even the grandest grande dame of society would commit such a *faux pas* with a man of his rank. A lady might offer the back of a gloved hand to be kissed, but only after having curtsied to him. Nevertheless, he found himself clasping her hand, keenly conscious of the warmth of her slim fingers.

"It was my pleasure," he murmured.

The feel of her bare silken skin heightened the intensity of her effect on him. He felt as giddy as a schoolboy meeting his first pretty girl. It made no sense, for he prided himself on being a man in firm control of his emotions and somewhat jaded by the allures of the fairer sex.

She must have sensed his reaction, for her gaze widened slightly and a rosy blush tinted her cheeks. Her expression held a frank curiosity about him, as if she, too, were puzzled by the unseen energy of attraction. As they stared at each other for timeless moments, Hadrian felt as if he were drowning in those gorgeous eyes. He had the strongest urge to reach out and unpin her hair, to see those sable tresses tumble around her shoulders and bosom.

It was only when she gave a tug that he realized he was still gripping her hand. He loosened his hold, and she stepped back, the sparkle of warmth on her features dimming to a mask of politeness. She lowered her gaze to the boy, who had wandered to the hearth and picked up a stick of kindling to poke at the fire.

"Put that away, Leo, and come along. Your bath is growing cold."

He abandoned the stick, but dug in his heels. "Don't want no bath."

"Proper grammar, please. And the bath is necessary, for tomorrow you are to meet your grandfather." She took hold of Leo's hand and guided him away, pausing only to toss a quick, heart-stopping smile over her shoulder. "Good evening, sir. Do pardon us again for the intrusion."

A moment later, they disappeared out into the corridor and shut the door. The muffled grumble of Leo's protests gradually died away.

It took a moment for Hadrian to feel like himself again. A trace of her alluring feminine scent lingered in the air. Now that she was gone, it seemed ludicrous that a stranger could affect his equilibrium to such a degree.

Her poised manner did not fit the lower orders, so he had been wrong about the boy being the offspring of servants. Rather, she must be an overnight lodger here, another traveler stranded by the freezing rain. He hadn't noticed a wedding ring, yet it seemed reasonable to assume that a husband awaited her upstairs.

Logic dispelled the remainder of Hadrian's undue reaction. She was the very opposite of his preferences, for he liked women who were dainty and sophisticated. Her appeal perhaps could be explained away by the fact that he'd discharged his latest mistress a fortnight ago and had been on the lookout for another to catch his interest. But he strictly confined his liaisons to willing widows and discreet courtesans.

Not mothers with young children.

He resumed his seat at the table and took up his newspaper, though the printed words failed to hold his attention. Instead, he frowned into the dying flames of the fire while his mind continued to mull over the intriguing encounter. Despite the faint accent, she had a refined mode of speech, possessed a natural grace, and displayed a charming blush.

Yet the handshake was curious behavior, indeed. She was clearly a rustic who was unfamiliar with the protocol of curtsying to a gentleman. Even if she was unaware that he was the Duke of Clayton, she ought to have recognized him as a man of consequence. He wasn't offended, only baffled as to what it might reveal about her background.

Devil take it. She would have to remain a mystery. Tomorrow, they'd each set forth to different destinations, never to cross paths again. He wouldn't waste another thought on a fleeting encounter with a nameless beauty.

Especially not when he was on his way to acquire the perfect bride.

Chapter 2

The following morning, Natalie Fanshawe was busy preparing for their departure when Leo vanished from the
tiny room under the eaves. One minute he was there,
playing on the floor with his miniature sailing ship, and
the next, he was gone.

Or perhaps more than a minute had passed. How long
had she been woolgathering?

Having discovered a dab of blackberry jam on his best
shirt, she had been scrubbing at it by the early morning
sunlight from the single window. Leo must look tidy
when they arrived at his grandfather's house today, for
so much depended upon this meeting. Although she
had sent a letter ahead—two letters, counting the one
posted last summer—Natalie could not be certain what
reception awaited them. Nor had she felt it wise to wait
months for a reply, for mail across the Atlantic was
slow and fraught with peril, despite the recent ending of
America's second war with England.

Now, the door stood open a crack.

Abandoning her task, she glanced out into the narrow
corridor. There was no sign of Leo. The aromas of bak-
ing bread and frying onions drifted from somewhere

downstairs, making her wonder if he had gone down to breakfast without her. It would be just like the little rascal to do so. He had an independent streak that alternately amused and frustrated her.

Natalie went back into the room to fetch a warm shawl. She scolded herself for not keeping a closer watch on him. He was her charge, the sole reason she had made the six-week journey across the ocean. She oughtn't have let herself dwell upon a stranger whose name she did not even know.

Ever since encountering that gentleman the previous evening, she had been preoccupied with the memory of his intent gray eyes and the firm clasp of his fingers. It was ludicrous, really, for he was too polished and proud for her taste, like the haughty British aristocrats that she'd heard tales about in her youth. Regardless, his masculine presence had caused a melting sensation deep in her bones. She'd scarcely been able to draw a breath while the warmth of his skin had been pressed to hers.

Why, oh why, had she unthinkingly offered him her hand?

His raised eyebrow had made it clear that she'd broken some silly rule of etiquette. She must keep in mind that things here were different than in America. Her late father as well as her friend Audrey often had decried the caste system in England, where a person's station in life was determined by his or her birth.

Who was the man, anyway?

Someone of consequence, no doubt, judging by his exquisitely tailored attire and superior manner. He likely had expected her to curtsy to him. Well, even if the proper decorum had been known to her, she still wouldn't have complied. She was *not* his inferior. A genteel handshake was perfectly proper in Pennsylvania, and that was that!

A rumble of laughter from downstairs yanked Natalie back to the present. She was doing it again, letting herself forget that her primary duty was Leo. It wasn't like her to be so distracted.

She closed the door and hurried down the narrow stairwell that led to the front of the inn. The taproom teemed with guests eating breakfast at planked wooden tables. A harried maidservant, her mobcap askew, rushed hither and yon delivering plates of food and refilling cups. The previous day's storm had filled the inn to the rafters, and Natalie counted herself lucky to have secured even an attic chamber.

She glanced around, but Leo's towheaded form was nowhere in sight. Could he have wandered into the private parlor for a second time? The possibility unsettled her. Though the opinion of a stranger oughtn't matter, she cringed nonetheless at the notion of being judged a slipshod guardian by those intense granite-gray eyes.

A few steps past the front desk took her to the private room. The door stood open, and the sight inside was measurably more serene than the noisy taproom. And glory be, her aristocratic nemesis wasn't present, after all. She saw only an elderly manservant in a neat black suit laying out gleaming silver on the white tablecloth.

"Good morning, sir. I hope I'm not disturbing you."

He looked up from his task, his face resembling a wrinkled prune. "This parlor is reserved. So if you've come to flap your eyelashes at His Grace, you'll be as disappointed as the last five twittering girls. I'll allow no one to disrupt his breakfast."

His Grace? In America, she'd only heard the appellation used to address an archbishop. Since she would bet her last penny that the toplofty gentleman of the previous evening was no religious cleric, perhaps the parlor was being used by a different guest today. Why that should disappoint her, she didn't care to examine.

"I'm looking for someone else." Walking forward, she twitched up the long linen cloth to peek under the table. She didn't know whether to be relieved or upset that Leo wasn't hiding there.

Where *was* he?

"See here, miss! You mustn't be touching His Grace's table."

"Forgive me. Have you perhaps seen a six-year-old boy with sandy hair?"

"If I had, I'd have sent the naughty child away. Begone with you, now!"

The peevish old gent came toward her, waving a linen napkin to shoo her out of the parlor. He looked so unreasonably sour that Natalie couldn't resist gliding to the doorway and then pivoting to flash him her most dazzling smile. "I'm sorry to have troubled you, sir. I hope you have a very pleasant day."

The door closed in her face. What a curmudgeon! It was just as well that Leo hadn't come here and encountered the snooty servant. But that still left her fretting about where the boy might be. She had to locate him before the mail coach arrived to carry them the remainder of their journey. Ever since the ship had landed at Southampton a few days ago, she had learned that the Royal Mail adhered to a very strict schedule and waited for no one.

A quick check of her pocket watch told her that not as much time had elapsed as she'd feared. She had over an hour in which to find Leo, eat breakfast, and convey their baggage downstairs. Still, she had come to learn that any activity involving a child tended to take longer than expected. And if they weren't ready to depart on time, they risked being stuck at this inn for another day.

Spurred into action, she spun around and ran smack into a solid wall.

A gasp choked her throat. In swift succession, she noted that the wall was actually a man's chest, that he was garbed in a fine blue coat and snowy cravat with a diamond stickpin, and that his clean male scent held a tantalizing familiarity.

Glancing up sharply, she realized that it was *him*. The gentleman from the previous evening.

He gripped her upper arms to hold her steady. Her own hands somehow had landed on his broad shoulders. Natalie had to tilt back her head slightly to look at him, an unusual circumstance since she matched the average man in height. Those eyes were even more spellbinding from up close. They were the gray of the stormy Atlantic in winter, though at the moment she detected a gleam of warmth in them.

His otherwise impassive face was a study in masculine angles, from the firm jaw and smooth-shaven cheeks to the dark eyebrows and rather haughty nose. He had toffee-brown hair, the strands as perfectly groomed as the rest of him. Crushed to him, she felt the strong beating of his heart against her bosom. The imprint of his tall muscled form and long legs pressed into her.

That melting sensation coursed through her again. It permeated the deepest parts of her body in a way that threatened to befuddle her brain. They stood as closely as lovers, a scandalous pose for a woman of six-and-twenty in the arms of an unknown man.

Natalie pulled free and retreated several steps. With luck, he wouldn't notice the flush in her cheeks. "I beg your pardon, sir! I was in a hurry and not watching where I was going. It's entirely my fault."

"Let me guess. Has Leo vanished again?"

The suggestion of a smile on his lips disarmed her. "Unfortunately so. I thought he might be hiding in the parlor, but he wasn't." She oughtn't tell her woes to a perfect stranger, but the confession tumbled out regardless. "I took my eyes off him upstairs for a few minutes, and when I turned back around, he was gone. I have to find him or we'll miss the mail coach."

"I see. Where is your husband? Can he not help you locate the boy?"

"Husband? Oh no, I'm not married, I . . ." Natalie paused, annoyed with herself for blurting out such personal information when she was traveling alone with a young child. The man was regarding her intently, and the last thing she needed was to be pestered by unwanted male attention. "I'm Leo's guardian. Now, if you'll excuse me, I must hurry."

She tried to slip past the man, but he stepped into her path. "Have you any idea as to where he might have gone?"

"Knowing Leo, he could be anywhere. But he hasn't eaten yet, so I'll start in the kitchen."

"Allow me to assist you."

The thought of being accompanied by this modish gentleman dismayed Natalie. He would only distract her when time was of the essence. "Thank you, but that won't be necessary," she said firmly. "I'm sure you're eager to be on your way this morning."

"I'm in no rush. You look around inside the inn, and I'll check the stables. Boys generally have an affinity for horses. We'll meet outside in ten minutes to compare notes."

He turned on his heel and strode away through the crowded taproom. A number of guests turned their heads to watch him, the buzz of conversation noticeably increasing. The younger women in particular gawked, and one stout maiden even jumped up to curtsy to him. He afforded her a polite nod before his broad-shouldered form disappeared out the door.

Natalie pursed her lips. He certainly had an air of authority that attracted attention. What a vexing man, to interfere as if *he* were the one in charge! Yet she had to concede it was obliging of him to search the stables. It wouldn't surprise her if Leo had slipped outside to watch the grooms at work. Back in America, the boy often could be found at the blacksmith's or the farrier's workshop.

She made haste down a cramped corridor to the tiny kitchen at the rear of the inn. The innkeeper's harried wife was alternately frying eggs, sautéing potatoes and onions, and shouting instructions at a half-grown girl who was toasting bread at the fireplace. The girl scuttled to lay out crockery plates on a table. Natalie had to wait until the woman was dishing out the hot food before questioning her about Leo.

"Nipped a link of sausage, I'll 'ave ye know," she said, pointing her spatula at Natalie. "Ye best keep a closer watch on the rascal!"

"Please add it to my account. Did you happen to see where he went?"

"'E run out the back door when I yelled at 'im. That one could use a good thrashing!"

Natalie murmured a quick apology and left the kitchen, heading in the direction that Leo had taken. Mercy, she should never have let him out of her sight! But at least she was on his trail now. With any luck, he soon would be safely back in her custody.

And this time, she would *not* take her eyes off him.

Pushing open the door, she stepped outside into the stable yard. The sleet storm of the previous day had given way to bright sunshine and the promise of fairer weather. Already the coating of ice on the roof and trees was melting, leaving the ground wet and muddy. Grooms were hitching horses to various carriages and wagons. From her stance by the inn, she did a visual survey of the area, but could not spot Leo anywhere.

A cold drip from the eaves landed on her cheek. Shivering, Natalie burrowed deeper into her shawl and debated whether or not to proceed to the stable. She didn't relish the notion of making her way through the lake of muck that had been churned up from the morning's activity. But could she really trust that fancy-pants gentleman to do a thorough search?

No.

She set forth, lifting her hem and staying at the edge of the yard where the ice-battered grass kept her half-boots relatively clean. Upon reaching the open double doors, she stepped inside and breathed in the familiar perfume of hay and horses. It took a moment for her eyes to adjust to the dimness. Several horses poked their heads out of the stalls to snuffle at her.

A man was descending a ladder off to her left. Her heart gave an involuntary leap as she recognized his tall, attractive form in the buff breeches and black boots. He jumped down from the second-to-last rung and dusted off his bare hands.

Unfortunately, he was alone.

She scurried to his side, saying without preamble, "The cook saw Leo heading out the back door a short while ago. But you didn't find him here?"

"No, and I've poked through every nook and cranny, including up in the loft." Brushing a few pieces of hay from his pristine coat, he added, "I questioned the grooms, too. None of them have seen the little brat."

Natalie bristled. "Leo isn't a brat! He's a very dear boy with a prodigious curiosity."

He cocked an eyebrow. "Whatever his personal proclivities, when he runs off without telling you, he becomes a brat."

"Well, then! Good day, sir. You needn't trouble yourself a moment longer on my behalf."

Incensed, she turned on her heel and charged out of the stable. The heat of her aggravation warded off the frosty nip in the air. Devil take that arrogant man! She hadn't asked for his assistance. He had bullied his way into her affairs without her consent. Let him go on his merry way.

If she felt a twinge of guilt at her harsh judgment, it quickly dissipated under the need to concentrate on her search. She was too anxious to waste time over trifles.

The inn was situated at the outskirts of a village. If Leo had gone exploring, then he couldn't have ventured very far in the twenty minutes or so that he'd been missing. Perhaps he'd taken a notion to look at the local shops.

Avoiding the muddy ruts down the center of the road, Natalie headed into the village. She hastened past a stone roundhouse and several thatch-roofed cottages, keeping her eyes peeled for his towheaded form. Smoke puffed from chimneys, but no one was outdoors in the damp morning chill, convenient to be asked if a little boy had passed by. She had reached the village green, where a flock of ducks huddled beside an ice-covered pond, when the scrape of footsteps came behind her.

"Miss!"

That male voice held a familiar ring of command. She turned in a swirl of skirts to see the stranger from the inn coming toward her, his strides long and swift. He had left without a hat, and the breeze stirred his light-brown hair into an attractive tousle. The autocratic fellow had no right to look so arrestingly handsome. What could he want now?

Hope sent her heart catapulting to her throat. She rushed to meet him halfway. "Did you find Leo, after all?"

He shook his head. "Regrettably not. I merely wanted to apologize for my rudeness. Pray forgive me for offending you."

Natalie regarded him with caution. Her anger, she knew, had been rooted in worry over the lost boy. It wasn't like her to lash out at someone who was trying to help, and in all fairness, she could not withhold clemency.

"Apology accepted," she said. "I suppose Leo *does* misbehave at times. It's just that I don't care to hear about it from a stranger."

"Then it seems introductions are in order if we are to work together to find him. Given the unusual circumstances, we shall disregard the rules of propriety. I am Clayton. And you?"

"Miss Fanshawe. Natalie Fanshawe. But you really needn't have followed me, Mr. Clayton. I'm quite capable of finding Leo on my own."

She started down the high street, though not before noticing Mr. Clayton had parted his lips as if to say something. He fell into step beside her, taking the outside even though it required him to tramp through the mud in his polished black boots. When he finally spoke, she had the strange sense that it wasn't what he'd first intended to say.

"I'd like to assist, if you'll allow me," he said. "I've already dispatched my groom to search the nearby woods. My footman is waiting at the inn with instructions to keep a watch over Leo in the event of his return."

The news gladdened Natalie, allowing her to disregard his peremptory manner. She flashed him a grateful smile. "Thank you, sir. That is one concern off my mind at least."

"I gather you think he might have come to explore the shops. But that doesn't appear to be the case."

The two of them glanced around the single street of the tiny village. The pitifully small number of establishments included a greengrocer, a cobbler, and a haberdashery, all of which were closed at this early hour. There was no sign of a naughty little boy with his nose pressed to a window.

"Might he have chased after a dog or a rabbit?" Mr. Clayton asked.

"Anything is possible." Her steps slowed as she peered down a deserted alley. "Oh, there are a dozen places where he might have gone! Back home, he was acquainted with everyone and they would bring him back whenever he wandered away. But no one here knows him."

"Never fear, he can't have gone far. What was he doing when last you saw him?"

"Playing with his toy sailing ship." Struck by an alarming thought, Natalie clapped her hand to her mouth. "I wonder . . ."

"Wonder what? Tell me."

"I wonder if he might have set out for Southampton. Yesterday evening at bedtime he said that he didn't wish to meet his grandfather today, and he begged me to take him back to the ship so that we could return to America."

"America?"

Preoccupied with the memory of Leo, she merely gave Mr. Clayton a nod. It had been heart-wrenching to see Leo's lower lip wobble, for he was normally a happy boy with a sunny disposition. She'd attributed his bout of melancholy to their being confined in a crowded coach for several days after having enjoyed long weeks of freedom aboard a ship. Then this morning he'd been unusually quiet, and she'd thought he only needed time to adjust to all the changes in his young life. Today, he would be thrust into yet another new situation when he'd scarcely recovered from the death of his parents the previous summer.

Certainty sank its talons into her. Yes, it was very plausible that he had decided to run away.

Mr. Clayton subjected her to a keen stare. "Southampton is more than a hundred miles away. He can't possibly think to walk so far."

"You don't know Leo." Shivering, she tightened her grip on the shawl. "He's only six and likely acted on a whim."

"Surely he wouldn't even know in which direction to head."

"Actually, there's an excellent chance that he would. He happens to be quite observant about his surroundings."

Fear squeezed her throat. Without thinking, she caught Mr. Clayton's arm and felt the firmness of his muscles beneath her fingers. "Leo is too innocent and trusting to know about the evils in the world. What if someone were to abduct him?"

Mr. Clayton gave her another of those intent looks, then briefly covered her hand with his, his ungloved skin warm and reassuring. "He can't have had much of a head start. Now, I don't suppose you would heed my suggestion to stay here, Miss Fanshawe. No? Then follow me if you like."

With that, he started at a swift pace down the road that led out of the village. Natalie dashed after him, determined to keep up even if it meant half running. But he had a distinctly longer stride, his legs unhampered by skirts and petticoats. As they left the hamlet behind, the gap between them widened and within minutes he had achieved a significant lead, appearing as small on the horizon as one of Leo's carved animals.

She soon grew warm from the hike over the rolling countryside. As she strove not to fall too far behind, the beauty of the scenery filled her senses. She passed a farm with fields plowed for planting, a meadow scattered with woolly sheep, and several stone cottages nestled in groves of barren trees. It was all so civilized compared to the wild frontier of America. If not for the dire circumstances, she'd have liked to wander down one of the lanes, listening to the birdsong and looking for signs of spring as she was wont to do at home.

Her attention was caught for a moment by the bucolic picture of a farmer letting cows out of a red barn, and when she looked ahead again, it was to realize that Mr. Clayton had halted in the distance. He was standing at the roadside, staring downward, his hands on his hips. Her eyes widened on the little figure in front of him.

"Leo!"

Lifting her skirts, Natalie flew toward the pair. Her half-boots churned up the sodden grass alongside the road. It seemed to take an hour to reach them, though it could only have been a minute or two. As she came to a halt, tears of relief and joy stung her eyes.

She bent down and hugged him, to assure herself of his well-being. "Leo, you naughty boy!" she said breathlessly. "I'm so glad that we found you!"

"The boy has something to say to you," Mr. Clayton observed. "Don't you, Leo?"

The toy ship tucked in the crook of his arm, Leo cast a cautious look up at the man towering over him. Then he shifted his attention to Natalie and shuffled his filthy shoes through the mud. "Sorry, Miss Fanshawe. I didn't mean to make you worry."

"And?" Mr. Clayton prompted.

Leo thought for a moment. "And it won't happen again. I won't never go anywhere without telling you. Gen-gentleman's promise."

Her heart squeezed. "I certainly hope so, for you frightened me half to death."

Heedless of the wet ground, she sank down on her heels and pulled him close again, reveling in the knowledge that he was safe in her arms. He was so sufficiently chastened that he didn't even grumble when she pressed a kiss to his brow or when she took out her handkerchief and wiped away a smudge of grease on his cheek, presumably from the sausage he'd nicked.

A pang struck her bosom. Leo was her last link to her best friend. In the final moments of her life, Audrey had begged Natalie to take the boy to his only remaining family in England. Natalie had agreed, even though everything in her had balked at the notion of making the long voyage to the country that she scorned. In the months since the death of his parents, Leo had become like a son to her. She dreaded to contemplate the inevitable moment when they would have to part forever. Since her own father was gone, Leo was all she had left in the world.

Yet she was bound by duty to give him up.

Swallowing hard, she arose and checked her watch again to see they had a mere half an hour to spare. She took Leo's small hand in hers. "Come, we must hurry, for there isn't much time until our departure."

As they started at a quick pace back toward the village, Mr. Clayton fell into step alongside them. She stole a glance at his finely chiseled features and felt ashamed to have initially refused his assistance. But though she owed him thanks, the words of gratitude stuck in her throat. He was gazing straight ahead as if he'd forgotten their presence. There was nothing in his cool, closed demeanor that encouraged conversation.

She talked to Leo instead. "What were you were thinking? It's a very long walk all the way to Southampton."

"I wanted to go back to the ship," he said rather dejectedly. "I liked it lots better there."

"But you haven't any money to pay for passage."

"Oh, I could be a cabin boy for the cap'n. I'd fetch his tea and polish his boots."

"I see," she said, smothering a smile. "That's very enterprising of you."

"What's enter . . . enterprising?"

"It means that you are strong and spirited and that you will grow up to become a very hardworking man someday."

Leo pretended to sail his toy ship in the air. "I'm going to be a sea captain and own the fastest ship in the whole world! Ships are much nicer than being squashed into coaches."

"Well, there won't be much more traveling, anyway. If all goes well, we should reach our destination today."

But all did not go well.

As they neared the outskirts of the village, the rumble of wheels and the pounding of hooves sounded behind them. Natalie drew Leo off to the side of the road, back onto the grassy verge, with Mr. Clayton joining them. Her gaze sharpened on the approaching vehicle.

Drawn by a team of four horses, the coach sped through the puddles in the road, sending out a spray of cold droplets as it barreled past them. But she scarcely noticed the mud that spattered her skirt. Her rounded eyes took in the distinctive maroon wheels and door, the curved body of the coach, and the guard in crimson greatcoat standing on duty at the rear.

She sucked in a breath. "Oh no! It's the Royal Mail."

Chapter 3

In a panic, Natalie picked up Leo and shoved him at Mr. Clayton. The startled look on his face made her aware she'd just assumed he'd be her ally. But any reluctance on his part couldn't be helped. "It'll be faster if you carry him. I'll run ahead to the inn. Hurry, there's no time to waste!"

She picked up her skirts and dashed down the narrow street. The distant blow of the horn announced the arrival of the mail coach. It would stop at the inn for only a scant few minutes; the post waited for no one. And she still had to fetch their belongings from the room and settle her bill. Why, oh, why had Leo chosen this morning to run away?

Hurtling past the shops, she tried to reassure herself that the mail was running ahead of schedule. That might buy her some time. With any luck, the driver would decide to make a longer stop to change horses, to use the facilities, or even to grab a quick bite to eat.

All was not yet lost.

But when she arrived panting at the inn, it was to see several passengers entering the coach and the guard shutting the door. She ran up to him just as he was jumping onto the running board at the rear.

"Wait, sir, I have a ticket. My little boy and I must be on this coach! If I might just fetch my bags—"

"Sorry, miss. We're full. Lots of stranded people, ye see."

As the whiskered guard tipped his tall hat to her, the driver sprung the horses. The Royal Mail coach took off with a drumming of hoofbeats and a clatter of wheels. In a matter of moments, the sleek black-and-maroon vehicle disappeared around a bend in the road.

Natalie stood staring after it, her mind awhirl. Now what was she to do? She had sufficient funds to spend an extra night here, but she needed to stick to a strict budget until her return voyage to America.

"Bad luck," Mr. Clayton said from behind her.

Turning to see him bend down to deposit Leo back on the ground, she seized the chance to vent her frustrations. "The mail came early! It wasn't supposed to arrive until nine o'clock." Reaching into the pocket of her gown, Natalie drew out the silver pocket watch that had once belonged to her father. "See, it's only eight forty-three!"

"Your watch appears to be slow."

"That can't be. It's always kept perfect time."

Mr. Clayton consulted his own watch, a fine gold filigreed specimen which he opened to display the face to her. The hands pointed to three minutes past nine. "This is the correct time. It's set in accordance with the Royal Observatory at Greenwich."

"But . . . I wind mine every night . . ."

Biting her lip, Natalie tried to ascertain if she had done so at bedtime the previous evening. With sinking awareness, she acknowledged having no such recollection. She had been preoccupied with getting Leo bathed and tucked in bed. Afterward, all she could remember was blowing out the candle and lying in the darkness, listening to the tapping of sleet against the window and trying to keep her thoughts from straying to a certain handsome stranger.

The very man who stood before her.

Natalie blew out a breath. "I suppose you're right. I must have forgotten, so I've only myself to blame—" She checked herself in mid-sentence, noticing for the first time the large smear of mud on the lower section of his otherwise pristine blue coat. "Oh no! That must be from Leo's shoes."

Mr. Clayton glanced down with a wry look. "So it would seem."

"Forgive me. I ought never to have required you to carry him. Will you allow me to clean the coat for you?"

It was the least she could do after the way he'd helped her. If she could cadge a cake of soap from the innkeeper and sponge the stain very carefully, perhaps the fine garment needn't be ruined.

"That won't be necessary. Chumley will see to it." At her inquiring look, Mr. Clayton added, "My valet. In truth, he'd be irate if I allowed anyone else to interfere with my wardrobe."

Mr. Clayton traveled with a valet as well as a footman and groom? Of course he did. He appeared to be a wealthy, influential man—which made it all the more surprising that he'd offered to assist her.

She regretted that it was time for them to part ways, that there would be no more opportunity to satisfy her burning curiosity about him. He intrigued her in a way no man had ever done. "Then I can only apologize once more. And I must thank you, Mr. Clayton, for your aid in finding Leo. It was very good of you to do so."

Natalie flashed him a warm smile. He *had* been kind

despite her initial mistrust of him. He had voluntarily searched the stables, chased after Leo, and in the bargain had given the boy a stern talking-to about proper behavior.

She had repaid the man by ruining his coat. The situation was rather mortifying, especially when she faced those inscrutable granite eyes. Perhaps the best way to express her gratitude was to remove herself—and Leo— from his presence.

"I wish you safe travels, sir. Good-bye." Turning away, she spied the boy standing at the corner of the inn, clutching his toy ship while watching the grooms in the stable yard. "Leo, come along now. I'll have to find another way to get us to Whitnash. And pray remove your muddy shoes before we go inside."

She needed to figure out what to do now that they'd missed the mail coach. The distance wasn't terribly far— only a dozen miles or so—but it might as well be across the ocean. Although fond of walking back home, she had two valises to carry and a little boy to shepherd. Between the muddy roads and the chill in the air, proceeding on foot would not make for a pleasant journey when Leo must already be tired from his aborted attempt at escape.

Perhaps she could spare a bit of her coin to hire a carriage or a local farmer with a dray. The innkeeper might have some recommendations.

She was supervising Leo as he sat down to take off his shoes when Mr. Clayton stepped to her side. Her heart skipped a beat as much from his sudden nearness as the intent look in his eyes.

"As it so happens, Miss Fanshawe, I'm heading in the direction of Whitnash, too. Perhaps you would permit me to escort you there?"

When Natalie left the inn an hour later, a groom was waiting outside to take her valises. He directed them to an elegant post chaise, then went to place their baggage in a second, plainer carriage. She wasn't accustomed to such service and still felt a certain trepidation at her decision to accept Mr. Clayton's offer. As she and Leo approached the stylish vehicle, black with gold trim, a poker-faced footman in forest-green livery sprang to open the door.

"May I ride with those men?" Leo asked, his freckled face alight.

Her gaze followed his pointing finger to the team of four matched grays. Two postilions, in livery identical to that of the footman, each were mounting one of the pairs of horses harnessed to the chaise.

"I'm afraid not," she said, with a consoling pat to his back. "They have an important job to do in getting us safely on our journey, and you might very well distract them."

"I'll be good. *Please?*"

"No, darling. Remember, it's important for you to be on your best behavior today since we are guests of Mr. Clayton."

The young footman gave a start, and she glanced up to see his hazel eyes rounded in surprise. He blinked rapidly while his face once again resumed a blank expression.

Natalie didn't know quite what to make of his reaction. Perhaps it was highly unusual for Mr. Clayton to take passengers. In truth, she felt a little intimidated by all the finely garbed servants in their host's retinue. She counted seven, including two outriders, two postilions, a valet, a footman, and a groom.

Mr. Clayton must be exceedingly rich, indeed.

That thought was further reinforced as she followed Leo into the chaise. It was smaller than the mail coach, but far more luxurious. The two seats were covered in buttery soft burgundy leather, the walls upholstered in brocade of the same rich hue. Gold tassels dangled from the curtains, which were drawn back to allow an expansive view of the outdoors.

Leo was bouncing up and down on one of the seats. Since there was no coachman, the chaise had the bonus of a front window as well as on the sides. "Look, I can watch the horses from here. Can this be my spot?"

Before she could reply, a baritone voice came from behind them. "Yes, so long as you do so quietly," said Mr. Clayton.

The boy instantly settled onto his knees, as still as a mouse, while peering out at the team.

From her place beside Leo, Natalie turned her head sharply to look at their benefactor. He'd startled her, for she hadn't seen him follow them outside. There could be no other reason why her pulse was racing and her cheeks felt warm. It certainly couldn't be due to the fact that he dwarfed the interior of the chaise, or that he'd changed into a fine claret coat with fawn breeches, his boots once again impeccably polished. Over his arm, he carried a multicaped black greatcoat which he tossed onto the empty seat.

His very elegance unsettled her. Though she'd known well-dressed people in America, Mr. Clayton had an aura of sophistication unlike any man of her acquaintance. In these close confines, he seemed larger and more masculine than ever. What did she really know of him beyond his name? Yes, he'd helped her find Leo, but was one good deed sufficient for her to place her trust in the man? Was it wise to put herself and Leo at risk?

She shook off her gothic misgivings. Clearly, he was not seeking to abduct them for some nefarious purpose. He was a well-mannered gentleman who wished to give aid to two stranded travelers. There was nothing more to it. And she had to admit it was nice to accept his help after handling matters alone for so many months.

As he sat down opposite them, Natalie was glad that she'd taken the time to tidy the boy, coaxing him into his best Sunday clothes and scrubbing the mud off his shoes. Since her hem had been badly soiled, an equal effort had been paid to her own appearance. Her best plum silk gown might not be up to the fashion standards of England, but she was quite pleased with the dramatic way it enhanced the green of her eyes. Luckily, she'd recently refurbished her bonnet with cream ribbons to coordinate with her slate-gray cloak. Between dressing and packing and settling their bill, she'd scarcely had time to grab a quick breakfast and gulp a cup of tea.

As the footman began to close the door, a white-haired gent in a black suit came hurrying up. She recognized him as the cantankerous servant who had been in the private parlor earlier.

"What is it, Chumley?" Mr. Clayton asked.

Chumley? This man was the valet, she realized in chagrin. Heaven help her, *he* was the one given the task of cleaning that muddy coat? Without a doubt, he would bear a grudge against her for causing him extra work.

Chumley's upper lip curled as he flicked a glance at Natalie and Leo. Then he bowed to his master. "Your Grace, as you've paperwork from Parliament to read, may I mention there is room aplenty for these persons in the baggage coach. I will happily surrender my own seat to them."

"Thank you, but that won't be necessary."

Natalie was discomfited to think they were a bother. "If we are inconveniencing you in any way, sir—"

"Absolutely not," Mr. Clayton said crisply. "The matter is already settled. Now we'd best be on our way."

That last remark was addressed to Chumley, who bowed again and retreated, though not before flashing Natalie a suspicious stare. Her skin prickled from the force of his disapproval. She remembered him griping about a bevy of girls coming to the parlor to bat their eyelashes at his master.

Chumley must view *her* as a flirt casting out her lures, although nothing could be more absurd.

The door closed and the post chaise began moving, leaving the inn yard for the open countryside. Though the road was rutted, the vehicle was smoother and better sprung than any ride in her experience. Yet she couldn't relax with her mind awhirl with perplexing thoughts.

She addressed Mr. Clayton, who was gazing out at the passing scenery. "Sir, I came upon your valet earlier in the private parlor. At the time, he referred to you as 'Your Grace.' But I find it difficult to believe you're an archbishop. Unless the religious clergy in England are very well heeled."

He turned the full force of his gaze on her, one of his dark eyebrows cocked. "It is the proper form of address for one of my stature. I am Hadrian Ames, the Duke of Clayton."

Duke?

The news jolted Natalie. Even in America, she'd heard of the highest rank of aristocrats who ruled English society and possessed vast riches, all of it inherited in a long line dating back centuries. Here, one's class depended upon heredity instead of hard work. The concept of possessing such wealth and power by a mere accident of birth disturbed her innate sense of fairness.

"You're not Mr. Clayton, then."

"No. I'm afraid you assumed that, and I saw no pressing reason to correct you."

Miffed, she sat back and studied him. Of course he

wouldn't tell her, he'd probably deemed her unworthy of the truth. No, that judgment was uncharitable given her scant knowledge of his character. Perhaps it was just that he wished to avoid any more fawning.

Remembering the buzz of interest in the taproom when he'd walked to the door, she realized that all the other guests had been privy to his exalted stature. But for her, there had been no opportunity to gossip with anyone. The previous evening, she and Leo had arrived late and had taken their meal in their room, after which he'd run downstairs to hide in the parlor while she'd gone to the kitchen to fetch his bathwater. Once she'd found him again, it had been nearly bedtime.

That was one mystery solved, at least. It explained why Mr. Clayton—*the duke*—had appeared disconcerted when she'd offered her hand instead of a curtsy. He would be accustomed to obeisance from all those beneath his lofty rank. Perhaps it was a blessing she'd soon see the last of him, lest such homage be expected of her now, too.

"I cannot pretend to know much about the English aristocracy," she admitted. "What am I to call you, then, if not Mr. Clayton? I cannot imagine myself saying *Your Grace* to anyone other than clergy."

He lifted his hand in a dismissing wave. "*Duke* will do. Or simply *Clayton*. Whichever one you prefer."

"All right, then, Clayton it shall be, though that, too, seems improper without the *mister*. It appears there are a number of things about the nobility for me to learn. In America, we are more egalitarian, you see."

Leo had been playing with his toy ship, but he piped up, "What's egal-i-tar-ian?" He sounded the word out carefully.

She turned her head to smile at him. "It means that

we do not have dukes and kings and nobles who inherit their position by virtue of birth. In America, one's success in life is entirely up to each person. You must work hard to raise yourself to a position of authority."

"Like a sea captain?"

"Precisely," she said with a laugh, combing her fingers through the mop of tawny hair that always became messy no matter how many times she tidied it. "Though perhaps your future occupation will depend in part upon the wishes of your grandfather Godwin."

Leo shrugged, returning his attention to sailing his ship along the back of the seat, making little sounds that she deduced were meant to be the crashing of waves. Her heart squeezed. At least she could be comforted that he now seemed more reconciled to meeting his grandsire for the first time.

If only she herself could accept the prospect of losing Leo.

When she returned her attention to the duke, he was leaning forward with his hands clasped, his brow furrowed, and his gaze unusually intent on her. "Godwin, you say? The Earl of Godwin?"

"Yes, his estate is called Oak Knoll. It's located near the village of Whitnash. Do you know him?"

An odd alertness on his face, Clayton didn't reply at first. He stared fixedly at Leo and then at her as if he were trying to see inside her mind. Without answering her question, he said in a strangely rough tone, "If indeed Leo's grandfather is Lord Godwin, who are his parents?"

"Audrey and Jeremy Bellingham. They were my dearest friends in America. I taught in their mission school on the frontier." Her throat caught. "Unfortunately, they're both gone now."

"Gone?"

The sharpness in his tone startled her, as did the stark expression on his face. Unwilling to use the word *dead* in front of the boy, she merely said, "Yes, Leo is an orphan."

The duke appeared shaken by the news. "May I ask what happened?"

She lowered her voice to a murmur. "I'm afraid it is best not to speak of that at present."

If only it were so easy to block that horrific day from her thoughts. Though she'd grown adept at locking away the memory, vivid flashes of the scene played in her mind. The surprise attack had happened on a sunny afternoon the previous summer at their fenced compound in the wilderness. She had been teaching a reading lesson to a group of children in the schoolhouse when a gunshot had sent her rushing to the window . . .

Now, despite the warmth of her cloak, Natalie fought off a shiver. She was hardly aware of gripping her gloved fingers in her lap. The acrid memory of smoke and blood twisted her stomach into knots. Though months had passed, she had not been able to shed the heavy burden of guilt for having survived when so many had died.

"Well," the Duke of Clayton said, "it seems that destiny has set you in my path, Miss Fanshawe. In truth, our meeting was a bona fide fluke of fate."

Her attention snapped back to him. His watchful stare gave her the unsettling sense that he'd guessed something of her dark thoughts. "Fate?"

"Yes. As it so happens, we are traveling to the same destination. My father was cousin to Lord Godwin. I'm on my way to pay his family a visit."

Astonished, Natalie tilted her head to one side. How could that be? His announcement seemed too farfetched to be true. But she could think of no earthly reason why he would fabricate such a connection. Nor could she detect any sign of deception on his strong features.

All other thoughts vanished as she tried to work through the tangle of family relationships. "Then Audrey would have been . . ."

"Lady Audrey was my second cousin. Which would make Leo my second cousin, once removed." One corner of his mouth curling in ironic humor, he regarded the boy at play. "Fancy that, the brat shares my blood."

She was too rattled to chide him again for the name-calling. Besides, the duke's expression showed a dash of the same amazement that captivated her senses. How extraordinary to think this lofty aristocrat was kin to her best friend. And to Leo.

"Then you've met Audrey," she said, eagerly leaning forward. "You must have known her when she was a girl."

"We grew up together at Oak Knoll. My father died when I was five, and Godwin was my appointed guardian. Being the same age, Lady Audrey and I were as close as siblings."

So, the duke was twenty-nine years of age, as Audrey would have been. How strange that her friend had never mentioned the connection. Then again, she'd seldom spoken of her life back in England.

"She never called herself *lady*," Natalie corrected. "Titles didn't matter to her. She once told me how relieved she was to have left all that pomp behind."

"It was her birthright, nevertheless. You're in England now, where proper forms of address matter."

"Not to me."

"Then permit me to warn you," he said with a darkening frown. "The Earl and Countess of Godwin will expect you to call them *my lord* and *my lady*. As well as to curtsy to them."

"Bah. In America we bow to no one, not even to President Madison."

"Here it is considered an obligatory sign of respect." His face was set in hard lines. "Pray recall the old proverb: when in Rome, do as the Romans. I would strongly advise you, Miss Fanshawe, to heed that advice."

Chapter 4

The journey to Oak Knoll took a little more than an hour. For that, Natalie was glad. After her expressed disdain of the class system, the Duke of Clayton had assumed the aloof façade of the aristocrat. His manner was polite but cool, indicating disapproval of her American opinions.

If she had a niggling suspicion that he had a valid point about heeding local customs, she set it aside. She had every intention of using her best manners with Leo's grandfather; rudeness went against her nature. But then, so did genuflecting to people whom she considered to be her equals.

He'd asked no more questions about Audrey, and Natalie had offered no further commentary about her life in America. Instead, they'd conversed for the remainder of the ride on bland topics like the countryside and the weather. He also held a lengthy discussion with Leo about sailing ships, including the mighty English man-o'-war.

That particular topic caused Natalie to grit her teeth, reminding her of the conflict between their two nations that had begun in 1812 and ended very recently. Too many of her fellow Americans had died due to encounters with English ships, and it had served to enhance her dislike of the British.

The post chaise turned off the main road and passed through a set of open iron gates. Earlier, Clayton had informed one of the outriders they were to go straight to the estate rather than stop in the village of Whitnash to drop off his passengers as originally planned. Now, the vehicle proceeded up a drive that wound through a vast wooded parkland.

"Welcome to Oak Knoll," he said with an inscrutable glance at her.

The early spring landscape was as stark and bleak as her heart. This was where she and Leo would part ways. Natalie fervently prayed she'd be allowed to stay long enough to help him settle into his new life.

She sought to assuage her somber mood by sliding her arm around the boy, drawing his sturdy little form close to her side. "We're here, darling, we're almost at your new home," she murmured, pressing a kiss to the top of his sweet head. "It's the end of our long journey."

Leo leaned into her trustingly, but only for a single poignant moment. Then he wriggled free to press his nose to the window. "It's all woods. Does my grandfather live in a cabin?"

The duke gave a low chuckle. "Hardly. Oak Knoll is a house so enormous you may get lost when playing hide-and-seek. But never fear, I'll show you around the place. There it is now, you can see it through the trees."

The boy knelt on the padded seat to peer through the front window. His eyes resembled big blue saucers. "Look, Miss Fanshawe! It's a castle!"

"So I see."

Situated on a low hill, a great gray fortress loomed ahead of them, complete with turrets and crenellated battlements and towers at either end. Oak trees crouched like trolls around it, poking the dark fingers of bare branches at the sky. Masses of dead ivy, brown from the ravages of winter, trailed over the stone walls. Only the rows of mullioned windows and the columned portico kept the place from looking like an evil wizard's citadel.

Scoffing at her own grim fantasy, Natalie strove instead to imagine the house in the fullness of summertime with flowers blooming and the trees covered in leafy green. The exercise did little to erase her trepidation, though she was glad that Leo didn't seem to notice anything amiss.

While the boy stared in rapt awe at his new home, the duke leaned forward, his granite eyes commanding her attention. "I must ask, Miss Fanshawe. Is Godwin expecting your arrival?"

"I wrote to him late last summer," she murmured, "and again in December, but I never received a response. I can only presume the war interfered with the mail."

"Are you saying he might not even know about—" His gaze incredulous, he cast a significant glance at Leo.

She firmed her lips. "I couldn't delay any longer. I was obliged to fulfill my vow to Audrey. Her last request was for me to bring her son to England with the utmost swiftness."

Her mind flashed again to that horrific scene, to her friend's dying words, to the grip of Audrey's bloodied hands. *Please, you must promise to do so, as soon as possible. Leo must go to England where he'll be safe.*

Swallowing the lump in her throat, Natalie looked starkly at the duke. "She wanted him to have the protection of his family, you see. So when news of the peace treaty came, I made immediate arrangements for our voyage. Surely Lord Godwin will be eager to welcome such a fine grandson."

"One would hope so."

On that cryptic remark, Clayton said no more, and his brooding expression stirred uneasiness in her. What if Leo wasn't welcome here? What if his blood relatives rejected him? But she didn't see what other choice there had been. Although sorely tempted to forget the vow, to keep Leo in America with her, she'd felt honor-bound to obey the wishes of her dear departed friend.

To her last breath, Audrey had desired only to shield her son from harm. Even if she didn't agree with the decision, Natalie could understand that urgency, given the ferocious attack that had cost so many lives. Yet she'd have been happy to keep him with her forever. Nothing had ever meant more to her than fulfilling the role of foster mother to Leo.

But now her fears rose to the fore. What life awaited him here? Who were these people that Audrey had felt compelled to flee at the age of eighteen? Why would she be so adamant about giving her son to a grandfather who might not even want him?

Fierce resolve steeled Natalie's spine. No matter what she had promised, she would never leave Leo in a harmful situation. She would remain with him until assuring herself that he'd be happy here at Oak Knoll.

And if he was not?

Then she would take him back to America and raise him herself.

Hadrian allowed Miss Fanshawe and Leo to alight first from the post chaise. While she turned to straighten the boy's collar, he glanced up at the familiar stone façade of the manor house. So many of his childhood memories lay within these walls. Although the estate looked dreary from the hard winter, he admitted to a nostalgic fondness for the place. On school holidays, he'd whiled away many an hour fishing at the pond, galloping over the hills, or joining his uncle in hunting parties during autumn.

He believed Leo could be happy here, too.

If, that is, Godwin was amenable to accepting the son of his runaway daughter. Long ago, the man had forbidden anyone even to speak her name. Having been away at Oxford at the time of the brouhaha, Hadrian had learned second-hand about the quarrel in which Audrey had declared her intention to wed the man she loved and Godwin had threatened to disown her if she did. It had long been understood that Godwin intended for Hadrian to offer for her, although Hadrian had always viewed her as a sister, and a rather pious one at that. He'd suffered no heartbreak when she had eloped, other than wishing he'd had the chance to renounce any claim on her in hopes she might have stayed in England. Godwin, on the other hand, had acted as if she were dead.

And now she was.

Hadrian's chest tightened. Moralistic or not, Audrey had been a familiar part of his youth and he had a keen desire to know what tragedy had befallen her and her husband. It had been something horrific, judging by the haunted expression on Miss Fanshawe's face and the way she'd refused to speak of it in front of Leo.

The massive front door clicked open, and a man stepped out onto the portico. The Earl of Godwin epitomized the proper gentleman in a nut-brown coat and nankeen pantaloons. His thick thatch of hair had receded at the temples, and age had dulled the color from a dark gold to the paleness of straw. Despite being of an unremarkable height and build, he exuded authority from his squared shoulders to the proud tilt of his jaw.

His welcoming smile vanished as he spotted Miss Fanshawe and Leo. A puzzled frown confirmed that he was not expecting their arrival.

Hadrian braced himself for an unpleasant scene. He didn't share Miss Fanshawe's belief that Godwin would be thrilled to acknowledge the boy. Yet he resolved to do whatever he could to facilitate this meeting.

For Leo's sake. And for Audrey's.

He offered Miss Fanshawe his arm, and for once she did not scorn gentlemanly protocol. Her gloved fingers curled around the crook of his elbow, gripping with a tightness that belied the pleasant curve of her lips. Given her independent streak, it surprised him to know that she could suffer from an attack of nerves.

Little did she realize, he admired her pluck in crossing an ocean for the purpose of fulfilling a vow made to a dying woman. None of the ladies of his acquaintance would have had such fortitude. Most would have needed smelling salts at the mere suggestion of leaving the comforts of society.

As they mounted the three wide steps to the entry, she held Leo's hand. Uncharacteristically shy, the boy stayed close to her skirts. Hadrian was reminded of himself at about that age, compelled to leave his widowed mother and live with his cousins. He could still remember his mother's weeping and his sense of being frightened and alone—but at least he'd had some familiarity with this house and the people here.

Leo had only Miss Fanshawe.

"Delighted to see you, Clayton," Godwin said. "I presume the ice storm delayed you? Richard was jesting that you'd lost your way. After all, it's been at least six years since you've deigned to visit Oak Knoll."

"We see one another often enough in London during the season, so the journey never seemed necessary. May I add, you're looking in prime health."

After the two men shook hands, the earl's affability vanished into a haughty stare directed at the others. "You've brought guests?"

"We met on the journey quite by happenstance. Lord Godwin, may I present Miss Fanshawe and Leo. They've come to call on you." Hadrian deliberately left off the boy's last name. And because he didn't wish to give Miss Fanshawe the chance to offer her hand in lieu of a curtsy, he hustled them toward the door, which was held open by a footman. "Come, let's get out of the chill."

The entrance hall wasn't much warmer than the outdoors. Hadrian had expected that from the long years of living here. Even if there had been a hearth, it would have been difficult to heat such a cavernous space.

Handing his greatcoat to the footman, he noticed that Godwin had not followed at once. As the man trudged toward them, his complexion looked rather ashen. Had he recognized Miss Fanshawe's name? Had he received her letters, after all?

Hadrian suspected as much, though it was difficult to be certain.

Her attention on the earl, Miss Fanshawe surrendered her cloak and bonnet. A hint of stiffness in her manner indicated she was unsure of her reception. She helped Leo remove his coat while allowing the boy to retain hold of his miniature ship.

When she turned toward Hadrian, a fist of desire struck him unawares. He was hard-pressed not to gawk at the shapely form revealed by the shedding of her voluminous outer garments. Not that there was anything indecorous about her appearance; rather, the simplicity of the plum gown served to accentuate her lustrous beauty. In London, she would attract a retinue of adoring gentlemen drawn by that stunning combination of upswept sable hair and luminous green eyes. With her head held

high and her shoulders squared, she looked fierce and
formidable. As if she were girded for battle.

"Lord Godwin," she began, "I believe you may know
who I am."

"Perhaps this matter is best discussed in private,"
Hadrian said smoothly. He willed her to understand that
it would only make Godwin hostile if they broached the
topic of a long-lost grandson in front of the footman.

She aimed a measuring look at Hadrian and gave a
small nod. Just then, Leo tugged on her skirt.

"Miss Fanshawe, look at all the axes and swords!"
Oblivious to any undercurrents, the boy was craning
his neck to view the collection of armaments mounted
on the paneled walls, and the suits of armor positioned
on either side of the broad oak staircase. "There's a real
knight! Two of them!"

She smiled down at him, smoothing his disheveled
hair. "So I see. Only imagine how heavy that contrap-
tion must have been to wear into battle."

"You have to be a big, strong man. When I grow
up, I want to be a knight. I'll kill the enemy with my
sword."

As the boy pretended to jab the air, Godwin's ice-
blue eyes narrowed. In a guttural grumble, he addressed
Hadrian. "The family is waiting for us in the drawing
room. The footman can escort these two to the kitchen
to wait. I will speak to Miss Fanshawe after luncheon."

"No," Hadrian stated. "They will accompany us upstairs."

The earl firmed his lips in a vexed expression that
Hadrian recognized from his youth. But Godwin was no
longer his guardian and knew better than to gainsay a
duke, especially one who directed an implacable stare at
him. Hadrian seldom pulled rank out of respect for his

father's cousin; however, this was a situation in which ducal status came in handy.

Godwin gave a stiff nod, then led the way up the staircase. Hadrian followed with Miss Fanshawe and Leo, who clutched his toy ship like a talisman. Though he kept close to his guardian's skirts, the boy gawked at the old shields on the walls as if he'd never seen anything quite so fascinating.

Hadrian took that as a good sign. Leo soon would come to know the colorful history of this house and eventually to appreciate his noble ancestry. Providing, of course, Godwin could be convinced to forget his damned pride and acknowledge his daughter's son.

Upstairs, they went along a dim corridor, through an arched doorway, and into a drawing room that was decorated in rich shades of green and gold. A crackling blaze in the fireplace made the room decidedly warmer than the rest of the house. At the entry of the newcomers, the two people sitting by the hearth rose to their feet. Hadrian strode ahead of Miss Fanshawe to greet Lord Godwin's wife, Priscilla.

Always fashionable even in the country, Lady Godwin wore a gown of saffron lutestring, with cream braiding beneath her generous bosom. Her salt-and-pepper hair was elegantly styled to enhance her swanlike neck.

She came forward with a smile and curtsied to him. "Your Grace, we're delighted you've arrived at last. Ellen in particular was sorely disappointed that you missed dinner yesterday evening. She went upstairs for a moment, but should be back down shortly."

For a second his mind went blank. Why would his much younger second cousin mind his absence? Then he remembered with chagrin the entire purpose of this visit. To assess Lady Ellen's suitability as a bride.

How had he become so distracted he'd forgotten that?

He gave the countess's cheek the obligatory peck. "The sleet made the roads impassable, I'm afraid. I was forced to take shelter along the way."

A young man with wheat-gold hair strolled forward to shake his hand. His tailored blue coat bore the look of Weston, though with that wiry build he undoubtedly required padding in the shoulders. Richard, Viscount Wymark, was heir to the earldom and Godwin's only son. At twenty, he'd already acquired a reputation in London as a gamester.

"I see you've brought visitors to liven up this dull party, Clayton. And just who might they be?"

Wymark flicked only the merest glance at Leo. A smile lifting one corner of his mouth, he fixed his gaze on Miss Fanshawe in a covetous manner that made Hadrian's blood boil.

Hadrian strove to alleviate the untimely spurt of anger. It was unlike him to allow emotion to cloud his judgment. Better he should get straight to the issue at hand.

"Lady Godwin, Lord Wymark, this is Miss Fanshawe, who was stranded at the same inn as I was. By chance, I discovered she was on her way here to Oak Knoll to bring tidings of grave interest to this household."

Lord Godwin's nostrils flared. Though he said nothing, he shot a piercing stare at Leo. Was he searching for a family resemblance?

Hadrian detected a similarity in the fair hair and the slight roundness of the blue eyes, perhaps also in the bone structure of the face. It was hard to be certain since a child's features were less defined than in adulthood.

Miss Fanshawe stood with one hand protectively resting on the boy's shoulder. "It's a pleasure to meet all of you. Leo and I have traveled quite a long distance to come here."

"And we're very eager to hear what you have to say." Hadrian stepped to the fireplace to pull the bell rope. "However, perhaps you'll agree this discussion is for adult ears only."

He'd have sent Leo downstairs from the start, but it was important that everyone have a look at him first. He went to the boy, hunkering down to his level. The wariness on that small face reminded Hadrian of himself at that age, sent here to live after the death of his father. Gently he said, "So, brat, would you rather stay here and listen to dull talk, or eat some cakes and biscuits in the kitchen?"

Leo had been hanging close to Miss Fanshawe's skirts, but his freckled features perked up at the prospect of treats. He cast a glance up at her. "May I, Miss Fanshawe?"

She stroked her fingers through his hair. "Of course. Just not too many sweets or you'll be sick."

Leo hesitated. "You won't leave while I'm gone, will you?"

"Absolutely not. I promise to come and fetch you shortly."

The warmth of her smile touched Hadrian more than it ought. It reached deep inside of him, stirring mawkish feelings that he didn't care to examine. One thing was clear, her devotion to Leo made her a strong advocate for the orphaned child. Hadrian could see why his cousin had entrusted her with the boy's care.

He went to give instructions to the footman who had appeared in the doorway, while Miss Fanshawe hugged Leo before sending him on his way. Upon Hadrian's return, he noted that the others were watching him—and Miss Fanshawe—with avid interest. Godwin appeared to be clenching his jaw, etching hard lines in his patrician features.

Wymark strolled to the sideboard. "Brandy, anyone?" he asked, waving the decanter. "You look as if you could use a drink, Clayton."

Hadrian declined the offer with a shake of his head. He'd as soon not had Wymark present, but could hardly evict him from the drawing room in his own home. Perhaps it was just as well the family hear this together. It would save him the trouble of multiple explanations.

Lady Godwin fluttered her pale hands. "What a shoddy hostess you must think me, dear Hadrian! Though it's nearly time for luncheon, I should have rung for refreshments."

"Not now," he said. "In fact, you may wish to sit down. All of you."

Looking mystified, she obeyed, resuming her chair by the hearth and arranging her skirts. Miss Fanshawe did likewise, sitting with perfect posture, her hands folded in her lap. The only unladylike aspect about her was the vigilant way in which she studied each individual in the group.

The other two men took nearby seats, while Hadrian opted to remain standing with his elbow resting on the fireplace mantel. "Now that we're all settled," he said, "I'm afraid I have unhappy tidings. As you know, Lady Audrey and her husband fled England a decade ago. I regret to inform you that Miss Fanshawe has come from America to bring us word of their deaths."

Lady Godwin gasped. "Oh no. How dreadful!"

Her expression held the appearance of sorrow, but the lack of tears was understandable in light of the fact that she had been Audrey's stepmother. As Lord Godwin's second wife, she had tended to favor her own children, Wymark and Ellen. Wymark himself looked less than grief-stricken, for he'd been a boy of only ten at the time of Audrey's elopement. He was leaning casually back in his chair, swirling the brandy in his glass.

The earl displayed no emotion whatsoever. His inscrutable face might have been carved from marble. As if to further shield his thoughts, he shifted his gaze to stare into the flames of the fire.

Yes, Hadrian judged, Godwin most definitely had received at least one or perhaps both of the letters sent by Miss Fanshawe, for he didn't appear to be at all surprised by the news. It was also apparent that he hadn't shared the content of those missives with his family.

"Whatever happened to the poor girl?" Lady Godwin asked, groping for a handkerchief and pressing it to her cheek. "Was it illness? Or some dreadful accident? Oh, I warned Audrey not to leave this house for such a wild, uncivilized country! And with a common curate, too!"

"Be that as it may," Hadrian said crisply, striving to hide his impatience, "there is no point in rehashing the past. As to what happened, our visitor is privy to the details. She was Audrey's closest friend." He sent Miss Fanshawe a penetrating look, wondering at what secrets lurked behind that lovely face. "Perhaps now she will be so kind as to enlighten all of us."

Chapter 5

Feeling the force of everyone's attention, Natalie returned their scrutiny with tense composure. She hadn't known what to expect from Audrey's relatives, but it wasn't this lukewarm reaction. Aside from the duke, the only person who'd expressed any sadness was the countess, though she seemed to be putting on a performance rather than exhibiting heartfelt grief.

Lady Godwin had been Audrey's stepmother, Natalie recalled. Audrey had once alluded that the woman had seemed pleased by the elopement. Apparently, the countess had never warmed up to her stepdaughter, the only child of her husband's first marriage.

That assessment applied also to Audrey's half brother, Lord Wymark, who seemed largely unaffected by the tragic news. He sat sipping his brandy, looking more avid than upset, as if he were hearing a bit of titillating gossip.

Lord Godwin merely gazed at Natalie in flinty silence. On the long sea voyage, when she'd imagined this moment, she had hoped the man would feel anguish over the death of his eldest daughter. That perhaps over the years, he had come to regret sending Audrey into exile and washing his hands of her. But his aristocratic features revealed nothing.

Did he truly feel so indifferent? Or had he already done his grieving weeks ago upon receiving one or both of Natalie's letters? He was too much a stranger for her to discern the answer.

The Duke of Clayton had shown the most genuine emotion. When she'd broken the news to him in the post chaise about Audrey's death, stark distress had flashed over his face. He had regarded his second cousin as a sister, he'd said, having grown up with her in this house.

At present, he stood somberly waiting for Natalie to speak.

She took a certain solace in his grave countenance. It was clear that the duke, at least, had felt an affection for sweet, generous Audrey, who'd never had an unkind word to say about anyone. She had been an admirable person of strong convictions, brave enough to leave behind a life of luxury to be with the man she loved with all her heart and soul.

They all needed to hear about that, not just her death.

Natalie swallowed the lump in her throat. "To understand what happened," she began, "first you need to know about Audrey's life in America. She and her husband, the Reverend Jeremy Bellingham, shared a deep love for each other and for God's word. They settled in the state of Pennsylvania and devoted themselves to preaching their faith to the people there. I first met them in Philadelphia about seven years ago. They were raising money to build a mission in the wilderness."

Wymark pulled a sour face. "Surely my sister wasn't begging."

"Seeking donations for a worthy cause is far from sordid," Natalie said sharply. "And your sister is to be commended for her dedication to helping the poor. Since I had connections in local society, I offered to help Audrey collect the necessary funds. She and I became fast friends. Even when she moved away, we kept in touch by mail. When she wrote two years ago to ask me to join them on the western frontier, I . . . welcomed the chance."

Natalie had to stop herself from admitting precisely why she'd been so eager to leave Philadelphia. Her own confession of woe had no place in a tale about Audrey.

Lady Godwin curled her lip. "The frontier? Are you suggesting that my stepdaughter lived among the savages?"

"There were native tribes in the area, yes," Natalie said coolly. "But they were friendly and we often bartered with them for wild game and cured hides. There were also a few farmers, as well, who had cleared the land to grow crops. The mission itself was a small settlement named Bellingham by the locals. It was enclosed by sturdy log walls, with a small church and a school inside the compound. I taught reading and arithmetic lessons to the children, while Audrey tended to the sick. She had a gift for healing, did you know that?"

Everyone else looked blank, but a slight smile lifted one corner of the duke's mouth. "She used to doctor her dolls in the nursery, as I recall. And if I ever so much as scraped a knee, she would insist upon playing nurse with all of her ointments and bandages."

Natalie caught herself smiling back, albeit only briefly. Once again, she felt the tug of that peculiar connection with him as if they understood each other on a deep, fundamental level. But it made no sense. Given her steadfast belief in equality, she could have nothing in common with an English duke. And surely at the grand old age of six-and-twenty, she was too prudent to be susceptible to a handsome face.

She went on. "Audrey studied medical textbooks and learned herbal remedies. She had a gentle way with people, especially those who were badly injured. I daresay she was part of the reason why settlers flocked to Bellingham. They felt welcome and safe there. Though we'd heard tales of skirmishes elsewhere during the recent war, it was a quiet and peaceful spot. At least until . . . one afternoon last August."

Natalie glanced away, fisting her fingers in her lap. Everything in her rebelled at the prospect of describing that event. She could still hear the screams and smell the blood and smoke. The mere thought of it chilled her to the bone.

"What then?" Wymark prompted, looking morbidly fascinated. "Pray go on, Miss Fanshawe."

Though she drew a ragged breath, it still took an effort to force out the words. "The gates were open . . . as they usually were during the day. We were accustomed to people going in and out, traders and farmers, locals we knew. But on that particular afternoon, a small group of strangers rode into the compound. One of them . . . shot Jeremy dead on the steps of the church. The others began to swing their swords, cutting down everyone in their path, chasing after those who tried to run, farmers, natives, children . . . and Audrey."

She closed her eyes for a moment, wishing the awful scene she'd witnessed from the schoolhouse window was not so vividly etched into her mind. She had tried to bury it, yet it still caused her nightmares.

Lady Godwin moaned. Her complexion was pale, her eyes rounded with fright. "Poor, dear Audrey! I always feared she would be killed by savages!"

"They were savages, all right," Natalie said in a grating tone. "And they wore the red coats of the British infantry."

The Duke of Clayton gave a start of shock. "Are you certain?"

"Yes. Though from the ragtag condition of their garb, they might have been renegades, separated from their unit."

"Bah, I don't believe it," Wymark said, setting his glass with a click onto a side table. "Our troops are too civilized to attack women and children, let alone preachers and farmers."

Natalie stared him down. "Then you do not understand the reality of war, sir. As Americans, we were the enemy. So were the native people who had made a treaty with us. And enemies are to be slain."

She firmed her lips to keep from berating him further. Perhaps it was unkind of her to speak so bluntly to these pampered aristocrats. *They* hadn't ordered the attack. Besides, she herself had been somewhat pampered at one time. She hadn't known then the evil that could lurk in the hearts of men.

Lord Godwin bestirred himself to say gruffly, "Where were you when this attack occurred, Miss Fanshawe? Why are you alive to tell the tale?"

"I was teaching a class in the schoolhouse when gunfire rang out. When I ran to the window and saw the bloody scene unfold, I knew I had to protect my students from harm. They were all little ones, none more than seven or eight years old. I hid them in a shed by the back fence, and strove to keep them quiet lest they be slaughtered like the others."

"Ohh," Lady Godwin whimpered. "This is too much! I cannot bear to hear of such violence. Richard, do fetch my hartshorn from the drawer."

Wymark dutifully arose and went to a cabinet, bringing back a small blue bottle, which he uncorked and waved under his mother's nose. Taking it from him, she alternated between sniffing the restorative and fanning her face with the lacy handkerchief.

"I forbid you to speak another word, Miss Fanshawe," the earl growled. "I will not have you distressing my wife in this manner. She is gently bred and not accustomed to such brutality!"

"You *will* hear out Miss Fanshawe," Clayton countered in an imposing tone. "She has more to say, though I hope perhaps we are past the worst of it."

He turned his intent gaze to her, as if to warn her to speak with care.

Natalie gave a small nod. She could understand his concern. They hadn't heard the worst, but her throat felt too taut to describe the carnage in detail, to articulate what had happened to her, or to relate her frantic attempt to stop the bleeding from the saber slash across her friend's abdomen.

Deathly pale, Audrey had opened her eyes. "It's too late for me . . . promise you'll take Leo to England where he'll be safe . . ."

Pulling herself back to the present, Natalie drew a long breath and released it. "Fortunately, several people had guns and were able to fight back. Perhaps half the settlement survived." She focused her attention on the earl, adding, "Including your grandson, Leo."

Lord Godwin's only reaction was to tighten his lips. But she was certain he did not look surprised. He had *known*.

"Grandson?" his wife repeated in a sharp tone that belied her show of debilitating weakness. She sat up straight in her chair, the hartshorn lying forgotten in her lap. "What do you mean? Surely you cannot be referring to that . . . that urchin!"

"That urchin is Leopold Jeremy Bellingham. He is six years old, and was Audrey's only child." Natalie returned her attention to the earl. "So you see, Lord Godwin, why I felt compelled to make this long journey. It was Audrey's dying wish that I bring Leo to England to live with his family. I wrote to you twice about the matter, yet you never replied. Did you receive those letters?"

A muscle worked in his jaw. His gaze flickered as if he resented being forced to admit the truth. "One," he said, "a fortnight ago. I had not yet decided how to respond."

Which meant he had put it into a drawer and ignored it.

Natalie felt a flare of anger that he could treat the blessed news of a grandson so cavalierly. It was unthinkable that he would carry a grudge against his estranged daughter so far. But giving the man a tongue-lashing would only stir more resentment in him. Her primary concern had to be Leo.

"Well, it seems that now you shall have to decide," she said evenly. "Leo is your own flesh and blood, after all. When Audrey died, the feud surely died with her. Whatever happened between the two of you ten years ago should have no bearing on the current circumstances."

"I will not be dictated to by a stranger in my house," he blustered. "This is a private family matter."

"I'm sure Miss Fanshawe means no offense," the duke said smoothly. "But you must allow, she has a point. You've a duty to rear the lad in accordance with his status as the grandson of a peer. You would not wish it to be known in society that you'd failed to see to his care and schooling."

The two men stared at one another. At least until Godwin blinked.

"Miss Fanshawe and the boy may stay in the nursery for the time being. However, she ought to have waited for my invitation rather than come here without permission."

"She had a vow to fulfill to Audrey," the duke stated. "And I for one believe it is an admirable trait to keep one's promises."

Natalie silently thanked him again for his support. It made her feel not quite so alone in this den of vipers. He appeared to have a good deal of influence over his father's cousin, despite the difference in their ages. Was it because a duke outranked an earl? If only she understood more about their antiquated class system!

Lord Wymark had been sitting in his chair, watching and listening. Now he leaned forward and said, "I presume, Miss Fanshawe, that you have the proper documentation to prove the child's parentage."

"His baptismal record unfortunately was destroyed when the attackers set fire to the church. However, I have an affidavit confirming Leo's identity that is signed by several members of Congress. It enabled me to obtain his travel papers."

"That seems highly irregular," Wymark said, one eyebrow lifting. "Why would these men vouch for him? Did they know Audrey and Jeremy?"

She shook her head. "Rather, they know *me*. You see, my father was a senator from Pennsylvania until shortly before his death two years ago. I often served as his hostess at parties in Washington and Philadelphia." She arose from her chair and surveyed the party. "The papers are in my valise. Shall I fetch them?"

"Later," Lord Godwin barked, with a dismissing wave of his hand. "Bring them to my study after luncheon. You may go look after the boy now."

Hadrian watched as a footman led Miss Fanshawe out of the drawing room. Slim and graceful, she walked with her head held high. Her blend of natural elegance and candid manner captivated him more than it ought.

One would never guess from looking at her that she'd survived a horrific massacre—and at the hands of British soldiers.

He suspected there was more to the ugly tale than she'd let on. The hint of torment in her eyes had spoken volumes. The story had left him feeling both sickened and oddly discomfited. Despite the pride he'd always taken in his rank, her experiences made his comfortable life seem . . . inconsequential. And it was sobering to reflect that he'd voted in Parliament to fund the war that had resulted in Audrey's death. He'd always shared the Englishman's contempt for the former colonies for having had the cheek to launch a successful revolt against their mother country nearly forty years ago.

But now he found himself curious to learn more about these Americans and their way of thinking. Miss Fanshawe, in particular.

The moment the woman disappeared from sight, the countess addressed her husband in a hissing tone. "Why did you not tell me of this letter, Archie? Why did you keep it a secret?"

Godwin shifted in his chair to pat her hand. "I didn't wish to burden you when I knew nothing about Miss Fanshawe. I'd intended to hire a man to look into the matter next week when we go to London. I'd have told you eventually, of course."

"I'm inclined to share your caution, Father," Wymark said as he unfolded his wiry frame from the chair and fetched himself another brandy. "For all we know, Miss Fanshawe may be a trickster."

Hadrian pivoted toward him. "What the devil is that supposed to mean?" he snapped. "You heard what she had to say. She clearly knew Audrey."

"Oh, I don't doubt *that*. But perhaps when Audrey was killed, Miss Fanshawe saw her opportunity. Perhaps that is when she devised a hoax." Wymark sipped his brandy, his blue eyes narrowed. "Having learned of my sister's noble connections, Miss Fanshawe may have decided to obtain forged papers, pass off her own son as Audrey's child, and then live the good life on my father's benevolence."

Lady Godwin gripped the padded gold arms of her chair. "Then she may very well be an adventuress angling for a portion of your inheritance!"

Hadrian listened to them first in incredulity, then in anger. He was ashamed to admit that that very suspicion had flitted through his own mind in the post chaise, when he'd first learned her story. But it had swiftly dissipated upon his assessment of her frank nature and, strangely, her disdain for the nobility. She struck him as too open and forthright to be a deceiver.

"This is preposterous," he said, frowning at each of them in turn. "You're casting slurs on the woman's character without a shred of evidence. She was your daughter's friend. Kindly remember she is a guest in this house."

"Clayton is right," the earl concurred. "We mustn't leap to conclusions. Nevertheless, I cannot simply raise a strange child without the proper legal proof that he is my kin."

"If indeed she is practicing deceit, you mustn't allow them to stay even a moment under this roof," his wife said. "You must send them away at once!"

"There is no reason for such hysteria," Hadrian said testily. "Miss Fanshawe poses no threat to anyone here. As for the boy, you've only to look at him to see the family resemblance. If it makes you feel more easy, I shall talk to Leo myself and see what he has to say about his mother."

"Miss Fanshawe may have coached him," Wymark warned. "I never knew you to be so trusting, Clayton."

"Nor you so cruel, cousin."

At that sullen look, Hadrian had a suspicion as to what was going on. Wymark must be deep in debt again and anxious to bleed his father's bank account. He coveted every penny he could squeeze out of stingy Godwin, and another claimant on the family fortune would only reduce Wymark's share.

The earl rose to his feet. "I'll summon my solicitor from London. He can examine the papers and pass judgment on their veracity. In the meantime, I will of course permit Miss Fanshawe and the boy to remain here."

"Leo," Hadrian said. "His name is Leo."

The earl gave a conciliatory nod. "Leo, of course. Though it's a pity this disruption should coincide with your visit. I cannot pretend to be happy about having to deal with a distraction at such a time."

"I must concur," Lady Godwin said. "Your Grace, you will be anxious to renew your acquaintance with dear Ellen. We mustn't allow any interruptions to spoil your stay. Ah, there she is now."

A movement drew Hadrian's gaze to the doorway of the drawing room. The slender young lady who hovered there brought to mind a shy goldfinch. Gowned in pale yellow muslin, with guinea-gold curls framing her dainty features, she exuded a fresh, winsome beauty.

A proud smile brightened Lady Godwin's face. Rising, she motioned her daughter into the room. "Come, my darling, make your curtsy to His Grace."

The girl dutifully glided forward and did a pretty genuflection. Large blue eyes peeped up at him before her lashes dipped modestly downward again. In a rehearsed manner, she chirped, "Good day, Your Grace. We are very happy that you've honored us with a visit."

So this was Lady Ellen.

The last time he'd seen her, she had been a flat-chested sprite of twelve who'd known how to wind her papa around her little finger. Hadrian had accompanied the family to a fair in Whitnash, where she had wheedled pennies from Godwin for ices, cavorted around a maypole, and giggled at a puppet show.

She had grown up in the intervening six years, her figure filling out in all the right places. Nevertheless, he felt like a lecher when he flicked a furtive look at her shapely bosom. His discomfiture had to be due to the fact that she was his second cousin, and that he'd known her as a little girl. Surely his qualms would pass as he and Lady Ellen became reacquainted as adults.

He sat down with her on the chaise. As her parents beamed at them, he felt as if he were a prize stallion being presented with a mare. "It's been a long time since last we met, Lady Ellen. Tell me, do you still laugh at Punch and Judy?"

She tucked her chin, affording him a timid glance from beneath her lashes. "Oh no, Your Grace. I've become quite dull, I'm afraid."

"Rather, you've learned proper behavior," her mother corrected. "You've become the perfect young lady."

"You do appear admirably ready to face the ton," Hadrian said to the girl. "The gentlemen will be thronging around you, vying for one of your lovely smiles."

The smile immediately vanished. "Me?" she squeaked. "But . . . I'm just a rustic, fresh out of the schoolroom. I wouldn't know what to say to them . . . or even to you."

He took her dainty hand and patted it. "There's nothing to fear. Just talk about whatever you like. They'll find you to be charming."

"I hope that *you* find her charming, too," Lady Godwin said leadingly.

He inclined his head in a polite nod. "I look forward to spending time with my cousin this week. We've much catching up to do."

So why the devil did he feel more like an older brother than a suitor?

Lady Ellen fit all of his requirements for the perfect wife. In appearance, she was a beauty with that glossy blond hair, the huge blue eyes, the delicate features. Her ancestry was impeccable, hailing as she did from a long, distinguished line of nobility. And he was twenty-nine to her eighteen, an ideal gap to ensure he was ready to settle down, while she was young enough to bear him healthy sons and to learn how to oversee the large households on his five properties.

Hadrian conversed with her for a few more minutes before excusing himself to change for luncheon. As he left the drawing room and bounded up the stairs, a sense of guilty reprieve filled him. He felt almost like a schoolboy escaping a particularly onerous Greek lesson.

Chatting with the girl had been something of a trial between her blushes and faltering, the difficulty in finding a subject of interest to her. Though prodded by her mother, Lady Ellen seemed lukewarm on the topics of riding, hobbies, and even the coming season. She was like a china doll on a shelf who served no other purpose than to look pretty.

But surely that impression would dissipate as she grew more accustomed to his company. They needed time to come to know one another better, that was all. He mustn't expect a young and inexperienced girl to be as lively and fascinating as the intrepid Miss Fanshawe.

Chapter 6

"Oh, miss, you mustn't be doing that!"

The dismayed voice made Natalie glance over her shoulder. She was standing on a chair, using a broom to swipe at a cobweb in a corner of the schoolroom. They'd eaten their lunch here, and now Leo was sitting at a table by the window, absorbed in playing with a set of tin soldiers he'd unearthed from a cupboard.

A maidservant in mobcap and apron came hurrying into the nursery. The girl couldn't have been more than sixteen. And she looked genuinely distraught. Her brown eyes were wide in a freckled face, her rusty-red brows drawn together as she set down her box of cleaning supplies.

Having successfully cleared away the sticky strands, Natalie stepped back down to the floor. "I'm sorry, did I alarm you by standing on a chair? I'm perfectly safe, as you can see. And who might you be?"

"I'm Susan. But, miss, you oughtn't be cleaning. 'Tis *my* duty."

"The place is coated in grime. Every surface will have to be wiped in order to make these rooms habitable. The task will be finished twice as fast if we both pitch in."

"But you're a *lady*!"

"Nonsense," Natalie said crisply. "I hail from America, where people aren't divided into classes. As a free woman, I won't stand by idly while you work. So let's combine forces and get on with it."

She grabbed a rag and began to dust the cabinets and bookshelves. Seeing that Susan still looked dubious, Natalie suggested, "It would be very helpful if you'd begin in the bedchambers, so that Leo and I will have somewhere clean to sleep tonight."

"Yes, miss." Susan bobbed a curtsy, then scurried with mop and broom down a corridor.

Natalie disliked the curtsy. But perhaps the duke was right, and she ought to embrace the local customs. She certainly didn't wish to make the girl uncomfortable. Susan had been trained to show deference to those she regarded as her betters, as were all English servants.

But it still bothered Natalie's sense of equality.

Her rag soon grew filthy, for the schoolroom appeared to have been neglected for a number of years. She went to the bank of windows and opened the casement, leaning over the sill to shake out a cloud of dust.

The mid-afternoon air had warmed from the chill of the morning, and the ice storm of the previous day seemed like a bad dream now, for the temperature was almost balmy. A soft breeze carried the scents of loam and freshness and the promise of springtime. With the nursery situated at the top of the house, she had a bird's-eye view of the rolling hills and the farmland in the distance, where the fields were being plowed for planting.

It all looked so tidy and civilized compared to the American frontier. Not that that entirely displeased her. There was a certain peace to this orderly landscape, a soothing serenity to be relished after spending more than a year living in the wilderness. Perhaps each locale had its merits.

Leaving the window open to air out the musty room, she went over to ruffle Leo's hair. "You're being rather quiet, young man."

"I'm setting up my battle. Bang, bang!" He waved the toy soldier in his hand at the opposing regiment, then glanced up at her, his eyes bright. "Will Mr. Duke come here? I want him to see the fight."

He'd adopted that name for the Duke of Clayton, and she'd given up on dissuading him from it. The innocent hope in his blue gaze tugged at her heart. He craved a man in his life, someone whom he could look up to as a father. But although Clayton had been supportive of Leo's right to live here, she very much doubted a nobleman of his stature would bother any further with a child, not even one who was related to him by blood.

"Perhaps another day, darling. He'll be visiting with his relatives today. Now, let me know if you grow cold and I'll close the window."

As Leo returned to his army, she focused her attention on dusting the pictures on the walls. Twenty-six of them comprised the alphabet, each letter cleverly depicted as a zoo animal. While she worked, Natalie had a vision of the duke sitting here in this schoolroom as a boy, learning his letters by gazing at these very drawings. It was difficult to imagine such a powerful man as a vulnerable boy grieving for his father.

On the ride here, he'd mentioned having attained his title at the tender age of five. He had come to live at Oak Knoll since his father's cousin, Lord Godwin, had been his appointed guardian. Where had his mother been? Had she moved here with him? Or had she died, as well?

Useless speculations. Better she should ponder Leo's fate.

Meeting his relatives had been a sobering experience. Lord Godwin had acted aloof, Lady Godwin self-absorbed, and Lord Wymark callous. None of them had appeared pleased to have a long-lost grandson land in their midst. The Duke of Clayton had been Leo's sole ally, and he was merely a visitor. Soon, he would go away and Leo would have no one to watch out for him.

The notion shook Natalie to the core.

A part of her fiercely wished she had never crossed the ocean to bring Leo to England. These aristocrats might be his blood kin, but they clearly had little interest in the boy. Everything in her balked at the notion of abandoning him among people who did not love him. She wanted to steal him away and take him back to America. Upon their return to Philadelphia, she could raise Leo herself while fulfilling her dream of opening a school there.

Yet she had promised Audrey. She had sworn an *oath*. And surely Audrey would not have made such a request if she'd believed her father to be a heartless tyrant. But how could she have still trusted the earl after the way he'd forsaken her? He'd disowned her for the sin of marrying a commoner.

Natalie frowned while dusting the framed drawing of a swan curled into the letter *S*. She had learned at her own father's knee about the exclusivity of the British upper class. Having grown up in England, Papa had disparaged their practice of wedding only blue bloods from within their closed circles. Godwin had cast off his daughter for daring to break that rule. And it remained to be seen if he would even accept Leo.

The muted sound of a knock broke into her brooding thoughts.

A young lady was peeping into the schoolroom. Clad in a gown of pale yellow with a black ribbon tied beneath her bodice, she had gold curls and china-blue eyes. Her gaze darted from Natalie to Leo and back again.

"Hullo," she said in a sprightly tone. "I hope I'm not intruding. I heard that I've a nephew who's come to visit all the way from America."

Nephew? This must be the half sister Audrey had once mentioned.

Natalie put down her dust cloth and wiped her palms on her apron. "Please come in. You're not intruding in the least. We were just sprucing up the place."

Gliding forward, the girl wrinkled her pert nose as she glanced around. "No one's used the nursery in ages. My name is Lady Ellen. And you are . . . ?"

"Miss Fanshawe." Natalie considered offering her hand, but felt loath to soil such pristine beauty with her dusty fingers. And she certainly would not genuflect to a girl who looked to be nearly ten years her junior. "That's Leo over there by the window."

Seemingly oblivious to Natalie's breach of protocol, Lady Ellen breezed on past and headed to Leo. She hovered over him, her slim hands clasped to her bosom. "Oh, what an adorable little boy you are! So very handsome!"

He craned his head back to regard her. "Who are you?"

"I'm your aunt Ellen, your mama's younger sister. Fancy me being an aunt and I didn't even know it until today!"

"Mama isn't here anymore. She's an angel in heaven now."

"Indeed, I've only just heard." The girl's face crumpled, her lower lip quivering. "You poor, dear child. It was so terribly sad—"

"It was many months ago," Natalie interrupted, unwilling to let him be reminded of that horror, especially since his nightmares had finally faded. "Now, perhaps Leo will show you his battlefield."

"Oh! Look at that. I remember my brother Richard playing with these very same soldiers. But do come, Leo. You must see all the other toys."

Natalie went to wash her hands in a basin of water. She watched over her shoulder as the girl motioned Leo to join her at a row of cupboards. There, with all the enthusiasm of a child, she dragged out skipping ropes and building blocks and wooden puzzles, leaving everything scattered in a messy heap. Leo sat down to play with a top, spinning it across the planked floor.

While Natalie dried her hands on a linen towel, Lady Ellen scurried over, saying in an abashed murmur, "I daresay I oughtn't have mentioned Audrey to him. How thoughtless of me! Papa thinks I'm entirely too impetuous."

Natalie kept her voice low, too. "It's just that Leo was inconsolable for a time after his parents died. It's good to see him contented again."

Those big blue eyes brimmed with tears. "Yes, I imagine so. And you mustn't think badly of me for my gown."

"Your gown?"

"I ought to have donned mourning, of course. But Mama says we needn't wear weeds since so much time has passed already and Audrey was estranged from us, anyway. I scarcely remember my sister, you see. But I did wish to honor her memory in some way. So I added this." She indicated the length of narrow black ribbon tied in a bow beneath her bosom.

Natalie was touched by the gesture. At least the girl was friendlier than the rest of her family and exhibited genuine caring for Leo. "How thoughtful. Audrey was my dearest friend, and let me assure you, she was too happy a person to have ever wanted people to drape themselves in black on her account."

"Then I needn't feel bad about it." Lady Ellen pursed her rosy lips. "I only wish there was something I could do for poor Leo."

"I'm sure he would enjoy an occasional visit from his aunt."

The girl brightened at that; then just as swiftly her face fell. "Oh, but my family and I will be departing for London next week for the season. And Papa believes children belong here at Oak Knoll."

Dismay shook Natalie. This was a twist she hadn't anticipated. Leo mustn't be abandoned here with only servants for company. "What do you mean by the season? The springtime?"

"Why, it's when all of society gathers in London, from Eastertide through June. Do you not have such a season in America? What a pity, for it is the most glorious time of the year, or so everyone says."

"You've never experienced it before?"

"No, this season shall be my very first one." She clasped her hands together and twirled around in a circle, her skirts flaring. "You cannot imagine how thrilled I am! There shall be balls and routs and parties and shopping . . ." She stopped, alarm wiping the vivacity from her pretty features, her gaze frozen on the door. Under her breath, she moaned, "Oh no. It's *him*."

Mystified, Natalie turned her gaze in that direction, and her heart cavorted against her rib cage. Meltingly handsome in a tailored blue coat that outlined his broad shoulders, the Duke of Clayton stepped into the nursery. His tall form seemed to dwarf the spacious room. She had a keen awareness of her own untidy appearance and had to resist the impulse to tuck in a few strands of hair that had come loose while she was cleaning.

His gaze flicked at her and Lady Ellen standing in the corner. He seemed a trifle surprised to see them together.

Beaming, Leo ran helter-skelter through the maze of toys and tables. "Mr. Duke! Mr. Duke! Miss Fanshawe said you wouldn't come, but I knew you would!"

One corner of his mouth curled up. "You're a clever one, brat. You remembered that I'd promised you a tour of the house."

"First, you have to watch my battle," Leo said, grasping Clayton's large hand and hauling him toward the window. "I've been working on it for hours and *hours*."

The duke let himself be towed in that direction. But halfway there, he paused to give them a courtly bow. "Ladies."

Lady Ellen sank into a deep curtsy, while Natalie acknowledged him with a cool nod that belied the quivering inside her bosom. His gaze lingered on her for a moment, and her skin tingled, sending sparks of awareness throughout her body. He seemed always to have this effect on her—to make her feel as flustered as a green girl.

She was too mature for such starry-eyed nonsense. Especially in regard to an English nobleman who was no better than herself. What she felt was merely an instinctive feminine reaction to an attractive man, nothing more.

Clayton proceeded to the table and crouched down to survey the tableau arranged there. "I see you've assembled two large armies. The mighty British infantry against the French forces."

"Oh no, Mr. Duke! It's the mighty 'Mericans against the British. We'll beat the lobster backs, push them right into the sea. Bang! Bang!" Leo used one of the soldiers to knock several of the others off the table.

He ruffled the boy's hair. "Then I had best play the part of the British before they're utterly decimated."

"De-cim-ated?"

"Destroyed. Trounced. Defeated."

"Ha! They *will* be de-cim-ated 'cause the 'Mericans are the bravest! Pow!" Leo sent another soldier flying.

Natalie parted her lips to remind him to behave politely, but stopped in surprise when Clayton went to his own side of the table and launched into an attack on the American troops, marching a company of soldiers forward into battle. The two armies fought in earnest with both man and boy uttering exuberant sound effects.

Watching the duke abandon his lordly demeanor brought a reluctant smile to her lips and a treacherous thawing to her heart. She would never have expected so lofty a gentleman to play with a child. Perhaps it was time to revise her initial impression of him being haughty and imperious.

No, he was still imperious, she amended. He was a man who had inherited his wealth and stature through an accident of birth. He'd never had to work a day in his life in order to earn the many luxuries that he enjoyed. She doubted he'd ever even spared a thought for all of the lesser beings who labored from dawn to dusk in order to make his life easy.

All of a sudden, she noticed that Lady Ellen was sidling toward the door. With her chin tucked down, she looked shy and reserved, unlike the lively girl of only a few minutes ago.

Natalie glided to her side. "Is something amiss?"

"No . . . *yes*," Lady Ellen whispered. "Oh, I thought I was *safe* in the nursery. I came up here to escape him."

Natalie kept her voice low, too, though the loud play across the room surely prevented Clayton from eavesdropping. "To escape the duke, you mean? But why?"

"Because my parents want me to *marry* him, that's why. Mama said he intends to offer for me."

The news jolted Natalie. No wonder the Duke of Clayton had made the journey to Oak Knoll; he was seeking a blue-blooded bride. But his second cousin? Even for the aristocracy, such an alliance seemed unpalatable. "He does appear to be quite a bit older than you."

"Nearly a dozen years," Lady Ellen groused in a barely audible hiss, her lower lip thrust out in a pout. "He's ever so dull and dreary."

Dull? Dreary? She might have been describing an entirely different man than the one who'd chased after Leo, offered them a ride when they'd missed the mail coach, and who was at this very moment engaging in imaginary combat with the boy. "Perhaps you only need time to become better acquainted with him."

"Bah." Lady Ellen dismissed that with a sniff. "He might be handsome enough, but he's going to ruin everything. I want to enjoy my first season, not be shackled to a fiancé. Besides, it was just some silly old arrangement my papa made with the duke's father. I don't see why *I* should be bound to it. After all, it wasn't *me* they meant for him to marry. It was— Oh! He's coming!"

Her gaze dipping downward again, she edged toward the door, taking tiny sidelong steps as if hoping Clayton wouldn't notice her.

"Miss Fanshawe," he said, his eyes intent on Natalie, "may I have your permission to take Leo on a tour? And yourself, of course, too."

She oughtn't agree. There was much to do in preparing the schoolroom for Leo, and she wanted everything to be perfect before she had to say her final, painful good-bye to him. Yet she'd been cooped up here all afternoon, and the prospect of a reprieve sounded infinitely more appealing than battling dust. "Yes, thank you. I'd love to see the rest of the house, if for no other reason than to learn my way around."

"Excellent." Turning his gaze to his cousin, he added in a smooth tone, "And you, Lady Ellen? It would be my great pleasure to act as your escort. I'm sure you know as much or more about this ancient pile as I do."

She halted in place, her chin tucked in, her demeanor bashful. "Forgive me, but I—I must go and change for dinner."

"Dinner is at seven. It's not even half past four."

"Yes . . . well . . . I've letters to write, too. Pray excuse me, Your Grace."

With that, she sketched a curtsy, darted out into the corridor, and vanished from sight.

The duke stood frowning after Lady Ellen. By his knitted brow, he appeared to be puzzled by her standoff-ish behavior. He clearly had no inkling that she regarded him as too old and dull for her vibrant young tastes.

But it wasn't Natalie's duty to enlighten him. He'd discover the girl's reluctance soon enough on his own. And if the rejection wounded his pride, it wouldn't be for long. A rich, handsome duke surely must attract flocks of eligible young women. He could hardly want for choices.

Unless, of course, he was determined to persuade Lady Ellen.

She was a beautiful girl, and perhaps he'd been an-ticipating the moment when he could court her in ac-cordance with that long-standing agreement. What had the girl said? *It was just some silly old arrangement my papa made with the duke's father . . . It wasn't me they meant for him to marry. It was—*

Lady Ellen had never finished the statement. If the arranged-marriage plan hadn't originally named her as the bride, then who?

As Natalie left the nursery with Leo and Clayton, a

wisp of memory stole into her mind. Shortly after be-friending Audrey in Philadelphia many years ago, the two of them had been sitting for an afternoon, rolling bandages for a local hospital. While chatting about their lives, Audrey had revealed that the reason she'd run away with her beloved Jeremy was not just that her father opposed the marriage, but that he had tried to force her into a betrothal with a nobleman. She'd wryly said, *Can you imagine me, a duchess?*

A duchess.

The truth blazed inside Natalie. That nobleman must have been the Duke of Clayton.

Chapter 7

"Your grandfather owns all the surrounding land," the duke said. "His estate extends as far as your eyes can see."

Leo knelt on the wide stone sill of the tower window and peered out the wavy glass. He pointed to a spot where the lowering sun glinted off water. "Look! There's a river!"

"I used to fish in that stream every summer. When it's warmer, I'll show you the best spot, at a bend where the trout like to hide among the rocks."

"Can't we go and see it right now?"

"It's too late in the day, brat. And mind you don't go there alone. Once when I was about your age, I hooked a trout so big that it pulled me into the water and swam away with me holding onto the rod for dear life. I'm lucky I didn't end up being dragged all the way down the river and into the sea."

Leo gaped at him. Then he spied the twinkle in the duke's eyes and giggled. "A fish can't do that. Except maybe a whale in the ocean."

"No? My nanny didn't believe me, either, when I came back with my clothes completely drenched."

Standing beside them, Natalie had to smile. The Duke of Clayton had displayed a knack for keeping both her and Leo entertained with amusing little anecdotes as they'd trekked through formal drawing rooms, morning rooms, a music room, dining chamber, library, and a huge ballroom with three enormous chandeliers covered in protective cloth. A few minutes ago, they'd climbed up a narrow, winding stone staircase into one of the towers.

If this large circular room had ever been used for defensive purposes in medieval times, that was certainly not its purpose anymore. Now, it had been turned into a storeroom that held a jumble of castoffs: chairs and cabinets, fireplace screens, broken candle lamps, stacks of shrouded paintings, and several old leather trunks.

Leo wiggled off the sill and jumped down to the stone floor. He pointed across the room at one of the trunks. "Can I look in that treasure chest over there, Miss Fanshawe?"

"*May* I," Natalie corrected. "And you must ask your grandfather before touching anything. These items don't belong to us."

"Was he the man who was frowning at me today?" Leo kicked the toe of his shoe against the floor. "I don't think he likes me very much."

His assessment of Lord Godwin broke Natalie's heart. When she had taken Leo's identity papers down to the earl's study earlier, it had been with the intention of arranging a time for him to meet with Leo. She would shame the man into acknowledging him if need be! But Godwin had been closeted with his secretary and had brushed off her request. It was inconceivable to her that the earl could reject his own grandson simply because his daughter had not married according to his dictates. The very thought stirred both her anger and her protective instincts.

She smoothed Leo's messy hair. "Well, I daresay you must give him some time. He doesn't yet know you, but he'll soon come to see you're a fine boy." She hoped so, anyway. He *must*.

Leo appeared satisfied by the answer. He craned his neck to peer up at Clayton. "Will *you* let me look in the treasure chest, Mr. Duke?"

Clayton waved his hand. "Pray explore to your heart's content."

His face alight, Leo darted to the large trunk and tugged at the clasp. The hinges squeaked as he lifted the lid. "Oh, it's just old clothes. For *ladies*."

His nose wrinkled in disgust, he moved on to another trunk and opened it. This one contained a miscellany of discarded objects. With great enthusiasm, he began digging through the items. "Oh, look, a bag of marbles! And a broken clock!"

"There may be something sharp in there," Natalie warned, "so mind that you don't poke yourself."

"I'll be careful," Leo said, his voice muffled as he continued to rummage for treasures.

"You needn't look so fretful," the duke murmured, stepping to her side. "He's only doing what all boys do. And if he dirties his clothes, we're at the end of our tour, anyway."

Natalie hadn't realized she was scowling. The truth was, she found it unsettling that Leo had ignored her edict about not looking in the trunks and had turned to the duke for permission. In the space of less than a day, her authority had been usurped by a man who scarcely even knew Leo.

An English duke, no less.

But when she looked at Clayton and saw one corner of his mouth quirked in a slight smile, her prickly mood evolved into something far more dangerous to her composure. She felt the startling desire to experience the brush of those lips on hers, to feel his arms clasping her close to his hard masculine form. The longing was so powerful that a flush of heat spread through her body and weakened her knees.

Nonplussed, Natalie reminded herself to maintain her distance from him. Not only did he represent the old guard of privilege, but their respective countries had been at war only a scant few months ago. "Thank you for the tour," she replied. "I must say, the size of your cousin's house is impressive. It's much larger than even the presidential mansion in Washington. Before the British burned it, that is."

"That happened last summer, did it not? I read about it in a dispatch." He gave her an enigmatic stare. "It was retaliation for the Americans destroying the grain mills at Port Dover in Canada and cutting off bread supplies to the British troops."

She bristled. "Retaliation? God must have been on our side, then. He sent a huge thunderstorm to put out the fires the enemy set in our capital. It drove them all back to their ships."

If she'd thought to shame him, the duke frustrated her with a grin. "Our nations have made peace, Miss Fanshawe. So perhaps you and I should call a truce, too."

That grin made him look younger, more approachable, less the snooty nobleman. Against her will, a sheepish smile tugged at her own lips. It would be churlish to cling to old resentments, Natalie supposed. Especially when the duke had proven himself to be a vital ally in protecting Leo in this unfriendly household. For that reason alone, she must court his good will.

"You're right," she conceded. "I do beg your pardon."

One of his dark eyebrows shot up. "Can this be the

nettlesome Miss Fanshawe? Pray don't curtsy, too, lest I think you've lost all of your spirit."

"Oh, *that* will never happen!" Turning away, Natalie strolled to the trunk of garments and picked up a gold-feathered demimask attached to a long stick. She held it to her face and peered impishly at the duke through the eyeholes. "There must have been a masquerade party here once. Perhaps hosted by a previous earl. I cannot imagine the present Lord Godwin unbending enough to don a frivolous costume."

"Actually, he did hold a masquerade ball," Clayton mused. "Strange, I'd forgotten about it until just now. It took place shortly after I came to live here."

As he stepped closer, Natalie lowered the mask to look inquiringly at him. She couldn't help but notice the unusual dark rim surrounding his gray irises. He really had the most captivating eyes, if one could see past that granite hardness. Together with his thick lashes and keen stare, his chiseled features held an allurement that hinted at sin and seduction.

He reached out and took the mask, his fingers brushing against hers. The slight contact raised a flurry of prickles over her skin and made her shiver. She rubbed her arms, pretending to warm them. "There's a chill in here. It's these stone walls."

His cocked eyebrow suggested he saw through her subterfuge and found it amusing. He tossed the mask aside and plucked a gold cape from the trunk, which he arranged around her shoulders. The aroma of lavender sachet wafted to her nose. As did the heady scent of his cologne.

"Come over to the window," he said. "The sunlight will warm you."

His hand resting at the base of her spine, he guided

her to the spot. The heat of his palm penetrated her more deeply than the sun ever could. It stirred the shocking desire for him to caress her bare skin. Needing a distraction, she stepped away and spun to face him, the cape swirling around her. "Tell me about this costume ball. What do you remember about it?"

The duke's eyes turned hazy as if he were looking into the past. "I recall peeking down through the balustrade at everyone in their fancy clothes. Aunt Sarah—that's what I called the first Lady Godwin—came upstairs to give Audrey and me a good-night kiss. She was draped in some sort of white robe with gold trim. And wearing that very cape, too. She looked like an angel."

Natalie tilted her head to the side. "She was . . . Audrey's mother?"

"Yes. Aunt Sarah died in childbirth sometime later, along with the baby. I couldn't have been much older than Leo, perhaps seven or so. I recall Audrey weeping and there being a weight of sadness in the house."

The Duke of Clayton had lost his surrogate mother, then, as well as his father. Where had his real mother been? Though intensely curious, Natalie reminded herself it was better to understand the present household. "The earl must have married the second Lady Godwin shortly thereafter."

He nodded. "I was away at Eton at the time. I came back at the end of my first term and she was here."

"Eton. That's a boarding school for boys, is it not?"

"Yes. So, its reputation has carried all the way across the pond, has it?"

Natalie refrained from revealing that her father had attended Eton a very long time ago. It wasn't necessary for the duke to learn her checkered family history. "Audrey may have mentioned it," she said offhandedly. "Speaking of her, I've been wanting to thank you for supporting Leo today. She would have been very grateful to you for watching out for her son."

The duke glanced at the boy who was sitting on his heels across the chamber, examining the contents of a small wooden box. "Audrey and I grew up together," he murmured. "So of course I would help her son. And I suppose in some way, I feel responsible for her departure from England."

"Why is that?"

"I was at Oxford when she and Godwin had their final quarrel. Had I been here at Oak Knoll, I'd have given my blessing to her marriage."

"Your blessing? Would that have mattered to the earl?"

"Yes. You see, he'd long intended for a match between Audrey and me. Then she fell in love with our local curate. Jeremy Bellingham was too pious for my taste, but he seemed a decent enough chap. If I'd had the chance to voice my approval, the happy couple might have remained here in England." He lowered his voice to a rough murmur. "And she might still be alive."

Natalie judged his regret to be genuine. He had regarded Audrey as a sister, not a potential bride, regardless of the pact between his father and Lord Godwin. So why, then, was he courting Lady Ellen?

Perhaps he felt less of a sibling bond with the much younger girl. They wouldn't have occupied the nursery together as he had with Audrey. He could view Lady Ellen as merely a lady with the proper noble lineage to suit a man of his high rank.

"Life is full of *what-ifs*," she said musingly. "No one could have guessed what would happen. Audrey and Jeremy chose of their own free will to emigrate to America, and they had ten happy years together. They never regretted leaving England."

Clayton's mouth twisted as if he couldn't quite

believe that. He stared out the window a moment, the sunlight picking out the caramel strands in his brown hair. When he turned back toward Natalie, she felt the burn of his gaze. "Speaking of Bellingham," he said, "I can't claim to know much about his background. Did he have family in England? If things don't work out with Godwin, would you be able to take Leo to them?"

"Jeremy was an orphan," she murmured, matching his hushed tone so that Leo wouldn't overhear. "He was living in a poorhouse when a kind vicar provided him a proper education after spotting his quickness with memorizing Scripture. I don't believe he had any relatives at all." Then the implication of what the duke had said struck her. She took a step closer to him and uttered in a harsh whisper, "Do you truly think that Lord Godwin will reject his own grandson? Is he so bitter as that?"

"He's a proud man with strict notions of propriety. Understandably, he was angry when Audrey defied him to marry beneath her rank."

"Understandably?" Somehow, it shocked Natalie to hear the duke casually confirm what her father had always said about aristocratic marriages. "Jeremy was a worthy, upright man. This obsession with inherited status is ridiculous."

"Nevertheless, it's our tradition in England. We can't all be upstart rebels like you Americans."

She mustn't be distracted by that playful glimmer in his eyes. "If you ask me, Lord Godwin behaved like a tyrant toward Audrey. After meeting him, I can't understand why she made me promise to bring Leo back here."

"Perhaps because she knew her father hadn't always been so hostile. At one time, he'd doted on Audrey. She had a happy childhood here, all in all."

"A doting father doesn't forsake his beloved daughter.

If he was truly attached to her, he would have made an effort to contact her after she left."

The duke shrugged. "We knew she'd emigrated to America, but not where. For that matter, why did *she* not write? She certainly knew where to find him."

"He'd cut her out of his life, that's why. He said that if she married against his wishes, she was no longer his daughter."

"As I said, her departure hurt Godwin deeply. He became colder, more withdrawn and unforgiving. He forbade us even to speak her name."

Natalie clenched her fingers around the fine cape. Having had a loving father herself, she found the earl's behavior reprehensible. "Well, none of this is Leo's fault. It isn't right that the earl should spurn his own flesh and blood."

If anything, that only made Clayton's face turn grim. Seeming to weigh his answer, he glanced across the tower room toward Leo, who was still busy delving for treasures. Then his troubled eyes seared into hers. "I hesitate to tell you this, Miss Fanshawe. But you deserve to know the truth."

"The truth?"

"Yes. The situation is more complicated than you realize. You see, my cousin suspects you of being . . . a trickster."

"What?" Of all the things he might have said, nothing could have startled her more. "I don't understand. How so?"

"It has been suggested that Leo is not really Audrey's son. That upon meeting her in America, you devised a scheme to inveigle yourself into a noble household. That perhaps Leo is *your* son—and you hope to gain an inheritance for him by means of fraud."

In the throes of shock, Natalie gaped at the duke. His piercing gaze seemed to be gauging her reaction, and he looked every inch the despotic aristocrat. It dawned on her that after she'd left his family at midday in the drawing room, the duke, along with his cousins, must have dissected her character. And they had judged her to be capable of felonious conduct.

Bile rising in her throat, she took a step backward, bumping into the stone wall. "Don't tell me *you* accept this nonsense, too! Why, Leo doesn't even look like me."

"That's precisely what I told them. Godwin has summoned his solicitor from London to examine the boy's papers, so the issue should be resolved shortly. And for pity's sake, I never said that *I* believed it." He closed the distance between them and grasped her hand, his fingers warm and firm around hers. "I'm on your side, Natalie. You can trust in me."

Could she trust him? She'd be a fool to do so. No doubt the nobility closed ranks at a perceived threat and repelled any attempt to breach the walls of their exalted status. As one of the elite, the powerful Duke of Clayton would pledge his loyalty to them, not to her or to an orphaned boy.

Yet his touch on her skin caused a treacherous softening inside her. As did the throaty sound of her name on his lips. He oughtn't address her with such familiarity, but she couldn't bring herself to correct him. Not when she had the most absurd notion that he wanted to kiss her. Those deep gray eyes tempted her with all the allure of a wizard's enchantment . . .

"Miss Fanshawe, Miss Fanshawe!"

Leo's voice broke the spell. The thread of woefulness in his tone awakened her maternal instincts with a jolt. Whirling around, she spied his small form standing by the wall at the other end of the circular room. An unusually solemn look on his face, he beckoned to her.

Natalie's first thought was alarm that he'd injured himself. There were a hundred ways he could have come to harm among these broken castoffs. And she had let herself be distracted by a handsome man.

She rushed to his side, weaving a path through the discards. "What is it, darling? Are you bleeding?"

His blue eyes like saucers, he shook his head, mutely pointing at a stack of framed paintings leaning against the wall. He had pulled the linen shroud off the first one. Since the canvas backing faced outward, Natalie turned the large, cumbersome picture around so that she could view whatever had disturbed him. And she sustained another jolt.

It was a life-sized portrait of his mother.

Seated on a gilt chair in the library, Audrey radiated a fresh, youthful beauty as she gazed into the distance with a dreamy expression on her patrician features. A cluster of pink rosebuds nestled in her blond curls, while a few tendrils of hair trailed along the slenderness of her neck. Against the fairness of her skin, a delicate string of pearls encircled her neck. An open book lay forgotten in the lap of her elegant white gown as if she'd stopped reading for a moment in order to contemplate a happy future.

Tears blurred Natalie's eyes. She blinked them away, not wanting to upset Leo. How amazing it was to see her dear friend again, if only in oil paints on canvas. How strange, too, to see her draped in such luxurious raiment. She felt a renewed admiration for Audrey, who had given up silks and jewels to wear homespun gowns in a simple cabin in the wilderness in order to be with the man she'd loved with all her heart.

Yet the Earl of Godwin had banished the likeness of his eldest daughter to this rubbish heap. He had hidden it away so that no one in the family could view Audrey again. How dare he treat her so shabbily?

Leo stood staring at the portrait, sucking on his forefinger, a babyish habit that Natalie hadn't seen him do in months. She pulled him close to her skirts, her arm encircling his small shoulders. "How lovely your mama was. It must have surprised you very much, didn't it, to come upon this?"

He reached out as if to touch the painting, then popped his finger back into his mouth, moving his head up and down in a mute nod.

The Duke of Clayton appeared at her side, and her muscles tensed from an awareness of his presence. He hunkered down in front of Leo. His voice low, he asked, "What do you say, brat? Is it a good likeness?"

Again, the boy nodded.

"I've often found that it's difficult to speak with a finger in one's mouth." Reaching out, Clayton lightly tugged on the boy's arm until the finger came out. "Now, you may answer properly. You do recognize who that is in the painting, don't you?"

"'Course. It's Mama." Leo turned his innocent face up to Natalie. "Is there a picture of Papa, too?"

"I'm afraid not," she said, brushing back a lock of his hair. "You see, your mama was Lord Godwin's daughter. She grew up in this house, in the very nursery where we are staying. That's why there's a portrait of her here."

He ruminated on that for a moment, then said in a small voice, "If nobody wants it anymore, can I—*may* I have it?"

Natalie's throat caught. "I'll have to ask your grandfather's permission."

"I'll speak to Godwin," the duke said, rising to his

feet. "In the meantime, brat, perhaps I could carry it to the nursery for you. We'll hang it in your bedchamber. Would you like that?"

Leo's eyes lit up. "Yes, *please*, Mr. Duke."

Natalie bit her lip to keep from saying that it might not be a wise idea to display a constant reminder for Leo of the mother he had lost. After all, he had only recently overcome his grief. But she couldn't bring up the topic of his nightmares while Leo was standing there, all ears.

The duke picked up the oversized painting and motioned to Natalie to lead the way back down the winding stone steps of the tower. Grasping Leo's small hand, she was conscious of a simmering resentment over what Clayton had said to Leo. *You do recognize who that is in the painting, don't you?*

He had been testing the boy. He'd watched and waited to hear the answer. No matter what he might claim to the contrary, the Duke of Clayton was just like the rest of his noble family.

He, too, harbored doubts that Leo was truly Audrey's son.

Chapter 8

Two days later, Leo vanished.

Natalie discovered his absence upon returning to the schoolroom after going into her bedchamber for a few minutes. She had left him sitting at one of the pint-sized tables, laboriously copying a list of words. Now, slate and chalk lay abandoned on the wooden surface and his chair was empty.

The toy cavalryman that had been on the table was gone, too.

"Leo? Are you here?"

Receiving no answer, she did a quick circuit of the large room to see if he was crouched on the floor, absorbed by a toy. She checked the cupboards to make sure he wasn't playing a game of hide-and-seek. Then she dashed back down the corridor and into the bedchamber opposite her own. It was empty save for his neatly made cot, a ladderback chair, and the portrait of Audrey hanging on the wall above a chest of drawers.

Dear God, she had lost Audrey's son again. It was just like a few days ago at the inn. Where could he have gone this time?

Natalie checked the other three bedchambers in the spacious nursery, but the boy wasn't there, either. Earlier, he'd been restless, wiggling in his chair, and grumpy at the prospect of more lessons. In retrospect, she ought to have realized that he needed the chance to run off his pent-up energy. They'd been stuck in the nursery for the past two days, and she should have taken him outside to explore the grounds on this fine, sunny day—never mind that his snooty relatives might object.

She stepped to the open door and glanced in either direction. "Leo?"

The only response was the echo of her voice in the narrow passageway. There was nothing else on this floor except for a few servants' bedchambers. Just then, she heard the scrape of footsteps and rushed to the stairs to see a maidservant with an armful of linens trudging up the steps.

"Susan! Did you happen to see Leo just now? He's gone missing."

Alarm flashed across her youthful features. "Nay, milady. Shall I look for him?"

"I'll go. Please stay in the nursery. If he comes back, make sure he remains right here."

Grabbing her chocolate-brown shawl from the hook by the door, Natalie hurried toward the staircase. She needed to find the boy before he wandered into a part of the house where he was not invited. Heaven knew, it could be a disaster for him to encounter Lord Godwin. Especially after the way the man had cast nasty aspersions on Leo's birth.

Ever since the Duke of Clayton had revealed that the family suspected her of being a charlatan trying to pass off her own son as nobility, she had resolved to keep Leo away from them. It was only for the time being, she told herself, until Godwin's solicitor arrived from London to verify the authenticity of the boy's papers. Then the earl would have to accept Leo as his grandson.

He would have no other choice.

Meanwhile, she didn't want Leo to be wounded by unkind remarks or cold scowls. He'd been happy since finding the portrait of Audrey, much to her relief. There had been no return of the nightmares he'd suffered after the massacre, and Natalie was determined to keep it that way.

She hastened along a downstairs corridor, her shoes silent on the plush carpet as she glanced into elegant rooms, retracing the route they'd taken on their tour with the duke. She even went up into the tower room, but the boy was nowhere to be found.

Every now and then, she called out his name. "Leo! Where are you?"

Descending to the ground floor by way of a side staircase, she turned a corner and almost collided with Lady Godwin. The countess wore a gown of military-blue silk that hugged her lavish bosom. With the lace cap on her salt-and-pepper hair, she might have been deemed stately if not for the way her lips were pursed in distaste. She attempted to look down her long nose, but Natalie was half a head too tall for the snobbish expression to have any effect on her.

"Miss Fanshawe. Did I hear you call that child just now?"

"His name is Leo," Natalie said testily. "And yes, he left the schoolroom when my back was turned. I don't suppose you've spied him anywhere?"

"If I had, I'd have sent him straight back upstairs with nothing but pap for his supper. See to it that you confine him to the nursery henceforth. I will not have strange boys wandering around this house."

"He is *not* a strange boy. He's Lord Godwin's grandson."

"That remains to be seen. Now, you had best find him before the earl discovers your negligence. My husband will not be so kind as I am." On that incendiary statement, Lady Godwin sailed away in a rustling of skirts.

Natalie took several deep breaths to dispel the heat of her anger. She could tolerate criticism toward herself, but not when it was directed at Leo. After losing his parents in that horrific attack, he needed love and compassion, not rejection from his only blood kin. For the umpteenth time, she entertained serious regrets about ever bringing him to England.

But she had promised his mother. Audrey had comforted Natalie after the untimely passing of her father, had given her a home and a teaching post. The least Natalie could do was to honor her friend's dying request.

After checking the ground-floor rooms, including an enormous library and a deserted dining chamber, she began to wonder if Leo might have left the house. From the nursery windows, they'd watched the gardeners at work far below them, digging in the winter-bare beds, preparing for springtime. They'd observed a pair of swallows building a nest in the eaves. Then this morning, they'd seen the duke out riding with Lady Ellen and Lord Wymark.

Natalie had stared at Clayton's fine form until the small party on horseback had disappeared into a copse of trees. Had he finally cajoled the girl into accepting his courtship? The probability of that stirred disquiet in the pit of her belly. They seemed an ill-suited couple—not that she cared a whit how the English aristocracy conducted their grand marital alliances.

Leo had asked rather plaintively when Mr. Duke would take him fishing as he'd promised. Natalie had made an excuse, fearing that Clayton's interest in the boy only extended to discovering whether or not he was truly Audrey's son. The duke had never actually intended to escort him down to the river . . .

The river. Of course! That must be where Leo had gone.

Galvanized, she headed toward the rear of the house and found a door that led out into the garden. As she stepped outside, the air held the tang of freshly turned loam. She loved the smell of spring, the warmth of the sun, the promise of new life. But at the moment her priority was to find Leo.

As she hurried over the paving stones, a grizzled old gardener who was trimming the rosebushes tipped his hat to her. She paused to ask, "Have you by chance seen a little boy out here?"

"Nay, milady," he said, scratching his brow and leaving a dirty streak on his teak-dark skin. "Can't say as I have."

Though tempted to correct that *milady,* Natalie thanked him and darted past his wheelbarrow, which contained an odorous mound of horse droppings. She clutched her skirts to protect her hem from other suspicious brown piles along the path. Perhaps Leo had departed the house by a different door.

Beyond the garden wall stretched a vast carpet of grass, with green shoots dotting among the dead brownness. The rolling landscape hid the river that had been visible from the upstairs window. But she knew the general direction and headed across the lawn and into a copse of trees. Here, tiny buds of leaves formed a soft green mist on the barren branches.

She tightened the shawl around her shoulders as a chilly breeze whipped a few dark tendrils from her bun. With every breath, she drew in the fecund aroma of fallen leaves from the previous autumn. Sunlight dappled the forest floor and lent a cathedrallike serenity to the scene. Strange how this English woodland could remind her of the American wilderness. At least she needn't carry a gun here for fear of encountering a bear or a wolf.

Just as her senses detected the burble of water and the glimmer of a stream through the trees, she saw someone standing near the bank. Her eyes widened. No, it wasn't one person, but *two*.

A man and a woman who were locked in a fervent kiss.

Natalie stopped in her tracks. Even from a distance, she recognized the woman from her golden curls, the slim figure garbed in a robin's-egg-blue pelisse. It was Lady Ellen, and she appeared to be fully engaged in the ardent embrace, with her head tilted back to allow the man to nuzzle her throat.

Was that the duke?

Warmth suffused Natalie from head to toe. To think Lady Ellen had professed to dislike him!

Then her lover lifted his head to coo at the object of his affection. Natalie blinked at him in surprise. Those youthful features most definitely did *not* belong to the Duke of Clayton.

Feeling oddly relieved, she decided to take a circuitous route to the river. She had no desire to be caught spying. This clandestine affair was none of her concern.

As she started to retreat, however, her shoes crunched on the dry leaves and the couple sprang apart. They both turned to gape goggle-eyed at Natalie. The man reached inside his fine coat and drew out a sheaf of papers, which he furtively handed to Lady Ellen. Then he absconded at a swift pace into the forest, heading in the opposite direction from the house.

Lady Ellen stuffed the papers inside her pelisse. Her

straw bonnet hung by its strings behind her neck, and she quickly drew it up over her head and retied it as she came hurrying toward Natalie.

"Miss Fanshawe! I daresay you're wondering who that was. Mr. Runyon is one of our neighbors."

"He appeared to be more than just that," Natalie said dryly.

"Well . . . he's besotted with me." A charming flush on her cheeks, Lady Ellen let her fingers flutter over the paper corner that protruded from her pelisse. "He writes the most marvelous poetry. He thinks I have eyes like glowing sapphires and skin like sun-kissed cream."

"I see." Natalie bit back a smile. It sounded precisely the sort of atrocious verse that would appeal to a green girl. "I thought you wanted to enjoy your first season unencumbered by a fiancé."

"But I do! I've no intention of accepting Mr. Runyon's offer of marriage." She clasped her hands to her bosom and twirled, her skirts swaying around her trim ankles. "It's just so lovely to have admirers. Mr. Runyon is going to London next week, too, with his family. We shall dance together at every ball."

"Then perhaps you should wait until then to see him again, when you can be properly chaperoned. I can't imagine your parents would approve of you two having assignations in the woods."

The girl demurely lowered her gaze. "Yes, Miss Fanshawe."

Natalie wondered if Lady Ellen's word was to be trusted, but she had problems of her own to solve. "By the way, did you happen to see Leo out here in the woods? He left the nursery and I thought he might have come down to the river."

"Oh, he didn't. Earlier, I saw him heading toward the stables."

The stables! That made sense, considering he'd taken his toy cavalryman. "He must have gone to look at the horses. Shall we walk back together?"

Lady Ellen made no objection, falling into step beside Natalie. "You won't tell Papa, will you?" she said a trifle anxiously. "About Mr. Runyon, I mean."

"I see no reason to be a tattletale. But is he really so ineligible that you must meet him in secret?"

"He's merely the third son of a baron. Oh, Papa will be *furious* if he learns about this. He and Mama want a grand title for me."

Though unwilling to encourage the girl to further misbehaviors, Natalie felt compelled to say, "If you love a man, then perhaps rank and money oughtn't matter quite so much."

"Bah, I could never give up everything as Audrey did. Besides, I don't even want to *think* about marriage just yet."

They emerged from the trees and strolled toward the stables that were situated a short distance from the fortresslike house. Despite the brevity of their acquaintance, Natalie felt a glimmer of sisterly sympathy for Lady Ellen. How sad it must be for her to know that society viewed her as a prize mare to be auctioned off to the highest bidder. "Well, it seems to me you're rather young to make any hasty commitment."

"That's what I told Mama, but she insists that I lure His Grace into making me an offer. She even made me go on a ride with him this morning." Lady Ellen wrinkled her pert nose. "She doesn't care that the duke is old and stodgy. Or that I never know what to say to him."

Natalie frowned. "I assumed by now he'd have charmed you into accepting his courtship."

"Charmed? Why, he isn't romantic in the least. Can you imagine *him* writing poetry to me? How absurd!"

The girl's eyes abruptly rounded, and a whimper escaped her rosy lips. "Oh no, there he is! Pray pardon me, Miss Fanshawe. I must dash away before he spots me!"

Picking up her skirts, Lady Ellen scampered off, making a beeline for a patch of rhododendrons alongside the garden wall. The girl crouched down so that her bonnet dipped below the thick shrubbery while she crept toward a side door of the house.

Natalie was hard-pressed not to laugh at the spectacle.

A moment later, the duke came striding through the rear garden. He was a sight to behold in a midnight-blue coat that fit his wide shoulders to perfection. A snowy white cravat adorned his throat, and a pair of polished black boots and buff breeches accentuated his long, powerful legs. He appeared as faultlessly turned out as if he'd stepped straight out of an exclusive tailor's shop, having purchased the most expensive attire available.

Old and *stodgy* were the last words Natalie would use to describe the Duke of Clayton. The mere sight of him took her breath away—even though he might well be as unreliable as the rest of his family. She would not quickly forget what had happened in the tower room, when he'd asked Leo if he recognized the woman in the portrait. As if a six-year-old boy could be convinced to lie about the identity of his own mother!

Leo. She still had to find him.

Ignoring the duke, who had veered in her direction, Natalie cut across the lawn at a right angle away from his path. The red roofs of the stable buildings appeared through a stand of elms. She had not quite reached her destination when he caught up to her, matching his stride to hers.

"Miss Fanshawe. Is there a reason why you're running away from me?"

Every fiber of her being quivered as she glanced up to

see a smirk resting on his mouth. The breeze blew a lock of brown hair onto his brow and lent him an endearing handsomeness. She ought not feel such a foolish attraction to a man who personified the very nobility that she opposed. "I'm not *running,* sir, but attending to my duties. Not all of us have the leisure to do as we please."

"Yet you were out on a walk with Lady Ellen just now. I saw you from an upstairs window. Where did she go, by the way?"

Natalie cast a furtive glance at the house. Luckily, the girl had vanished from sight. "You just missed her. She went inside already."

"The two of you came from the direction of the woods. What were you doing out there?"

An inquiring directness in his eyes seemed to peer deep into her thoughts. Did he guess that Lady Ellen had had a rendezvous with another suitor? A young neighbor who was the duke's rival for her affections?

But that was not Natalie's secret to reveal.

"As a matter of fact, she was helping me look for Leo," she invented. "I thought he might have gone down to the river, but he wasn't there."

"Ah yes," he said affably. "Lady Godwin mentioned that the brat is missing. That's why I came out here, to see if you'd found him yet."

So why hadn't he said so from the start? Why all the questions?

Natalie drew a breath that filled her lungs with his provocative masculine scent. "Leo isn't a brat. And I was just on my way to check the stables."

"I'll join you. If he's run off again without permission, the *boy* could use another lecture on proper behavior."

The twinkle in the duke's eyes proved a distraction as he took hold of her elbow. His touch seared straight through her sleeve to wreak havoc with her insides. It would be ill-mannered to refuse his escort, she reminded herself. Aside from Lady Ellen, he was the only one who had exhibited any concern for Leo's welfare. Natalie might not approve of the English class system, but her pragmatic side acknowledged the value of having a duke as an ally. If indeed she could trust him after the way he'd questioned Leo.

Perhaps the best way to put a period to her unwanted attraction to him was to bring his marital plans out into the open. "You came here to Oak Knoll to court Lady Ellen, did you not?"

Slowing his steps, he sent her a piercing look. "Is it so obvious?"

She reduced her pace to match his. "The other day, she mentioned something of your interest in her."

"Did she? What exactly did she say?"

"Very little, really," Natalie hedged. "Only that there was a long-ago agreement between her father and yours."

"They were fast friends as youths. They fancied it a fine notion to pledge their children and strengthen the family ties. Since my ducal seat is only twenty miles from here, the marriage also would enable Lady Ellen to remain reasonably close to her parents." Clayton's mouth twisted wryly. "Though I confess, she doesn't seem to be very taken by the match."

Was he in love with her? Or just determined to fulfill a family obligation? It was difficult to tell. "Perhaps she's hesitant because it was Audrey you were supposed to wed. No one likes to be second choice."

"You may be right," he mused. "I can't imagine any woman would appreciate that."

His gaze roved over Natalie's face, and when he glanced at her mouth, his eyes lingered for a second. She knew enough about men to recognize that flicker of heat. A reciprocal warmth swept her with the desire to

be clasped against his hard body and to experience his
burning kiss. The sensation was so strong that it seared
her insides.

Then a chilly gust of wind slapped her back to her
senses. What madness had scrambled her brains? She had
no interest in any Englishman—least of all a duke who
was on the verge of betrothing himself to one of his own
kind.

"Well," she said lightly, "if you're looking for ways
to charm Lady Ellen, you could always try your hand at
writing poetry to her."

"Poetry?" The horror on Clayton's face was almost
comical. "You can't be serious."

"It was just a thought." Biting back laughter, Natalie
took pity on him. "By the way, if that coat is the same
one I remember from a few days ago, I'm happy to see
that your valet did an excellent job of cleaning the mud
left by Leo's shoes."

Clayton glanced down at the pristine garment.
"Chumley is a gem."

The conversation ended as they arrived at the stable complex, which included an enormous barn, a red-
brick carriage house, and several paddocks where some
horses had been turned out for exercise. The yard had a
fair amount of activity under way. In front of the barn, a
young groom shoveled a pile of fresh manure into a wheelbarrow. A handyman stood on a ladder and touched up
the white trim with a paintbrush. Another worker could
be seen through the open doors of the carriage house,
polishing the brass fittings of a coach in preparation for
the family's departure to London in a few days.

Natalie didn't want to think about the future just
now. It was too wonderful to breathe in the perfume of
horses and leather. She had always loved the freedom
of riding, the rush of the wind in her face, the excitement

of discovering what lay over the next hill. Several fine mounts pranced inside the fenced enclosures, tossing their manes in the sunshine.

"Oh, I do miss riding!" she said impulsively. "Are all stables on English estates so large and well kept?"

Clayton turned an appreciative smile at her. "We Brits love our horses. Racing is a national pastime. I myself run a breeding program at a property I own in Suffolk near Newmarket. It has twice the capacity of this stable. Last year's champion was sired by one of my stallions."

"Newmarket. I remember my father mentioning that racetrack. He raised horses, too, on our farm just outside of Philadelphia." At least until he had died suddenly and she'd been forced to sell the place.

"Did he, indeed?" His expression alive with interest, the duke raked her with an assessing look. "He must have visited England, then."

"In his youth."

"You mentioned he was a senator, too, a politician as well as a horse breeder. He sounds rather like our English aristocrats."

The topic made her uneasy, for he'd ventured too close to the truth. What would he say if he learned of her shady family connections to the nobility? Natalie had no wish to enlighten him, for she firmly believed that the blue blood conferred by birth made a duke no more worthy than any of the workers in this stable yard.

Luckily, she had reason to change the subject. "Look, there's Leo. I'll go fetch him."

Natalie hurried ahead toward the boy, who was galloping his little cavalryman along the white slats of the paddock fence. Her mind was set on scolding him when an angry equine snort broke into her thoughts. The livid sounds of an enraged stallion came from within the paddock.

In swift succession, she noted that Lord Wymark was mounted on a large bay at the far end of the enclosure, and that he seemed to be having difficulty controlling the agitated animal. He shouted at a groom, who hastened to unlatch the gate.

The stallion reared, its front legs pawing at the air. The iron-shod hooves hit the dirt and the horse sprang forward.

Just as Leo wandered past the open gate.

Chapter 9

Hadrian had been admiring Miss Fanshawe's shapely figure as she walked ahead of him toward Leo. She wore that cinnamon gown again, the same one as in their first meeting at the inn, when she'd come looking for the brat who'd been hiding underneath the table. Now, as then, he wondered how a long-sleeved frock with a modest neckline could be so titillating. The brown shawl over her shoulders made her gown even more provocative, affording him glimpses of a slender waist, womanly hips, and a delightfully curvy bottom.

Perhaps it was not the trappings at all, but the woman herself who fascinated him. Natalie. An uncommon name for an uncommon lady. Her bold, forthright nature made him suspect that she would be equally passionate in bed. He had no intention of finding out if that was true, but the thought inspired his lustful imaginings nonetheless. He was entertaining a vision of exploring the silken skin beneath her skirts when an irritated whinny brought the fantasy to an abrupt halt.

His gaze snapped to the paddock. Only then did he realize that Wymark was mounted on Thunder, his new bay stallion. The horse was dancing to the side, tossing its head and snorting. His cousin sawed at the reins in an attempt to keep the spirited animal in check. Fool! Hadrian had warned the pup that he lacked the experience to control the volatile beast.

Just then, Thunder reared, front legs kicking the air. Wymark clung for dear life, by some miracle avoiding a toss into the dirt. The bay came back down onto all four hooves and surged forward.

Straight at Leo as he strolled past the open gate.

Natalie dashed toward him, frantically calling out his name. But she was hampered by her long skirts. She'd get herself killed along with him.

Hadrian sprinted forward, his legs pumping, his heart pounding. Time slowed to a crawl as if he were running through a bog of treacle. His mind played a prayer over and over. *Please, God. Please, God. Please, God.* The nightmare of Leo and Natalie lying mangled and bloody spurred him onward, the effort utilizing every ounce of his strength.

The boy looked quizzically toward her. His freckled features showed wide-eyed curiosity. Then he must have heard the hoofbeats, for he swung his tow-haired head toward the paddock and froze.

The massive stallion surged toward him, hooves hammering the packed dirt of the yard. One of the workers shouted a warning. The horse faltered for a split second, long enough for Hadrian to hurtle past Natalie and grab Leo.

He seized Natalie's waist with his other arm, and in one continuous motion yanked them out of the animal's path. They went tumbling down in a heap near the paddock fence.

Just in the nick of time. As Hadrian covered them with

his body, the horse galloped past so close that clods of earth sprayed them. He felt a jolt as one of the hooves grazed his shoulder.

He glimpsed a groom at the edge of the yard waving his arms to stop the runaway horse. Spooked, Thunder reared again and this time succeeded in dislodging his rider. Wymark went tumbling to the ground as the bay took off like a shot across the lawn, its silken mane streaming in the wind.

Hadrian turned his attention to the rescued pair, fearing he might have injured them in the hard fall. Natalie appeared stunned, her bosom heaving, her lips parted to gasp out, "Leo . . . ?"

The boy was already squirming to free himself. "I'm squished! What's wrong with that horse, Mr. Duke? Why's he so mad?"

"He needs training, that's all." Worriedly, Hadrian shifted position to scan the boy. "Are you all right, brat? Any pain in your arms or legs?"

"No, but I lost my cavalryman," he wailed tragically. "I gotta find him!"

As if he hadn't just escaped death, Leo nimbly scrambled to his feet. He scurried off, bending over to peer at the ground for his toy. Work resumed in the stable yard, and Hadrian heard the scrape of a shovel somewhere nearby, the creak of the painter's ladder against the stable, the muted voices of several grooms discussing the near-accident a short distance away.

Then the rest of the world vanished as he turned his gaze downward at Natalie. He lay sprawled on top of her, his hard frame cushioned by her soft feminine curves. The delight of full-body closeness seared him. A lightning flash of hot blood flamed into his groin, bringing him to instant arousal. It was the very devil of a time in which to be struck by lust, but he relished the sensation nonetheless.

He couldn't bring himself to release her. Not just yet. Not until he had a moment to savor her womanly form. Was she experiencing the same urgent hunger as he felt?

As he watched, the look in those sunlit green eyes altered subtly from shock at the close call to a carnal awareness of him. Her thick dark lashes lowered slightly, though she didn't glance away in maidenly shyness. She continued to hold his gaze, her bosom rising and falling beneath his chest, one of her hands still clutching his forearm.

He read a certain reserve in her lovely features. Clearly, she knew as well as he did that any intimacy between them could only lead to disaster. She was wary of him, for she had made her low opinion of the nobility very clear.

Not that *wary* precisely described Natalie Fanshawe. She had survived a brutal attack on the American frontier. She had rushed into danger just now without hesitation. And she had an audacious way of speaking her mind that he found curiously refreshing . . .

"Clayton," she said rather breathily, "you'll need to move if I'm ever to stand up."

Her body stirred beneath him in a way that threatened to drive Hadrian over the verge into madness. With effort, he cudgeled his lusty mind back into the realm of sanity. A gentleman oughtn't be contemplating the seduction of a respectable woman. As much as he might crave to do so, he could not lie here forever in the cradle of her body.

Especially not in a damned stable yard in full view of the world.

He eased off her, stood up, and drew in a lungful of

cool air to clear his head. Extending a hand, he assisted Natalie to her feet. She shook out her wrinkled skirt and smoothed the fabric in a quintessentially feminine manner.

"Forgive me for tossing you to the ground like that," he said. "I hope you aren't too badly bruised."

"It's nothing. Leo and I are alive, and that's all that matters." Her stark gaze focused on his face. "If anything, I must thank you for acting as swiftly as you did. When I saw that horse coming straight at him, I feared . . ."

Shuddering, she adjusted the shawl that had fallen from one of her shoulders. Tears glinted in her eyes as she glanced away, blinking hard in a palpable effort to master her emotions. Until that moment, Hadrian hadn't realized just how much she loved Audrey's son. He had a powerful urge to fold her into his arms, to offer her comfort and protection, and damn anyone who might be watching.

But no sooner had he taken an involuntary step toward her than she managed a wobbly smile. "Well! It's over now and we're fine. And you'll no doubt be embarrassed to be seen with me. I must look a fright!"

Lifting her hands, she attempted to straighten the tumble of sable curls that had come partially undone in the fall. Several strands streamed down past her shoulders to curl around her bosom. With her cheeks flushed from the encounter, she looked the precise opposite of frightful. She made such an adorable picture that a soppy warmth stirred in the region of his chest. It was a feeling so foreign to his customary cool hauteur that it threw him off-kilter.

"Nonsense," he said roughly. "You're the most—"

"Oh no!" she broke in. "You're bleeding!"

Natalie was staring in dismay at his left shoulder. He glanced down to see that a portion of his upper sleeve had been ripped open, the shirt beneath it torn as well.

Blood oozed from a laceration the size of a hoof. Now that she'd brought it to his attention, his shoulder ached like the very devil.

"One of Thunder's feet clipped me, that's all. It's nothing serious."

"Another inch or two, and it might have been your skull!" She dug in her pocket and whipped out a folded handkerchief, gently pressing it to the wound. "Thunder—that's the horse's name?"

"Yes." Hadrian ignored the pain and concentrated on her closeness, savoring her enticing feminine fragrance. "Wymark recently purchased the stallion. The beast is too excitable to be ridden by someone so inexperienced."

Those gorgeous eyes lifted to his. "An animal with such a high-strung temperament won't be easy to tame."

"Precisely why my cousin should never have mounted Thunder. Bert is his trainer. That's Wymark's groom."

"I see." She lifted the square of linen to examine the injury, not a difficult task since she was barely half a head shorter than him. He hadn't realized until this moment how irksome it was to a man of his height always having to gaze down at much daintier women. "There may be some bandaging supplies kept in the stable," she said. "Hold this in place to stop the bleeding, and I'll find out."

"That won't be necessary," he said, tucking the handkerchief inside the torn fabric so that the intact portion of his coat held it in place. "Chumley will doctor me."

"Your valet is a man of many talents. However, I very much doubt that he'll be able to fix the damage to your coat without sending it to a tailor. The tear is jagged and you'll likely need to replace the entire sleeve."

"Don't look so glum," he said, warmed by her concern. "A ruined jacket is no great tragedy when compared to the safety of you and Leo."

"You're very kind, Mr. Duke. Especially as it appears your expensive wardrobe isn't safe around either of us."

Smitten by her smile, he said impulsively, "My name is Hadrian. I hope you'll consider me enough of a friend to use it."

"Then do call me Natalie." She paused, a hint of irony twisting her lips. "Unless you fear your cousins might object to any familiarity with a provincial upstart."

"Leave them to me." A smudge of dirt marred her cheek, and without thinking, he brushed it away with his thumb. The rose-petal softness of her skin jolted his pulse beat, a reminder of the temptation she posed. "If you'll excuse me, I'll have a word with Wymark. It appears that Thunder managed to unseat him."

Hadrian forced himself to walk away from her. He headed toward Wymark, who was sitting on the grass, rubbing his knee. The damned sprout was lucky he hadn't broken his neck. He deserved that and more for having come within a hairsbreadth of trampling Leo and Natalie.

Speaking of luck, she had interrupted him at a critical moment, pointing out his injury just when he'd been about to declare her the most beautiful woman of his acquaintance. She'd spared him the inadvisability of voicing that gushy tribute. Natalie Fanshawe might be strikingly attractive with that combination of deep green eyes and sable hair, and her curvy form, but she was far too egalitarian to be his wife. They came from vastly different worlds. Within his elevated sphere, he had his pick of far more suitable ladies.

Including Lady Ellen.

He winced from more than just the ache in his shoulder. By letting himself be distracted, he'd forgotten all about his intended bride. He mustn't let that happen again.

Nevertheless, his thoughts strayed back to Natalie. His intense desire for her could not be faulted. Any adult male not on his deathbed would find her enticing. But he would admire her from afar and control his baser impulses.

They'd be friends. Just friends, nothing more.

Natalie used the pinning of her hair as an excuse to watch the duke—*Hadrian*—walk away. He strode directly to his cousin, who was sitting on the ground, rubbing his knee. The husky, dark-haired fellow in workman's clothing who stood over Wymark must be Bert, the groom. When the duke reached them, he and Bert pulled Wymark to his feet. The younger man proceeded to slap the dust from his buckskin breeches and green coat.

Dragging her gaze away, she looked for Leo. The boy was lying on his stomach beside the paddock fence, playing with his toy cavalryman as if nothing untoward had happened. He deserved a sound scolding, but she was still too shaken to summon the energy to administer one.

It was more than the near-tragedy that disturbed her. It was also the experience of lying beneath Hadrian in the aftermath. She had a vivid memory of his hard body, heavy and masculine, pressing into her bosom and hips. The alluring feel of him had awakened a hunger unlike anything she had ever known. Excitement had sizzled like wildfire in her depths, along with the giddy desire to let him do with her as he willed. Her body still quivered with the afterglow of warmth.

Heaven help her. He was an English lord, the highest rank of the nobility. It was absurd to feel so drawn to a man who was all wrong for her.

Wasn't it?

Then again, any woman would be attracted to the Duke of Clayton. Even if one ignored his title, he was a tall, well-built man who exuded an air of competence and strength. The breeze tousled his thick brown hair, the sunlight picking out lighter caramel strands. But it was more than just his devilishly handsome features that appealed to her. In the gray eyes that she'd initially found cold and impenetrable, she had come to see intelligence and humor. She'd enjoyed the byplay of their conversations. And although his countenance was often serious, he also had an ironic wit that made him stimulating company. He'd parried her teasing well, and she'd always appreciated a man who could laugh at himself.

At the moment, though, he appeared to be in full ducal mode.

It was clear from those stern features that he was in the midst of issuing a severe reprimand to his cousin, who wore a sullen scowl. The family dynamics sharpened her curiosity. Although she didn't know Wymark's precise age, he looked to be perhaps twenty, not quite having reached his majority. Any young man on the cusp of manhood would resent being dressed down by an older relation.

The breeze carried the sharp rumble of Hadrian's voice, though she could not quite discern his words. But she noticed that it was utterly unlike the warm, husky tone he had used with her. A memory teased her mind. In the instant when she'd noticed his injury, he'd been in the middle of saying something to her.

You're the most—

The most . . . what? The most outspoken woman he'd ever met? The most vexing? The most beautiful?

She shook her head to deny the treacherous melting inside her. How ludicrous. Hadrian doubtless found her quite ordinary. He must be acquainted with dozens—perhaps hundreds—of elegant ladies who had the luxury to do nothing but pamper themselves all day. He would never sing the praises of a provincial American who had taught school in the wilderness, who refused on principle to curtsy, and who had managed to lose a wayward six-year-old boy twice in a matter of a few days.

No, if Hadrian had any interest in her at all, it could not be respectable.

Her father had grown up in England, and he'd spoken disparagingly of the noblemen who dallied with commoners while marrying blue-blooded ladies. Papa's father—Natalie's grandfather—had been a member of those exalted circles. A dislike of the aristocracy had been a primary reason why her father had emigrated to America as a young man. She'd be foolish to ignore the wisdom of his experience and form an attachment to any lord.

It was best to relegate the duke to the role of useful ally.

With that firm decision, she focused her attention on what was truly important. "Leo, please stand up. You and I need to have a talk about why you left the nursery."

He stopped his cavalryman in mid-gallop. After taking one cautious look upward at her unsmiling face, he clambered to his feet and hung his head. "I didn't want to practice my letters no more. I already know them."

"Anymore," she corrected. "And that doesn't give you the right to wander about wherever you please." *This isn't America,* she wanted to say, but lacked the heart to remind him of his old life. "I spent the better part of an hour looking for you all over the house and the grounds."

"Sorry," he muttered, kicking the dirt with the toe of his shoe.

He *did* look repentant, but she sank down to his level anyway, placing her hands on his small shoulders and gazing into the grimy, freckled face that had been squeaky clean this morning. "By coming here to the stables without permission, you put yourself in harm's way. That horse very nearly knocked you down. You might have been badly hurt."

"Mr. Duke knocked me down instead. He saved me."

Hero worship shone in his blue eyes, and Natalie felt a pang in her heart. She prayed that Hadrian would not disappoint the boy once she left here. Then she swallowed hard, not wanting to think about the future. "Well, you're very lucky he was here. But you must promise never to run off like that again. Is that clear?"

"Yes, Miss Fanshawe."

"Excellent. Let's return to the nursery now. You'll need a wash-up after playing in the dirt."

To his credit, Leo didn't argue as she rose to her feet and grasped his small hand. The route back to the house required them to walk toward Hadrian, who was still deep in conversation with his cousin at the edge of the stable yard. Nearing them, Natalie had the prickly sense of being watched.

And it wasn't by the duke.

Her gaze fell on Bert, slouching against a fencepost. Arms crossed, the brawny groom was staring openly at her. He had curly black hair and a crude handsomeness marred by a crooked nose. As he caught her eye, his lips peeled back into a leering smile that made her skin crawl.

She pulled her shawl tightly around her and assumed a look of icy scorn before turning her attention from him. It was an expression that she had perfected to ward off sailors and other ne'er-do-wells who would take advantage of a lone woman.

Just then, Hadrian beckoned to her. "Lord Wymark wishes to say something to you and Leo."

Judging by the sulkiness on the younger man's face,

she very much doubted that he wanted to speak to her at all. He turned and gave her a stiff bow. "I beg pardon for endangering you and the boy. It was not intentional."

"Apology accepted. I know how difficult it can be to control a spirited horse."

If anything, her response seemed to anger him, his frown deepening, and Natalie realized she oughtn't have added a comment that a proud young lord would interpret as a veiled jab at his riding skills.

The duke, however, appeared satisfied. "Come," he said, taking hold of her arm. "I'll escort you and Leo back to the house."

As they turned away, she had one last glimpse of Wymark's resentful features. He seemed to begrudge their very presence here at Oak Knoll. Of course, the family suspected her of being an imposter, attempting to pass off her own son as Audrey's. Nevertheless, Wymark ought to show at least *some* warmth toward Leo, who might be his nephew.

Perhaps, like his parents, he simply disdained the boy for being sired by a commoner and raised in the wilds of America.

Whatever the cause, his antipathy left Natalie deeply troubled. Wymark was a reckless young lord who had endangered a child—and he didn't even seem to care. It was yet one more reason for her to feel reluctant to leave Leo with his only blood kin.

Chapter 10

"I'm gonna be a cavalryman when I grow up," Leo announced.

Having departed the stable yard, they were strolling along the gravel path that led back to the house. Natalie could see that the duke appeared to be in a more relaxed humor now that he had dealt with his cousin.

"A cavalryman?" Hadrian said in mock surprise. "What about your ambition to become a sea captain?"

"I'd rather ride my horse into battle. Then I can kill the frogs with my sword. Take that, you Frenchie! *Argh*." The boy pantomimed stabbing the air, then crumpled dramatically like a fallen enemy onto the grass alongside the path.

A gleam in his eyes, the duke halted to gaze down at him. "Well, brat, at least you finally have your adversaries properly straightened out."

Leo sprang back to life and sat up, his face furrowed. "What's ad-ver-saries?"

"Your enemies. They are no longer the British, I see."

The boy thought about that for a moment, then shrugged and skipped ahead of them, the embodiment of childish unconcern for adult matters.

"You may thank Susan, the nursery maid, for his transformation," Natalie explained as they resumed walking. "She's been entertaining him with hair-raising tales about Britain's war with the French."

Natalie had overheard them talking while the maid gave him his bath the previous evening, and then again this morning after delivering their breakfast. In a matter of only a few days, Leo was setting aside the land of his birth and altering his loyalties to align with his new home here in England. She felt a twinge of sorrow at the thought.

Hadrian gave her a commiserating look that seemed to penetrate her very soul. Reaching out, he gently squeezed her hand. "It was bound to happen, you know. If Leo is to live here as the grandson of an earl, he'll have to conform to our way of life."

His enveloping touch warmed her blood, scattering her thoughts, so she pulled her fingers free. "That doesn't mean I have to like it."

He seemed amused by her retreat, one corner of his mouth lifting. "Point taken. However, adaptation is for his own good. So is proper behavior. He oughtn't have left the schoolroom without permission."

"I've already spoken to him about that."

"Perhaps it would help for him to hear it from someone else, too. Hey, brat. Come back here."

As Leo trotted toward them, pretending to hold the reins of an invisible horse, the duke guided Natalie to an oak tree beside the path. He waved her toward a stone bench that overlooked the house and the vast sweep of lawn. "Shall we sit for a moment?"

She hesitated, glancing at his shoulder, where blood had seeped through the makeshift bandage of her handkerchief. "What about your wound? Doesn't it need tending?"

"It's nothing. A few more minutes won't matter."

When she sank down, he settled beside her. Thankfully, the bench was long enough to allow a circumspect few inches between them. She oughtn't be tarrying in his company, not after that sizzling encounter in the stable yard. His mere presence stirred a flight of butterflies inside her rib cage.

But the early spring afternoon was too lovely to be cooped up in the nursery just yet. A flock of sparrows soared against the blue of the sky, and the gentle breeze carried the scent of freshly turned loam. The tree had not yet leafed out, so there was enough sunshine through the spreading branches to keep her from being chilled.

Leo stopped in front of them and gave Hadrian a cautious look. "Was I running too fast, Mr. Duke? I didn't mean to!"

Hadrian leaned forward, his elbows on his knees, his face level with Leo's. "No, it's your sneaking out of the nursery without permission that concerns me. You knew it was wrong."

The boy's chin dipped. "Yes, sir."

"You caused Miss Fanshawe a great deal of worry today. A gentleman doesn't behave that way."

"But I'm not a gentleman. I'm just a half-pint. That's what Papa used to call me."

Natalie's heart squeezed. She'd feared that at his young age, his parents might fade completely from his mind. Many months had passed since their deaths. But ever since the portrait of Audrey had been hung in his bedchamber, Leo had mentioned them a few times. He no longer seemed as distraught by the memories as he'd been in the weeks after the attack.

"Even half-pint gentlemen need to follow the rules," Hadrian stated. "Henceforth, you must listen to Miss

Fanshawe and do exactly as she instructs. Is that understood?"

His head bobbed up and down. "Yes, sir, Mr. Duke."

Affording him a shrewd look, Hadrian added, "There's another very good reason for you to mind your manners. If you show me that you can behave, I'll buy you a pony."

"*What?*" Natalie sputtered. Just like that, all of her good will toward the man vanished like smoke in the wind. "You can't—"

"A pony? A real pony?" Leo's excited voice drowned her out. His face lit up, his eyes big against his dirt-streaked face. "Can I—*may* I learn how to ride him, please?"

"Of course. Riding is an essential part of every young gentleman's education."

"Yippee! I'll be the bestest gentleman *ever*!"

"Excellent. Now go and play. But stay where we can see you."

In a burst of boyish exuberance, Leo cantered off across the lawn.

The instant he was out of earshot, Natalie rounded on Hadrian, her fists clenched in her lap. He was smiling indulgently, clearly pleased with his promise of a costly gift and unaware that he'd undermined her efforts to raise Leo according to the values of his parents. "You *bribed* him! That isn't the way to teach a child. He must learn that proper conduct is its own reward."

"Nonsense. He's of an age when he ought to be learning to ride. I merely used the pony as an incentive."

"A far too lavish incentive! I wouldn't mind if you wanted to buy him a lemon drop in the village. Or give him a pat on the head and a kind word. But not *this*." All of her fears for the boy's future rose to the fore. "I won't have Leo spoiled as you were, growing up in the lap of luxury, with your every wish indulged. It will ruin his character!"

All trace of pleasure vanished, leaving his features hard, his lips thinned. "Is that what you think of me? I've given you no cause to question the merits of my character."

Aware she'd gone too far, Natalie said stiffly, "I didn't mean to impugn your honor. But as a duke, surely you must have been raised with all manner of affluence and extravagance."

"My childhood wasn't like that at all."

"Oh? I suppose a duke played with sticks and leaves as Leo did in America. Or with a handful of wooden animals carved by one of the settlers. No, *you* had that vast army of tin soldiers up in the nursery, along with a host of other expensive toys. *And* a pony, no doubt."

Hadrian clenched his jaw, his brow furrowed, as if he were wrestling with an inner demon. "If you must know, those soldiers belonged to Richard—Lord Wymark. So did most of the other things in the cupboards. When I was Leo's age, Godwin was a skinflint who didn't approve of an excess of toys. He seized most of the ones given to me by my mother. It was only when he married the second time that he relented and indulged their two children—Richard and Ellen. But by that time, I was already living most of the year at boarding school." Hadrian's piercing gaze bored into her. "When I came here at the age of five, I had to make do with very little. So did Audrey. Perhaps that's why she was able to adapt so well to living on your American frontier. Being the same age, we were raised together, and I doubt you'd have called *her* spoiled."

His tirade left her somewhat chastened. His posture was rigid, as if she'd struck a nerve. Maybe his childhood hadn't been quite the bed of roses that she'd presumed.

He had, after all, made a good point about Audrey, who had never behaved as one born to privilege.

As her anger ebbed, Natalie found herself curious about Hadrian. It seemed there was more to him than initially met the eye. "Forgive me, I oughtn't have made assumptions. But . . . if your mother was alive, why did you have to come here to Oak Knoll? Why couldn't you have remained with her?"

"Godwin was my legal guardian. My father naturally made provisions for his successor to be raised by someone who could be trusted to oversee my education and my inheritance."

"Couldn't the earl have done that without separating you from your mother? It seems unnecessarily harsh for you to lose both parents when one was still capable of seeing to your care."

His mouth twisted ironically. "You don't know my mother."

"Then tell me about her, please. Was she unfit in some way? Negligent, perhaps? Uncaring?"

"None of that—she's very devoted to me, in fact." He gazed into the distance for a moment as if struggling to find the right description. "The duchess is . . . frivolous, blithe, sentimental, someone who can fuss over a maid with a sore tooth or weep copiously at the death of a fictional character in one of the novels she likes to read. She's impulsive and extravagant, too, without the slightest notion of the value of money. As a child, I used to visit her for a week twice a year, and she would buy everything in the toy shop that caught my fancy."

"And she sent those things back here with you, only to have Lord Godwin take them all away?"

Hadrian conceded that with a nod. "I was allowed to keep only one item, and the rest was donated to charity.

Now, don't look so aghast, it built character and kept me from becoming too spoiled."

Natalie smiled rather abashedly to hear her own accusation mocked. For Leo's sake, it was a relief to learn that not all upper-class children were overindulged. She glanced up at the castlelike house, picking out the nursery windows at the top floor and imagining Hadrian arriving here as a grief-stricken little boy who had been denied even the comfort of his mother. "How did your father die?"

"A fall from his horse during hunting season. To be honest, I scarcely remember him. There's just the impression of a tall man who would pick me up and swing me in the air to make me laugh. Other than that . . . nothing."

"Your poor mother, to lose both her husband and her son all at once. It still seems cruel to me that you were removed from her care."

"For company, she had my younger sister, Elizabeth, who *was* given everything she desired and consequently picked up all of our mother's habits of impetuosity and overindulgence. But one cannot dislike Lizzy for her faults since she also inherited Mama's generous heart. And my sister has wisely married an extremely wealthy marquess, though she may yet beggar Wrenbury before all is said and done."

In his half-smile, Natalie detected a genuine fondness for his mother and his sister. It touched her heart, and she felt a slight crumbling in the wall she'd erected against him. "Do you see them often?"

"Enough to make up for the years apart." Hadrian gave her a sardonic grin. "I devote a fair amount of time to scolding them about their spending. I haven't given up yet on reforming them."

"And here I believed all aristocrats to be useless wastrels."

"I'm neither miser nor saint. Yet I might very well have squandered my fortune as a gambler and profligate had I remained in my mother's keeping."

Natalie braced her palm against the cold stone of the bench in between them. "Regardless, I still think it's wrong to separate a child from his mother."

He glanced away, his gaze pensive. Then he looked back at her and shrugged. "The past is done. Growing up at Oak Knoll, I learned moderation and discipline. As a boy, I thought Godwin too strict, but now I can appreciate his tutelage, for he taught me to be a shrewd investor and a prosperous landowner." Hadrian smiled mischievously, his gray eyes showing a hint of blue in the brightness of the sun. "So, Natalie, have I redeemed myself in your critical estimation?"

His smile charmed her with all the power of a wizard's enchantment. He was only being affable, so why did she feel like a moonstruck girl?

Matching his light tone, she said, "I stand corrected, of course. You were not precisely *spoiled* as a child. Only unfairly elevated to a privileged stature by an accident of birth."

His chuckle held a note of irony. "My rank is an immutable part of who I am. It's not something I would change, even if I could. So if you wish to start a revolution here in England, that will make us enemies, and I would far rather count you as a friend."

Friend. Could she truly be the duke's friend when she felt assailed by this relentless tug of attraction to him? When she felt a pang of regret that they were from two utterly different worlds? For the sake of her sanity, Natalie reminded herself that their relationship was merely temporary. It would last only until she could secure Leo's future and feel confident that he had at least one strong ally before she returned to the United States.

An ally who would help keep the boy on the right path.

"Then as a friend," she said, "I have to question why you would indulge Leo with an extravagant gift—a pony that he doesn't deserve for being naughty. It makes me wonder if you see yourself in him. And if you're instinctively trying to compensate for things *you* were denied as a boy."

Hadrian appeared startled by the observation. He swung his gaze toward Leo, who was kneeling on the ground outside the garden wall, using a stick to poke at something in the dirt.

"Don't be absurd!" he growled before tempering his tone. "Well . . . at least I hadn't intended it that way. Do you really think that could be true?"

"It's a possibility. Did *you* have a pony?"

"My mother once bought me one, a fine chocolate-brown fellow just my size. His name was Mud."

Her heart melting, she pictured him as a little boy. The gift must have meant a lot to him since he still remembered it so clearly. "Mud?"

"I was only six. The pony was my favorite gift, and Mama took me to the park in London so that a groom could teach me to ride him. But Godwin sold Mud. He said that ponies gobbled far too much grain and I could learn to ride on one of the stable hacks . . . but I suppose that proves your point."

He cast an annoyed look at her, but she merely lifted her eyebrows, deciding it was best for a man of such lofty pride to draw his own conclusions.

"Well, *blast*," he said with feeling. "The brat needs a pony no matter what convoluted motives you may ascribe to me."

"What if Godwin sells that pony, too?"

"He won't dare, by God. I'll make certain of that. And pray recall that Audrey was like a sister to me. If Leo is her child, I ought to be allowed to behave like an uncle to him."

Natalie stiffened. "*If?* You told me that you believe he *is* her son. Or are you saying that you still have reservations about Leo just as the earl does?"

Surprise flashed across Hadrian's face. He pivoted on the stone bench and leaned toward her, his brow drawn in a frown. "Of course not. When I said *if* Leo is her child, it was nothing more than a manner of speaking, and poor wording on my part. I apologize."

Natalie gazed steadily back at him. His earnest expression made her want to believe him. But she had to be certain for Leo's sake. "In the tower room the other day, you asked Leo if he recognized who was in that painting of Audrey. You seemed to be testing him."

"Only because I'd promised Godwin that I would look into the matter, that's all. I myself was already convinced." He reached for her hand, gently squeezing her fingers as if to convey his sincerity. "You're a woman of good sense and intelligence, Natalie. So tell me, would I buy the boy a pony if I truly thought you to be an imposter?"

Her pulse leaped at his warm touch, and she felt the tug of that peculiar connection with him, as if they were one mind and heart. It was illogical, considering they'd only met a few days ago and had so little in common. Yet the feeling persisted nonetheless, enhancing the pleasurable sensation of his strong hand around hers.

She scrabbled for the thread of their conversation. "I concede your point. However, we haven't yet agreed that you're buying Leo a pony."

"Then I must devote myself to the task of convincing you."

Bringing her hand to his lips, he brushed a soft kiss over the backs of her fingers. His gaze glimmered at her as if he were issuing a challenge that he fully expected to win. Her lips curved in response to his roguish air and she felt an irresistible longing sweep though her body. Just how did he intend to persuade her? And why did she feel so eager to find out?

Attraction sparked between them, as bright and intense as the sun. It melted her innermost depths and she glimpsed heat in the slight lowering of his dark lashes as he stared at her. That look held ardor and temptation and the promise of pleasure.

Then, just like that, his warm expression altered subtly. A cool mask came over his masculine features, a shuttering of the candor in his eyes, a restraint of his playful smile. It was as if he'd remembered that she was merely a commoner, the temporary governess of his cousin's son. Natalie needed that reminder, too. She must never forget that Hadrian was the Duke of Clayton, a powerful nobleman who clearly had a talent for charming women.

He rose from the stone bench, drawing her to her feet before releasing her hand. "I've kept you long enough. We'll talk about this another time."

With a nod, Natalie matched his neutral tone. "Tell Chumley to wash your shoulder with soap before he bandages it. Audrey was a firm believer that cleanliness helps to keep a wound from festering."

"Sound advice. Shall we go?"

They proceeded to the garden fence to collect Leo, who had acquired damp patches on his knees and a smear of mud on his face. He opened his grubby palm and excitedly showed them an earthworm, then had to be persuaded by Hadrian that the squirmy creature belonged in the dirt and wouldn't make a very good pet.

Watching them, Natalie remembered the close call with the stallion in the stable yard. Lord Wymark had only grudgingly apologized for his negligence. Between his careless manner and the unwelcoming coldness of his parents, Oak Knoll seemed a perilous place for a vulnerable little boy.

She told herself the duke would protect Leo when she returned to America to open her school. Yet worry settled into her bones. How could she depend on Hadrian when he would soon go back to his life in London?

"Dear heaven!" Priscilla exclaimed from the window. "Archie, you must come and see this!"

A few minutes ago, she had entered her husband's study to discuss the preparations for their daughter's debut. Priscilla was planning a spectacular ball that hopefully would also include an announcement of the girl's betrothal to the Duke of Clayton. It was necessary to squeeze a generous budget out of her miserly husband. The earl was by nature the tightest of skinflints, begrudging every penny spent, even refusing her pleas for the family to travel to London early since he didn't wish to incur a month's extra expense in opening Godwin House for the season.

He must be made to realize that procuring the exalted title of duchess for their daughter did not come cheaply.

For that reason, she had brought him a snifter of his favorite brandy and wore the marine-blue silk that he'd always admired. She might no longer be the blushing bride that he'd married, but Priscilla had worked hard to maintain an elegant figure. Over the years, she'd learned a few tricks to coax him into prying open his locked purse.

One of which was to take up a stance by the window so that the sunlight enhanced her full-breasted form. Like any man, he could be most easily manipulated when he was distracted by lustful thoughts. The trouble was, all of her scheming had flown away when she'd glanced outside and spied a sight shocking enough to chill the heart of any matchmaking mama.

Pivoting, she saw the earl was still sipping brandy in his leather chair by the fire. "Godwin," she snapped. "For pity's sake, come here at once!"

The earl grimaced—not a promising sign for sweet-talking him—but Priscilla feared there might be a bigger crisis in the making. She waited impatiently while he put down his glass and arose to join her at the window.

"What is it?" he asked.

He was ogling her bosom and she had to tug on his arm to get his attention. "Look outside! Clayton is with Miss Fanshawe. And they appear to be far too cozy!"

Godwin cast a desultory glance out the window. "They're merely walking toward the house."

"They were sitting very close together beneath the oak tree just a moment ago. Worse, the duke was kissing her hand and gazing into her eyes! If you'd come when I first called, you'd have seen it for yourself."

"You must be mistaken. Even if Clayton had an interest in her, he's too much the gentleman to conduct an affair in full view of the house."

"An affair? That isn't what I meant. What if that colonial upstart tries to steal him away from Ellen right under our noses?"

"Bah, he'd never marry a woman so far beneath him. Miss Fanshawe is beautiful, I'll grant you. She's precisely the brazen sort that a man looks for in a mistress. Since Clayton dismissed his latest *chère-amie* some weeks ago, it's likely he's merely seeking to replace her."

Priscilla frowned as the duke and Miss Fanshawe collected the boy and then disappeared into the house. Despite her husband's nonchalance, she felt a cold prickle. Noblemen *did* make mésalliances from time to time. Only look at the duke's own mother.

"We mustn't underestimate Miss Fanshawe," Priscilla insisted. "I've seen how she puts on airs. When I met her in the corridor earlier, one would have thought *she* was the lady of the manor. You don't suppose . . ."

"What?"

The nagging thought took shape in her mind. "There's something familiar about her dark hair and green eyes. And it just now struck me. You don't suppose she's related to those dreadful Lincolnshire Fanshawes, do you?"

"Balderdash. She's an American."

"Well, *I* believe she has designs on Clayton. Pray recall that she's already trying to trick us about the boy."

He scowled. "We don't know that for certain."

His continued refusal to denounce the child worried Priscilla. She had the sinking suspicion her husband believed it was *not* a hoax, that Leo truly was Audrey's son. That must be why he was behaving even more tight-lipped than usual. He'd been deeply distraught over his daughter's elopement all those years ago, and the sudden appearance of a possible grandchild had ripped open the old wound.

It would have been better for everyone if Leo had never come here at all.

Besides, Priscilla had brought a considerable dowry to her marriage many years ago, and she didn't wish to see a penny of it go to a boy not of her blood. Nor did she intend for such a rich matrimonial prize as the Duke of Clayton to slip out of her fingers.

She sidled closer and stroked her husband's sleeve. "I'm only trying to help, darling. Pray keep in mind that Miss Fanshawe isn't to be trusted. She may well be scheming to nab the duke as an alternate plan to placing her son in this house."

Godwin's expression hardened in spite of her effort to charm him. "Enough with these useless speculations!

Until my solicitor arrives, I will hear no more about this matter."

Turning, he marched to the table and picked up his glass, tossing back a drink. Priscilla glared at her husband. Men! At times they were too stubbornly blind to see what must be done. It would be up to her to find a way to discredit Miss Fanshawe.

To force the woman to take that bothersome boy back to America where he belonged.

Chapter 11

"Do you enjoy poetry?" Hadrian asked Lady Ellen at dinner.

Seated directly across the linen-draped table, she looked up, her blue eyes wide and startled. Gainsborough himself could not have painted a lovelier image of a young lady. In the softness of candlelight, Ellen had delicate features, rosy lips, and golden curls. A strand of seed pearls adorned her slender throat as was proper for a girl just out of the schoolroom.

"Poetry?" She sounded wary, almost alarmed. "Only seldom, Your Grace."

She instantly lowered her gaze and resumed toying with her dessert, swirling the tines of her fork in the raspberry cream icing. She'd eaten very little of the cake, Hadrian observed, having seen her nibble only a few crumbs.

That she could find her food more fascinating than him was a source of mild frustration. Over the course of the meal, he had attempted a number of conversational ploys, asking her about her interests, her friends, her plans for the upcoming season. But nothing he'd said had drawn her out of her shell for more than a minute or two.

"You needn't be shy, darling," Lady Godwin said from the foot of the table. She, too, had been trying to coax the girl to little avail, and the smile she aimed at Hadrian seemed strained. "Ellen adores Shakespeare's sonnets, Your Grace. I'm sure she has some favorites that she could quote to you."

Lady Ellen rolled her eyes. "That was when I was *fifteen,* Mama. I won't have time for reading, anyway, once we go to London next week."

Wymark drained his wine goblet. "I daresay you might like Lord Byron's verses, sis. He's all the rage with the ladies. Not that I would read such silly drivel myself."

"Richard," the countess said in a chiding tone, "that is most impolite when His Grace has expressed an interest in poetry."

Actually, Hadrian cared not a whit for such useless nonsense. He had only brought up the topic because Natalie had suggested he try his hand at writing a love poem to Lady Ellen. Thank God she seemed disinterested. He would have detested having to scribble clichéd cantos—words that had to *rhyme,* for pity's sake—just to win her affections.

"It's quite all right," he said. "Horses are a topic of greater interest to myself and Wymark. How is that new nag of yours, cousin? The one you purchased for a song from Lord Ludington last week."

The younger man slid a glance at his father, who was signaling to the footman to take their plates. It was obvious Wymark would rather his sire not find out about the near-accident in the stable yard. Hadrian might have had sympathy if the stallion hadn't almost trampled Leo and Natalie.

"Thunder is no nag," Wymark said defensively. "He

comes from a line of winners. I'll soon be able to collect high stud fees for him."

Godwin drilled him with a sharp stare. "You had better pray so," he told his son. "That harebrained purchase wiped you out for this quarter and the next. Don't come begging me for any advances, either."

"But I saved forty guineas off the going rate at Tattersall's—"

"You'd have saved a great deal more by not buying that wild beast at all. I've already received a complaint from Snodgrass. The animal tore across his newly planted fields and nearly flattened one of his tenant farmers."

"Baron Snodgrass?" Lady Ellen perked up. "Whom did he send over to deliver the note?"

"That youngest whelp of his. Never can remember his name."

"Jasper," the girl supplied brightly, then glanced around rather abashedly and lowered her gaze to her plate. "At least I believe that's him."

Hadrian detected a spark of interest in her and wondered if he had a competitor for her hand. The possibility disturbed him less than he'd have expected.

Before he could wonder why, Lady Godwin arose from the table. "Ellen, shall we leave the men to their port? We can wait in the drawing room."

Lady Ellen displayed an eagerness to depart the table. A vision in pale rose silk, she sprang up from the chair and trailed her mother out the doorway.

Watching her depart, Hadrian thought it a pity she couldn't be more like Natalie. Two women could hardly be more dissimilar in temperament. Where Ellen seemed to shy from meeting his eyes, Natalie had a saucy confidence and a readiness to voice her opinions. He'd had no trouble whatsoever conversing with her; in fact, he'd vastly enjoyed it. They might not always agree, but he appreciated Natalie for being open and forthright. That must be why, despite the obvious differences in their stations, he'd come to regard her as his equal.

How peculiar to admit that. For all of his adult life, he had been accustomed to being the one in charge. To having people behave with deference toward him. It wasn't something he demanded of anyone, it simply *was*. Those beneath his rank asked his opinions and yielded to his decisions. They bowed or curtsied to show their respect.

Except Natalie. She alone refused to pander to him. Her disregard for convention had disarmed and intrigued him.

Perhaps that explained why he'd confided in her today. From any other woman, such personal questions would have earned a frosty stare from him. Instead, he'd blurted out truths about his childhood that he'd never before revealed to anyone else. Memories such as the lack of toys in the nursery. Being separated at the age of five from his mother and sister. His pony Mud that he hadn't thought about in years. At least he'd had the sense not to mention the part about crying himself to sleep for a week after Mud had been sold.

Natalie had listened closely and then apologized for misjudging him. But she had not backed down about him buying a pony for Leo. Although Hadrian hated to admit it, she was probably right about the wisdom of rewarding the boy for bad behavior. But damn it, he didn't want Audrey's son to be deprived of the joys of childhood as he himself had been.

Wait. *Had* he been deprived? Natalie couldn't be right about that, too, when he'd convinced himself otherwise.

"Pray leave us," Lord Godwin said.

Jolted out of his reverie, Hadrian realized the earl was addressing his son. Wymark lounged in his chair, a nosy expression on his narrow features. "Is this about my sister? Is there to be an announcement forthcoming?"

"Out," the earl repeated, more sharply this time. "I'd like a private word with His Grace. What we choose to discuss is no concern of yours."

"Fine. I'll go, then." Rising, Wymark grabbed his wine goblet and saluted Hadrian with it. Clearly tipsy, he swayed as he sauntered out of the room, pausing to throw over his shoulder, "Better get the ring on her finger quickly, Clayton, before the other fellows see her!"

A flush of disapproval tinted Godwin's cheeks, a contrast to his graying fair hair. Dismissing the footman, he picked up the crystal decanter and poured two glasses, pushing one toward Hadrian. "I apologize for the lad. He can be a trial at times, especially when he's in his cups."

"No harm done." Hadrian took a sip of the rich, ruby wine. His father's cousin might be a pinchpenny, but he kept a decent cellar. "This port can make up for anything."

Godwin held up his glass to the light from the candelabrum on the table. "It *is* a beauty, isn't it? My last bottle of this vintage."

They discussed the merits of several varieties of Spanish and Portuguese grapes before the earl said, "If I may, I would like to confer with you on the matter that Richard mentioned. I'm anxious to know your intentions toward my daughter, now that you've seen her for the first time in some years. Does she meet with your approval?"

Hadrian had anticipated the question although he was not entirely ready to answer it. "Lady Ellen is a well-mannered young lady. One cannot deny she has all the qualities to make an excellent duchess." He paused, then decided to be blunt. "However, I have my doubts as to whether or not *she* wishes to fill that role."

"Ellen can be bashful at times. She is only eighteen,

after all, and newly out of the schoolroom." Godwin frowned as if frustrated. "But I can testify that she's usually a more lively girl. Perhaps being confronted by a man of your stature has frightened her into silence."

"That may be so," Hadrian agreed noncommittally.

He glanced down into his glass, swirling the port and wondering at his vague sense of reluctance. He was making a grand alliance, not a love match, and Lady Ellen adequately filled his requirements. She had been trained since birth in how to manage a nobleman's household. As for her shyness, that surely would resolve itself in time. Hadn't he already decided, anyway, that he wanted a woman who wasn't too chatty or opinionated? He had no intention of spending the rest of his life shackled to a wife who would give him no peace.

But meeting Natalie had thrown that prerequisite into question. *She* was most definitely chatty and opinionated, yet he'd very much relished talking with her. They'd shared the repartee of friendship, a valuable commodity he'd only ever found with his male friends. Strange as it might seem, he felt more *alive* in her presence. Their closeness of minds and souls made no logical sense considering they'd known each other for only a scant few days. And the hell of it was that he could have conversed with her for hours.

At least he'd thought so until the moment when they had bantered about Leo's pony. He had brought her hand to his lips for a playful kiss, gazed into her sparkling green eyes, only to be rocked by an irresistible rush of desire. Her softened features and slightly parted lips assured him that the passion was mutual. In that mad moment, he had been sorely tempted to lay her down in the grass and damn the consequences . . .

Godwin cleared his throat. "I do hope we can come to a satisfactory agreement on this matter."

Matter? It took Hadrian a moment to recapture the direction of their discussion. Ellen. Marriage. His own qualms.

"It might be best to allow Lady Ellen to enjoy her first season unencumbered by a fiancé," he said tactfully. "Let her experience society, where she can have the chance to hone her conversational skills and gain her confidence. Rushing her will only make her unhappy."

Godwin grimaced. "I take your point. However, let us not forget that it was your late father's wish—and mine—that our families be joined in a closer bond. A pity things did not work out quite as we'd intended back then."

"Because of Audrey." A dormant anger awakening in him, Hadrian leaned forward to study the harsh lines of that aristocratic face, the man he had once feared to disappoint as a boy. "You haven't spoken her name in the past ten years. Don't you think it's high time that you did?"

The earl stared stonily at him. "She cut herself out of our lives. It was her mistake, not mine."

"It was a decision, not necessarily a mistake. One you should have respected and accepted. She might have stayed in England, then, and never died in that massacre." His throat thickening, Hadrian shook his head. "And just so you know, I wouldn't have courted Audrey, anyway. Not so long as she loved another man."

"Love! She had a duty to marry well. She let this family down."

"She let *you* down. Because of a bargain she'd had no part in making."

Nor had Lady Ellen or himself, he reflected. That was why he'd never coerce the girl if she was unwilling. In truth, the arrangement between their fathers was beginning to leave a bad taste in his mouth, making him question his own judgment.

"It's all water under the bridge now." Godwin tossed back the rest of his port. "There's no need to speak of it anymore."

"Yes, we do need to speak of it. Audrey's son is in this house at this very moment, up in the nursery. And you have a chance to make things right by accepting Leo as your rightful grandson."

The earl glanced away, his jaw tight. "I will rely on the advice of my solicitor. Musgrave is an excellent man of the law. He should arrive in a day or two."

Frowning at that stubborn face, Hadrian strove for calm. The earl had had a decade in which to harden his heart against his eldest daughter, and it wouldn't be easily softened. Besides, Hadrian had seen something flicker in those blue eyes. A shadow of pain that gave him hope that all was not lost.

And if things didn't work out?

By God, he would not allow Leo to bear the brunt of his grandfather's acrimony. Natalie was right, the boy *did* remind him of himself at that age, alone and bewildered, grieving for his father and denied the comfort of his mother. Leo's situation was that much worse, considering Godwin's reluctance to acknowledge the child.

"What if your solicitor has no clear answer?" Hadrian asked. "How familiar is he with foreign documents?"

"We shall find out soon enough."

"But what would you do in such an instance? You cannot abandon the boy after Miss Fanshawe endured an ocean voyage to bring him to you."

"Miss Fanshawe." The earl's gaze sharpened. "That reminds me. This afternoon, Priscilla saw you with her from the window of my study. The two of you were seated together beneath a tree."

Hadrian restrained a curse. Though he'd done nothing wrong, it irked him to know that the countess had been spying on a private moment. "I walked back with her from the stables. We were enjoying a bit of sunshine while Leo played on the lawn."

"Is that all? My wife noticed a decidedly cozy manner between you two."

"Cozy?"

"Yes, you were seen kissing Miss Fanshawe's hand. Good God, Clayton. One would think you'd have the sense to show more discretion. Keep a mistress if you like, but don't seduce her under my roof. I won't have my innocent daughter exposed to your dalliances."

Hadrian's glower turned icy. He clenched his jaw to keep from lashing out and throttling the man. Never in all his years of living here had he ever felt such a cold fury toward his former guardian.

He shot to his feet. "And *I* won't tolerate slurs cast at Miss Fanshawe. She was your daughter's friend, and her moral character is beyond reproach. You should be thankful that your grandson was entrusted to her care, but instead, you're too mired in your own bitterness."

Hadrian sent one last glare at Godwin's startled face before turning on his heel to stride out of the dining room. It was either depart the man's company, or do something he might later regret.

In the shadowy nursery, Natalie opened the door to the room opposite hers. She tiptoed to the cot in the corner and held up her lamp so that its golden glow fell upon Leo. He lay curled on his side beneath the blankets, his tawny hair mussed, his eyes closed in childish innocence. The toy cavalryman that he'd been holding had fallen to the rug, so she picked it up, placing it on the table beside his bed.

Her heart squeezed. How she dreaded the time when she would have to depart! Alas, that day was fast approaching.

Lord Godwin's solicitor had been summoned from London, though no one seemed to know exactly when he might arrive. It comforted her to think that even once Leo's papers were verified, she would still have a little more time left with him. A new governess would need to be hired through an agency in the city. Natalie would happily fill the post herself even though it would mean delaying her plan to open a school in Philadelphia. But she knew the Earl of Godwin would never permit his grandson to be taught by an American.

That meant she might have only a week or two more with Leo. She intended to treasure every moment of it. But was she doing the right thing to leave him here with a family that resented his very existence?

The troublesome worry had kept her awake. She had tossed and turned in her bed for well over an hour before deciding to head down to the kitchen for a glass of warm milk. With the nursery maid sleeping in the next room, Leo should be perfectly safe.

Natalie quietly closed his door and wended a path through the darkened schoolroom. The chill in the air made her glad for her old woolen robe. As she descended the steep staircase used by the servants, the feeble light of the lamp barely penetrated the gloomy shaft.

It must be near midnight. The house felt as still as a tomb, the silence broken only by the faint scuffle of her footsteps. The eerie atmosphere raised prickles over her skin, but it wasn't ghosts that she feared.

Rather, it was the notion of Leo growing up in such an oppressive place, deprived of affection as Hadrian had been. The duke had not precisely said that he'd yearned for love as a little boy, but she could read between the lines.

Having met Lord Godwin, she could well imagine him to be a cold, forbidding guardian. Hadrian would have received no warmth from a stiff-necked man who had sold even a child's treasured pony. Was it any wonder that the duke wanted to indulge Leo?

The boy had been remarkably well behaved for the rest of the day, talking nonstop about the promised pony. Natalie had decided to subdue her objections. If Hadrian wished to present such a magnificent gift to his young relative, then she had no right to stop him.

After all, Leo had entered a world of privilege. As the grandson of an earl, he would be educated in the best schools and take his place someday among the aristocratic elite. The land of his birth, the parents who had loved him, the woman who had brought him across the ocean, would fade to distant memories.

She swallowed past the lump in her throat. At least Hadrian seemed interested in being a father figure in Leo's life. But did the duke truly mean to visit Oak Knoll more often? Having been raised with a natural cynicism toward the nobility, she dared not make any assumptions. Especially since he'd given her reason to suspect there was another motive for him to seek their company.

He desired her.

Nearly missing one of the wooden steps, Natalie clutched at the newel post to steady herself. How absurd to feel so addled over an English duke. They were as far apart as the moon and the sun. Nevertheless, her heart beat faster as she dwelled on the memory of him holding her hand to his lips. The hunger in his eyes had been intense and unmistakable.

He wanted to bed her.

She reminded herself of what her father had once told her, that English aristocrats sought their pleasure from women of the lower orders. Seduction would mean ruin for her, while the Duke of Clayton walked away with his reputation intact. That was why there could never be anything between them beyond a tenuous friendship.

As she entered the cavernous kitchen, a glow came from the banked fire in the massive hearth while the rest of the chamber lay in darkness. She held up the candle and headed into the larder. There, the shelves held a variety of foodstuffs that gave off a delicious aroma: hams and sausages, preserves and pickles, sweets and spices. More pungent scents came from the bundles of dried herbs that hung from the ceiling.

After a short hunt, she located a canister of cold milk and poured a measure into a small saucepan. The handle felt a bit loose, but she didn't want to dirty anything larger. She set the pot onto a trivet over the grate and added a pinch of cinnamon and sugar. Using the fire iron, she poked at the glowing embers. Flames licked upward, radiating heat that warmed her chilly hands. As she stirred the milk with a spoon, Natalie felt cheered by the blaze and comforted by the familiar aroma of cinnamon.

The simple pleasure of performing a familiar task brought back memories of life in the American wilderness where she had learned to cook out of necessity. Though it wasn't her greatest skill, she had taken pride in the challenge of creating nourishing meals for herself and Audrey's little family.

Leaving the milk to heat, she walked past the long worktable toward a shelf that held crockery mugs and dishes designated for the servants. She would sip her relaxing drink, then return to bed. She would try to have faith that the situation with Leo would work out . . .

The sudden creak of wood broke the silence.

Startled, she spun toward the deeply shadowed corner from which the noise had emanated. A large black form separated itself from the gloom.

Chapter 12

Like a bear emerging from a cave, the hulking shape stepped into the light of the fire. The nape of her neck prickled. She knew that crudely chiseled face with its crooked nose and leering smile, the mop of curly dark hair.

Lord Wymark's groom, Bert.

Clad in a homespun shirt and brown trousers, the man stared at her, his avid gaze lingering on her robed figure. "'Evenin', miss. Ye're up late."

Natalie grasped the lapels of her wrapper, wishing she had a knife in her pocket. She took several breaths to calm her surging heartbeat. It wouldn't do to show fright, so she raised an eyebrow and glared at him. "Why did you not make your presence known at once? Why were you hiding in the shadows?"

"I was here first. Ain't my fault ye didn't see me."

"You oughtn't be in the house so late at night." The grooms slept in the stables. Although unfamiliar with customs in grand English homes, she took a guess and added, "The door was locked, so you must have broken in."

Bert shrugged as he brushed a few crumbs off his

wrinkled shirt. "A little jiggle of the handle, that's all. Needed a midnight snack. And 'twould seem I got more of a treat than I intended."

As he sauntered toward her, the lust in his dark eyes unleashed an avalanche of ice down her spine. They were isolated here in the cellars. Most of the servants slept up in the attic, and the housekeeper and cook had quarters at the other end of the corridor.

They were too far away to hear her scream.

Natalie edged back, hoping to put the worktable between the two of them. The knives must be in one of the many drawers, though she didn't know which one. If she attempted to search, he would be on her in a moment.

What else would serve as a weapon? The fire iron. It must be behind her, for she remembered propping it against the hearth.

Pretending a confidence that went only skin-deep, she said coolly, "If you value your position here, you'll keep your distance. I won't hesitate to inform Lord Wymark of any uncouth behavior."

"Now, what've I done? There ain't no law against admirin' a pretty lady." Judging by his smirk, Bert appeared to enjoy stalking her as she retreated. "His lordship won't mind, anyhow. He said ye've been livin' with savages in America. Ever laid with one?"

His denigration of her character was infuriating enough, but worse was his belittling of the Shawnee natives. She had encountered many good, kind people who traded animal skins and dried meat in exchange for various goods. They'd smiled and used gestures when she couldn't understand their broken English. She had been studying their dialect in the weeks before the massacre had changed everything.

"You overstep your bounds," Natalie said in her sternest

schoolteacher voice. "I've heard quite enough of your insults. Leave this house at once!"

Bert slowed his steps, his voice lowering to a croon as if she were a mare in need of taming. "Calm down, missy. Don't matter to me who's had ye. I only want to touch that soft skin. To undo yer braid, see yer hair spread over your nekkid bosoms."

Natalie resisted a shudder. He would attempt to force himself on her. She had seen that predatory intent once before.

Trying not to panic, she neared the fireplace. Though her gaze remained fixed on Bert, she could feel the heat of the flames and hear the snapping of the wood. The bubbling milk in the pot gave off a slightly scorched scent.

She inched closer to the hearth, furtively groping behind her for the slender rod. The roughness of the brick met her fingertips.

The groom sprang like a panther.

He seized the fire iron along with the ash shovel, stepping back to hold them aloft like war trophies. "Watch out there," he said, snickering. "Wouldn't want ye to hurt yerself."

He flung both implements across the kitchen. They clattered to the stone floor and skittered into the deep shadows.

Natalie fought off a wave of fright. What now? Threats and admonitions had proven to be no deterrent. He was a broad man, bulky with muscles, and the odds were in his favor. Although taller than the average woman, she knew her limits. He could overpower her with brute force.

Her only hope was to catch him off guard. She must behave like a frightened ninny, make him believe her to be weak.

She willed herself to cower by hunching her shoulders and lowering her chin. "Please, sir, don't hurt me," she said, adding a quiver to her voice. "I'm a respectable woman."

He stood a scant few feet from her. Shadows cast by the firelight gyrated over his gloating expression, proof that he'd been taken in by her sudden submissiveness. His lips peeled back in a grin that showed two rows of yellowed teeth. "Now, that's more like it. Many a wench puts up a fight at the start. But they're all eager for a taste of the big boy in my breeches."

His meaty fingers began to undo the front buttons of his flap. As he glanced down to watch his progress, Natalie saw her chance. Using the folds of her robe to protect her fingers from the hot handle, she grabbed the pot and hurled the boiling contents at him.

He must have caught her movement from the corner of his eye. Cursing, he started to raise his arm as a shield. Some of the scalding milk struck his sleeve and upper trousers. The rest splashed onto the exposed skin of his face and hands. Bellowing with pain, he clutched at his groin as hot white liquid dripped from his chin and down over his clothing.

Before she could so much as blink, he charged like an enraged bull. Natalie acted on sheer terrified instinct. She swung the pot at him with all of her might.

His fingers bit into her shoulders at the exact moment that the saucepan clanked against the side of his head. His neck jerked back and his grip slackened, his forward momentum propelling her against the brick of the hearth. Pots and crockery clattered to the floor. She parted her lips to scream, but only a squeak emerged as she went tumbling down beneath him.

His eyes were shut.

She lay entombed beneath the heavy mass of his

body, choked by the stench of sour whiskey. Had she killed him? Was he dead? A buried memory burst forth to swamp her senses, adding fuel to her wild panic. Dear God, no! It was just like before. She couldn't escape, couldn't see, couldn't breathe. Her heart pounded so hard that blackness encroached on her vision. In a mad frenzy, she shoved and kicked at his large, inert form.

In the next instant, his weight abruptly lifted from her. She sucked blessed air into her lungs and then rolled onto her hands and knees before scrambling to her feet. Dazed, she saw Hadrian. He held Bert by the scruff of his neck, his grip strong enough to lift the husky groom onto his tiptoes.

Before her chaotic mind could even feel relief, he spun the groom around and slapped his cheek several times until his eyes opened.

Bert blinked in befuddlement. "Duke—"

"Good, you're awake. It goes against my principles to strike an unconscious man."

Hadrian hauled back his arm and smashed his fist into Bert's face. The groom staggered sideways into the worktable, knocking it askew as he thumped to the floor like a sack of grain. Blood ran copiously from his nose and from the corner of his mouth. Head lolling, he grappled for his shirttail and used it in an attempt to stanch the flow. "Ow! Ow! Ye broke m' nose!"

"Be thankful you're alive. You are never to touch Miss Fanshawe again. Is that clear?"

"Wasn't gonna hurt her—"

Hadrian reached down and gave the man's ear a hard wrench. *"Is that clear?"*

"Ow! Aye, Yer Grace. Never!"

The duke stepped back, coldly regarding the groom.

"Now, take your miserable carcass out of here. You're to collect your belongings and leave Oak Knoll at once."

Bert lurched to his feet and stood swaying, his face raw with burns beneath the milk and blood. He also had a darker red mark on the side of his cheek where she'd struck him with the pot. In a nasally tone, he whined, "I work for Lord Wymark. Can't nobody send me away but him."

"Wymark is underage. You work for his father. And in case you've forgotten, Lord Godwin is the magistrate. If transport to Botany Bay is your wish, then by all means, stay here to plead your case."

The groom fell silent at that, though he continued to snuffle loudly. He flashed Natalie a resentful glare before turning away, lumbering to the antechamber that led outside. Hadrian followed the man and they disappeared from sight. A moment later, she heard the duke's clipped tone, then the door opened and shut. The key rattled in the lock.

Natalie trembled as tension continued to vibrate along her nerves. She could scarcely comprehend the danger was over. Her insides felt tied in knots as she surveyed the mess in the kitchen, the spilled milk, the broken crockery, the table pushed awry. If Hadrian hadn't come in when he did . . .

Feeling on the verge of being sucked back into that dark horror, she quickly busied herself with action. She mustn't allow herself to reflect. Better to just forget about it. She'd done so once and she could do it again. Her movements jerky, she bent down to pick up the copper saucepan.

Eyes widening, she stared at the damage. "Oh no!"

Hadrian materialized beside her, his broad palm

lightly resting between her shoulder blades. "Natalie? Are you injured? Did he hurt you?"

She raised her stricken gaze to his face. "I broke the handle! Cook will be furious."

His expression relaxed, though his pose remained vigilant. He gently removed the pan from her death grip and examined it. "The rivets must have come loose, that's all. Consider it your badge of honor for a deed well done. If Cook dares to fuss, I'll buy her an entire new set of pots."

That ought to have reassured her, yet Natalie was the farthest thing from calm. She felt herself teetering on the brink of irrationality. "I don't want you to buy me things! I can do it myself!"

Turning away, she grabbed a pile of folded rags from the counter and knelt to mop up the puddles of milk with frantic sweeps. White dots were scattered across the stone floor, along with smears of blood near the chair. If it took all night, she would wipe away every last trace of the incident. She would scrub and clean and scour as she'd done after the massacre . . .

Hadrian reached down and drew her to her feet. He flicked the rag from her grip. Then he folded her against him, tucking her face into the lee of his shoulder, his fingers cradling the back of her head. "It's all right, my dear," he murmured into her hair. "You're safe now."

His manner radiated a quiet, reassuring protectiveness. Nevertheless, Natalie stood rigidly in the circle of his arms, her breathing taut and shallow. Flashes of Bert's menacing face merged with that of the soldier at the massacre until they both seemed one and the same. She didn't want to dredge up that terrible memory from the buried depths of her soul. Nor did she seek comfort.

It was *her* cross to bear, not Hadrian's.

But his muscled form provided a safe harbor from the outside world. He wore no coat or cravat, only a cambric shirt and black breeches. His body heat penetrated her robe and nightdress and skin, reaching to the very center of her being. The painful knot inside her began to unravel, rising to her throat in a choked sob.

She swallowed hard in an effort to displace the lump. But once unleashed, that one cry turned into a torrent that proved impossible to control. A deluge of tears breached the wall of her willpower. Her knees crumbled, and she buried her face in his shirt, grateful that the strength of his arms kept her from dissolving into a spineless heap.

His embrace became her anchor in the storm of weeping. All the while he stroked her hair, murmuring to her, though she knew not the meaning of his words. She was too lost in a sea of anguish to fathom anything beyond the dreadful images in her mind.

"I didn't want to kill him," she cried, as the wild tide inside her crested. "*I didn't.* Why did he have to attack me?"

The hand on her back paused for a moment before again soothing away her tension. "Hush, now. He's gone. I'll protect you from harm. You've nothing to fear anymore."

Hadrian's firm, coaxing voice summoned Natalie back from the void. Beset by one last convulsive shudder, she took the folded handkerchief that he pressed into her hand, using the square of linen to wipe her damp face. Sanity trickled back into her brain, bringing her to an awareness that she'd been bawling in the arms of a duke.

Why it should matter what a nobleman thought of her, she couldn't imagine. Yet it *did* matter, and she felt too drained to determine why.

Tilting up her chin, she blinked at him through matted

lashes. Rather than exhibit distaste for her unrestrained lapse, he was frowning at her in concern, as if puzzling over something. Dear God, she'd been blathering in the midst of her weeping. What had she said?

Anxious to deflect any questions, she glided her fingers over the damp patch on his chest and the hard ridges of muscle. "I—I didn't mean to be a watering pot all over your shirt. I seem to be forever ruining your clothing."

"It keeps Chumley busy." His gaze watchful, Hadrian glided his thumb over her moist cheek. "Are you quite certain you're all right, Natalie?"

She managed a decisive nod. It was best to let him think that tonight's incident with Bert was the sole source of her distress. "It's just that . . . the groom startled me. I never expected anyone to be hiding in the shadows. All I wanted was a mug of hot milk."

"Ah. I'll wager *you* couldn't sleep, either."

"Either?"

One corner of his mouth curled into a half-smile. "I was reading in the library and came down to the kitchen in search of apple tarts. Cook knows they're my favorite and she baked me some."

"Oh." Natalie realized she hadn't even wondered why Hadrian had appeared at such an opportune moment. "I saw a plate of tarts on the shelf in the larder."

"Then pray excuse me while I find them."

With a gentle squeeze of her shoulders, he released her and headed across the kitchen. She felt bereft without his closeness. Her legs still rubbery, she sank onto the edge of the table, too depleted of energy to attend to the mess just yet. She blew her nose and then tucked his crumpled handkerchief into the pocket of her robe. How mortifying to have broken down like that! She didn't know quite what had come over her. It wasn't like her to lose control when she prided herself on being a strong, independent woman.

And to do so in front of Hadrian! What must he think of her?

It oughtn't matter. Yet she couldn't deny that it felt good to have a man to lean on. She had been alone for too long. Having grown up the only child of a widowed father who'd often included her in political discussions, she had always enjoyed conversing with men. But of late, there had been no one but Leo in her life—and as much as she loved the boy, he was no substitute for adult company.

When Hadrian returned, bearing a dish covered by a linen towel, she had recovered herself enough to stand up straight. "I suppose I shall have to warm another pot of milk. Would you care for some?"

"Actually, I believe we could both do with something stronger. Let's go upstairs to the library. It's warmer than this blasted cellar, anyway."

He came forward as if to take her arm, but Natalie shook her head. "I can't leave the kitchen looking like this. And the fire needs to be banked."

"The maids will tidy up in the morning." He set the plate on the table. "As for the fire, allow me."

"You know how?"

"Of course. Dukes are not entirely useless creatures." His mouth quirked in a droll half-smile, he glanced around the hearth. "Although I confess, I don't see any fire tools."

She pointed across the kitchen. "Bert threw them over there."

His smile vanishing, Hadrian gave her a grim look before heading in that direction. Had he guessed at her failed attempt to use one of the tools as a weapon? He couldn't begin to imagine just how terrified she'd been.

Or that the shock had wrenched open the door to a certain hideous memory . . .

Stifling a shiver, Natalie folded her arms over her midriff and hugged herself. There was no need to dwell on that event from the previous summer. The past was best left buried. In the months since then, she had put it all behind her. She had focused on caring for Leo, comforting him when he suffered nightmares, packing their few belongings, arranging for their travel papers. Hoping the passage of time would help her forget, she had kept herself busy and active so that she'd have no time to reflect . . .

"Does this pass inspection, milady?"

Natalie blinked, realizing that Hadrian had already shoveled ash over the embers. The flames had died down, leaving only a glow on the grate. The hearth, at least, appeared tidy, if not the rest of the kitchen.

"Perfect, Your Grace."

"I thought you'd sworn never to call me that," he said while propping the shovel beside the fire iron.

"That was before I knew you had any useful skills."

"I've a few others, as well."

The hint of rakishness in his smile ignited a feeling inside her much like the banked fire. There was no denying that she admired his virile handsomeness, the slightly mussed brown hair, the masculine angles of his face. His shirt was open at the throat to reveal a triangle of broad chest, and his gray eyes looked as soft as smoke . . .

His gaze lingered on her for another moment before he dusted off his hands and went to pick up the tray. "Come, I'll blow out my candle. Yours should be sufficient to light the way."

She picked up the pewter lamp, the flickering flame enclosing them in a golden cocoon. As they proceeded out of the kitchen and along the shadowy corridor, Natalie wondered why she felt so safe with Hadrian. After that vicious attack, she ought to be cautious of spending time alone with a man in the middle of the night, especially when she was garbed in her bedclothes.

And especially when the man in question was as tempting as sin.

Chapter 13

As they approached the library, their footsteps echoing in the great hall, Hadrian was aware of the heavy beating of his pulse. He must be mad to prolong their time together. Their lives were poles apart, and besides, she intended to return to America soon. Yet tonight he could not maintain his usual air of cool detachment.

He motioned for Natalie to go ahead of him. As she glided through the doorway, he caught a hint of her tantalizing scent, something soft and deeply feminine. It reminded him of holding that curvaceous body in his arms. In the kitchen, it had never even occurred to him to sit her down in a chair and let her cry it out from a safe distance as he did with his mother and sister. Like any sane man, he'd sooner face the hounds of hell than a woman's tears. Yet a powerful protective instinct had compelled him to clasp her close, to let her know that she could trust him to shield her from harm.

For as long as he lived, he would never forget the sight of her swinging that pot at Bert, knocking the man out cold, and then collapsing under his dead weight. The moment that it had taken for Hadrian to reach her had seemed to stretch out forever. He'd derived great satisfaction from smashing his fist into the brute's face. Had it not been for fear of further traumatizing Natalie, he'd have killed the bastard without an ounce of remorse.

Burying the memory, Hadrian followed her into the library with its floor-to-ceiling shelves of tooled-leather books. It was vital that he display a relaxed, unruffled manner. Despite her seeming calm, she surely still felt distraught and shaken.

He felt certain, too, that it wasn't just tonight's attack that had caused her emotional collapse. Something else was at play. He craved answers, yet what gave him the right to pry into her private life? He was merely an acquaintance, a friend. They were bound together only by their mutual wish to protect Leo.

Regardless, Hadrian found himself noticing how the play of candlelight and shadow in the library created an intimate retreat. The night scene looked tailor-made for seduction. Unaccustomed to the strict rules of society, Natalie might not realize just how inappropriate it was for them to be together. Should they be discovered, the scandal would sully her reputation.

Though of course, she was going back to America, he reasoned, and no one else was awake, anyway. The rest of the family had retired hours ago. Besides, he was perfectly capable of keeping his desires in check. He'd give her a brandy to steady her nerves, assure himself of her recovery from the attack, and then send her off to bed.

Alone.

Slim and willowy, she headed to the marble mantelpiece where a fire flickered. A pair of coffee-brown settees faced each other with a table in between them. He'd been sitting there a short while ago, perusing a book, when he'd been struck by the compulsion to go down to the kitchen. Odd, that. He was too rational a man to believe in premonitions. Yet the connection he felt with

Natalie made him wonder if he'd somehow sensed her peril.

Now, she stood gazing down into the low-burning flames. With her hair plaited into a glossy dark braid that draped over one shoulder, she looked young and vulnerable, in contrast to her usual intrepid self. It struck him that this was a woman who could endanger his carefully ordered life.

The notion rattled him. He had no intention of altering his plans. He had already made his choice for a wife.

Yet the ground seemed to be shifting beneath him. Wouldn't his London friends laugh if they knew that after a string of elegant mistresses, he could feel so drawn to a provincial spinster? That he found well-worn flannel to be more titillating than a filmy negligee? That having selected his blue-blooded bride, he lusted instead for an eccentric, lively, and outspoken American?

Devil take it. This was a moment out of time, that was all. Tonight, nothing else mattered to him but Natalie.

Setting down the plate of tarts, Hadrian went to her side. He took the candle from her and placed it on the table. Lacing her cold fingers with his, he guided her to the settee that he'd occupied earlier. "Your skin is like ice. Come and sit near the fire."

As she took the seat closest to the hearth, Natalie seemed to make a concentrated effort to rally herself. "I haven't yet thanked you."

He sank onto one knee and clasped her hands between his to warm them. He was keenly aware of the softness of her skin, the delicacy of her fingers. It felt like cupping a small bird between his palms. "Thanked me?"

"Yes, that's the second time today that you've saved my life." She turned over his hand, examining the reddened area on the back. "First you hurt your shoulder on my behalf. And this time, you've skinned your knuckles."

"The incident with the stallion was a fluke. As for to-night, *you* brained the villain yourself. I merely delivered the coup de grâce." He cocked an eyebrow. "Remind me never to venture too close when you're wielding a pot."

His jesting tone brought a sparkle to her eyes. "Behave like a gentleman and you've naught to fear. And by the way, *gentleman* has little to do with exalted birth. I've met fine, honorable gentlemen from all walks of life. What's important is courtesy, principles, and respect for others."

"I do hope you'll include a duke in that group."

"If I didn't, I wouldn't be here right now."

Absurdly pleased to be the recipient of her approval, he arose and went to a nearby cabinet. "Would you care for a glass of sherry? Or something stronger, a brandy, perhaps?"

"Brandy, please. I often enjoyed that or a whiskey with my father."

Hadrian wasn't surprised by her unconventional tastes. He busied himself with filling two glasses from the de-canter. "You're right to believe that character matters. I know aristocrats who possess none of those qualities. But I suppose every class of society has its bad apples."

"In America we have no classes," she pertly reminded him. "No one rules over others by birthright."

The mild jibe only amused him as he handed her one of the tumblers. "An egalitarian system of gover-nance seems to work well in a fledgling country like the United States. However, we're much more entrenched in our ways here in England. The aristocracy has been around since the time of William the Conqueror. To change it now would risk chaos and societal collapse, as happened in France during our parents' generation."

"Hm." She held up her glass in a mock toast. "Well, I could hardly wish the guillotine on my twice-savior, could I? How *is* your shoulder, by the way?"

The glow of those green eyes scrambled his brain, and he required a moment to comprehend that she was referring to the stallion's kick. "A slight twinge now and then, nothing more."

In reality, he felt a persistent dull throb, but the brandy should take care of that. He tossed back half his drink, then went to the hearth and added fuel to the fire, poking it with the fire iron so that a shower of sparks flew up the chimney. He needed to get a grip on himself. This hunger he felt had no place in a cordial association with an American governess. Having been awarded the designation of gentleman, he didn't want to ruin his image by succumbing to the urge to kiss her senseless.

Hadrian turned back around to see her paging through the book that had been lying on the table. She glanced up, frowning slightly. "This atlas has a marker at the map of North America."

"I was looking at it earlier, hoping to locate the settlement where you and Leo lived. Bellingham, you said it was called, after Audrey and Jeremy."

Sampling her brandy, Natalie nodded. "It's in the southeastern part of Michigan territory, but it's too new to be on this map."

"Ah. I'd wondered. I'm not entirely familiar with the country, so I was probably looking in the wrong spot, anyway."

He took a place on the settee across from her. It was best to keep a circumspect distance. That way, temptation could be easily resisted, a necessary precaution since she looked entirely too pretty in the soft firelight.

He had no sooner taken a drink than she arose. Carrying her brandy glass and the atlas, Natalie came around the table and seated herself right beside him. Her nearness was a jolt to his senses. What was it about her that made him feel as besotted as a schoolboy infatuated with his first girl?

She regarded him a little doubtfully. "I hope you don't think me too forward. It's just that you sounded interested in viewing the map."

"I *am* interested. Very much so."

Damn, now *that* sounded forward. But she either didn't notice the double entendre or chose to disregard it. She spread the open atlas across their laps, so that the right half rested on his thigh and the left on hers, with the spine in between them.

"The reason you couldn't find Bellingham," she said, "is that the mission was built only seven years ago, and this map appears to be outdated by over a decade. See? It lists Ohio as part of the Northwest Territory."

"Then where is Bellingham?"

"Right here, close to the western end of Lake Erie and just above where the Ohio border is now."

He moved the lamp from the side table so that the light fell on the place where she was pointing. "Ohio . . . is that now part of the United States?"

"Yes, it was added over ten years ago. I remember in particular because my father was involved in passing the Enabling Act, which established a procedure for creating new states. I must have been about fourteen, then. Old enough to recall the celebrations, including a parade and a special dinner at my house for members of Congress. I was allowed to join them for the dessert course."

He picked up the plate. "Speaking of dessert, would you care for a tart?"

She accepted one of the small pastries and smiled her thanks. While her attention was focused downward at the page, he took the opportunity to study her classic profile. She had long dark lashes, tipped in gold by the firelight. He ached to know if her cheek felt as petal soft as it looked. How he would enjoy kissing her, nuzzling her throat, opening her robe and . . .

To distract himself, he wolfed down a tart. The cinnamon apples and flaky crust melted on his tongue, but he'd have traded it in an instant for a taste of her bare skin.

While studying the map, Natalie nibbled on her own tart. "Look," she said, her fingertip touching the page. "Here's Philadelphia, where I was born. It's also where I first met Audrey, when she and Jeremy came to raise the funds to build their mission." Her finger trailed lower. "And here's our capital, Washington, where I spent quite a lot of time, too."

"Your father was a senator."

"Yes, my mother had died at my birth, so Papa asked me to be his hostess when I turned sixteen. It was both an honor and a challenge to plan parties for the president and foreign dignitaries. I learned the importance of being organized, and how to deal with crises like unexpected guests or fallen soufflés."

The vivacity that lit up her face charmed Hadrian as much as the diversity of her experiences intrigued him. "So, before your time in the wilderness, you were accustomed to being at the center of American society."

"Yes, due to Papa's position." A wistful note entered her tone. "I do miss him very much. He was a fine man, kind and generous to a fault, along with being a great orator. And he wasn't just an empty talker like some politicians, he was genuinely devoted to helping people. If you were caught in a snowstorm, he would give you the coat off his back, even if it meant he himself would freeze."

"A true gentleman, then. May I ask what happened to him?"

"He was struck down by a heart spasm two years ago.

He'd only just retired from Congress, intending to spend more time on our horse farm." She cast a somber look toward the fire. "We were planning to go for an early ride that morning. But when he didn't come down for breakfast, I went upstairs and found him, still lying in bed. He looked . . . so peaceful . . ."

When her voice faltered, Hadrian placed his hand over hers. He himself scarcely remembered his own sire. How much harder it must have been for Natalie since she'd been close to her father into adulthood. "I'm sorry. Perhaps there's a certain solace to be had in knowing he didn't suffer."

She drew a deep breath. "Yes, I'm grateful for that. I've many happy memories of him, too."

"You haven't mentioned any other family. Did you have cousins, aunts, uncles to comfort you?"

"I'm afraid there was no one. My mother was an only child. And my father . . ." For no apparent reason, her manner took on a certain reserve. She withdrew her hand from beneath his, ostensibly to brush a few crumbs off the atlas. "Well, his family lived very far away."

He had the distinct impression he'd probed too deeply into her private life. A pity, because he burned to know why she'd never married. It seemed only natural that a lovely, vibrant woman would have had many suitors, especially if she'd lived in the public eye. Perhaps she'd merely been loath to leave her beloved father.

Setting aside the atlas, he arose to fetch the decanter and refill their glasses. "So Audrey's family became your family. I'm curious, why did she and her husband choose such a remote locale for their mission?"

"Jeremy attended a lecture in Philadelphia, by a traveling preacher who spoke of a great need to bring the word of God to the natives on the frontier. They went where they felt they could accomplish the most good."

"Were they not concerned that it was dangerous? I recall there being a dispute about the Northwest Territory. It was claimed by the British and the Canadians, as well as the Americans."

"When they built the settlement, the area was peaceful. Leo was born there, and they took it as a sign from God that they were meant to stay. They befriended the local natives, shared their faith with them, and strove to demonstrate that they could all live together in harmony."

Hadrian tried to imagine dainty, fair-haired Audrey living in a rough cabin on the frontier with a baby and a preacher husband. Even surrounded by a log fence, an outpost in hostile territory had to be a perilous place. "Why didn't they leave when the war began? And what about you? You must have traveled there in the midst of the war."

"Bellingham was located some twenty-five miles from the nearest battle site, at River Raisin. Anyway, a year had passed with no further skirmishes in the area. I'd always enjoyed teaching, and after Papa's death, I thought it time to find another way that I could be useful."

"Yet Bellingham didn't turn out to be quite so safe a refuge, after all," he murmured.

Abruptly, torment shadowed her face and robbed her beautiful eyes of their brightness. Natalie surged to her feet, her fingers tightly clutching the wrapper at her throat. "I—I'd rather not talk about this anymore. It's late."

Silently cursing himself, Hadrian arose, too. Why had he stirred up painful memories by alluding to the massacre? It was none of his concern. He had a strict policy of not involving himself in other people's troubles. Especially in situations where intense emotional outbursts might occur.

But she had survived a harrowing attack. It was clear

that the experience still weighed heavily on her. And he simply couldn't abide the thought of her suffering alone.

He stepped closer, placing his hands on her shoulders. She felt rigid to the point of trembling, and he gently massaged her tight muscles. "Are you certain you don't wish to talk, Natalie? I suspect more transpired during the massacre than you've let on. When the British soldiers attacked the settlement, you said that you were in the schoolroom. And that you hid the children in a shed. What else happened?"

She glanced away, biting her lip. "You're better off not knowing."

He cupped her cheek, turning her face back toward him. "But *you're* not better off," he said softly. "I suspect this has been eating away at you, that it's the true cause of that bout of weeping in the kitchen. You said, *'I didn't want to kill him.'* You couldn't have been referring to Bert because you'd just seen him walk out of the room, very much alive."

Her bleak gaze fixed on Hadrian. But he had the sense that she wasn't really seeing him, that she was looking inward at some horror from the past. "It serves no purpose to rehash the past."

"Yet it can't be doing any good, either, to let it fester inside of you. A burden is easier to carry if it's shared."

He wasn't sure where that knowledge had come from. It was precisely what he'd avoided doing in his own life. His friends wisely respected his aloof reserve and knew better than to pour out their personal problems. Until this moment he'd never wanted anyone to confide their darkest secrets in him.

But he did now.

Their gazes clung for a moment. Then she drew a ragged breath and stepped away from him, her arms wrapped around her middle. "It all . . . happened so fast.

After I ushered the children to safety, Leo included, I put one of the older boys in charge of the little ones. They were to remain in the shed and stay quiet. I couldn't just cower there with them, you see. I had to go and help my friends and neighbors. They were *dying*."

Chilled, Hadrian watched her pace back and forth in front of the hearth, the hem of her robe swishing around her ankles. "My God, what did you think you could do against armed troops?"

"I had my pistol. My father taught me from a young age how to defend myself. Upon leaving the children, I made haste toward the sounds of gunfire and . . . and screams. But as I went toward the front of the school-house, a man came at a fast pace around the corner . . . one of the British soldiers."

Hadrian gripped his fingers into fists to keep from going to her. It was clear from her tense posture that she'd erected a wall around herself and would reject comfort. Especially from an Englishman.

Shifting her gaze to the fire, she continued in that flat tone, "He was so close, only a few feet away. He sprang at me, a sword in his hand. There was such bloodlust in his eyes, it was like looking into the face of a . . . a demon. Retreat was out of the question, for it would mean leading him back toward the children. I raised my pistol, but it misfired and then he knocked it out of my hand. He threw me to the ground and tried to push up my skirt. But he didn't know . . . that I had a knife in my pocket. I . . . I cut his throat."

On that last sentence, her voice wobbled. She buried her face in her hands, her body shuddering.

Hadrian hastened to wrap his arms around her slender form. Would that he could absorb her pain! Stroking the tautness of her back, he murmured consoling phrases that he'd have thought trite under any other circumstances. But there was simply nothing else to say that would cleanse her of the dreadful memory.

At the same time, fury gripped him that any man, let alone a British soldier, would dare to attack her—and Audrey. On his return to London, he'd have a few choice words with the War Secretary about the behavior of the troops toward civilians, women in particular.

Gradually, Natalie melted into him, her breath warm on his neck and her arms circling his waist. A powerful wave of tenderness replaced his anger. Though not a particularly religious man, he uttered a silent, heartfelt prayer of thanks that her life had been spared. That she could be here in this moment with him, safe within his embrace.

When she raised her head, he half expected another storm of tears. But her haunted gaze held only sadness. "Why did I survive and not Audrey?"

Torment vibrated in her voice, and he felt at a loss to assuage it. The truth, he suspected, was that Audrey had been a healer, not a fighter. Her genteel upbringing had proved a liability in time of crisis.

He brushed away a lock of sable hair from Natalie's cheek. "Perhaps because you were armed and willing to fight back."

She considered that a moment. "It's a terrible thing to kill someone. I still have nightmares about the blood . . . and seeing the life fade from his eyes."

"You did what you had to do," Hadrian said with tender intensity. "He deserved to die."

"That doesn't make it any less gruesome. I was trapped beneath him for a time before I was able to free myself. Tonight, when Bert collapsed onto me, it all came rushing back. That's why I . . . I fell apart." She glanced away. "Forgive me, Hadrian, I never meant to involve you in my troubles."

With a light clasp of her chin, he turned her face back toward him. "There's no need to apologize."

"But I've never in my life wept like that, not even after the massacre."

"Come, sit down." He guided Natalie to the settee and tried not to notice how perfect she felt nestled in the crook of his arm, her bosom cushioned to his side. Only a cad would be having lusty thoughts when she'd just confessed a horrific experience. "I think you're remarkably levelheaded, and I admire your pluck. In the space of a few years, your father died, then your best friends. Maybe you've kept this experience hidden away simply because you had no one left in whom to confide."

Hadrian wondered at his own intense empathy for her. As a rule, he avoided speaking about deep sentiment, preferring to use banter and witticisms as a foil. But tonight he craved more than mindless repartee. He wanted to explore the complexities of this woman who had every reason to be wary of men.

Her expression softened, her eyes as luminous as emeralds in the firelight. She angled herself toward him, placing her palm in the center of his chest. That warm, light pressure made his blood sizzle in spite of his firm resolve. "You're right, Hadrian. There *was* no one—until you."

Chapter 14

Natalie wondered at her own boldness. She had not made a conscious decision to touch him; her hand seemed to have a mind of its own. With only the fine cambric of his shirt separating her palm from his bare skin, she reveled in the heat of hard-muscled flesh. It wasn't like her to make overtures toward a man. Especially not one who was utterly wrong for her.

A duke. She had grown up despising the British aristocracy for reasons best left unspoken.

Yet tonight Hadrian had become a flesh-and-blood man, and she could no longer disdain him for an accident of birth. Confessing her painful secret had deepened their bond. Somehow, they had gone beyond being mere acquaintances or friends, though exactly what existed between them remained a tantalizing mystery.

Searching herself for sorrow, she found herself blessedly free of that heaviness. Strange, how little the past seemed to matter anymore. She felt lighter, less burdened by all that had happened. And it was largely due to Hadrian. He made her feel protected and cherished in a way that she hadn't known in a long time. Perhaps forever.

Which meant he was a very dangerous man.

Her sense of safety was an illusion, at least in part. A nobleman would never offer her anything more than a moment's passing pleasure. In fact, it was probably nothing out of the ordinary for him to be with a woman in the middle of the night. A man of his wealth and charm would have left a string of broken hearts across England.

She had no wish to become one of them.

Nevertheless, the mellow glow of the brandy and her soul-deep yearning proved more powerful than common sense. The very air seemed charged with energy. Did Hadrian feel it, too? She could swear that the heavy thump of his heartbeat against her palm had accelerated.

He glided his fingertips over her cheek, leaving a trail of sparks. "I'm glad you confided in me, Natalie. I only wish I'd gone down to the kitchen sooner and spared you the anguish."

"But then I would still have the pain bottled up inside of me. Releasing it was very liberating, you know. So was my confession, more than I could ever have imagined." Done with all the drama, she adopted a lighter, teasing tone. "To be honest, when we first met at the inn, I never would have taken you to be such a good listener. You struck me as too imperious to heed beings lesser than yourself."

One corner of his mouth twitched into a half-smile. "I beg to differ. I was remarkably well mannered considering that a little brat had dashed into my private dining parlor, interrupted my dinner, and hidden himself underneath my table."

"You were reserved and aloof," she countered. "Still, when you helped me find Leo the next morning, I quickly learned that beneath all that cool hauteur lurked a kind, chivalrous gentleman."

His eyes gleamed. "I hope you'll never repeat that to

anyone. I've worked hard to maintain that aura of cool hauteur."

"I'm sure it comes naturally to one of your rank, without the least bit of work at all." Natalie couldn't resist sliding her hand over the hard wall of his chest as she gave him a saucy smile. "So, what did *you* think of *me* at our first meeting? An ill-mannered provincial, no doubt, since I failed to curtsy. And one who was vulgar enough to commit the cardinal sin of shaking your hand."

"Rather, you were the loveliest and most unusual woman I'd ever met, though perhaps a trifle irritating—"

"Irritating? Because I didn't bow and scrape to you, I presume."

"Don't interrupt, you ill-mannered provincial," he said with a glint of deviltry. "The truth is, I found you to be fascinating. And I confess to having had a keen desire to unpin your hair."

"My hair?"

"I wanted to see it free and flowing. I still do. May I—" Caught in the wizardry of his words, she nodded. He reached for her braid and nimbly untwined it, allowing her hair to tumble into heavy coils. Then he sifted his fingers through the long, dark strands so they wafted in loose disarray across her shoulders and bosom. "It's even prettier than I expected. As soft and luxurious as sable."

A thrum of desire burrowed deep inside her. It seemed startlingly intimate to let a man fondle her unbound hair. As if it were an act to be done in the bedchamber by a husband . . . or a lover. She sternly reminded herself that Hadrian could be neither. "I thought you found me irritating."

"We were speaking of first impressions. And you have to allow that I was bound to be a little irked when my privacy had been invaded by strangers." Hadrian brought her hand to his lips and pressed a kiss to her knuckles. "But any minor irritation I felt then has long been surpassed by my admiration for your beauty—both inside and out."

The mask of reserve had vanished entirely, and his eyes looked as warm as smoke. Did he truly find her beautiful? Against all caution, Natalie ached to believe that he spoke from the heart. That he felt as uplifted by their closeness as she did. As they gazed at each other, a powerful eroticism pulsed between them. She could no more resist its magnetic pull than she could cease breathing.

It seemed inevitable when he brought his head down to brush his lips over hers. A delicious little shiver coursed through her, and she closed her eyes to savor the sheer pleasure of his kiss. She hadn't realized until that very instant just how much she'd been longing for it. His hands cupped her face as if she were precious to him, while his mouth glided lightly over hers. Though it held the tender testament of affection, the effect was also deeply sensual, tingling throughout the most hidden places of her body.

Heaven help her, the man was enticing. Nothing in her experience could match the bliss of this moment. It was hard to believe they had met for the first time only a few days ago. She felt as if she had known Hadrian forever.

All too soon, he broke the contact, and when she lifted her lashes, a molten silver blaze burned in his eyes. Her heart skipped a beat at that passionate look even as his hands dropped to her shoulders. His tense jaw and sudden stiffness of manner contradicted the naked desire on his face.

"Natalie," he said in a gravelly tone, "it's time for you to go."

She blinked at him in confused dismay before understanding emerged from her passion-fogged thoughts. Of course. He'd witnessed the attack on her in the kitchen. He'd seen her weep uncontrollably. He'd listened to her tale of horror. It had been a night of raw emotions for her, and his innate sense of honor forbade him from seizing any advantage over her.

But she didn't want to part from him. Not just yet. Not even in light of the peril he posed to her heart.

She lifted her arms to encircle his neck and rubbed her cheek against the raspy growth on his jaw. "Don't be a gentleman, Hadrian," she whispered. "At least not for a little while longer."

The fire in his eyes burned brighter. His thumb tilted up her chin as he keenly studied her. Then he released a harsh breath. "God help me, you're far too tempting."

Without further ado, their mouths met again by mutual consent. This time, he kissed her with skillful mastery and unbridled passion. The knowledge of his desire for her was like a torch to tinder as liquid fire flowed through her veins, seeping into even the marrow of her bones.

He parted her lips and came inside to taste her deeply. The mating of their tongues felt remarkably enticing and even more seductive than the stroking of his hands over her face and hair. Having known only chaste pecks from long-forgotten suitors, she gloried in the new experience. It was as if Hadrian had awakened her dormant nature and filled her with a thirst for something more. Seeking that elusive prospect, she pressed closer to him, her fingers slipping into the rough silk of his hair as she returned his kiss with brazen eagerness.

In the midst of it, Natalie knew she would always remember this moment. The captivating pleasure of being clasped to his male form, the dark taste of brandy in his mouth, the shivery excitement of his caresses, all of those impressions were seared into her mind. Knowing that their embrace could not last, she would tuck it away in her heart and hold it there forever.

His fingers tracked down the smooth column of her neck, lingering a moment over the rapid pulse beat in her throat, then sliding beneath her wrapper to caress the bare skin of her shoulders. He brushed aside a few stray curls of her hair to allow his lips to follow the same path.

Natalie quivered as the velvety dampness of his tongue tasted her tender flesh. She tilted her head back, reveling in the intoxicating sensations he aroused so easily in her. It seemed only natural when he parted her robe to continue his exploration. Adrift in enjoyment, she was barely aware as he unbuttoned the front of her nightgown until his hand slipped inside to cup her naked breast. When his thumb stroked over the puckered tip, heat flowed down to her core and wrested a gratified gasp from her.

He used his other hand to tilt her face for another deep, languorous kiss; then he rubbed his whiskered cheek against hers so that she felt the warmth of his breath on her skin. "I want you, Natalie," he said in a rough whisper. "I crave you, all of you."

His passionate declaration swamped her defenses, as did the voluptuous delight of his fingers plying her sensitive flesh. Inundated by a sea of giddy sensuality, she finally understood the powerful instinct to mate with a man. She hungered to be ravished, to let him take their closeness to its inevitable conclusion, despite the wisp of rationality that warned her against it.

Her fingertip traced the outline of his damp lips. "Hadrian . . . I never knew I could feel so . . . so *alive* as I do right now with you."

"Yes."

The possessiveness imbued in that single word ought

to have irked her. Yet under the burn of his touch, she found herself glorying in his attentions and wanting to give herself to him. Especially when he lowered his head to take her nipple into his mouth.

The lap of his tongue fed fuel to her inner fire, and she caught her breath at the shocking pleasure of it. Her fingers moved restlessly over his broad shoulders and into the thickness of his hair. With every skillful tug of his lips, an insistent throbbing pulsed deep within her, making her edgy and eager, crumbling the last of her defenses. All of her awareness focused on the provocative delight of his suckling. There was only the here and now; nothing else mattered but Hadrian. Hadrian, who had become as essential to her as air to breathe. She ached to learn everything that he could show her . . .

He suddenly drew back. His grip tightening on her shoulders, he sat up straight. Cool air washed over the exposed skin of her bosom. She opened her eyes in confusion to protest his abrupt manner. "What—"

His finger over her lips silenced her. All trace of warmth had vanished from his face. His granite gaze was trained on a spot somewhere beyond her. In the next instant, she heard what had distracted him.

The distant rattle of a lock in the great hall. The muffled click of a door opening and closing. The staccato approach of footsteps.

Hadrian swore viciously under his breath as he yanked the edges of her robe together. "We can't be seen like this," he muttered. "You'll be ruined."

Comprehension doused her desire. It was like a dash of ice water to realize how far she had ventured beyond the bounds of proper behavior.

The sensual spell shattered, Natalie jumped to her feet and tidied herself. He did likewise, stepping away to don his coat, which had been lying on a chair in the shadows. She had barely retied her wrapper and combed her fingers through her tangled hair when footsteps approached from outside the library.

Lord Wymark stepped into the room. His gait was somewhat unsteady as he ambled toward them, his garb disheveled, his untied cravat hanging loose around his neck. "Ah, Miss Fanshawe," he said, slurring his words. "Spied the light in here. Thought 'twas Clayton . . . ah, there y'are, old boy."

Hadrian stepped out of the shadows. The passionate lover of a few moments ago had vanished. An expression of chilly detachment on his hard features, he stared at Wymark. "I thought you'd gone to bed."

"Slipped out the back door. Took a stroll down to the Hare and Hound for a game or two. Won't tell the earl, will y'?"

"It's no concern of mine if you choose to ruin your life."

"The Duke o' Decorum. Never steps a toe out o' line." Wymark aimed a sly glance at Natalie. "But I see y' found your own amusement tonight."

Natalie sucked in an indignant breath. Yet her conscience stopped the protest that sprang to her tongue even as the heat of embarrassment stung her cheeks. What could she say, really, when he'd spoken the truth?

Hadrian's face turned frosty. Fists clenched at his sides, he took a step toward his cousin. "I'll make allowances for you being foxed, Wymark. The fact of the matter is, Miss Fanshawe has endured a frightening experience tonight, thanks in part to you. She was just on her way back upstairs."

Hadrian watched her depart. He'd braced himself for an argument from Natalie that would have made his defense of her reputation that much trickier. But she'd had the wisdom to calmly bid them good night.

Gliding toward the door of the library, she looked magnificent, tall and slender in the dark gold wrapper, her head held high. Not for her, the weepy reproaches of a wronged lady. She had a stately bearing that hid all sign of the steamy interlude they'd shared. He took fierce satisfaction in the fact that he alone knew of the passionate woman hidden inside of her. It was a mind-altering revelation that ought never to have happened.

And he suffered not a morsel of regret.

Realizing he was staring like a mooncalf, Hadrian pulled his gaze from the now-empty doorway and pummeled his thoughts back into a semblance of rationality. Luckily, Wymark hadn't noticed.

His second cousin had gone straight to the cabinet to pour himself a drink. Turning, Wymark lifted his glass in a salute that sloshed brandy onto the oriental carpet. "Foul stuff they serve down at the pub. One thing I'll say for my pinch-fisted sire, he does keep a good cellar."

As the youth took a swallow, Hadrian went on the offensive. "Your groom assaulted Miss Fanshawe in the kitchen tonight."

Wymark sputtered and coughed, lowering the glass. "What? Bert?"

"You heard me. The scoundrel tried to force himself on her when she went downstairs for a glass of hot milk. I walked in as she hit him over the head with a cooking pot. He also received a sample of my right hook."

Wymark ran unsteady fingers through his messy, wheat-gold hair. "I don't believe it. She must've . . . must've led him on—"

For the second time that evening, hot rage surged in Hadrian. Only a thread of coherence kept him from leaping forward and inflicting physical violence. "I ought to lay you out for that slur."

Looking startled, Wymark stumbled back into a chair and sat down abruptly. "Apologies, coz. Meant nothing by it."

Hadrian took several deep breaths to calm himself. It would only raise suspicions that would hurt Natalie if he behaved in a way that was at odds with his usual self-possession. When he felt restrained enough to speak, he said tersely, "Bert left Miss Fanshawe in a wretched state of distress. I've had the very devil of a time calming her nerves this past hour." Although other matters also had affected her state of mind, it was best to convince Wymark it was entirely due to the groom.

"Hope y' told her not to press charges."

"I've dismissed the scoundrel. He's gone."

"Gone?" Wymark shot back to his feet, nearly toppling over in the process and spilling the last of his drink. He glanced angrily at the empty glass, then hurled it toward the hearth. His drunken aim kept it from shattering, so that it merely rolled across the carpet and under a table. "You can't do that, Clayton. He's *my* groom, not yours!"

"It's too late. You'll have to find yourself someone else."

"But . . . he's the only one with the skill to handle Thunder! My stallion needs weeks o' training. Else he won't be ready to race!"

"That is neither here nor there. A violent abuser of women cannot be permitted to remain at Oak Knoll. I'm sure your father would agree."

At the mention of Godwin, gloom clouded Wymark's features, along with a measure of resentment. "That's easy for you to say with your piles of gold. Good trainers don't come cheap, and Bert was working for free in exchange for a cut o' the prize money. I'll never be able to pay off my vowels . . ." He glanced sullenly at Hadrian. "Never mind. You wouldn't understand."

Hadrian was not without sympathy for a man in a tight spot, although he himself gambled only on occasion as a matter of social amusement. He had the discipline to know when to cut his losses. But for the past year or so, he'd seen troubling signs in Wymark that wagering was fast becoming an obsession.

"You're underage," he pointed out. "You can't be held liable for gaming debts."

Wymark looked appropriately scandalized by the notion. "The devil you say! Stiff my friends? I could never hold up my head again."

"I'm glad you value your honor, at least. If you want to avoid ruin, your first step is to stop wagering. Your second is to sell that blasted stallion. There's a reason why you were able to purchase him on the cheap. He's too volatile to ever be a decent competitor."

"Thunder won't bring a fraction o' what I owe."

"Then make a vow to your father that you'll stay away from the gaming tables in exchange for him settling your debts."

"Bah! The old man will only tighten the screws. I'll never hear the end of it." He stood swaying, a sly look appearing on his face. "Don't suppose you'd spring me a few thousand, would you, old chap? Considering we'll soon be brothers-in-law."

Wymark didn't know that Hadrian's intention to wed Lady Ellen was currently in limbo. Hadrian had informed Godwin after dinner that any betrothal must be put off for a few months in order to allow the girl sufficient time to overcome her shyness. To further complicate matters, the episode with Natalie had cast his once-ordered future into utter disarray. He needed time to think and consider. But his marital plans were too private a matter to discuss with his drunken cousin.

"No loans," he stated firmly. "It's time for you to man up and find a way out of this mess yourself."

Glowering, Wymark trudged to the cabinet for another drink. The fool had been indulged by his mother, Hadrian knew, but perhaps this crisis would be the making of him. Suffering for a time might prove to be the best teacher.

His cousin turned and cast a defiant, resentful scowl over the rim of his glass. "Not so high-and-mighty as you pretend," he mumbled. "Only a cad would cheat on m' sister."

"I beg your pardon?"

"Saw the way y' looked at Miss Fanshawe. The earl might be keen to know you and her were so cozy here tonight. Of course, I might be persuaded to keep m' mouth shut for—for the right price."

A powerfully hot vibration shook Hadrian's core and exploded like a flow of lava. It was like nothing he'd ever felt in his life. Propelled by a red blast of rage, he strode forward to seize his scrawny cousin by his lapels and drag him up off his feet. "I wouldn't advise you to try to blackmail me, Wymark."

"N-not blackmail, just—just a loan—"

Hadrian tightened his grip until Wymark's blue eyes bugged in alarm. By God, he would not allow this young pup to besmirch Natalie's name. "Let me explain the terms of our bargain," he said in his iciest tone. "You will not receive so much as a farthing from me. And you will bide your tongue in regard to Miss Fanshawe. Do I make myself clear?"

Wymark gulped, apparently even in his drunken stupor recognizing the deadly intent on Hadrian's face.

"S-sorry, old chap. Didn't mean no harm. M' lips are—are sealed."

The cringing fear on those weak features was enough to penetrate the volcanic fury that had enveloped Hadrian's brain. Loosening his grip, he thrust Wymark away in disgust. The youth wobbled backward, collapsing onto the settee, where he cowered like a chastened little boy.

"I intend to hold you to that pledge," Hadrian snapped.

Turning on his heel, he strode out of the library. The sharp echo of his footsteps in the great hall served to work off his anger. As his mind resumed a semblance of its normal function, he mulled over the episode. Restraint had always guided his life and his actions. He'd prided himself on having firm mastery over his emotions. Yet tonight the foundation had tilted beneath him. Now, he detected an odd sense of exultation in himself that was unsettling, to say the least.

It all had to do with Natalie.

As he mounted the staircase, his thoughts swerved inevitably to her. To the memory of her trembling with passion in his arms. To the softness of her lips opening beneath his. To the taste of her skin and the arch of her spine, lifting her perfect breasts to his mouth. If not for that interruption, he would have pressed her down onto the settee and made love to her right there in the library.

Reckless fool! He knew better than to treat respectable women so cavalierly. Even as a green youth, he hadn't behaved so irresponsibly. It didn't matter that she'd wanted to kiss him, too.

As irksome as Wymark's arrival had been, it had come at a fortuitous moment. Hadrian had always restricted his sexual affairs to experienced women. Despite Natalie's worldly knowledge in other matters, there was an unmistakable innocence about her. The penalty of consummating their lust would have been grave.

Or *was* it mere lust?

No other woman had ever brought him to the point of abandoning all reason and logic. The rarefied world of the ton was filled with an endless array of English beauties who were drawn to his title and fortune in the hope of becoming the next Duchess of Clayton. It wasn't a circumstance he'd encouraged or sought, it was simply a fact of life.

Though a few had caught his eye over the years, he'd never found any lady who could engage his interest beyond a light flirtation. Nor had he realized until now that he desired more in a wife than just a pretty face and an exalted lineage. He craved wit and conversation, depth and intelligence, resilience and spirit, warmth and excitement.

Natalie possessed all those qualities in abundance. Tonight, the thread of connection he'd sensed between them had tightened into a strong silken bond. He wanted to claim her, to protect her, to bind her to him forever. Yet duty required him to wed Lady Ellen or another blue blood like her. Not an ineligible American governess who scorned the aristocracy.

Riveted by the direction of his thoughts, Hadrian came to an abrupt halt in the shadowed corridor outside his bedchamber. Was he truly considering marriage to Natalie Fanshawe?

Sheer, utter madness.

A man of his rank did not wed a woman so far beneath himself, let alone a foreigner. His pulse should *not* be surging at the prospect. She was an outsider who knew nothing of the myriad rules of the ton, and likely wouldn't obey them anyway. All the snoots and chinwags would make her the topic of nasty gossip. Though he could silence them with a freezing stare, he was loath to pitch Natalie into the lion's den of the haute ton.

Of course, that was presuming she'd even consider becoming the Duchess of Clayton. He wasn't so blindly arrogant as to think that one hot kiss would be enough to win a woman of her character. In fact, he had a strong suspicion that if he were to offer for her, she'd run screaming for the next ship back to America.

He'd never see her again.

His mind in a whirl, Hadrian braced his hands on the wall and stared fiercely down at the ivy-leaf pattern on the carpet. He'd embroiled himself in one hell of a sticky quagmire. And just when he'd believed that his future was as good as settled.

Only one clear thought emerged from the vortex. It would take time to allay Natalie's deep-seated disdain of the nobility. Somehow, he had to keep her in his life until they had a chance to see if they truly suited one another.

That also meant keeping quiet about the change in his marital plans. She wouldn't wish to be courted by a duke. So for now, he must keep it a closely guarded secret.

Chapter 15

"Oh, I *wish* it weren't raining so hard," Lady Ellen said on a sigh. "I was hoping to go for a walk in the woods."

"Rain makes mud," Leo replied. "I like mud, but Miss Fanshawe won't let me play in it."

Standing side by side, they had their noses pressed to the window of the nursery as they watched the slide of raindrops down the glass panes. Lady Ellen had wandered into the schoolroom a short while ago just as Natalie and Leo were finishing their luncheon. Now, both aunt and nephew commiserated over the dreary state of the weather.

Observing them from her seat at the governess's desk, Natalie found it difficult to focus on the task of organizing the next day's lessons for Leo. She lacked the concentration even to assign the boy his afternoon reading lesson. At least the gray skies served as a damper to her buoyant mood. After the passionate interlude with Hadrian the previous night, she'd had trouble keeping her feet planted firmly on the ground.

Twirling her quill pen, she swept the feather along her jawline. The absentminded action brought a reminder of his thrilling kisses. He had unbuttoned her nightdress, caressed her bare bosom, closed his mouth over one peak—and she had loved every scandalous moment of it. The provocative memory stirred a bone-deep longing to experience it all over again.

But that was impossible. No decent woman behaved with such abandon, especially with a nobleman. It could only bring her to ruin.

Sighing, Natalie dipped the nib of her pen into the ink pot. Instead of composing simple addition and subtraction problems, however, she found herself doodling two entwined hearts on the paper. She'd gone to sleep dreaming of Hadrian and had awakened this morning to the quandary of being infatuated with a duke who belonged to the nobility that she despised.

Well, perhaps *despised* was too strong a word. Since arriving in England, she had discovered that like people in all walks of life, there were decent aristocrats along with the bad ones. For instance, while Lady Ellen had a kind and generous nature, her brother, Lord Wymark, was a drunken lout.

How mortifying that he'd nearly caught her in Hadrian's embrace. The memory of his sly stare made Natalie's skin crawl. There was something about Wymark that made her uneasy, something she didn't quite trust. But as embarrassing as it had been, she was glad he'd arrived when he did.

If not for that interruption, she'd have allowed Hadrian more liberties. Never had she known that desire could erase the ability to think rationally. Now, in the light of day, she knew it had been a mistake to linger in his company. A mistake to deepen their closeness by confessing her secrets. A mistake to engage in intimate activities that belonged between husband and wife. There could never be anything lasting between them. Her life was in America, where she planned to open a school.

A trill of laughter drew her attention back to Leo and his aunt. They appeared to be having a good-natured quarrel over which raindrop would slide faster down the windowpane. The girl looked like a perfect English rose today, blond and petite in a blush-pink gown.

Abandoning all pretense of work, Natalie set down her pen and rested her chin in her hands. It was time to face the most discomfiting aspect of her behavior the previous night. Not once had she spared a thought for Lady Ellen.

Natalie had known that Hadrian was courting the girl. For that reason alone, it was wrong of her to have acted as she did, and wrong of Hadrian, too. They had both been swept away by the moment. His caresses had awakened a hunger in her that continued to entice her thoughts and feelings. But it mustn't ever happen again. Lady Ellen might be skittish now, yet once she danced with him at society balls, how could she help but fall for his charm?

A cloak of gloom stifled Natalie's spirits. She pressed a hand to her bosom in an effort to allay the heaviness in her heart. Surely it couldn't be envy. She had no interest in the rarefied world of the upper crust. Besides, Hadrian would never offer her marriage—nor would she accept him if he did.

Dallying with a duke could only lead to misfortune and disgrace. As much as it pained her, she really had no choice but to avoid his company in the future.

It was Leo she must focus on. With Lord Godwin's lawyer due to arrive any day, she needed to treasure the precious time that she had left with the boy. It would break her heart to say good-bye to Audrey's son, for she had grown to love him as dearly as if he were her own child.

Just then, he and Lady Ellen joined hands and danced

around in a circle, while he sang, "Rain, rain, go away, come again another day."

"Little Leo wants to play," Lady Ellen chimed in. "Rain, rain, go to Spain. Never show your face again."

Giggling, they collapsed together on the wood floor. There was still much of the child in the girl, Natalie noticed. By this time next year, would Lady Ellen be a wife with a baby on the way? Would she be Hadrian's wife?

Natalie drew in a deep breath. She should be glad, for perhaps the two of them would be agreeable to keeping an eye out for Leo's well-being . . .

The boy looked up at his aunt. "Why should the rain go to Spain?"

"I don't know," Lady Ellen said. "I suppose because the words rhyme."

The teacher in Natalie demanded a correction to that. "Actually," she said, arising from the desk to join them, "the song celebrates the British navy defeating the Spanish Armada over two hundred years ago."

"What's an armada?" Leo asked.

"It's a very large fleet of ships. The Spanish were the rulers of the sea at the time." Natalie pointed out the location of the countries on the globe. "Spain wanted to conquer England, so they sent over a hundred galleons outfitted with cannons. The British had a much smaller fleet. But a terrible storm blew up and scattered the Spanish Armada, sinking many of the galleons so England could easily defeat the rest."

Leo listened with rapt attention. "When I grow up, I want to fight the Spanish Armada. I'll be the captain and order my sailors to fire the cannons. Boom!"

"You can be Admiral Bellingham," Lady Ellen declared. "Then you would command the entire fleet."

"Admiral Bellingham," Leo repeated as if cherishing

the title. He fetched his toy ship, making it sail over imaginary waves along the windowsill.

Watching him, Natalie wondered wistfully what sort of man he would become someday, and if she would ever even know. Impulsively, she turned to Lady Ellen and took her dainty hands. "I do hope that when I leave here, you'll write to me and let me know how Leo is doing."

"Leave?" the girl asked naïvely. "But why can't you stay?"

Natalie drew back her hands. "My home is in America. I plan to found a school in Philadelphia. I'm here only until the earl's solicitor arrives, and they can sort out all the legalities in regard to Leo."

Natalie's troubled gaze lingered on the boy before a tug on her arm pulled her attention back to Lady Ellen. Her china-blue eyes were wide with surprise.

"But Miss Fanshawe, he *is* here! Mr. Musgrave, I mean. He arrived in time to take luncheon with us."

"The solicitor?"

"Yes, he and Papa went into his study a little while ago."

A knell of alarm struck Natalie's breast. While she'd been mooning over Hadrian, the moment she'd dreaded had finally arrived.

"I must go." Smoothing her hair, she regretted having worn this old cinnamon muslin gown instead of her best plum silk. But there was no time to waste in refurbishing her appearance. "Will you stay here with Leo until the nursery maid returns?"

"Certainly. I ran up here when I saw the duke coming my way." Lady Ellen wrinkled her nose. "I was afraid I'd be stuck playing cards with him or walking in the picture gallery. But where are you going?"

"I wish to hear what Mr. Musgrave has to say."

"You mustn't! Papa doesn't like to be interrupted in his study."

"He shall have to endure my presence this once."

On that bold declaration, Natalie rushed out of the schoolroom and down several flights of stairs to the ground floor. She remembered noticing the location of Godwin's study when Hadrian had taken her and Leo on a tour. It overlooked the gardens at the rear of the house.

When she arrived there, the door was closed. She put her ear to the panel, but the wood was too thick for her to hear anything more than the muffled sound of male voices. They seemed sharp and upraised, lending the impression of a dispute in progress.

Lifting her hand to knock, she paused, beset by sudden qualms. Having spent most of her time in the nursery, she had not encountered Lord Godwin since her first day here, when he had glowered at her with chilly dislike. What if she angered him and he banished her from the house at once? What if he didn't even allow her to stay with Leo until another governess could be hired?

The day of parting would be upon her. Today. Without any time to prepare Leo . . . or herself.

She swallowed hard. No, that wouldn't happen. She need only remain calm, reasonable, and respectful. If she could mediate political clashes between opposing senators at her father's dining table, then she certainly could handle one haughty English earl.

Natalie rapped on the door. A moment later, it swung open. Her pulse did a wild dance as she found herself facing Hadrian.

The Duke of Clayton, she revised, for in his snowy cravat and tailored coat of dark blue superfine, he appeared every inch the English nobleman. No trace remained of the charming lover of the previous night. His tousled brown hair was now neatly combed, his raspy jaw shaven to perfect smoothness, his warm affability exchanged for his signature expression of cool hauteur.

For the barest instant, she glimpsed a softening of his gaze, then decided it must have been a trick of the rainy daylight. The granite intensity of his eyes gave no hint whatsoever that he was pleased to see her. Quite the contrary, in fact, judging by his frown. Had their passionate kiss meant so little to him?

She buried the knot of disappointment inside herself. Well, of course the encounter had been nothing special to Hadrian. He was no doubt accustomed to fondling women in the dark of night. And let that be a lesson to her. When it came to dukes, it served no purpose to dream.

He gave her a slight bow, his manner reserved. "Miss Fanshawe. I'm afraid you've interrupted a private meeting. You'd best come back later."

Glancing past him, she had a partial view of the study. Lord Godwin sat behind a broad mahogany desk, while on the other side of it, a stranger occupied one of the two chairs. Papers littered the surface of the desk.

Natalie lifted her chin, glad that she was not a petite, well-bred English miss who would retreat in cowed defeat. "If this is about Leo, I daresay I've every reason to be here."

As she stepped past Hadrian and entered the room, Lord Godwin's steely blue stare bored into Natalie. He bristled with annoyance, and she again had the uncanny sense of having interrupted a quarrel. "Why are you here?" he demanded. "You should be upstairs in the nursery with the boy."

"It's because of Leo that I'm here, of course."

"Actually, her arrival is quite timely," Hadrian said, in a smooth reversal of his initial attempt to refuse her entry. "I was about to suggest that we send for her. After all, it's imprudent for us to speculate any further when we could ask her to provide the necessary clarifications."

"I'd be more than happy to answer any questions you might have," Natalie concurred.

Godwin gazed with pursed lips at the duke before giving a curt nod. "Oh, very well, then," he said testily.

Hadrian went to the desk and pulled out the chair beside the one occupied by the stranger. "Pray sit here, Miss Fanshawe." All gentlemanly courtesy, he waited for Natalie. His grave expression made her revise her impression of hostility. Rather, he appeared disturbed about something else entirely, his tense manner seeming to indicate that trouble lay ahead.

She lowered herself into the chair and folded her hands in her lap. Hadrian must have occupied the seat before her arrival, for the leather cushion still held the warmth of his body. A faint whiff of spicy male soap made her keenly aware of his close presence. Perhaps she was foolish to feel comforted, but he was the only one present who might be considered an ally.

Hadrian performed the introductions. "Miss Fanshawe, may I present Mr. Musgrave, the earl's solicitor. He's been examining the legal papers that you provided."

Musgrave had slickly combed brown hair and a dark suit of clothes. He was slightly bucktoothed and that and his plump form brought to mind an overfed beaver. A pair of gold-rimmed pince-nez rested on the bridge of his short nose, which accounted for the way he lifted his chin to gaze at her in a superior manner.

He cleared his throat and glanced at the earl, who, with a wave of his hand, gave permission for the solicitor to proceed. "Miss Fanshawe," Musgrave began in an officious tone, "I am given to understand you are a citizen of the United States of America. Is that correct?"

"Yes, I was born in Philadelphia."

"And you are the temporary guardian of a six-year-old boy named"—he paused to consult a paper—"Leopold Jeremy Bellingham."

"Indeed I am. Leo is the son of my late friends, Jeremy and Audrey Bellingham." She decided it wise to emphasize, "Lady Audrey was Lord Godwin's eldest daughter."

"Have you any proof of that?"

"Proof? The earl may have disowned her, but he cannot deny her very existence."

Musgrave looked down his nose at her again, the glasses magnifying his squinty brown eyes. "I meant, have you proof that the woman you knew in America was in fact his lordship's daughter?"

Natalie bristled. "Of course she was Audrey. Shall I relate what she told me of her father tossing her out of this house for marrying a commoner? And how else would I have known to bring her son here? But if you desire evidence, then allow me to say that she was the same woman depicted in the portrait that was consigned to the tower storage room here at Oak Knoll."

Lord Godwin had been sitting in his chair, listening, but now he planted his palms on the surface of the desk and half rose to his feet. "Who gave you leave to go snooping? You and the boy were to remain in the nursery."

"I wasn't snooping."

"She was with me," Hadrian said, stepping forward to coolly address the earl. "On their first day here, I took Miss Fanshawe and Leo on a tour of the house. Leo spotted the portrait and recognized his mother at once."

Lord Godwin sank back down. "And you're quite sure of that?"

"It's the truth," Natalie reiterated. "Leo would never have mistaken the identity of his own mother."

Musgrave tilted his head up to address Hadrian, who loomed over him, all impressive, imperious duke. "Your Grace, I feel compelled to ask, when the portrait was discovered, is it possible that Miss Fanshawe had a few moments alone with the boy, long enough to whisper in his ear?"

Natalie gripped her fingers around the folds of her skirt in an attempt to contain a surge of anger. How dare he imply that she had coached Leo to lie. But of course, the solicitor was merely looking out for the earl's interests. It had been on that day in the tower room, just before they'd found the portrait, that Hadrian had warned her of the family's suspicions.

When Hadrian didn't immediately reply, she said in her chilliest tone, "I beg your pardon, Mr. Musgrave. I would never instruct a child to tell a falsehood. And I resent you calling my character into question."

"Miss Fanshawe has every right to be offended," Hadrian said. "Leo's reaction to the painting was that of a grieving boy for his mother. I've no reason to believe his demeanor was anything other than genuine."

Natalie appreciated his support. But he also had hesitated for a few seconds, long enough to cast the doubt that she could see in the earl's narrowed eyes. When Leo had discovered the painting, she *had* rushed ahead to comfort the boy in his distress. However, Hadrian surely knew that nothing deceptive had occurred. Didn't he?

Whose side was he on?

Though it was necessary to leash her temper, she could still make her feelings known. "Lord Godwin, your grandson asked if he might keep Audrey's portrait in the nursery. The duke gave permission for it to be hung in Leo's bedchamber. I presume you've no objection."

That proud, patrician face seemed to pale. His lips thinned and his jaw tightened. He stared at her for a moment as rain tapped against the window glass. Without bothering to answer, he turned his sour attention to the solicitor and abruptly changed the subject.

"Musgrave, you've raised an issue with the boy's papers."

The man adjusted his pince-nez on the bridge of his nose. "Yes, it's about this affidavit in regard to young Leopold. It is my understanding that birth records in America are handled in much the same way as here in England. So why, Miss Fanshawe, have you not provided a notarized copy of the parish register?"

This was the question she'd expected. "As I told the earl, Leo's parents perished in a raid at their mission on the frontier. The attackers burned a number of buildings, including the log church where the register was kept. Leo's baptismal record was destroyed in that fire. My only recourse was to have a lawyer draw up a document with my sworn statement attesting to Leo's identity."

"That is highly irregular, to say the least. And who are these two witnesses who signed this affidavit? John Condit and Henry Clay."

"They are well-respected congressmen who were friends of my father's. Mr. Condit is a senator, while Mr. Clay is presently the House Speaker."

"Were they acquainted with Lady Audrey?" the solicitor asked.

Natalie shook her head. "No, I'm afraid not. However, they've known *me* since I was a girl. They respect my sworn word."

"I see." Musgrave looked down his snub nose at her. "Then his lordship must take into consideration the lack of any actual evidence to support your story. And there is no guarantee, either, as to whether or not these witnesses are themselves reliable."

"In America, they are held to be extremely reliable.

We may not have an aristocracy, but we do have honorable leaders who are highly respected in their communities."

Hadrian had been prowling around the study, but now he stopped to say, "Might I add, Miss Fanshawe's father served as a senator for a number of years before his death. As his hostess, she had occasion to meet many high-ranking officials in the government."

Natalie would have preferred for her word to be believed on its own merits. Yet if a paternal reference was what it took for the earl to accept her sworn statement, then so be it.

"Politicians," Godwin said with a snort. "If they are anything at all like the elected members of the Commons—"

A sharp rapping on the door cut him off. He cast an irritated glance in that direction. "Who the devil is interrupting us now?"

Hadrian started forward. "I'll see."

"Allow me, Your Grace." Arising, Mr. Musgrave lumbered across the study with the single-mindedness of a beaver on his way to gnaw a tree. Just as he reached for the knob, the door swung open and smacked into him. He staggered back a few steps, making a grab for his pince-nez before it could slide off his nose.

In a whirl of olive-green skirts, Lady Godwin swooped into the study. She was followed by Lord Wymark, who appeared rather bleary-eyed after his overindulgence in drink the previous night.

"Archie, I need a word with you at once." The countess took in the scene at a glance, and her gaze narrowed on Natalie seated in the chair. "Why is Miss Fanshawe here? This gathering should be strictly for family members."

Rising, Lord Godwin cast a baleful glance at his

wife. "Rather, it's for whomever I deem necessary. And I'm afraid that doesn't include you, Priscilla. Or you, Richard."

"You'll change your mind," Wymark told his father, "when you hear what Mama has just discovered."

Hadrian paced toward them, his manner impatient. "This is no time for gossip or idle chitchat. Unless it concerns Leo, it can wait until later."

"It most certainly does have a bearing on this situation, Your Grace," the countess asserted. She glided to Natalie's chair, her lip curling with disdain. "Miss Fanshawe, may I ask if your sire's name was Benjamin?"

Natalie stiffened under the jab of that pointed question. "Yes," she admitted cautiously. "Benjamin Fanshawe was my father."

"And was he born here in England? One of the Lincolnshire Fanshawes?"

She gave a reluctant nod. Though the possibility had lurked at the back of her mind, Natalie had not really expected anyone in England outside the family to remember him after so many years. What did the countess know?

Her gaze flitted to Hadrian, who regarded her with a startled frown before he turned his attention to Lady Godwin. "I fail to see why Miss Fanshawe's ancestry would have anything to do with Leo."

Lady Godwin swung toward him. "Oh, but I assure you it does, Your Grace. You'll understand in a moment. It took me some time to recall the gossip from thirty years ago, back when the Fanshawes were still admitted to society. That was before Sir Basil Fanshawe—Miss Fanshawe's grandfather—was expelled from the best circles for reneging on his debts."

The earl cast an assessing glance at Natalie that seemed to tar her with her grandfather's sins. "Good God. I'd forgotten all about that miscreant."

"Scapegraces, the whole family," Wymark bestirred himself to say. "I knew a Fanshawe at Harrow, a year ahead of me. Giles the Gypsy, he was called. Come to think of it, he had Miss Fanshawe's black hair and green eyes."

"That is due to the taint of Romany blood from Sir Basil's grandmother," Lady Godwin said with derision. "Or so the rumor goes. But that isn't the worst of it. Just now, as I was paging through *Debrett's,* a memory struck me that one of Sir Basil's offspring had immigrated to America—Miss Fanshawe's father. If I may put it delicately, he had few prospects here in England since he was born on the wrong side of the blanket."

Natalie found herself the subject of attention from everyone present. She pinched her lips together to keep from lashing out when she needed to bide her tongue for Leo's sake. So what if Papa had been baseborn? He'd had more virtue and honor in his little finger than any of these supercilious aristocrats who would disparage him for an accident of birth.

In particular, Hadrian watched her with a cool, enigmatic stare. It pained her to think he could be regretting their passionate encounter. Or worse, that he might be speculating that her tarnished heritage made her fair game for seduction.

"I'm still waiting to hear how all this relates to Leo," the duke said, shifting that imperturbable gaze to Lady Godwin. "Miss Fanshawe's family connections are irrelevant to this case."

"Might I suggest it speaks to her character, Your Grace. Her father was the illegitimate son of a disreputable family. Deception is in her blood." Lady Godwin stepped closer to her husband. "You must see that, Archie. Miss Fanshawe is precisely the sort of female who would concoct a wicked scheme to defraud you."

Lord Godwin's lined features wore a disgruntled expression. "This is all gossip and speculation when it is facts that are needed. Musgrave, I presume you know of a discreet investigator who can be dispatched to America to make inquiries into this claim. One who will not cost me too dearly."

"Of course, your lordship," the solicitor said, scribbling a note on a paper in front of him. "That certainly can be arranged."

"But with an ocean voyage there and back, it could take months," Lady Godwin objected. "Meanwhile, the child is living here, under our roof!"

"You bring up a salient point," Hadrian said, speaking to the others while keeping his watchful gaze on Natalie. "I believe Musgrave would agree that under the law, Godwin has no obligation to house Leo until a positive identification can be made."

Natalie's jaw dropped. A positive identification? Hadrian had led her to believe that he trusted her word, that he had no doubt Leo was Audrey's son.

The duke's betrayal was like a kick in the stomach. Pain reverberated throughout her body as she absorbed the raw truth that whatever tenderness and affection he'd shown her the previous night had been all a sham. Was Hadrian just as horrid and cruel as the rest of his family? It was too much to bear!

All of her hard-won restraint shattered under an avalanche of icy fury. She'd had enough of this intolerable meeting and these haughty aristocrats who would reject a precious little boy, a child of their own blood.

Natalie shot to her feet. "For shame, all of you! You've made it very clear that Leo isn't wanted in this house. As for you, Lord Godwin, you've no right to treat your own grandson like a pariah simply because your daughter thwarted you by marrying the man she loved. It's beyond my comprehension why her last request was for a man as callous as you to raise her son."

The earl stood in stony silence, though he had the good grace to glance away. Lady Godwin's mouth flapped with speechless outrage. Lord Wymark smirked in that sly manner of his. As for Hadrian, she wouldn't give the traitor the satisfaction of even looking at him.

"Miss Fanshawe!" Musgrave chided in sanctimonious horror. "Do mind your tongue before your betters."

"They are *not* my betters, and it would behoove you to recognize they are not yours, either," Natalie snapped. "Lord Godwin, you needn't waste your precious gold on an investigator. I shall be taking Leo back to America at once. And rest assured, you'll never hear from either of us ever again."

In high dudgeon, she turned and marched toward the door, only to find the duke with his hand on the knob, blocking her exit. She was sorely tempted to kick the scoundrel in the shins if he tried to stop her.

As she lifted her chin to glare at his diabolically handsome face, he wasn't even looking at her. His attention was on the earl. "Go ahead and send that investigator, Godwin. Miss Fanshawe and Leo needn't depart England just yet. They can come to London to stay with me."

Chapter 16

Noting the dangerous flash of those gorgeous green eyes, Hadrian caught hold of Natalie's arm and hustled her out of the study before his stated intent could sink fully into her consciousness. His family wore wide-eyed expressions that ranged from shocked to scandalized, but he didn't give a damn what they thought. He cared only about Natalie's reaction.

The explosion came almost at once.

The instant the door closed behind them, she jerked herself free and spun to face him. "How dare you presume to speak for me! I most certainly am *not* going to London with you. I wouldn't suffer your company long enough to walk with you to the end of this corridor. Good-bye—and good riddance!"

The finality of her tone struck him deeply, as did the contempt on her face. It was a stark contrast to the way she'd regarded him the previous night, with softness in her eyes and a warm smile on her lips. His chest squeezed with the fear that she might never again look at him that way. Had he pushed matters too far just now?

She had to be made to understand the necessity of

what he had done. That he wanted to protect her and Leo, to keep them safe under his care.

As she set off at a brisk stride down the echoing passageway, Hadrian paced at her side. "If you'll slow down and listen, Natalie, I can explain—"

"It's Miss Fanshawe to you. And I've done quite enough listening to people I cannot trust. Go back to that nest of vipers where you belong."

"For pity's sake, you've misread my purpose. What I said in there, about Godwin having no obligation toward Leo, was merely a contrivance to get the two of you out of this house."

"Well, congratulations, then. You've succeeded quite admirably. We will be departing for Southampton at once."

"And by what means will you travel there?"

She looked nonplussed for a moment, then tossed up her chin. "We'll walk to the village. There must be a posting inn. I'm sure I can arrange some form of transportation."

"Whitnash is three miles away. It's pouring rain outside. And it's mid-afternoon already, which means it will be nightfall before you arrive. That's presuming you don't get lost on the way."

He'd be damned if he'd offer them conveyance in his chaise. Not if it meant sending her out of his life. Forever.

"I'll manage," she asserted.

"With a six-year-old child? I won't allow it."

"Allow it!" The words echoed in the vastness of the entrance hall as she stopped near one of the suits of armor by the staircase. With a glance at the footman who was trimming the lamps in the library, she lowered her voice to a hiss. "You may be able to order other people around, Mr. High-and-Mighty Duke, but not me."

Hadrian clenched his jaw. Never before had he met a more exasperating woman—or a more alluring one. There was a dash of pink color in her cheeks that enhanced her wild beauty and stirred the fiery urge to pull her into his arms. But this time she wouldn't melt; he'd be more likely to feel the sting of her slap. As much as he admired her independent spirit, it frustrated him, too.

For a moment, he considered using Leo as bait. He would be well within his rights to lay claim to the boy on the basis of their blood relationship. Any judge in the land would award him custody due to his rank. Natalie would then be obliged to go to London if she wanted to see the boy. But she would never forgive him such a trick. He would win the battle and lose the war. Already, she'd erected a barrier against him as if he were the enemy.

Blast it. He was accustomed to people heeding his words, not scorning him as if he were of no consequence.

Struck by an awareness of his own arrogance, he tried to see matters from Natalie's perspective. She had survived a bloody massacre, taken charge of an orphaned child, crossed an ocean to a despised foreign land in order to deliver Leo to his family, only to find herself caught in a web of hostility where her very character and integrity were attacked.

Worse, she'd given the gift of her trust to Hadrian, and he had repaid her with what she perceived to be a betrayal.

Looking at the situation in that light made him feel like a knave, so he strove for a more conciliatory tone. "Forgive me, I oughtn't have been so presumptuous. What I meant was that Leo would be drenched if you were to depart in the rain. He might even fall ill. Please understand that I only wish to do what's best for him." And for Natalie, too, though he didn't dare say so in her present state of indignation.

His apology appeared to smooth her bristles to a degree. Her tense expression relaxed somewhat. "What's best for Leo is to leave this house where he isn't wanted."

"You're absolutely right. He needs to be in a place where he's welcome." When Hadrian reached out to grasp her hand, he was relieved that she didn't flinch from him. Warmth flowed up his arm and set his pulse to racing. He lightly stroked his thumb over the backs of her soft fingers, marveling that such daintiness could belong to such a strong, valiant woman. "Will you grant me a few minutes of your time to discuss this? Please."

Her teeth sank into her lower lip as she regarded him searchingly. "All right, then. But don't think I'm agreeing to anything else."

It was a victory, albeit a grudgingly given one. He shifted his hand to the small of her back, guiding her into a dimly lit salon off the entrance hall. As the room was seldom used, the family preferring the more modern drawing room upstairs, the furnishings here were a collection of musty medieval pieces, with tapestries on the stone walls and a heraldic shield above the oversized hearth.

He left the door open a crack for propriety's sake. The chill in the air made him consider lighting a fire, but Natalie was already looking skittish enough to bolt at any delay.

She stepped away from him, taking up a stance by a carved, thronelike chair. "Now, kindly explain why I shouldn't go straight back to America and spare Leo the pain of knowing that his grandfather detests his very existence."

She folded her arms in a defiant pose that drew Hadrian's attention to her bosom. His mind served up the vivid memory of caressing the rose-petal skin of her breasts, feeling the tip pucker into a bud under the laving of his tongue, hearing her moan with pleasure. He banished the image at once. As delectable as she might be, now was not the time for distractions. His most pressing goal was to convince her to accompany him to London.

Fixing his attention on her face, he said, "Audrey asked you to bring Leo to England for a reason. She wanted her son to go to the best schools, to have all the advantages of her family's status. And since she and I were like siblings, I'd like to think that she wanted him to know me, as well."

Natalie arched an eyebrow. "Why should I believe anything you say? You still have doubts about Leo's identity."

"Doubts?" He shook his head emphatically. "No, I don't. Not in the least. I'm confident the investigator will deliver the proof Godwin needs. Perhaps it seemed otherwise just now in the study, but only because I wanted an excuse to remove Leo from this house."

Her gaze skeptical, she curled her fingers around the back of the chair. "It didn't appear to me that the earl needed much of an excuse at all. He was looking for any reason to banish Leo."

"He can be a stubborn old bird. It's still a bruise to his pride that Audrey defied him and left England. But he'll come around eventually. Let him conduct his little investigation. If we take Leo to London for a few months, it will give Godwin time to adjust to the notion of having a grandson."

"Months! I was intending to depart for America within a week or two."

Gazing at the vibrant beauty of her face, Hadrian felt the grip of alarm. She couldn't leave England. Not when he had just found her. Now he understood why he'd taken such a detached, logical approach to marriage; he had never met any woman quite like Natalie. In the gray dullness of the rainy day, she had expressive features and an adorable sparkle that lit up the room. Her candid manner and sharp wit made her utterly unlike the artificial beauties of the ton.

But the strength of his attachment to her was entirely too new. It would take time to determine if they belonged in each other's lives forever. And time was the one thing he didn't have—unless he could coax her to go to London.

He paced back and forth to contain his restless need for her. "You've been here for barely a week. It's far too soon to give up on your vow."

"If Leo isn't wanted here, then there's no point in delaying."

"But he *is* wanted. By me." It was true, Hadrian realized with a pang. He liked the brat, though he'd seldom before heeded young children, aside from his nephew. "I'm more than happy to provide Audrey's son with a home. But he needs you here with him, too, at least for a while. Is there a pressing reason why you must go back at once?"

"Yes. I wish to open a school in Philadelphia for the autumn session. There are so many things that need to be done, finding a building to rent, hiring teachers, purchasing supplies, advertising for students."

The keen glow in her eyes struck Hadrian. This was a wrinkle he hadn't expected, her determination to educate children. She had firm plans for her future that didn't involve him. "Some of those tasks could be accomplished from afar. An estate agent could locate a suitable place on your behalf. With your father having been a prominent man, surely you have connections."

"Perhaps." She glanced away, her gaze thoughtful, before she returned her wary attention to him. "But going to London won't solve the issue of Lord Godwin's coldness. He's made no attempt whatsoever to forge a bond with his grandson. Not once in the past week has he asked to see Leo. Instead, I was to keep him hidden in the nursery like a dirty little secret. If the earl stubbornly refuses to believe Leo is Audrey's son, then we'd be better off returning to America where I can raise him myself."

"I'm sure you'd be an excellent mother to him," Hadrian said in all sincerity. "However, allow me to point out that Godwin may not be quite the ogre he seems. He merely has a strict view that young children should tend to their lessons out of sight of adults. As a boy, I myself had few dealings with him until adolescence, when he began to take me riding over the estate for training in land management, dealing with tenants, methods of animal husbandry, and the like."

Natalie frowned, her gaze penetrating. "So you're saying that when you were a fatherless little boy like Leo, the earl paid no attention to you, either?"

The appalled note in her voice startled him. "I wasn't neglected," he hastened to say. "Before I went off to Eton, there were nursemaids and governesses and tutors, of course. And I reported to the earl once a week so that he could evaluate the progress of my studies."

"That's hardly a stirring endorsement! What a dreadful way for a boy to grow up. All children need love and attention. Not just from servants, but from their parents, their family. Boys in particular need a father figure."

Feeling unaccountably defensive, Hadrian prowled to the window to gaze out at the rainswept hills. He had both respected and feared his guardian, as was proper. It was simply the way that upper-class children were raised.

Yet somehow, Natalie's critical assessment had resurrected a host of buried memories from his boyhood. He recalled falling down and skinning his knee, and being berated for running by a stern governess. Whenever he was ill, a succession of nameless maidservants had tended to him. At least for a time there had been Audrey's mother, the first countess, who had come each night to press a kiss to his cheek. He'd been heartbroken at seven when she'd died since he'd seldom been allowed to visit his own mother.

A gust of wind tossed a flurry of raindrops against windowpanes, bringing him back to the present and reminding him that he hadn't responded to Natalie. He turned back around. "Perhaps you just need time to accustom yourself to our English ways. Gentlemen seldom have much to do with the rearing of children."

"Fiddlesticks. My father raised me after my mother died at my birth. Although I had a governess, Papa made sure he and I spent time together every day, playing games and telling stories, discussing current events. I never once doubted that he loved me—and *he* certainly was well versed in English ways from having grown up here."

Hadrian seized the opportunity to satisfy his curiosity. "Ah, yes, the Lincolnshire Fanshawes. Why did you never mention that you had family in England?"

"I never thought it important," she countered with a shrug. "But perhaps you think my father's birth makes me an unsuitable guardian for Leo."

"Don't make assumptions. I'm merely interested . . . as a friend." In so many ways, she was a tantalizing mystery to him. There were depths to her that he suspected would take a lifetime to fathom. But it was too soon to voice his strong feelings when he couldn't quite define them himself.

Natalie studied him a moment. With all the grace of a medieval queen assuming her throne, she seated herself in the chair with its high carved back and lifted her hand in a languid wave. "Do sit down, Duke, and I'll be happy to fill you in on the more titillating aspects of my family history."

Hadrian obligingly took the chair opposite hers. Leaning back, he stretched out his legs and let his eyes feast on the sight of her lovely features, caressed by the soft rainy light. "I'm listening."

"As you know, my father was the baseborn son of a baronet, Sir Basil Fanshawe. Apparently, Sir Basil was an infamous rake in his prime, and one of his many affairs was with an opera singer. When she conceived his child, he supported her financially, though he didn't wed her, of course. Like all English aristocrats, he chose a well-bred lady to be his wife."

Hadrian didn't want her believing that was always true. "Commoners *have* married into the nobility from time to time."

"Perhaps in rare instances when the woman is an heiress, but that wasn't the case here. According to Papa, his mother—my grandmother—left him as a swaddling babe with Sir Basil. She was heading off on a European opera tour, you see. My grandmother later married an Italian *conte* and became a *contessa*, only to die of a fever shortly thereafter, poor soul."

"You don't resent her for abandoning your father?"

Natalie sighed. "Singing was her passion. And I like to believe she wanted a more permanent life for her son than constantly moving from city to city like a vagabond. I give credit to the baronet, too, who tried to do right by my father. Though Sir Basil's personal affairs were in a shambles, he scraped up the funds to educate Papa at Eton and Cambridge. But Papa came to realize that his bastardy was a liability here in England. Though he was raised a gentleman, he was barred from many of the best homes."

That explained quite a lot to Hadrian about her dismal view of the aristocracy. "So he emigrated to America."

She nodded. "As a young man, Papa went in search of a place where he would be judged not on the blueness of his blood, but on the worth of his character. He embraced liberty with great enthusiasm and became a citizen as swiftly as possible." A challenging smile lit her face as if she relished the story and hoped to shock him with it. "There, Mr. Duke, now you know my shady past. I'm sure it's quite a bit more risqué than your own."

Hadrian found himself smiling back. "Actually, I've a few rebels and miscreants among my ducal ancestors, a smattering of commoners, as well. I'll tell you about them sometime. But getting back to your father, it seems he made a great success of himself."

"Yes, Papa had a knack for business and land management, and was so well spoken that he could sell a swamp as arable farmland. Not that he ever did so. He was scrupulously honest in his dealings, which is why we were comfortable but never wealthy. Eventually, he was persuaded to become a senator by friends in the state legislature."

"A tribute to the value of an English gentleman's education," Hadrian couldn't resist saying.

"I certainly can't fault your schools here," she agreed. "Yet he also had a somewhat chaotic upbringing, with Sir Basil forever with his pockets to let, from all his gambling debts. His other relatives were much the same. I suppose you could say that Papa was the only ambitious, hardworking one in a dynasty of wastrels. You've heard of the black sheep of the family? He used to chuckle that he was the one white sheep in a family of black sheep."

Hadrian found the tale enlightening. Natalie might speak flippantly, but the fact remained that bloodlines meant a great deal to the ton. Even a tainted genteel ancestry was considered superior to a common one. He himself had been brought up to believe that to be true.

But ever since their fateful meeting during the ice storm, he'd felt a shift inside himself, a desire to challenge long-held convictions. He wasn't yet certain where it would all lead. However, he did know that with the proper patronage, a striking beauty like Natalie would take society by storm.

If, that is, he could convince her to set aside her preconceptions of the aristocracy. And *if* he could persuade her that she would be happier with him than opening a school in America.

"Did your father keep in contact with Sir Basil?"

"Yes, they did correspond somewhat erratically. Papa had a half brother and half sister, too, though they're gone now. After my father's death, Sir Basil wrote to offer me a home with him and his two other grandchildren, my cousins. It was kind of him, but I declined, of course."

Of course. She didn't wish to live in England, nor did she care a fig for rank. It would be a challenge to change her mind, but Hadrian craved the chance to earn her respect. "Perhaps Sir Basil will be in London for the season," he said. "Will you call on him there?"

Her posture stiffened slightly, the aura of warmth evaporating. She eyed him with the same cool hauteur she'd accused him of possessing. "I haven't agreed to go to London."

Hadrian leaned forward, his elbows on his knees, his hands clasped. He searched for the words that would appeal to her. "I very much hope that you will. Leo would enjoy visiting the Tower, the circus, even the ships at the docks. You can't leave England without seeing the sights in its finest city."

"And we'd reside with you," she said, frowning.

"I'd be honored to have you both as my guests. Clayton House keeps a wonderful nursery stocked with toys and books for any guests. There'll be an army of servants at your beck and call. The accommodations are first-rate, the chef is excellent, the library huge. You'll not find better amenities anywhere."

At that description, Natalie appeared even less thrilled. Much to his perplexity, her eyes sparked displeasure as she rose to her feet. "I gather there would be strings attached."

He stood up as well. "Strings?"

"I won't be your mistress, Hadrian. If I gave you a wrongful notion last night, that was a mistake. One kiss doesn't mean I'm willing to be your kept woman."

The source of her offended state cleared the fog from his brain. Having learned scorn for the nobility at her father's knee, she had presumed Hadrian's intentions to be dishonorable. If only she knew how wrong she was!

"Allow me to put your mind at rest," he said. "If I harbored such a wicked design, I certainly wouldn't have invited you to stay at Clayton House. My mother lives there."

"Your mother? But . . . I thought you were estranged from her."

"As a child, yes, when I was allowed to visit her only twice a year. Once I reached my majority, however, I took control of my properties, including the town house. That has always been her primary residence, and I saw no reason to evict her. In truth, we rub along quite well together—so long as I can keep her from beggaring me with her shopping."

"Oh."

Natalie looked charmingly nonplussed by the revelation. The sight of her blushing confusion aroused tenderness in him as well as desire. He ached to draw her into the circle of his arms and kiss away all of her worries.

But there would be time enough later to woo her, once he had her under his own roof.

"You'll be adequately chaperoned," he went on. "As well as having my mother underfoot, we'll undoubtedly see quite a lot of my sister, who lives nearby. I didn't ask you to come to London for any nefarious purpose."

"You didn't ask me, period. You issued a decree."

He smiled ruefully. "Forgive me. Miss Fanshawe, will you and Leo kindly consent to stay as guests in my house? Mama will adore the brat, judging by the way she dotes on her one grandson, who is near Leo's age."

Natalie still looked uncertain. "Won't the duchess object to my presence? She might agree with Lord Godwin that I'm a fortune hunter."

"Hardly. My mother has never forgiven Godwin for taking me away from her all those years ago, so there's nothing to fear in that quarter. Besides, if you'd wanted to run a scam, you'd have set your sights on *me* the moment we met. Becoming a duchess would reap you far greater rewards than scheming to place a little boy in an earl's household."

Natalie stared at him, then gave a trill of laughter, amusement adding a bloom to her lovely features. "Now, there would be a mésalliance! As if *I* would ever think that a lofty English duke would wed a common upstart like me!"

He smiled blandly, intrigued that she could have so little notion of her own allure. "I'd never presume you to think any such thing, Natalie. By the way, we *are* back to first names again, I hope. Formality would be awkward while living under one roof. If you and Leo will accept my hospitality, that is."

She considered his words before nodding. "All right, Hadrian, I suppose we could stay with you and your mother for a few weeks."

The thrill of victory welled in him, though he was careful not to show just how much her assent mattered to him. It would take time and patience to ease her strong disapproval of the aristocracy. "Excellent," he said. "Then you'll wish to do your packing. We'll depart at first light in the morning."

But she made no move toward the door, her gaze intent on his face. "You *are* fond of Leo, aren't you? I believe you'd make him an excellent father."

"Me?"

"Yes. And Lady Ellen will be a good mother to Leo. She'll give him the affection that he truly deserves."

Lady Ellen? What had she to do with anything?

Hadrian gaped for a full five blinks before remembering that Natalie still believed he meant to wed the girl. He almost corrected her, then thought better of it. If she knew he was considering altering his marital plans in her favor, she might very well rescind her agreement to go to London.

"I'll keep that in mind," he said noncommittally.

He would do no such thing, of course. Although he liked the novel notion of adopting the boy, a part of that included Natalie filling the role of his wife and Leo's mother. Best of all, Hadrian would have her in his bed each night. Their passionate kiss had been a mere taste to hone his appetite for her.

It struck him that he'd never entertained a single lascivious thought about Lady Ellen. With Natalie, however, it was a constant battle to keep himself from visualizing the feminine curves beneath her gown. He craved to glide his hands over her lush bottom, to trace the slender indentation of her waist, to cup the breasts that filled his palms to perfection.

But it would be an uphill battle to soften her resistance to a man of his high rank. Was he wrong to think he could convince her to stay in England? Wrong to hope she could somehow fit into his world? Wrong to believe she'd find him worthy enough to give up her life in America?

At the moment, she was eyeing him with determination, a charming flush in her cheeks. "There's something else I need to say," she told him. "I oughtn't have encouraged you to kiss me last night. It was my fault and utterly unfair to Lady Ellen. It must never happen again."

The air suddenly seemed to hum with charged energy. They stared at each other, and he could see in her direct gaze that she, too, felt the scorching bond between them. He himself recalled every moment of their embrace with searing clarity. The brandy tang of her mouth, the eager softness of her lips, the pressure of her slim body arching against him. He burned to touch the silken smoothness of her breasts again, this time to strip away her clothes, to discover every hidden secret of her body, to sink into her welcoming heat.

In two steps, he could close the distance between them and have her in his arms again. It wouldn't take much effort to coax her into returning his fervor, despite what she was saying. But it would be far wiser to wait until they were away from this house. Once in London, he could devote himself to enticing her.

He tamped down the blaze of desire. "Neither of us were unfair to Lady Ellen," he stated. "I'm not betrothed to her. In fact, Godwin has agreed she should be free to enjoy her first season."

Frowning, Natalie appeared to be keenly inquisitive about the situation. "But . . . you *do* intend to marry her, don't you?"

"That remains to be seen," he hedged.

She firmed her delectable mouth. "If you don't, what will happen to Leo? I don't want him to be raised in this house, Hadrian. Especially not after what happened with Lord Wymark."

"Happened?"

Natalie glanced over her shoulder at the door, then lowered her voice. "That incident with the stallion, of course. I shudder to think of how close Leo came to being trampled. If truth be told, there's something reckless about Lord Wymark that gives me a cold chill. I don't trust him."

Hadrian's first impulse was to scoff. Richard was simply a careless young fool who had been spoiled by his mother.

But Natalie looked so genuinely concerned that he considered the matter from her perspective. All she'd seen of Richard was his sulky manner, his lack of control, his penchant for drinking and gambling. That, combined with the cold reception she'd received from Lord and Lady Godwin, had fostered a very real fear in Natalie for Leo's welfare.

Blast his cousins for treating the two of them so badly.

Abandoning his resolve to keep his distance, he stepped closer and placed his hands on her shoulders. Her vital warmth coursed through him as he lightly kneaded the tension from her muscles. "You mustn't let Wymark alarm you. Once we leave here, your paths aren't likely to cross."

"Nevertheless, I dislike spending even one more night in a household where Leo's very presence is begrudged."

With his hands on her shoulders, he felt the shiver that rippled through Natalie. It communicated a twinge of worry to him, as well. Despite his reassurances to her, there was always the chance that he could be wrong.

He ran his fingertips over her petal-soft cheek. "Then perhaps it would make you feel easier if we were to depart straightaway."

Luminosity entered her green eyes. "Right now? Today?"

"There's a few hours of daylight left. How quickly can you be ready?"

"At once."

Watching the sway of her hips as she hastened to the door, Hadrian felt caught in the throes of fierce protectiveness. The sooner he had her and Leo safely under his care, the better. Grimly, he knew without an ounce of doubt that he would kill anyone who tried to harm either of them.

Chapter 17

Emerging from the post chaise two days later, Natalie thought there must be some mistake. Surely the grand structure towering before her could not be a house.

Built of honey-colored stone, the residence had an impressive portico with tall columns topped by a stately triangular pediment. The classical style reminded her of the president's house in Washington, though this building was much larger and more magnificent. She counted a dozen immense windows stretched across the ground floor alone. It was a crown jewel compared to the more modest brick town homes that lined the square.

A tug on her skirts brought her gaze down to Leo, who stared up with rounded eyes. "Does the king live at this palace with Mr. Duke?"

Laughing, Natalie tidied his tousled hair. "No, darling. Though it does look vast enough to hold a royal court."

"Never fear," Hadrian said, "you'll learn your way around Clayton House soon enough."

Her heart quaked at the sound of his deep voice. He'd just dismounted after having ridden on horseback for much of the journey, leaving the luxurious post chaise to her and Leo. Although he appeared the perfect gentleman

in his greatcoat and hat, there was a banked heat in his
eyes, a rakish curve to his lips, that once again made her
doubt the wisdom of accepting his invitation to London.

He desired her. Their passionate kiss had merely whet-
ted his appetite. She felt a slow burn deep within her
core every time he looked at her.

Despite his assurances, Natalie was aware she didn't
truly know the Duke of Clayton. Nor could she shake the
vague suspicion that he had some unspoken reason for
bringing her and Leo here. He had appeared entirely too
satisfied when she'd finally acquiesced.

During the long hours of travel, she'd had ample time
to ponder. He had visited Oak Knoll for the purpose of
affiancing himself to Lady Ellen. Yet he'd seemed eager
to clarify that he was not yet betrothed. What did it
mean? Had he finally realized the girl had no interest
in a man much older than herself? Or was he intending
to win Lady Ellen's hand over the course of the season?

And how did she herself fit into the picture? She'd
grown up hearing her father decry the indiscretions of
the nobility, and their arrogant manner of using women
they perceived to be of the lower orders. Yet Hadrian
could hardly be scheming a seduction with his mother
in residence.

Perhaps she was reading too much into the matter,
Natalie thought. Perhaps he merely wanted her here for
Leo's sake.

It was a dispiriting thought. Imprudent though it might
be, she wanted to matter to Hadrian. She wanted him to
toss and turn at night, dreaming of her. She wanted him
to miss her when she departed for America. As much as
she herself would miss him . . .

"In my experience, brat, some ladies are frightened by
a mouse. But it appears that Miss Fanshawe is frightened
by a house."

The low rumble of Hadrian's voice pulled her back to reality. So did Leo's giggle at the rhyme. She blinked to see they were regarding her with shared male amusement. Realizing she was frowning, Natalie immediately corrected her expression with a smile. "Don't be silly. Though it *is* by far the largest house I've ever seen."

"You *are* afraid. And here I believed you to be intrepid."

Hadrian appeared perfectly serious, the image of ducal hauteur, though his gray eyes held a glint of humor in the sunlight. Aware of a treacherous weakening in her knees, she scolded herself for being affected by his teasing charm. It wouldn't do to encourage any more familiarity between them.

Before she could respond, Leo piped up. "What's intrepid?"

"Bold," Hadrian said. "Fearless. Since Miss Fanshawe finds bravery in short supply today, perhaps she should hold on to me for courage."

As the duke offered his arm, Natalie was half tempted to stick out her tongue. But that would be undignified when they were surrounded by footmen and grooms, including Chumley, the sour old valet who even now was casting baleful glances her way as he supervised the unloading of the baggage.

"You can hold my arm, too, Miss Fanshawe," Leo said gallantly. "'Specially if you're afraid."

She glanced down to see the boy crook his elbow in a pint-sized imitation of Hadrian. Nothing could have been better designed to squeeze her heart. Smiling, she reached down to accept the assistance he offered, then curled the fingers of her other hand around Hadrian's arm.

"Why, thank you, kind sirs. Now, I can feel protected by *two* gentlemen."

Leo looked delighted and proud. It was a poignant reminder that he needed a strong male influence in his life, a man he could emulate as a model of courtesy and proper behavior.

If only she could convince Hadrian to adopt the boy. He had been noncommittal when she'd brought up the topic, but she intended to persuade him to do so over the coming weeks. Leo deserved to be loved, rather than abandoned to the guardianship of a grandfather who resented him.

As the three of them mounted the marble steps to the portico, a peculiar notion swept over Natalie. She fancied they were a family, returning home after a long absence. A bone-deep longing clutched at her heart, but she banished the illusion at once. Such a scenario would require her to be an English duchess. How absurd!

It was dangerous, too. By allowing herself to fall prey to such fantasies, she would be more susceptible to Hadrian's magnetism. He would never propose marriage to her, nor would she accept him if he did. She had a life of her own back in America, a plan to open a school, and she must not be distracted by dreams that could never be.

A white-wigged footman in forest-green livery held open the door. As they proceeded into the house, their footsteps echoed in the vastness of the entrance hall. The interior was even more awe-inspiring than the outside, and Natalie scarcely knew where to look first.

Untying her bonnet, she turned slowly around to view the tall marble columns with gilded capitals, the life-sized classical statues in niches, the domed ceiling that was painted with frolicking nymphs and cherubs. On either side of the room, a pair of matching staircases swept upward to meet at a marble balcony worthy of a soliloquy from Romeo to Juliet.

Several servants in neat dark garb waited with square-shouldered posture. Natalie was glad Hadrian remained at her side. If truth be told, she *did* feel a trifle intimidated by this splendid house and the array of staff members, especially the distinguished middle-aged man in black who came forward, accompanied by a hatchet-faced older woman with a ring of keys jingling at her stout waist.

"Welcome home, Your Grace," the man intoned, bowing as his female counterpart bobbed a curtsy to the duke.

Hadrian introduced them to Natalie as Winkelman and Mrs. Darrow, the butler and the housekeeper. "My guests have recently arrived from America," the duke told them. "Master Leo Bellingham is a cousin of mine, and Miss Fanshawe is his temporary guardian. She was a friend of Leo's mother, my late cousin Audrey."

Blinking in surprise, Mrs. Darrow glanced at Natalie, then back at the duke. "Forgive me, Your Grace. When we received your message yesterday, I presumed Miss Fanshawe to be the boy's governess and would stay in the nursery. Shall I prepare a guest bedchamber for her, then?"

"Yes, please do," he said, handing his gloves and greatcoat to the butler, who then passed the items to a footman.

"Please don't," Natalie dissented. "I'll be perfectly fine in the nursery. Mrs. Darrow, you really needn't go to any trouble on my behalf."

"Nonsense," Hadrian said crisply. "You're not in my employ. It would be remiss of me to give you accommodations designed for a governess."

"Might I suggest the daffodil suite?" the housekeeper said, siding with her master while giving Natalie a commiserating look. "You won't be terribly far from the lad, miss. The stairway to the nursery is directly beside the bedchamber. 'Tis a mere hop up one flight of steps."

Natalie turned her gaze to the little boy, who had wandered to the far end of the entrance hall. He stood with his head tilted back, studying a gigantic painting of some ducal ancestor wielding a sword and mounted on horseback.

"But . . . my place is with Leo."

Hadrian's warm fingers wrapped around hers, lightly squeezing. "Never fear, the brat will be perfectly safe. My staff will keep him well supervised whenever you're unavailable. During the day, you'll be free to spend as much time as you like with him. We both will. Besides which, it would be good for him to become familiar with his new station in life."

Natalie opened her mouth to protest, then closed it.

When he put it so reasonably, with that subtle reminder that she'd be leaving eventually for America, she felt foolish for objecting. *Was* she being overly protective? She might not approve of the way servants raised the children of the aristocracy, but once she was gone, this would become Leo's world. Perhaps she ought to allow him the space to adjust to it without her hovering over him too much. Oh, but the prospect did rip at her heart!

Winkelman coughed discreetly. "Your Grace, the duchess returned from Bond Street not half an hour ago, along with Lady Elizabeth. She requested that you bring your guests to her suite straightaway. She, er, mentioned having something to give the child."

"Bond Street?" the duke said. "Let me guess. Tuttle's Toy Emporium."

The butler's impassive features betrayed a trace of humor in the minuscule elevation of one eyebrow. "There *were* a number of packages with that distinctive wrapping."

"Well," Hadrian said, a weighty exasperation conveyed in the single word. "Will you mind coming along,

Natalie? You can meet my mother and sister while your rooms are being prepared."

A footman whisked away her cloak and bonnet; then she collected Leo and they headed up one of the twin staircases. Hadrian took the opportunity to point out highlights of the house, including a portrait of an uncle who had been an admiral, and a nick in the woodwork where Hadrian had struck it as a boy while attempting to ride his sled down the stairs. It was clear that he was proud of his domain and very much wanted to make them feel at home.

Natalie found that touching, though she was still too wonderstruck to imagine living in such grand surroundings. The place was in stark contrast to the modest frame house in which she'd grown up, and the cozy log cabin she'd shared with Audrey and her family in the wilderness.

Reaching the upper balcony, she glimpsed several magnificent reception rooms before they continued up another wide flight of steps, headed along a carpeted corridor, and arrived at a door that stood partway open. The duke rapped loudly on the panel. When Leo would have darted inside, Hadrian held him back, a twinkle in his eye. "Ladies first, brat."

Natalie hesitated. Despite having forded raging rivers and ridden through wild lands, she found herself leery to cross this threshold into the private quarters of a duchess. Her reluctance made no sense. What could there possibly be to fear in meeting Hadrian's mother and sister? They were, after all, potential allies in securing a happy future for Leo.

Holding on to that thought, she marched inside and found herself in a sitting room that abounded with gilded splendor: chairs with embroidered pillows, shelves and tables crowded with dainty objets d'art, flower paintings on the rose-papered walls. Even the air smelled rich with a perfumed scent.

Just then, a yapping spaniel sped around the corner and stopped in the arched doorway as if to guard entry to the bedchamber. The dog was followed by a chestnut-haired beauty in a mint-green gown.

This must be Hadrian's sister. A softer, feminine version of her brother, she showed the unmistakable roundness of pregnancy as she swooped forward with a glad cry. "Hadrian! I *told* Mama I heard a knock!"

He gave her a peck on the cheek before reaching down to scratch the floppy ears of the spaniel. "Well, Lizzy. I understand that you're up to your old tricks, encouraging the duchess to beggar me at the shops."

"That old tattler Winkelman! Now, don't be a fussbudget and spoil our fun. We had a delightful morning preparing for your guests." Her china-blue eyes roved with interest over Leo and Natalie. "And here they are!"

Hadrian took the hint and introduced her as Lady Elizabeth, the Marchioness of Wrenbury. "I must warn you," he told her, "that Miss Fanshawe is too egalitarian to embrace the custom of curtsying."

"Egal-*what*?" She playfully swatted his arm. "Conceited prig, you use big words on purpose since you know I was never very attentive at my studies."

"It means 'Merica doesn't have dukes and kings," Leo spoke up. "Miss Fanshawe told me that."

Lady Wrenbury leaned down to address him. "Why, aren't you a clever fellow! Do you know, I've a son about your age. We call him Finny. Perhaps once you've settled in, you'd care to play with him sometime?"

Leo considered it. "Can Miss Fanshawe and Mr. Duke come, too?"

"Why, of course! Miss Fanshawe is always welcome."

A burble of mirth sprang from her. "And so is . . . *Mr. Duke*."

Natalie smiled back at her. "Please call me Natalie, Lady Wrenbury. I hope I won't offend you with a simple handshake."

"Certainly not!" the woman said as they briefly clasped hands. "And I am Lizzy. Lady Wrenbury sounds so terribly ancient! Anyway, curtsies are rather a bore, especially in a receiving line. I'm always petrified I'll step on my hem and go tumbling to the floor in front of everyone. Now do come and meet Mama."

Feeling more relaxed, Natalie followed. It was a relief to discover that she liked Hadrian's sister. Her earlier hesitation must have been due to a dread that his immediate family might be as hostile as Lord and Lady Godwin. She had no desire to spend the coming weeks in another uncomfortable situation, scorned as a devious hoaxer.

She entered an enormous bedchamber done in the same rose décor as the sitting room. Swaths of pink satin, drawn back by gold cords, framed the tall windows. The canopied bed featured chintz hangings, numerous feather pillows, and an elaborate crest on the gilt headboard. Fine objects of crystal and porcelain cluttered every available surface, including an ormolu clock that ticked softly on the mantelpiece.

The effect was overwhelmingly feminine, a retreat where any male was bound to feel out of place. Glancing back over her shoulder, she was amused to see a hint of steely forbearance in the set of Hadrian's jaw. Even Leo appeared dumbfounded by all the girlish opulence as he stayed close to the duke's heels.

Fluffy tail wagging, the spaniel dashed across the plush carpet toward a plump woman who sat on a chair, engaged in sorting through mounds of large and small parcels wrapped up in green-striped paper tied with yellow ribbons. She was richly gowned in violet crepe with a silk turban in a slightly lighter shade on her head. Amethysts glinted on her fingers, at her wrists and throat.

The Duchess of Clayton appeared quite imposing and stately—at least until she raised her head and smiled radiantly at them, in particular, her son. "Hadrian, darling! Thank heavens you're home!"

She held out her arms, and he went forward to press a kiss to her cheek, extracting himself before being drawn into a full embrace. As he attempted to step back, however, she clung to his hand with both of hers, gazing up at him with tragic blue eyes in a face that might have been ordinary if not for the devoted sentiment that brought her lined features to life.

"Oh, my dear boy, *do* assure me there is no betrothal. Your note was *entirely* too brief."

"There is no betrothal . . . yet."

Natalie felt his gaze flick toward her, though she didn't know quite what to make of it. Was he warning her not to say anything of his courtship of Lady Ellen?

His mother sighed in relief and let go of him to fan her face with a piece of striped paper. "Bless me! I never understood how you could wish to marry a girl who is scarcely out of the schoolroom, one you haven't seen in *years*. Especially the daughter of such a man—"

"We'll speak of this later," Hadrian said firmly. "First, Duchess, may I present cousin Audrey's son, Leo Bellingham, who has been delivered here from the wilds of America by Miss Natalie Fanshawe."

The spaniel hopped into the duchess's lap, and she stroked him with her beringed fingers while turning her regal attention to Natalie and Leo. Solemnly studying them both, the duchess seemed a curious mix of formidable and approachable, and Natalie had to squelch the surprising impulse to genuflect.

Perhaps that explained at least part of the reason why people curtsied and bowed. It gave them something to do while being inspected.

As if they'd passed muster, a smile warmed the duchess's face. "Welcome to Clayton House. Pray sit down and we'll have a cozy chat." She waited while Natalie and Hadrian found chairs, then told Natalie, "I've been on pins and needles since receiving my son's note yesterday. Men can be such terse letter writers, can't they? They gloss over the most *important* details. And I must say, Miss Fanshawe, I'm surprised he never mentioned you to be such a strikingly lovely young woman."

Embarrassed by the compliment, Natalie glanced away to see Lizzy cast a measuring look at her brother, who in turn observed the scene with his usual cool hauteur. "I—thank you," she said. "I'm sure the duke had more important things on his mind. Leo, for instance."

The duchess smiled at Leo. "*Such* an adorable little boy! Come closer, darling, and you may pet Orlando. I am a sort of cousin to you by marriage, did you know? You may call me Auntie Millie."

Leo trotted forward and patted the dog in her lap, giggling when the animal licked his chin. "That tickles! Can I play with him, Auntie Millie?"

"Certainly! Though I think you may rather wish to play with the things inside these parcels."

Leo's eyes rounded to saucers as he glanced at the mounds of wrapped packages. "But it isn't my birthday."

She fluttered her fingers, her rings flashing. "Oh, these are just a few little welcoming gifts."

He touched one of the parcels as if he'd just stumbled upon a pirate's golden treasure trove. "Look, Miss Fanshawe! Can I open them? *Please*?"

Natalie told herself to bide her tongue and avoid offending her hostess, but she could not remain silent. She was too appalled by the extravagance. "Not yet, darling. You're very thoughtful, Duchess, but really, this is far too much. In America, Leo was accustomed to playing with sticks and stones."

"Oh, the poor, dear child," Lizzy exclaimed unhelpfully. "Think of all he's missed!"

"Nevertheless, Natalie is right," Hadrian said, looking sternly from his sister to his mother. "Especially as the nursery is already well stocked."

"But I only wish for him to be happy here," his mother said with a pout. "You sound just like Cousin Godwin! When you were a little boy, he was forever sending scolding letters, warning me to cease spoiling you. Why, the pinchpenny brute even had the audacity to *dispose* of the toys I gave you."

"That was a long time ago. And there *is* something to be said for austerity. We've spoken of this a number of times."

The duchess groped for her handkerchief, dabbing the corner of one watery eye. "Oh, pray don't be cruel, Hadrian. My purpose is only to be kind."

He appeared nonplussed by the sudden glint of tears, but there was something sham in the way she gazed up at her son that gave Natalie the suspicion that his mother could turn the waterworks on and off at will.

In an effort to settle the dispute while Leo was distracted by examining the boxes, she said quickly, "You *are* kind, Duchess, to have gone out of your way to make Leo happy. Might I suggest that you give him a parcel to unwrap today, and save the others for later? So long as he behaves himself, of course."

"One per week would be a reasonable compromise," Hadrian said with a slight smile at the boy. "Go on, brat. You may choose one to open right now."

Not surprisingly, Leo selected the biggest box and knelt down to rip off the yellow ribbon and striped paper. His face lit up. "Look, it's the Royal Mail coach! With horses, too. There's even a coachman! Thank you, Aunt Millie!"

He jumped up to give her a quick hug while everyone dutifully oohed and aahed. Tail wagging, Orlando leaped down from the duchess's lap to watch Leo play with his new toy. Natalie noted the fine detail of the miniature set and fretted at the obvious expense. It also gave her an inkling as to why Lord Godwin had found the duchess's indulgence of Hadrian to be excessive.

While the boy was occupied, the duke turned to his mother. "I'm wondering if you might be acquainted with Miss Fanshawe's grandfather," he said. "Sir Basil Fanshawe."

Her eyes widened with interest. "Sir Basil? From Lincolnshire? Why, that rogue was a beau of mine back in my debutante days, though he was much older than me. I haven't heard his name in ever so many years."

"He lost his place in society over some unpaid debts quite a long time ago," Natalie said. "It was shortly after my father emigrated to America. To be perfectly frank, my family history is somewhat checkered."

"Oh, bosh, so is ours, and *I* am a part of the reason why," she said matter-of-factly. "I shouldn't think my son has mentioned *my* lineage to you, for by ducal decree of my late husband, it was swept under the rug ages ago."

Intrigued, Natalie glanced at Hadrian to see him

regarding his mother with a hint of exasperation. "I'm not in the habit of regaling everyone I meet with an accounting of my parentage," he said. "Now, about Sir Basil."

"Ah yes," the duchess said. "Have you kept in touch with him, Miss Fanshawe? Is he still among the living?"

"We exchange letters from time to time. I've an address for him here in London, in an area called Covent Garden." Natalie looked at the duke. "If it isn't asking too much, Hadrian, perhaps you wouldn't mind lending me your carriage one day so that I might visit him?"

Even as he inclined his head in a nod, Lizzy sat up straight in her chair, glancing from her brother to Natalie. "Hadrian, is it? I'm surprised he allows you to call him by his given name."

"Indeed," her mother concurred, her speculative gaze on Natalie. "My son seldom permits anyone to address him with such familiarity. He is Clayton or Duke or Your Grace to all but a handful of intimates. Like his father, he's always been stuffy and proper that way."

Was that true? As the women stared at her, warmth crept into Natalie's cheeks. Hadrian seemed to find amusement in her discomfort, judging by the smirk tilting up one corner of his lips. Afraid the ladies might guess about that passionate kiss, she tossed out a distraction. "We've been working closely in an effort to do what's best for Leo, that's all. We agreed it wasn't wise to leave him with Lord Godwin at the moment."

The duchess took the bait. "A sensible decision, I must say. Oak Knoll is a horrid place for a young child, so cold and grim, like a fortress."

"That's precisely what I thought, too," Natalie said.

"*I* have never even been there," Lizzy commented. "But I've met Lord Godwin here in London, and he seems a severe sort of fellow. I confess, I'm eager to learn what happened during your visit."

"We'll discuss it later," Hadrian said, flicking a meaningful glance at Leo, who was playing with his toy coach on the floor. "Getting back to Sir Basil, Natalie will be calling on him, in addition to taking Leo to the park and various amusements around town. It would be obliging of you, Mama, to assist her in acquiring the proper London wardrobe."

Natalie felt as if she'd been poked with a pin. "What? I've ample clothing in my valise." That was a brazen lie, she acknowledged to herself, comparing her paltry few dresses to the fashionable creations worn by the other two women. "Though perhaps you'd be so kind as to direct me to a shop where I might purchase materials to sew another gown or two."

"Sew? Yourself?" The duchess appeared scandalized by the notion. "Certainly not! I would be a poor hostess indeed if I expected my guests to labor all day stitching their own clothing. We shall visit my mantua-maker in the morning. Madame Barbeau is the finest in London. She will not require an appointment, for she often says I'm her best customer."

"A splendid notion," Lizzy chimed in, clapping her hands. "Such beautiful sable hair you have, Natalie. And those green eyes! She would look very fine in saffron or jonquil, don't you think, Mama? As well as dramatic colors like claret and damson. And Madame showed me the loveliest bronze silk the other day, so rich and shimmery."

Flustered, Natalie shook her head. "Forgive me, I know you only mean to be helpful. But the truth is, I simply cannot afford to acquire an extensive wardrobe."

The duchess fluttered her beringed fingers. "Oh, my dear, it is but a trifling expense to *me*. It shall be my reward to you for traveling all the way across the ocean to bring young Leo to his kin."

"Yet I must refuse. I could never accept such a lavish gift. And that is final."

Her words fell like stones into the serenity of the rose-pink bedchamber. She expected the duchess to turn cool and haughty that a foreign upstart would dare to address her in such a manner. Instead, Her Grace appeared crestfallen, the corners of her mouth turned downward, as if she were a child denied a special treat. There was even a wounded glimmer to her eyes, and not the crocodile tears she'd directed at her son earlier.

Natalie felt small and mean for having spoken so harshly. On impulse, she knelt in front of the older woman, taking hold of her hands. "I *am* sorry, Your Grace. I truly don't wish to upset you. It's just that I'm accustomed to providing for myself."

"As I am accustomed to purchasing things," the duchess said on a sigh.

"It *is* her greatest pleasure," Hadrian confirmed dryly.

Natalie flashed a scowl up at him, for he wasn't helping matters. He must have known his mother would leap at the chance to outfit Natalie. And deep down, it struck at her pride to think that he might find her appearance to be lacking.

"I have the very solution!" Lizzy exclaimed. "Last autumn, before realizing I was in a delicate condition, I ordered a number of new gowns. Alas, they won't fit me now that I've grown as large as a house." She lovingly rubbed her rounded belly. "So perhaps, Natalie, you would be so good as to take the dresses. You're taller, but my maid can let down the hems. It won't cost you a penny, and you'd be doing me a *great* favor, for they are cluttering up my dressing room. By the time I'm able to wear anything so slimming again, they'll be out of style. Remember the violet sarcenet, Mama? It would look heavenly with her hair and eyes."

The duchess perked up. "Indeed, and I've a spangled shawl that would be the perfect accent. Why, I've never even worn it, after deciding that it brought out the gray in my hair."

As the two women began to chatter excitedly about various other accessories that could be contributed to the cause, Natalie stood up, aghast at this new scheme and confounded as to how to halt it. She abhorred the notion of accepting charity—which this very much felt like— yet the ladies were so enthusiastic that she lacked the heart to voice another refusal.

Hadrian appeared at her side, an irksome grin tilting one corner of his mouth. "It's useless to fight them," he murmured. "They always get their way. Shall we proceed to the nursery now?"

Chapter 18

On their way upstairs, Hadrian carried Leo's new toy. The boy bounded up the steps in a state of jubilant talkativeness. "I like my mail coach very much. The little horses, too. Even if it's not the same as having a *real* pony."

Natalie caught the hopeful, sidelong glance he cast up at the duke. Still reeling from the extravagance of his mother and sister, she said firmly, "Leo! You are not to be expecting a pony anytime soon. One gift per week is all we agreed upon. And that's only if you behave yourself."

"I will, Miss Fanshawe. 'Specially if I have a real pony!"

Hadrian chuckled. "I haven't forgotten my promise, brat. In the meantime, you may practice your riding skills on the hobby horse in the nursery."

"What's a hobby horse?"

"A large wooden steed designed for a fellow just your size. Go inside, you'll see it over by the window."

The boy dashed ahead of them through the doorway and into the sunlit schoolroom. A pair of maidservants stood waiting, one old and one young. The girl helped

Leo onto the carved horse and showed him how to rock back and forth, which he did with great enthusiasm. Both servants curtsied to the duke, eyeing Natalie with friendly curiosity.

Hadrian set down the miniature mail coach on one of the small tables, then went to the middle-aged woman and planted a kiss on her wrinkled cheek. "Why, Tippy, I might have known you'd still be in charge of this nursery. Miss Fanshawe, this is Mrs. Tippet."

Setting aside her own woes for the moment, Natalie greeted her warmly, liking the woman's briskness and air of competence. She had a grandmotherly plumpness in a serviceable gray gown and white apron, and brown eyes that twinkled beneath her mobcap.

"I was nursemaid to His Grace for his first five years, and then whenever he came to visit. The girl here is Flora. She grew up with younger brothers and knows how to keep little boys occupied so's they stay out of trouble."

Flora smiled shyly before going to help Leo dismount from the hobby horse. She seemed energetic enough to keep up with an active boy, especially one who was eagerly darting around the large play area to view the many toys.

While the duke directed him to check out the contents of the cupboards, Natalie strolled around the schoolroom, examining the well-stocked educational supplies. Although the textbooks dated back to Hadrian's youth, they would do well for her to use in teaching a six-year-old.

At least for the time being, she thought with a pang. Then a new governess would be hired, and Natalie would return to America. She would say good-bye to Leo—and Hadrian—forever.

Now, why was she feeling such a lump in her throat? That day wouldn't arrive for many weeks. And anyway, she *wanted* to resume a normal life in Philadelphia, where she could proceed with her plans to open a school.

Mrs. Tippet was standing beside Hadrian, watching as Leo sat down to assemble the pieces of a wooden puzzle with Flora's assistance. "Ah, it's good to have a child at Clayton House again. It's been far too long since you were a little tyke." She shook her finger at Hadrian. "This nursery would be full of youngsters, if Your Grace would only do his duty."

Hadrian chuckled. "Never fear, I'll oblige you soon enough."

His enigmatic gaze flicked to Natalie. Even though she knew he must be referring to Lady Ellen, a shiver stirred over her skin, coursing through her bosom and down to her depths. She resisted the errant sensation with ruthless resolve. Their arrival at his London house had only underscored the fundamental differences in their worlds. It would serve no purpose to indulge such longing when nothing could ever come of it.

"Tippy, I trust you'll watch over Leo while I show Miss Fanshawe to her rooms."

"'Twill be a pleasure, Your Grace. Rest assured, me and Flora will keep the mite safe and happy."

That prediction was confirmed by Leo himself. He scarcely even looked up from his puzzle when Natalie told him she'd return in a little while. On her way out the door, she caught a glimpse of his towheaded form bent over the table, swinging his legs and giggling at something Flora said to him.

Hadrian's hand came to rest at the small of Natalie's back as he guided her down a nearby staircase. "Leo is a very adaptable lad. And you won't be too far from him, I promise."

Realizing that he must have seen a trace of worry on her face, she confessed, "He's been my sole responsibility for so many months that it's difficult to leave him in the care of someone else."

"It'll be good for him. You'll see."

Natalie hoped so. She reminded herself it would be cruel to keep the boy dependent on her, making their eventual parting all the more difficult. But she didn't want to think about that now. Not with Hadrian so close to her.

The light pressure of his palm felt unbearably intimate, its warmth penetrating her gown like a lover's touch. A tingling desire flowed through her veins and wreaked havoc with her equilibrium. If she fretted about anything, it ought to be her desire for a man who could have no place in her future.

At the bottom of the staircase, he ushered her through a nearby doorway and into a large bedchamber done in a pleasing décor of pastel blues and yellows. She gazed in delight at the dainty French furniture, the glass-fronted bookcase, the elegant writing desk. Gauzy curtains on the windows rippled in the breeze and cast a filtered sunlight over a seating area with a sofa and gilt chairs.

To one side stood the loveliest canopied bed she had ever seen. Swaths of silk in robin's-egg blue with lemon-yellow trim draped the four posts. The white coverlet was embroidered with the daffodils that gave the room its name.

A maid in black uniform and snowy apron, a mobcap over her brown hair, had just finished plumping the row of feather pillows. She bobbed a respectful curtsy. "'Tis ready, Your Grace. Fresh linens, the room is aired, and the lady's valise unpacked. There's only the windows to close again."

Natalie smiled at her. "I'll do that in a little while, thank you. You'll have me feeling entirely too pampered."

She *did* feel pampered. After living in a log cabin in

the wilderness, the luxurious surroundings made her feel as if she'd tumbled into a dream world.

The fresh, cool air drew her across the room to the bank of windows. She parted the filmy curtains and peered out at an expansive garden below, where pebbled pathways meandered among mature trees and shrubbery. Green shoots in the flower beds heralded springtime, as did the leaf buds on the trees. The scene looked so bucolic that only the distant rooftops confirmed that she was in the midst of a great city.

"I trust the accommodations meet with your approval."

Hadrian's voice at her shoulder made her spin around. His nearness caused a fluttering in her bosom. He stood only a scant foot away, his gray eyes smoky in the diffused sunlight. A slight smile tilted his mouth, as if he harbored wicked thoughts that involved kissing . . . and more.

In the absence of all common sense, she burned to feel his strong arms holding her close, his lips pressed to hers, his hands caressing her bare skin. A tantalizing warmth spread through her body until she scarcely noticed the bracing breeze from the windows. It would be so easy to forget her vow to resist him . . .

When one of his eyebrows lifted inquiringly, she realized he was waiting for her response. "The room is perfect, and you're right, it's close enough to the nursery. In truth, it's so lovely that I feel as overindulged as Leo." Edgy in his presence, she glanced past the duke's broad-shouldered form toward the bed. It was then that she noticed they were alone. "Where is the maid?"

"I sent her away."

"You know very well it's improper for us to be alone in a bedchamber. You'll have to leave at once."

Hadrian made no move to depart. With his slightly aquiline nose and aristocratic features, his snow-white cravat and tailored blue coat, he looked every inch the English duke, the master of all this luxury and wealth. "Since the door is open, only a stickler would call it an impropriety," he said reasonably. "As for Leo being overindulged, I don't wish for that to happen, either. You made an excellent compromise with my mother."

"Did I?" Aware of a bottled-up tension, Natalie brushed past him to pace the soft carpet, her hem swishing around her ankles. "A gift every week, when he already has more than enough playthings in the nursery. That's fifty-two presents a year, not counting birthday and Christmas."

"It's an improvement over him receiving them all at once."

"Fiddle! He isn't accustomed to owning even a fraction of that. He's a sweet, unselfish boy, and I shudder to think of him growing up spoiled. No one should require so many *things* to make them happy. You yourself spoke to your mother about the benefits of austerity."

Hadrian stood listening to her tirade, a faint frown on his brow. "Are we quarreling about toys—or about your gowns?"

"Toys! Oh, *blast*." Natalie bit off her words at the astuteness of his observation. The tension inside her *did* have a deal to do with him wanting to array her in fashionable garb. "Now that you mention it, I find that expenditure appalling, too. Though it's kind of your sister to offer the gowns, it's a tremendously costly gift—and from someone I only met this very day."

"Lizzy can be very generous, and so can my mother. You saw how happy it made them."

Natalie couldn't dispute that. The ladies had been delighted to be given the task of replenishing her wardrobe. And she couldn't deny, either, that in the depths of her soul she harbored the same covetous desire as any woman for new clothes. But not when those items must have cost a king's ransom.

"I've never accepted charity, and I don't wish to start now," she explained. "I'd sooner go without than feel beholden to someone else. And don't try to tell me there's no expense involved. Your sister could sell those gowns back to the shop and recoup at least a portion of their cost."

He leaned his shoulder against the bedpost and watched her pace back and forth. "That's very practical-minded of you," he said with a slight smile. "But it's also practical to spruce up your apparel for those times when we'll be taking Leo out and about town to see the sights. It's likely we'll encounter acquaintances of mine, and you'll want to look your best when meeting the fashion plates of society."

She stopped in her tracks, glaring at him. "Are you saying you're ashamed to be seen in the company of a dowdy mongrel from America?"

His smile vanished, his dark eyebrows clashing in a frown. "Of course not. You couldn't be more mistaken."

"Oh? It sounds as if you believe the upper crust won't accept me as I am. Never fear, I'll borrow a few of the gowns and make myself presentable enough to pass muster with your friends."

He strode forward to fasten his hands to her shoulders. "Listen to me, Natalie. You've taken this all wrong. I could never be ashamed of you even if you were garbed in sackcloth and ashes. You're a beautiful woman, inside and out, and should anyone in society dare to scorn you, they will know my wrath."

The ringing sincerity in his words went a long way toward easing her wounded pride. He looked fierce and formidable, a nobleman who would use his power to protect those who mattered to him. The knowledge that he would do so on her behalf burrowed deeply into Natalie's heart, dissolving the rest of her anger and leaving her vulnerable to the rise of an unruly warmth.

Shaken, she covered her confusion by saying, "They'll know *my* wrath, too, I'm afraid. So I may embarrass you yet."

A grin flickered over his lips, then vanished. Reaching up, he tucked a loose strand of hair behind her ear. "Then you'll want to be well armed for the battle. Society can be judgmental, and fashion is one essential part of a lady's armor against the gossips. That's all I meant, Natalie. You'll feel far more at ease if your appearance meets the standards of the ton."

She felt foolish for having misapprehended his purpose. Proper dress had been important in Washington, too, when she had acted as her father's hostess. A remorseful smile touched her lips. "I owe you an apology, then. I shouldn't have assumed the worst."

His eyes warming, he caressed her shoulders a moment before dropping his arms to his sides. "I ought to have explained myself better. And by the way, you needn't feel like an outsider. It's likely you're related to a number of England's best families. My mother will be more than happy to pore over *Debrett's* and help you decipher your ancestry."

"Debrett's?"

"It's a book that records the family histories of all the peerages and baronetages. My mother delights in tracing my lineage, since her own is not included."

The prospect intrigued Natalie, though she reminded herself that noble bloodlines oughtn't matter. Then his implication struck her. "Are you saying the duchess was born a commoner?"

He nodded wryly. "As common as grass. She's the only child of a wealthy nabob who made his fortune in

India. My late grandfather was angling to wed her to royalty, but he settled for a mere duke instead."

"So that's the secret the duchess said your father had swept under the rug! Was it an arranged marriage, then?"

"Yes, she was eighteen and, according to her, a bit starry-eyed."

Natalie absorbed the news in startled silence as she studied Hadrian's patrician features. Given his noble bearing and commanding manner, she would never have imagined that he had anything but the bluest of blue blood coursing through his veins.

No wonder the Earl of Godwin had been named his guardian. Hadrian's father wouldn't have wanted a mere commoner to raise his heir. Yet it still seemed unnecessarily cruel to have separated mother and son. Even now, many years later, the duchess resented Godwin. That had been clear by her relief at learning her son hadn't betrothed himself to Godwin's daughter.

Would Hadrian tell her he still intended to court Lady Ellen? He'd been tight-lipped about his marital plans ever since leaving Oak Knoll.

Natalie pushed away the image of the two of them wrapped in each other's arms. It was none of her concern. If a smoldering kernel suspiciously like envy burned in her breast, she must never allow Hadrian to guess its existence.

"No witty retort?" he said. "I should think you'd enjoy learning that I'm as much a mongrel as you are."

A droll smile on his face, he stood watching her, and Natalie found herself smiling back. She liked a man who could mock himself. "Luckily for you, I happen to find mongrels far more interesting than purebreds. And at least *you're* not dowdy."

"Now, I never called you that. It was *you* who pinned that tag on yourself. Quite unfairly, I might add."

His appreciative gaze swept downward over the skirt of her best plum silk, then back up again, lingering on her bosom long enough to cause a wild disturbance there, before returning to her face. His eyes caressed her features, and his expression refined into a look of intense desire. She caught her breath as the air suddenly seemed to sizzle. Though they stood a foot apart, her body tingled as if his hands were beneath her gown, stroking her warm flesh.

Oh my. She was *not* supposed to allow lascivious thoughts into her mind. He was far too dangerously attractive a man. Especially when they were alone in her chamber with the inviting expanse of the bed directly behind him.

Seeking a distraction, she said, "Will you tell me about the other parts?"

"Parts?"

"Of a lady's armor against society. You said that fine clothing is one. If there are more to be known, you'd best warn me."

"Those will pose no problem, for you already possess them in abundance. Charm. Grace. Wit." His expression intensifying, he stepped closer and skimmed the backs of his fingers over her cheek, melting her heart in the process. "And the beauty of confidence, of course. *I* may be the one in need of armor and sword to fight off all of your admirers."

At that light touch, the passion simmering between them flared like a flash of lightning. It seared away all rational thought, leaving only an acute awareness of him beating in her blood. His eyes darkened, and she sensed a banked tension in his masculine form, a desperate need that matched her own.

She couldn't say who moved first, but suddenly they were in each other's arms and she was reveling in the firmness of his muscled chest against her bosom. He brought his head down, his gaze searching hers, his warm breath caressing her face as if to give her a chance to refuse him. But she could no more resist him than she could cease breathing.

Reaching up, Natalie looped her arms around his neck. "Hadrian, I shouldn't want you so much . . . but I *do*."

A ravenous growl emanated from deep in his throat in the moment before their mouths met. The heat of the contact sent desire coursing through her veins to every part of her body. A madness descended upon her, a craving for all the sensual pleasure he could give her.

This kiss was even more fervid than the first one they'd shared. In the three days since then, she had existed in a state of acute awareness of him. It was most intense at night, while lying alone in her bed, wishing he was there with her. That had been her most secret fantasy, an indulgence reserved for darkness, when she would toss and turn, beset by an unbearable ache that instinct told her only he could appease.

Now, his kiss made her weak-kneed and delirious. She relished the glide of his hands down her back, following the curve of her waist and hips. As he shaped his palms around her derriere and lifted her to him, she moaned, aware of the shocking urge to writhe against him in an effort to assuage the burning demands of the flesh.

Brushing kisses over her face, he left a trail of heat. "Natalie . . . I've had the very devil of a time keeping my hands off you."

"Mm. A pity, for you do have the most *skillful* hands."

His deep chuckle tickled her skin. "That's quite the praise, darling, when you've had only the merest sampling of pleasure."

Darling. Was she truly his darling? She wanted to believe so, if only to ensure that she meant more to

Hadrian than just a passing fancy. He had a deft charm that must have been honed by abundant experience . . .

All lucid thought abruptly vanished as a wave of giddiness made her unsteady. Feeling on the brink of swooning, Natalie instinctively locked her arms around his lean waist for support. In the next instant, she realized that the unbalanced sensation was no illusion. She was indeed in motion, tumbling backward, her spine meeting the silken cushion of bedcovers and goose-feather mattress.

As Hadrian settled over her, she absorbed the heavy weight of him even as her feverish senses recorded the novel details of lying beneath a man. His masculine scent of leather and spice. The burning intensity in his hooded eyes. The swift beating of his heart that matched the frantic fluttering of her own. More than anything, she quivered from a keen awareness of his loins nestled into the cradle of her hips. Her experience might be sorely lacking, but she recognized the rigid length pressing against her.

On some hazy level, Natalie knew she ought to be alarmed, that she ought to push him away and banish him from the bedchamber at once. Yet fascination lured her deeper into a realm of passionate desire. He was just too sinfully tempting to relinquish after only one kiss.

Their mouths joined again for long, leisurely minutes that left her exhilarated and breathless. Rife with infatuation, she let her hands rove over the hardness of muscle in his back and shoulders, then upward to discover the dense silk of his hair. He ended the kiss to nuzzle her throat, his faintly whiskered cheek deliciously abrading her tender skin. She tilted her head back, the better to enjoy his ministrations. At the same time, he stroked her silk-clad bosom to spectacular effect, fanning a fire that spiraled downward and into her core.

It was then that she realized his hand had descended

to cup her mound, rubbing in a way that felt darkly delightful. Her hips moved instinctively even as the breath lodged in her throat.

He feathered a kiss across her lips. "We needn't complete the act in order for you to enjoy my touch. Will you trust me to show you?"

Judgment and reason sent out a feeble warning. Yet his devilish enticement overwhelmed her tattered sanity. With all her heart and soul, she craved to explore the mysteries of her desire for him. And the strange thing was, she *did* trust him. "If . . . if you promise not to go too far."

His chuckle held a strained quality. "I swear it, on my honor as a gentleman." He bent and kissed her again, quite thoroughly, before adding, "But for this, we'll want privacy."

It took Hadrian all of half a minute to shut the door and stride back to the bed. He stripped off his coat on the way and slung it toward a chair without looking to see where it landed. With single-minded purpose, his gaze remained fixed on the woman lying on the white coverlet.

Natalie. In all his life, he had never seen a more bewitching sight.

She had pushed herself up onto her elbow to watch him. Their episode of kissing and caressing had loosened her upswept hair so that a few dark strands curled down around her shoulders and bosom, and her breasts appeared in danger of overflowing her bodice. Her lips were rosy, her eyes slumberous, the dark lashes half lowered as she waited for him.

As he approached, she moistened her lips with the tip of her tongue. All the blood from his brain went rushing to his groin. He craved to possess her with a ferocity that

made him tremble. With effort, he leashed the powerful
urges that burned inside him.

This was for *her* pleasure, not his.

Yet, if truth be told, it was also about softening her resistance to being courted by a man of his rank. She had
expressed her opinions about his aristocratic world in no
uncertain terms. He wanted to break down the barriers
between them and win her body, heart, and mind.

He lay down beside her on the bed, sliding his arm
around her slender waist to bring her onto her side. Then
he lifted his hand to her face to trace her lovely features.
She returned his gaze with characteristic brashness,
though her green eyes also held a hint of wariness.

"I oughtn't be here with you," she said frankly. "This
may very well be the worst mistake of my life."

He couldn't stop a grin. That was part of what he liked
about Natalie. She seldom said the expected, and he was
jaded enough to deeply value the trait. "Shall I leave,
then?"

Her arms tightened around him. "Certainly not!"

"I was hoping you'd say that."

Drawing closer, he blended their mouths, relishing the
pliancy of her lips and the swiftness of her response. Any
slight inhibition in her vanished as she kissed him back
with an unrestrained zeal that made his blood surge.
Then she did something that nearly shattered his iron
control. She brought her hand up and cradled his cheek
as if he were precious to her.

All the suggestive moves that women had used to entice him over the years paled before that one feather-
light touch. A tidal wave of lust inundated him. Her
taste, her scent, her femininity tempted him to the verge
of madness. For one mindless moment, he could think
only of stripping her naked, sinking into her heat, and
staking his claim on her.

His fingers were seeking the buttons at the back of her gown before Hadrian caught himself. A thread of rationality made him acknowledge the danger of losing mastery of himself. Better he should focus on pleasing her.

He curled his hand around the ripe curve of her bosom and stroked her through the silk fabric, working his fingers inside the tightness of bodice and corset. She made a small sound of delight as her nipples tightened to buds and her body moved sinuously on the bed. Little did she realize, it was just a prelude to what she truly desired.

Hadrian scattered kisses over her face, reveling in her feminine scent and the satin of her skin. Only then did he reach beneath the hem of her gown. Blessedly, her skirts were not twisted, permitting him to glide his hand upward over her slim calves and past the garters that held her silk stockings. As his fingers slipped inside her lacy undergarment and parted her slick, hidden folds, she gasped, catching hold of his arm. "Oh!"

He lightly swirled his thumb over her most sensitive nub of flesh. "Let yourself feel this pleasure," he murmured. "You're safe with me, darling."

A sigh of surrender eddied from her as she opened her legs to grant him access. Her lashes fluttered shut, her fingers curling into his shirt. Awed that this strong-willed woman would yield to him, he buried his own turbulent needs and focused on using his expertise to guide her up the path to ecstasy.

Any initial qualms she'd displayed vanished as he explored her honeyed secrets. She arched her head back, uttering small mewling sounds while moving her hips in wanton enjoyment, slowly at first and then with increasing desperation. He kissed her throat, murmuring sweet nothings, sensing her rising turmoil and reveling in it. She surged against his hand, seeking, searching, moaning. A moment later, she gave a keening cry as rapturous release rippled through her slender body.

Hadrian buried his face in her hair as he strove to steady his ragged breathing. His loins burned with a fierce fervor that required all of his willpower to stifle. He tugged down her skirts, his every muscle taut with restraint.

Natalie lay spent with her face tucked into the lee of his neck, her slowing breaths teasing his hot skin. Although her supple body tantalized him to the point of pain, he wouldn't have moved for the world. It just felt too perfect to hold her in his arms.

After a time, she wriggled languidly and opened her eyes to gaze at him in blushing wonder. "Oh my," she murmured. "I can see why we unmarried ladies are warned never to be alone with a man. That was pure bliss."

She looked so tempting that he wrestled with the urge to kiss her again, to take their mutual desire to its natural conclusion. She was a passionate woman who would find as keen an ecstasy in their lovemaking as he would. But in the aftermath, she would regret succumbing to him. He would succeed only in confirming her worst beliefs about the lecherous habits of noblemen.

Already, the hint of flustered awareness in her manner told him her senses were on their way to being restored. Being a virtuous woman, she would feel unsettled by her wild passions. It was best to give her time to adjust to her newly awakened sensuality.

"It's my pleasure to make you happy." He skimmed his mouth over hers and forced himself to add, "But I really must go now."

Her fingers tightened, one hand on his shoulder and the other cupping his neck. With her hair mussed and her lips rosy, she was the image of a satisfied woman. A woman who desired more, much more. Despite his better judgment, he felt a wild surge of hope that she would invite him to stay.

Then her teeth sank into her lower lip. She glanced away before returning her resolute gaze to him. "Yes . . . yes, I suppose you must."

Chapter 19

Late the following morning, Natalie sat alone in the plush confines of the ducal carriage on her way to meet her grandfather.

Her gloved fingers were tightly clasped in her lap. She gazed out at the passing scenery, the buildings of brick and stone, the throngs of people, the elegant vehicles competing with workmen's drays and hansom cabs. She'd always believed Philadelphia and Washington to be bustling cities, but London was so much larger and more crowded. The air rang with the raucous cries of street sellers and the constant clatter of traffic.

At any other time, she'd have been fascinated by the vast variety of new sights in this foreign metropolis. But today she felt too tense and preoccupied. She had lain awake for half the night, pondering that remarkable encounter with Hadrian, only to awaken with a firm resolve in her mind.

A young maid named Hetty had delivered one of the new gowns from Lady Elizabeth, the hem already let down to suit Natalie's height. From her, Natalie was able to learn that the duke had left the house directly after breakfast and wasn't expected to return until mid-afternoon.

It had been an immense relief not to have to face him. With the coast clear, she could make the arrangements for her plan.

Directed by the maid through a maze of corridors, Natalie had gone to the duchess's suite. There, she'd found Hadrian's mother lounging in a pink peignoir, enjoying a cup of cocoa with her nose in a novel. Her Grace had been delighted to help and had declared her heart touched by Natalie's eagerness to meet her grandfather without delay. She'd suggested Natalie pen a note to Sir Basil requesting permission to call on him at his earliest convenience, then dispatched a footman to deliver it. On the basis of her former acquaintance with Sir Basil, Her Grace had even hinted rather broadly of a desire to accompany Natalie.

That wish had had to be firmly quashed. The duchess must have no inkling as to the true purpose of the visit.

While awaiting Sir Basil's reply, Natalie went to the nursery to check on Leo. He was playing tin soldiers with a solemn, brown-haired boy, who turned out to be Lizzy's son, Finny. The Earl of Finley, Mrs. Tippet fondly identified him. Apparently, it was the custom for the eldest son of a peer to take one of his father's lesser titles, just as Lord Godwin's heir was a viscount, Lord Wymark. It served to underscore to Natalie how very different the lives of the nobility were from those of common folk.

Now, she smoothed her hand over the fine gold silk of her gown and prayed that all would go according to plan. She intended to prevail upon her grandfather to allow her and Leo to live with him. She must not stay even one more night under the same roof as the Duke of Clayton.

The previous day's incident had made it alarmingly clear how easily passion could spin out of control. She had believed herself to be strong and principled, capable of proper conduct with men. After all, she'd had considerable practice in her twenty-six years.

Yet she'd fallen straight into Hadrian's arms.

She had been an enthusiastic participant in their torrid embrace, well nigh handing herself to him on a silver platter. Several times, he'd given her the opportunity to put a halt to their lusty encounter, most notably, when he'd left the bed to close the door. Instead, she had yielded to the wild beating of her blood, permitted him to reach beneath her skirts, and responded to his expert touch like a wicked wanton.

Even now, the memory of that splendid pleasure made her throb with the desire to experience it all over again. Every kiss, every whispered word, every alluring stroke of his fingers down *there* was branded in her memory. And how was she ever to forget that stunning burst of ecstasy?

She blushed at her wanton cravings. Although Hadrian had honored his promise to leave, the intensity of passion on his face had indicated a keen desire to stay. For a moment, she had sorely wanted to invite him to make love to her. But she knew a man of his rank would never offer her marriage—nor would she ever accept. The only other option was to become his mistress, and that was out of the question.

Therefore, the rational solution was to remove herself from Hadrian's sphere. Then the siren call of temptation would be mitigated, and she could salvage her virtue before it was too late. Because if truth be told, she simply could not resist him. And if the prospect of departure hurt her heart, she would forget her longings eventually. He was an English duke and she was an American schoolteacher, and that made for an impossible situation.

On that dismal thought, Natalie felt the carriage begin to slow. She peered out to see a road lined by brick row houses. A group of boys playing a raucous game of ball almost knocked over an old woman, who shook her cane at them. Laundry flapped from the upper windows of several houses. The neighborhood was decidedly more rundown than the wealthy streets of Mayfair.

The carriage came to a halt, the footman opening the door and letting down the step before helping her disembark. She gazed up at the narrow house before her, noting how cramped and tiny it appeared, but she supposed anything would seem small compared to a ducal mansion. At least it looked tidier than the peeling paint and drying wash of the adjacent homes.

As she walked toward the house, the young footman darted ahead of her. Startled, she said, "James, it isn't necessary to come inside with me."

"I'm to announce you, miss, that's all. Her Grace would insist upon it."

Natalie held her tongue. The British aristocracy had many archaic rules, but now was not the time to make a fuss over protocol. For all she knew her grandfather was a stickler, and she didn't wish to commit a faux pas. Not when she desperately needed to persuade him to give her and Leo shelter.

When the servant knocked, the curtain twitched at the front window and she glimpsed a pale feminine face framed by a mass of dark hair. The door was opened a moment later by a mobcapped older woman with careworn features.

"Miss Fanshawe to see Sir Basil Fanshawe," the footman intoned.

The maidservant looked past him to pin Natalie with an inquisitive stare. "So, ye're the one from America!

Come in, come in! The master's been waitin' on pins and needles ever since yer note arrived."

The footman returned to the carriage, while Natalie stepped into a foyer barely large enough to hold a single chair, a framed print of a landscape, and a narrow staircase. She removed her bonnet and cloak, which the servant hung on a wall hook. Just then, an adolescent girl in rose muslin rushed out of a nearby doorway. Her bright hazel eyes and upswept curly black hair identified her as the one who'd been peeking out the window.

"I'll take her to Grandpapa, Mrs. Beasley." She linked arms with Natalie and towed her down a cramped passageway. "Hullo, I'm your cousin Doris. I'm sixteen, and Grandpapa says I'm now the lady of the house. Oh, I *adore* your gown, that gold silk is so very stylish. Do you know, my brother has the very same green eyes as you?"

Amused by the disconnected chatter, Natalie had not a moment to get a word in edgewise before they entered a small parlor, where two men awaited them. "She's here!" Doris announced. "Our long-lost cousin Natalie!"

An elderly man with a full head of white hair stood by the unlit hearth. Tall and distinguished, Sir Basil looked dapper in a slate-gray coat and dark trousers. A smile lit his lined features as he walked forward with the aid of a silver-topped cane. "My dear child! What a delightful surprise to receive your note! Why, I never thought to meet you in person."

Natalie found herself enfolded in a bear hug tinged with the scent of pipe tobacco. After a brief hesitation, she hugged him back, moved by the sentimental emotion that flooded her bosom. Growing up, she'd only had her father, and an occasional letter from these distant relations in England. Her grandfather had not quite seemed real to her until this moment.

Drawing back, he looked her up and down, his green eyes misty. "Ah, a true Fanshawe, you've the look of your papa. Now, here's your cousin Giles."

Giles Fanshawe was a lanky young man with a Romany handsomeness and a pleasant smile, who pumped her hand up and down. "Have you really come all the way from America? Is it true your father owned an estate where he bred horses?"

"Yes," Natalie said, "though it was merely a small farm."

"Giles wants to breed racehorses," Doris confided. "But Grandpapa hasn't the funds. We even had to lease out our estate in Lincolnshire."

"Now, don't be bothering our guest with your chatter," Sir Basil said, his smile taking the sting out of his words. "Do sit down, dear Natalie, and tell us what has brought you to our fair shores."

Natalie was directed to a well-worn leather chair that she suspected was her grandfather's favorite, since a pipe and pouch lay on the table beside it. As the others took seats opposite her, she gave them an abbreviated summary of the massacre that had taken the lives of Leo's parents, her promise to deliver him to his grandfather, and the problem involving his birth papers.

"Lord Godwin dared to accuse my granddaughter of lying?" Sir Basil said indignantly, rapping the tip of his cane on the threadbare carpet. "I knew that pompous oaf when he was a mere pup. Why, I've a mind to call him out for that craven insult!"

"Pray don't do that, sir," Natalie said, alarmed by the notion of him challenging Lord Godwin to pistols at dawn. "His cousin, the Duke of Clayton, has the matter well in hand."

"Is it true you're staying at Clayton House?" Doris asked, looking starstruck. "Your note was written on his mother's stationery. I nearly swooned to see the gold crest."

All eyes turned to Natalie. Realizing that now was her opportunity, she took a deep breath. "Yes, I am, but only because Leo is a distant relation of the duke's. Yet I confess to having misgivings about being there. You see, His Grace has expressed an intention to seek a wife this season, and I fear that Leo and I are a hindrance, what with all the entertaining he'll be doing. That's part of the reason why I came here today. Grandpapa, I was hoping that Leo and I might find a home with you while we're waiting for his papers from America to be verified. It need only be temporary, of course, since I'll eventually be returning to Philadelphia."

Sir Basil frowned. "My dear, you flatter me, but I've little to offer in these miserable rooms when you are staying in the highest kick of style."

"Clayton House is the grandest residence in London," Giles added. "The duke must be a miserly fellow not to find some corner of that huge pile for you to lay your head."

Unwilling to sully Hadrian's reputation, Natalie said hastily, "Oh, don't misunderstand me, he's been all that is gracious! It's just that I feel I'm imposing on his good will. And being from America, I'm not accustomed to such luxury, either. I'd be far more comfortable here among my own family."

They all stared at her as if she'd gone mad.

"Oh, but you *must* stay at Clayton House," Doris said. "Especially since His Grace is seeking a bride. Why, he might very well choose *you*, Natalie."

"You're devilish pretty," Giles said frankly. "Being under his roof, you'd have an advantage over all the other ladies. You'd need only to flirt with him."

"Yes, indeed," Sir Basil added, snapping his fingers.

"Why, this is a brilliant notion! Only think what an auspicious marriage it would be. My granddaughter, the Duchess of Clayton!"

Doris clasped her hands to her bosom. "Society would accept us again if you'd sponsor my come-out, Natalie. Just think, I'd be able to dance at balls and meet the man of my dreams. Oh, I never thought it was even possible!"

Dismayed, Natalie cast about for a way to dampen their enthusiasm. "I'm a nobody from the wilds of America. I have a life there, and I intend to return to it. The duke will choose a lady of impeccable background. Not a woman whose father was born on the wrong side of the blanket."

"Bah, you're a Fanshawe," Sir Basil declared. "You've noble lineage, and even a few royal connections dating back to the time of the Conqueror. As for your papa's birth, I always acknowledged him as my own, so I'll hear no more talk of you being a nobody."

Just then, Mrs. Beasley appeared in the doorway to announce luncheon. Her grandfather invited Natalie to join them, and she accepted with alacrity. She dared not leave without having accomplished her purpose. It was far too dangerous to remain at Clayton House and be tempted into another indiscretion.

Giles went out to inform her coachman to return in an hour or two, then they all proceeded into a tiny dining chamber and sat around a table covered by threadbare linen that was darned in several spots. Luncheon consisted of a platter of cold meats and cheeses, sliced wafer-thin, with bread cut so transparent that Natalie fancied she could see right through it. It was painfully obvious that her family had stretched their meager rations to include their honored guest, and she was careful to keep her portions small.

Try as she might, she had trouble tilting the conversation in favor of her objective. While asking questions about her life in the United States, they pointed out how much more civilized England was, where a lucky lady might wed a duke and live in luxury. When prevailing on her to describe the décor of Clayton House, including the nursery, they were quick to say that Leo wouldn't care to give up his many toys. Besides, the duke was bound to oppose his little cousin's being taken away and forced to live in cramped quarters.

That particular point did worry Natalie. Hadrian was fond of Leo and would object to his departure. But at present, *she* was the boy's guardian at the dying request of his mother and she was prepared to battle the duke if necessary.

Over a dessert that consisted of minuscule servings of rice pudding, she answered their many queries about Hadrian and his mother. Not wanting to fib too much, she strove to make them sound extremely elegant and top-lofty, far out of the league of a provincial American. But her relatives only seemed to find those qualities natural and admirable in those of a ducal rank.

"I *do* wish you'd stop calling yourself rustic," Doris said earnestly. "You're as charming and lovely a lady as I've ever seen."

"The duke would be fortunate to win your hand," Giles avowed, looking half in love with her himself.

"I have no dowry," Natalie said bluntly, in an attempt to bring them back down to earth. "He'll wed a wealthy heiress, just as his father did in marrying the present duchess."

"Clayton is one of the richest men in England, so he can afford to follow his heart," Sir Basil said. His lips curved in a reminiscing smile. "Speaking of the present duchess, did you know that I courted her a long time ago, when she was plain Miss Millicent Jones? Alas, her papa was holding out for a fancier title than a mere baronet."

"Actually, she *did* mention it—" Natalie stopped short upon seeing a shrewd interest light up her grandfather's face.

"Did she, now?" He snapped his fingers. "By Jove, that puts me in a mind to call on Millie and renew our acquaintance. And there's no time like the present. Yes, I do believe I shall accompany you back to Clayton House!"

Her plans in shambles, Natalie returned to the ducal mansion with Sir Basil. Her father had always said that his sire was a quixotic man, prone to impulsiveness and romanticism, and now she could see that side of him. He seemed a bit of a schemer, as well. Once he'd settled on the idea of visiting his old flame, there had been no dissuading him.

"Her Grace may be out," she warned as they stood in the entrance hall, waiting for the footman to return. "Or perhaps she won't want visitors."

"Bah. I might be twenty years her senior, but Millie always did have a soft spot for me." Sir Basil looked confident and dashing for an elderly man, his cane more a fashion statement than a necessity, as he craned his neck to view the splendor of the vast room. "Look at this place! Imagine yourself mistress of it all!"

She'd be a mistress, all right, if ever she succcumbed to temptation. Then an even more unsettling thought struck her. "Grandpapa, promise you won't mortify me by hinting to her of a match with the duke."

"My dear girl, I wasn't born yesterday," he said, patting her shoulder. "Such matters require finesse. You may be certain I shan't ruin your chances."

His words didn't exactly reassure her. She fervently prayed that the duchess would be unavailable, but her hopes were dashed a few minutes later, when

the footman came back to say that Her Grace would receive them. As they mounted the stairs, Natalie was half
tempted to escape to the nursery. But she needed to be
present in case it became necessary to avert disaster.

They proceeded down an ornate corridor, through an
arched doorway, and into an immense chamber taste-
fully decorated in gold and blue, with gilt furnishings
and priceless artwork. As the footman announced them,
Natalie noticed several ladies sitting with Her Grace,
along with Lady Elizabeth.

And there, in the thick of them, was Hadrian.

He arose from his chair, his gaze honed on her. He
looked so perilously attractive in his charcoal-gray suit
and white cravat that her insides curled into a tangled
knot. Was he, too, remembering the scandalous intimacy they'd shared the previous day? Under the scrutiny
of those penetrating eyes, she felt a clench of desire so
strong that it left her breathless.

She hadn't expected to find him here, entertaining
callers. In fact, she had little knowledge of day-to-day life
in a grand ducal household. Had she committed a blunder
by bringing her grandfather here without permission?

But Hadrian could not have been more cordial. Stepping forward, he bowed. "Miss Fanshawe, Sir Basil, welcome. Do come and join us."

As they followed him toward the others, Natalie slid
a glance at her grandfather to see him waggle his white
eyebrows at her as if to convey his approval of the duke.
A flush crept up her neck, and she sent a warning frown
back at him. Unfortunately, he had turned his attention
to Hadrian's mother.

Her plump form draped in a bronze-green gown, the
duchess sat on a chaise with one hand pressed to her
magnificent bosom and her pet spaniel nestled in her lap.
"My stars! Is it truly you, Basil?"

He swept a courtly bow and then took her other hand, reverently kissing the back. "Indeed so, Your Grace. I'm happy to see that the years have only added luster to your beauty."

"And *I* see that you haven't lost your skill at blarney." To her other guests, she said, "You must forgive us. We are old friends."

"Old?" Sir Basil objected. "Perhaps I am, but not *you*, Your Grace. Why, I can only think you must have drunk from the fabled fountain of youth."

The duchess giggled. "Flatterer. Pray call me Millie, as you were always wont to do. Now, sit down and we shall catch up on decades of news."

When she patted the place beside her on the chaise, Sir Basil seated himself there with alacrity, earning a smile from Her Grace for scratching the spaniel's ears and proclaiming him to be the handsomest dog in all England. Natalie took a chair in between them and Lady Elizabeth, partly because she liked Hadrian's sister, and partly because she wanted to be close enough to eavesdrop, ready to intervene if her grandfather strayed onto forbidden topics.

The three visiting ladies regarded him with a skeptical curiosity, and she wondered if the elder one would remember the thirty-year-old scandal about how Sir Basil had been drummed out of society for nonpayment of gambling debts.

Toward her, they exuded a distinct note of hostility, despite their polite smiles as Hadrian made the introductions. Arrayed in high style, Lady Birdsall had come with her daughters, Lady Cora and Lady Eugenie. The two were so remarkably alike in their blue-eyed blondness that Natalie would have thought them twins had not their mother mentioned that Cora had made her bows the previous season, while Eugenie would do so this year.

As the other ladies monopolized Hadrian's attention for a moment, Lizzy leaned closer, her eyes sparkling as she examined Natalie's gown. "Stunning," she murmured. "The gold suits your coloring far better than mine."

Natalie felt guilty for her initial rejection of the gowns. "Forgive me for not properly thanking you yesterday. I was too bowled over by your generosity."

"Oh, it's nothing, really! My maid will be bringing more soon." Lizzy rubbed her gently rounded midsection. "Oh, but I do envy your slender figure."

"You'll regain yours soon enough," Natalie consoled, wondering if she'd ever experience the miracle of bearing her own baby. Her gaze inexplicably strayed to Hadrian, only to find him watching her, and she looked hastily back at his sister. "And the end result will be well worth any discomfort."

"That's what Wrenbury always reminds me," Lizzy said with a sigh. "Three months to go yet. The trouble is, I've never been very good at *waiting.*"

"Whatever are you two whispering about, Lady Wrenbury?" Lady Birdsall called out, a brittle smile on her hawklike features. "Do share it with us."

"I was speaking of babies, and how dreadfully long they take to make their appearance."

Lady Cora and Lady Eugenie twittered and blushed, apparently unaccustomed to hearing talk of the natural functions of a woman's body.

Even Lady Birdsall appeared disconcerted for a moment. "Well! Speaking of children, I was intrigued to hear a rumor that His Grace has adopted a little orphaned boy."

"I *told* you the gossip would spread like wildfire, Hadrian," Lizzy teased. "It's so unlike the very proper Duke of Clayton to take in strays."

Proper? Natalie remembered thinking of him that way at first. But no more. He was captivating, seductive, able to tempt a woman into sin with one smoldering look . . . like the one he was directing at her right now.

Thankfully, he returned his gaze to the others. "Leo is hardly a stray. He's our second cousin, once removed. As for adopting him, I haven't as yet."

As yet. That might happen when he married Lady Ellen. Or perhaps another lady like Cora or Eugenie. Natalie clenched her teeth, telling herself it was concern for Leo's uncertain future that caused her inner turmoil.

"Miss Fanshawe, you must be governess to the boy, since you accompanied him here from the States," Lady Birdsall said. "It's very generous of His Grace to give you time off from your duties to sit with us."

The snide note in the woman's voice irritated Natalie. Lady Birdsall seemed to be fishing for information as to Natalie's place in the household.

"Actually, I'm Leo's guardian," she said. "His mother was a dear friend of mine. She and her husband were slain in a bloody massacre, and as she lay dying in my arms, she begged me to bring Leo to his family here in England."

The ladies looked aghast at her blunt description. But she wouldn't retract a word. It was the truth, and she had even withheld the disturbing fact that it had been British soldiers who had committed the atrocity.

"Merciful heavens," Lady Birdsall huffed. "Clayton, will you permit her to speak of such violence before these innocent young ears? Only look at how she's horrified my sweet, lovely daughters."

Everyone turned toward the girls. Despite their suitably shocked expressions, Lady Cora and Lady Eugenie appeared be enjoying the attention. They made little moues of distress and batted their lashes at Hadrian.

Natalie had been debating whether their hostility toward her had stemmed from her neglecting to curtsy to them, or simply because she was an American and not of their world. Now, the real reason dawned on her. Lady Birdsall viewed her as competition for her daughters in winning the duke's favor. Nothing could be more ludicrous!

"Miss Fanshawe risked her life to save Leo," Hadrian said. "I would rather advise the young ladies to admire her bravery."

His cultured tone bore a hint of steel that silenced Lady Birdsall. She pursed her lips and slid a telling glance at her daughters.

"Hear, hear!" Sir Basil said, his fingers wrapped around the silver fob of his cane. "I was just enumerating my granddaughter's many fine qualities to Millie. Few young ladies would have the pluck to cross an ocean in order to fulfill a promise to a dying friend."

"We are delighted to have her as our guest," the duchess added with a fond smile at Natalie. "My dear, you must never, ever feel that you aren't welcome in our home."

"Not welcome," the duke repeated with a frown.

"A mere misunderstanding, Clayton," Sir Basil said smoothly. "Natalie expressed a desire to reside with me since she feared she was imposing on your good will. But Millie has kindly assured me that is not the case."

"I see."

The keen stare that Hadrian turned on Natalie made her want to squirm. She'd been so anxious that her grandfather would blurt out his marriage scheme that she hadn't even considered he might reveal her plan to leave Clayton House.

Not that she'd done anything wrong.

She coolly met the duke's gaze. He must know that

her purpose had been to put an end to the temptation they posed to one another. And now that her plan had been thwarted, the question was, what would be his next move?

She subdued a quiver of anticipation.

Chapter 20

Natalie didn't find out the answer until two days later.

At ten o'clock in the morning, she headed downstairs with Leo, having received a note from Hadrian, written in bold black script and delivered by a footman. The message had been specific on the time, but vague on details. She knew only that they were to dress for an outing.

The prospect of an excursion to an unknown destination stirred a thrill in her. It wouldn't be wise to examine how much of her eagerness was due to a desire to see Hadrian. Though she'd expected him to confront her about the attempt to live with her grandfather, she hadn't laid eyes on him since then.

In the interim, Natalie had avoided venturing anywhere in the house where she might encounter the duke. Most of her time had been spent in the schoolroom, where she'd devoted herself to teaching Leo his lessons, taking her meals there, and befriending the two nursemaids, Flora and Tippy.

The duchess and Lizzy had come to the nursery the previous morning, and she'd enjoyed a nice long chat with them, too, while Lizzy's son, Finny, played with

Leo. She'd reluctantly turned down their invitation to join them for luncheon and also nixed their plan for her to attend a society event. Although she was intensely curious about Hadrian's world, she knew that in order to survive the coming weeks, it was better to behave as a governess, not a guest.

Clinging to her hand, Leo hopped down from step to step on the curved staircase in the entrance hall. "Listen to my feet echo, Miss Fanshawe."

"You sound like a big bear tramping through the woods."

"I *am* a bear. *Grr.*"

"Beware, James," she called out to the young footman on duty. "There's a bear on the loose."

A grin twitched as he opened the front door. "So I see, miss. Best to let the wild beast outside, then."

With Leo still growling, they stepped out onto the portico. Her gaze immediately veered to Hadrian, who was standing beside an open carriage parked on the circular drive. He was inspecting the wheels while a groom held the pair of horses.

Her heart cavorted within the confines of her corset. The duke was the model of the dashing man-about-town in an iron-gray coat, fawn breeches, and glossy black boots. His hat was set at a jaunty angle on brown hair that looked as rich as caramel in the sunshine.

Her knees felt in danger of melting, for the mere sight of him brought back the memory of that dazzling intimacy. Perhaps she ought not to have come, after all. Perhaps she should have sent Flora to accompany the boy.

Abandoning his bear persona, Leo pulled his hand from her grasp and scampered down the marble steps. "Mr. Duke! Mr. Duke! Are you taking us for a ride in your carriage?"

Hadrian caught him by the waist and swung him up

onto the seat. "Indeed, I am, brat. Now sit very quietly lest you startle the horses."

Only then did Natalie take closer notice of the sleek phaeton with its ebony body and gilded wheels. Its lightweight construction suggested it was designed for racing, and the single seat stood alarmingly high off the ground.

She made haste to Hadrian's side. "Is he safe up there alone?"

"He won't be alone for long. May I?"

The question was mere pretense as Hadrian fastened his hands around her waist and brought her closer so that her bosom brushed the solid wall of his chest. She tilted her head back to look at him. The gleam in those smoky-gray eyes made her giddy, and she was startled by the beguiling thought that he meant to kiss her right there in front of any passersby.

Even more startling, she *wanted* him to do so. The craving burned in the depths of her body and thrummed in her blood.

She was half disappointed when he did nothing of the sort. Tightening his fingers, he boosted her onto the high perch to sit beside Leo. As Hadrian bounded up and took the reins, she was keenly aware of his side pressing into her. She promptly moved Leo in between them.

"You'll be safer here," she told the boy.

"So will you," Hadrian murmured. "Especially as you're looking exceptionally pretty today. The green is a perfect match for your eyes."

A devilish smile lurked at the corners of his mouth, and she found her own lips curving up, too. If only he knew, she'd twirled in front of the mirror this morning, admiring the Pomona-green gown with its matching pelisse and trying not to feel guilty at the expensive gift from his sister. "Why, thank you."

She turned her head away, hoping the brim of her straw bonnet hid the warmth in her cheeks. It was clear that he had not given up on charming her. Imprudent as it was, she felt an acute interest to learn his next maneuver.

Hadrian deftly guided the phaeton onto the street, and the rhythmic clopping of the horses' hooves lulled her nerves. Proceeding past the square with its tall plane trees, they saw only two other carriages, but once on the main road, they encountered all manner of vehicles, from wagons to chaises to cabs.

"Can I—*may* I drive?" Leo begged, perched on the edge of the seat.

Hadrian cast an indulgent glance at him. "Not here, brat, there's too much traffic. But once we reach Hyde Park, you may help me."

Hyde Park. So that was their mysterious destination. She'd glimpsed the vast green space on the last leg of their journey into London, and it seemed the perfect place to go on such a fine, sunny day. In fact, she hadn't realized until this moment what a gloriously beautiful morning it was, with a mild breeze blowing and the promise of spring in the air.

"What about you, Natalie?" he asked. "Would *you* like a turn at driving?"

She glanced covetously at the reins in his hands. Back home, before her father's death, she had enjoyed tooling around Washington and Philadelphia in her gig. "Not now, but perhaps later, once I know my way around London a little better. Such gorgeous matched grays you have!"

Like any lover of good horseflesh, he launched into a recital of their superior qualities, from hocks to withers to flanks. Since her father had bred horses, she could easily hold up her end of the conversation. Soon, they approached a set of open stone gates that led into the park.

"This road is called Rotten Row," Hadrian said. "In late afternoon, it's crammed with horses and carriages as the ton comes to show off their finery."

At present, only a pair of gentleman riders cantered far ahead of them. Tall trees shaded the wide, sandy avenue. "Rotten? But it's lovely!"

"There are various explanations for the name, but most likely it's a corruption of *Route du Roi,* the King's Road. Over a hundred years ago, King William III liked to walk here from Kensington Palace to St. James's. Come, brat, since it's quite deserted, you may drive now."

He settled Leo between his legs and let him hold on to the reins, while Hadrian did most of the work. The boy's small face wore a look of absolute bliss as the horses pranced ahead of the carriage, their silken manes rippling in the sunshine. "Look, Miss Fanshawe, I'm driving!"

"Indeed you are. And very well, for your first time."

Natalie took advantage of the chance to watch Hadrian. The duke appeared to be enjoying himself, and she marveled at his patient instructions when Leo tried to pull on one leather ribbon or the other. After they'd traveled a distance down the road, he steered the team onto a narrower path, stopping the phaeton at a spot where they had a view of sunlight gleaming off a large body of water through the trees. A scattering of stylishly clad people strolled along the bank, as well as a few commoners in plainer garb who walked at a faster pace, perhaps taking a shortcut through the park.

"Welcome to the Serpentine," the duke said. "The lake was formed nearly a hundred years ago when a dam was built to capture water from the River Westbourne." With nimble grace, he leaped down from the phaeton. "Come, brat, I've something to show you here."

The boy scrambled down with the agility of a monkey. "A surprise?"

"You'll see in a moment. First, though, we oughtn't leave Miss Fanshawe stranded on her high perch." Hadrian stretched up his arms to her. "My lady, may I offer my assistance?"

The smirk on his handsome face dared her to leap into his embrace. She was sorely tempted to do just that, to be held against his powerful form again, if only for a moment. Then dignity won out. "I can manage."

Presenting her back to him, Natalie proceeded to clamber down on her own, stretching the toe of her shoe to feel for the small iron step. The height of the phaeton and the tangle of her skirts made the descent something of a challenge. Nevertheless, she felt confident of success, until disaster struck.

The hem of her gown caught beneath the sole of her shoe and unbalanced her. She grabbed at the body of the carriage in an effort to right herself. Instead, she found herself tumbling backward, pulled by a pair of large hands that were clasped firmly around her waist.

As her feet touched the ground, her backbone met Hadrian's broad chest. She was caught against his muscled strength, surrounded by his captivating scent of leather and dark spice. Her heart thudded as a rush of intense desire permeated her body, especially when his hands slid in a slow caress over her hips.

He bent his head down, his warm breath stirring the fine hairs at the nape of her neck. "How fortunate that I was here to catch you," he murmured in a flirtatious undertone. "The high perch can be difficult for ladies."

Natalie subdued a delicious shiver. Aware they were in a public park where anyone might see them, she twisted out of his arms and turned to face him. "I'm sure you've had ample experience with ladies."

"Jealous?"

"Indifferent."

His chuckle conveyed disbelief as he tossed his hat in the phaeton and then sauntered toward Leo, who had wandered away to stare at a saddled brown pony tethered beneath a nearby oak tree. A wiry man in dark, neat garb was standing with the animal. At the duke's approach, the man bobbed his head in a servile manner and then trotted over to hold the team of grays.

Struck by surprise, Natalie recognized him as one of Hadrian's grooms. She hastened toward the duke in time to hear Leo utter a loud "Yippee! A pony! You remembered, Mr. Duke!" The boy flung his arms around him, his head barely reaching the man's waist.

Looking slightly embarrassed, Hadrian ruffled Leo's hair. "Enough of that, it's time to learn how to ride."

Natalie watched from the edge of the clearing as he lifted the boy into the saddle, then showed him how to fit his small feet into the stirrups and to properly grasp the reins. Taking hold of the bridle, Hadrian led the pony on a slow walk around in a wide circle, while Leo hung on, looking torn between fear and glee. As he obeyed Hadrian's instructions to sit up straight and to use gentle but firm control of the animal, it wasn't long before he began to relax.

"Miss Fanshawe! I have a pony!"

"And a very handsome one, I see."

His delight was infectious, and she smiled, deciding not to let her issues with Hadrian mar her enjoyment of the day. Though she had been leery of him buying the pony, not wanting to Leo to be spoiled, she ruefully acknowledged that her concern had been misplaced. Her father had often said the English aristocracy was horsemad, and if this was to be Leo's world, then he deserved the chance to learn the proper techniques.

After a time, Hadrian allowed the boy to ride unassisted as he walked alongside, keeping a close eye and correcting him when necessary. They spent half an hour riding sedately in the clearing before Hadrian suggested it was time to give the pony a rest and that Leo might like to feed the ducks.

The boy agreed with alacrity, and after leaving the pony with the groom, Hadrian went to the phaeton, reaching into a hidden nook to produce a small sack of bread crumbs. During the short walk to the lake, the boy queried Natalie and Hadrian about possible names for his new pet.

It struck her that the pony fit the description of the one that Lord Godwin had cruelly sold when Hadrian was a little boy. "Mr. Duke once had a chocolate-brown pony named Mud."

"Mud! I like mud! May I call him that, Mr. Duke?"

"Certainly."

The boy went to the water's edge and began tossing bread crumbs willy-nilly. He was soon surrounded by quacking ducks and having the time of his life feeding them and giggling at their greedy antics.

Natalie cast a meaningful glance at Hadrian. "Something tells me you're reliving your own childhood through Leo."

He gave her a slightly sheepish look. "He deserves to be happy after losing his parents."

"Where did you find such a fine, well-behaved pony?"

"Tattersall's—it's a horse auctioneer not far from here, at Hyde Park Corner." He watched her with a hint of wariness. "You don't mind, then?"

She shook her head. "I don't want Leo to be pampered, but riding *is* an important skill for a boy to learn. And he's certainly old enough to begin."

Hadrian's expression eased, his gaze becoming warm and penetrating. "I recall you mentioning that *you* like to ride, too. Why don't you join me here in the park one morning? I've the perfect spirited mare for you in the stable, and I'm sure Lizzy has a habit you can borrow."

Yearning flooded Natalie with the wish to gallop down Rotten Row, to feel the wind on her face and the power of a fine mount beneath her. As a girl, she'd even occasionally ridden bareback on her father's farm, but of course that would be far too hoydenish behavior here. Nevertheless, it seemed like forever since she'd ridden purely for pleasure. Forever since she'd done so with a handsome gentleman who made her heart race.

But it would be a mistake to encourage Hadrian. He must have a reason for flirting with her. Since it couldn't possibly be marriage, that left only seduction. The very thought made her feel altogether too breathless.

She glanced at Leo, who had distributed all the bread crumbs and was now collecting stones along the bank and putting them into the empty sack. "I'm afraid that's impossible. I mustn't neglect Leo's studies. He's already had far too much disruption in his life."

"So you'll continue to hide in the nursery, hm?"

The rough vibration of humor in the duke's voice brought her head whipping back toward him. "I'm not *hiding*." Seeing the corner of his mouth curl in a knowing smile, she murmured, "All right, then, I *am* trying to keep my distance. I have no interest in engaging in a . . . a sordid affair."

"Nor have I." He stepped closer, his eyes caressing her face. "I can't imagine anything between us ever being sordid."

Nor could she. His seduction would be conducted with gentlemanly finesse, with passionate kisses and tempting touches. Heavens, it was herself she didn't trust. Even now, she longed to feel his lips on hers, his hands on her body.

She glanced out over the lake for a moment, trying to

draw calm from the serene blue water, before returning her resolute gaze to him. "You're perfectly aware that I've a weakness for you, Hadrian. However, I also know that noblemen regard seducing women as a game."

He reached for her gloved hand and raised it to his lips. "This is no game, Natalie, I promise you that. My intentions toward you are honorable."

Oh, those eyes. The sunlight picked out flecks of blue in the deep, gray depths. When he looked at her like that she was ready to believe every word he uttered even though it had to be nonsense. She felt the pulse of that ever-present bond between them, eroding her willpower and inviting her to forget all the reasons why he was so dangerous to her. The firm clasp of his fingers radiated a persuasive appeal. She could almost taste his kiss, feel the rasp of his cheek against hers, relish the stroke of his fingers between her legs . . .

An old woman in a shawl coughed as she walked past them. The spell broken, Natalie pulled her hand out of Hadrian's grasp. She stepped back and drew a deep breath to steady herself.

"See, that's what I mean," she murmured, irked more with herself than with him. "You're forever bewitching me. That's why I'd vastly prefer that Leo and I live with my grandfather."

"I thought Sir Basil had refused your request."

"He didn't know of our passionate embrace." She lifted her chin defiantly. "Perhaps I should tell him."

Hadrian mustn't guess that she'd sooner cut out her own tongue than admit such a thing to her grandfather, who might very well challenge the duke to pistols at dawn if he refused to make an honest woman of her.

He cocked an eyebrow. "I can't stop you from leaving if that's truly your desire. However, Leo should remain in my house."

"But Audrey placed him in *my* care."

"She charged you to deliver him to his family, a duty that you've fulfilled quite admirably. By the way, you'll be happy to hear that my solicitor is petitioning the court to assign legal custody of Leo to me."

Natalie felt as if she'd been poleaxed. *"What?"*

He frowned slightly. "I thought you'd be pleased. You *did* say that you wanted me to adopt him. You don't want Godwin to be his guardian, do you?"

"Of course not!" She turned her stricken gaze to the boy, who was kneeling in the grass beneath an oak tree, building a tower out of the stones he'd collected. The thought of losing him wrenched her heart. She reminded herself that this was what she'd planned, for Hadrian to raise Leo. Yet she'd assumed that day wouldn't come for many weeks, until the duke had affianced himself to Lady Ellen. "This means . . . I'm no longer responsible for Leo. He doesn't need me anymore."

"Nonsense, he needs you more than ever. You're the only mother he has." His voice low and rough, Hadrian caught hold of her hand again. "I never meant to distress you, Natalie. I want you to stay at Clayton House for as long as you wish."

She swallowed hard, realizing that her reluctance to leave England was due at least in part to Hadrian. "It will take a little time, I suppose, to advertise for a governess."

"And also for Leo to be completely settled into his new home. As you've said, he's suffered far too many changes in his life—"

The approach of hoofbeats cut him off. Muttering what sounded like a curse, he released her hand as two gentlemen on horseback approached. They were the same pair of riders she'd spied earlier on Rotten Row. Both appeared to be of an age with Hadrian, one with fair hair and sharp blue eyes, the other stout with a bull neck and ruddy features.

"Ho there, Clayton," the blond one called. "Where have you been hiding this mysterious beauty?"

"A fine one, indeed," observed his companion. "It seems only sporting to make her known to the rest of us fellows."

Hadrian's lips tightened into a cool smile. He introduced the blond as the Honorable Mr. Barford and the heftier man as Lord Comstock.

"So you're the American," said Lord Comstock, appreciatively eyeing her. "The town is abuzz with the news that Clayton has taken you into his home, Miss Fanshawe, along with an orphan child. So very unlike him!"

"And now it's clear why he's kept you all to himself," Mr. Barford added, clapping his hand over his heart. "You're a diamond of the first water. An absolute paragon of perfection."

Despite her earlier tension, Natalie found herself amused by the exaggerated praise. The scowl on Hadrian's face diverted her all the more. He'd accused her of jealousy, but it seemed *he* was the one bitten by that bug.

Unable to resist teasing him, she aimed a flirtatious smile at his friends. "How very kind you both are. It seems that English gentlemen are not so cold and aloof as I'd believed."

"Don't judge us all by Clayton," Lord Comstock said with a sly look at Hadrian. "The fellow's always been a stuffy stick-in-the mud, even back in our school days. Shall I call on you sometime and tell you more?"

Hadrian, stuffy? His friends clearly had no notion of the enthralling man underneath all that cool hauteur. Still, the prospect of learning more about his past intrigued her. "Thank you, I'd very much enjoy hearing those stories."

"I'm afraid that's impossible," Hadrian said in a clipped tone. "Comstock, your wife may object to your visiting a lovely young woman. The same goes for you, too, Barford. Now, if you'll excuse us, gentlemen."

As she and Hadrian took their leave, Natalie found herself a little disconcerted to learn the men were married. It was just that they'd admired her in the manner of carefree bachelors. But that, apparently, was the way of the ton. In the future, she must be more careful not to give the wrong impression.

The Duke of Clayton was enough of a flirt for one woman to handle.

Chapter 21

Hadrian's day went from bad to worse when, shortly after luncheon, he was summoned from his study by a footman bearing the message that Lord and Lady Godwin had come to call.

Though in no humor to entertain his father's cousin, he put away his papers and strode down a long corridor toward the front of the house, his heels ringing on the marble floor. He and Godwin had parted on bad terms nearly a week ago, and he felt duty-bound as head of the family to broker peace. After their disastrous last meeting, in which the earl's solicitor had cast doubt on Leo's identity and Lady Godwin had accused Natalie of attempting to defraud them, Hadrian had departed abruptly from Oak Knoll with Natalie and Leo.

But now he had an obligation to deal with the fallout.

Mounting the stairs, he hoped this meeting would go better than the morning's excursion. That had started out well, with Natalie softening toward him, until he'd mentioned his legal guardianship of Leo. The stricken expression on her face had been a dagger to his chest. Blast it, he'd expected her to be pleased, not dismayed.

Then, just as he was smoothing her ruffled feathers, Comstock and Barford had arrived.

Natalie had enjoyed their flirtatious compliments, at least until she'd learned the truth about those two rakes. Much to Hadrian's vexation, the incident had only confirmed her beliefs about lecherous noblemen. There'd been no chance to reassure her on the way home, either, for Leo's presence had prevented any private conversation.

You're perfectly aware that I've a weakness for you.

Her frank words stirred the memory of that intimate interlude in her bedchamber several days ago. Ever since, the lust to possess her had burned in Hadrian. But he was mindful of the fact that for once, his rank put him at a disadvantage. Unlike the ladies of the ton, Natalie was a free spirit who had no interest in marriage to a man of wealth and power.

A man who belonged to the aristocracy that she scorned.

He clenched his jaw. At least he could feel reasonably certain that she wouldn't depart for America straightaway. For one, she wanted Leo to have a suitable governess, and that would take time. For another, she was loath to part from the boy. Her affection was evident in the tender warmth on her face whenever she gazed at the brat. Now, if only she would look at *him* that way.

Fool! Had he fallen so low that he could envy a child? Apparently so!

Mastering his dark mood, Hadrian entered the blue salon and started toward the group of people gathered at the far end of the long chamber. Seated in their midst, his mother appeared strained by the task of playing hostess to a branch of the family that she heartily disliked. And they were all here, Lord and Lady Godwin, Lady Ellen, even Lord Wymark.

Abruptly, Hadrian's gaze was riveted by the object of his frustrations.

Strikingly beautiful in the soft green gown she'd worn earlier, Natalie sat on a chaise with her hands folded in her lap. As always, that stunning combination of dark sable hair, emerald eyes, and creamy skin stirred a fierce admiration in him. She looked perfectly at home with his family, too. Her serene expression and proud posture lent her the noble aura of a duchess.

If only she aspired to become one.

Her grandfather was seated beside her, dapper in a cobalt-blue coat that looked a decade out of style. Hadrian surmised that Sir Basil had summoned her to the salon, for Godwin certainly wouldn't have done so. The earl would as soon forget that she and his grandson even existed.

On that grim thought, he went forward to greet his cousins. The tension in the air felt thick enough to cut with a knife, and he wondered what had been said before his arrival. His mother, in particular, regarded him as a savior. Her fingers clutched at the skirt of her claret silk gown as if to keep herself from scratching out Godwin's eyes. "My dear boy, you're here at last!"

The earl afforded him a stiff nod. "Ah, Clayton. I trust you've been well."

Lady Ellen and her mother arose to curtsy to him. Lady Godwin gave him a perfumed peck on the cheek. "We arrived in London late yesterday, so we have honored you with our first call. It seemed fitting since we never had a chance to say a proper good-bye. Isn't that so, Ellen?"

The girl peeped shyly up at Hadrian. She looked like a pretty pink confection, her fair hair curling, her rosebud lips smiling. In a rehearsed manner, she murmured, "We've missed you, Your Grace."

She seemed a mere child. He must have been mad ever to have wanted to wed so young a girl. Out of duty, he kissed her hand. "Welcome to Clayton House."

Wymark bowed to Hadrian. "It was quite unlike you to leave Oak Knoll in such haste, coz. And in the company of the beauteous Miss Fanshawe."

The hint of slyness in his tone made their departure sound sordid. Frowning at him, Hadrian recalled when his cousin had stumbled drunkenly into the library to find him with Natalie. Wymark had sworn never to speak of the incident. If the damned pup dared to sully her name . . .

Natalie fixed Wymark with a cool stare. "Leo left with us, too. Your nephew—remember him?"

There was a moment of charged silence in which Wymark scowled, his mother pinched her lips, and his father's face turned stony.

Then Sir Basil harrumphed. "Beauteous, eh?" he bluntly asked Wymark. "My granddaughter is indeed a rare beauty, but you're a mite wet behind the ears to come sniffing at her heels."

Lady Godwin bristled. "I beg your pardon! My son could never have the slightest interest in a penniless woman of dubious ancestry, especially one who is firmly on the shelf."

"She's no more on the shelf than your fresh little peach of a daughter." With a cagey smile, Sir Basil looked at the duchess. "Shall we tell them your plan, Millie? The one we were discussing before these callers interrupted us."

Her face lit up with such delight that Hadrian had a stoical expectation of this plan costing him a great deal of money. "Go on," he said.

Her candid blue eyes met his. "Darling, I've had the most marvelous notion. I wish to host a grand ball to introduce Natalie to society."

Lady Godwin huffed out a breath, while Lady Ellen clapped her hands. "Oh, famous! Will *we* be invited?"

"Hush," her mother chided. "I'm sure His Grace will have something to say about such an unsuitable scheme!"

All eyes turned to Hadrian. He suspected this had been Sir Basil's ploy, judging by the man's reputation as a wily rascal. It would benefit him to have his granddaughter accepted by society, opening doors that had been closed to him for thirty years. But it was Natalie's reaction that interested Hadrian the most. She flashed a beseeching look at him, clearly opposing the idea, while being reluctant to disappoint his mother and her grandfather.

Hadrian had a sudden keen desire to partner her in a waltz, to hold her close as they whirled around the dance floor, to see her eyes sparkle in the golden glow of a thousand candles. He had a strong hunch she'd enjoy it, too. "There hasn't been a ball at Clayton House in years," he said. "A brilliant notion, Mama. Would a fortnight give you ample time in which to prepare?"

"That will be perfect! Oh, it shall be the event of the season. I'll begin the guest list at once. Perhaps, Natalie, you will be so kind as to help me write out the invitations?"

"Of course."

Despite her tranquil reply, Natalie aimed an accusatory glare at Hadrian. He smiled, lifting his shoulders slightly to convey that there was no stopping his mother once she took an idea into her head.

Lady Godwin rose to her feet. "Well! Since you insist on pursuing this mad scheme, Duchess, we shall leave you to your preparations."

Lady Ellen and Wymark spoke their good-byes, but Godwin addressed his wife. "I need a word with Hadrian. Take the carriage and I'll walk home."

"But we were to visit the Norwoods—"

"Do as I say, Priscilla."

At his stern look, she nodded stiffly and sailed out of the salon with her children. Then Hadrian found himself the focus of that gimlet stare.

"Is there a place where we might speak in private, Clayton?"

"Of course."

Hadrian cast one last glance at the graceful sway of Natalie's hips as she went to the writing desk to fetch paper and pen for his mother's guest list. Then he led the way downstairs. The earl said nothing, not even a pleasantry. His manner radiated a disapproval that reminded Hadrian of his boyhood, being summoned to face Godwin's wrath over some minor transgression.

But he was no longer a child, longing for his guardian's approval. Now he would be the one sitting behind the desk.

Reaching his study, he waved Godwin into a leather chair and went to the cabinet to pour two brandies, handing one glass to the earl. The years had cut deep lines into the man's harsh features and reduced his gold hair to a thinning straw color. His grumpy expression reflected the fact that he also was growing more bitter with age.

Godwin took a sip before speaking. "I'm surprised you'd allow your mother to associate with that infamous old rogue."

Hadrian had his qualms about Sir Basil. But if he ever hoped to win Natalie, he could hardly banish her grandfather. Taking his seat, he said, "The duchess is perfectly capable of choosing her own companions."

"Mark my words, he's after her wealth. He was a trickster thirty years ago, and old habits die hard."

"The danger is slight. You know as well as I that the bulk of her fortune is under my control." Hadrian took a drink, relishing the burn of brandy down his throat. "Now, I doubt you're here to discuss the duchess. If you're angry about my abrupt departure from Oak Knoll, you've only yourself to blame."

Godwin narrowed his cold blue eyes. "I had business with my solicitor this morning. Musgrave reported hearing a rumor that the Duke of Clayton has filed a petition with the court seeking guardianship of an orphan boy."

Ah, so *that* was what had raised the man's dander. "It's no rumor," he said coolly. "Since you refuse to acknowledge Leo Bellingham as your grandson, I've taken it upon myself to assume responsibility for him."

"I never said I wouldn't accept him eventually, presuming his papers are properly verified. But there was no need for such swift action on your part. If his connection to me is revealed too soon, my family will be subjected to vile gossip. People will wonder that I didn't take him in myself."

Hadrian clenched his jaw. Was that all that mattered to the man, his reputation and not the boy's welfare? "People need know only that Leo is a distant cousin of mine. More than a decade has passed since Audrey eloped to America with her missionary. It's doubtful anyone will associate the name Bellingham with you."

Godwin looked far from satisfied. "If you insist upon going through with this folly, it is your duty to take the precaution of betrothing yourself to my daughter. At least then there might be justification for your custody. We could say that the two of you wish to raise the boy as your own."

Duty. How many times had duty been drummed into his head as a child? Godwin had taught him to be a confident, steadfast man with a strong sense of responsibility as befitting his rank. Until a few weeks ago, he'd had no qualms with that. He'd even been ready to court Lady Ellen in order to fulfill a long-ago vow made between his father and Godwin. But now Hadrian rejected being caged in by such a false obligation. He would not marry to please anyone but himself—and the woman of his choice.

If, that is, Natalie would even have him.

"We've already discussed this matter," he said tersely. "Lady Ellen has shown no interest in my courtship. And since leaving Oak Knoll, I've decided she is not the wife for me."

Godwin jerked up his chin as if he'd been struck. "It's that American woman, isn't it? Miss Fanshawe has bewitched you. Based on a pretty face, you've taken her and the boy into your house when those papers may be false."

"Unlike you, I made sure to learn her character. That's why I don't need additional proof. I judge Miss Fanshawe's word to be true."

"For pity's sake, you've known her less than a month. She has appalling family connections, a baseborn father, and a disgraced grandfather. You should know better than to host a ball for such a common female. It will tarnish the dignity of your rank!"

A bolt of fury flashed through Hadrian. He gripped the arms of his chair to keep from lunging across the desk and throttling the earl. Springing to his feet, he towered over the man. "Enough! I will not tolerate your insults toward her. Is that clear?"

Godwin stared up at him, an awareness that he'd gone too far dawning on his taut features. Then he arose to give Hadrian a jerky nod. "Forgive me if I spoke too harshly. Nevertheless, I cannot approve of this. I pray that you may yet come to your senses."

His shoulders squared, the earl turned and walked out the door.

Hadrian stood fuming over the man's unconscionable coldness toward Natalie and Leo. Was this what his mother had endured in her dealings with Godwin? This scorn for her common birth? This self-righteous arrogance?

He only wished he'd recognized before now the full extent of the man's rigid pomposity. Perhaps Comstock was right; under the earl's tutelage, Hadrian *had* become a stuffy stick-in-the mud. He had been bred to a life of privilege and power, raised to believe in his own superiority, but now he needed to break free of those chains. He *must* do so, or in time, he would become as bitter and snooty as Godwin.

Hadrian prowled to the window, pushing back the blue draperies and peering out at the sunlit garden. Usually, the neat pathways and greening trees had a calming effect. But today his mind was too preoccupied with sorting through the shifting chaos of his thoughts. Foremost was his powerful reaction to hearing Natalie disparaged as a temptress. *She's bewitched you.*

Bewitched. That was as good a term as any for this fascination he had for a woman who didn't fit the conventional standard of a duchess. Never in his life had he felt so tied in knots. Yet he suffered no regrets about it, either.

Because of her, he had opened his mind to change. Happiness was an aspect he'd never considered essential to a marriage until meeting Natalie. Now, he craved her spirit and wit and vivacity. Yet it remained damnably uncertain if he could win her heart. How could he ever convince her to give up her freedom, her dream of opening a school, even the very country of her birth?

Perhaps it was time to reveal the truth to her. To put his hopes for their future out into the open.

Despite the chilly air of early evening, Richard, Viscount Wymark, felt the trickle of sweat down the back of his neck. The thought of what he'd just done made him feel weak, almost faint.

He sagged against the door frame, sucking in shallow breaths that were tainted by the stink of rubbish. This narrow, filthy street lined by rackety brick buildings made his skin crawl. He'd despised having to come here, but he'd had no choice.

Damn his miserly father for refusing to settle those gaming debts. Godwin had coldly commanded Richard to make arrangements to repay them from his measly quarterly allowance. He also had strictly forbidden the countess to slip her son any funds, as she was wont to do. Richard didn't dare beg his friends for yet another extension. He'd already been warned that he'd be cut from their exclusive clique and barred from the best gaming hells if he didn't hand over their winnings at once.

His life would be reduced to an endless parade of dull society events, dancing with virtuous debutantes and playing whist for pennies with prune-faced old ladies. He might as well put a period to his existence. Even now, his fingers itched for the roll of the dice. It was a sickness in him, one he could not cure no matter how hard he'd tried.

The weight of gold from the moneylender made his coat pockets sag. He'd hated taking the two sacks from those greasy fingers, had quivered like a blancmange at being warned of violent retribution if he failed to repay the loan—plus a hefty interest—within a fortnight. Somehow he had to come up with five thousand pounds by the end of two weeks.

It might as well be five million.

A hazy thought took shape in his head. It had lurked like a dark shadow at the edge of his mind ever since he'd visited Clayton House the previous afternoon. The sinister plan involved his nephew. Audrey's son.

Mama had admitted to him that Leo was likely the earl's grandson and must eventually be given an inheritance. It was enormously unfair since Audrey had cut herself off from the family by eloping to America with that missionary. Richard had few fond memories of his pious half sister. Ten years his elder, she'd been forever with her nose in a prayer book. Who'd have ever thought her whelp would be Richard's key to collecting five thousand pounds?

If, that is, he dared to put the scheme into motion.

His gut churned. If Clayton got wind of the plan, he'd be more fearsome to face than the moneylender. Only look at how he had nearly throttled Richard for insulting Miss Fanshawe. As much as Richard loathed his cousin, he didn't relish another confrontation.

He desperately needed an accomplice. But who?

Then inspiration struck. He knew just the ruffian to handle the dirty work. Recently, he'd spotted the fellow lurking at the racetrack in Newmarket.

Bert, his former groom.

Heading toward his carriage, Richard smiled for the first time in days. How perfect. Clayton had dismissed the groom for trying to kiss Miss Fanshawe. Hiring Bert for this job would be a way for Richard to thumb his nose at the duke.

And to take revenge by confiscating a tidy chunk of his wealth.

Chapter 22

As Wymark was laying his plans across town, Leo went missing again.

Natalie had spent most of the day in the duchess's suite, writing out invitations while Hadrian's mother and sister enthusiastically discussed all the details for the ball. It was dusk before she finally headed up to the nursery. There, she found the two maids in a dither, Mrs. Tippet wringing her hands and Flora with tears in her blue eyes.

The girl ran straight to Natalie. "Oh, miss! Master Leo has vanished!"

Natalie's heart lurched. "When? What happened?"

"'Twas just a few minutes ago. He was playing with his mail coach when I went down to the kitchen to see about his hot cocoa. The footman never brung it, you see, and Tippy said maybe there was something wrong with the bell rope. But I wasn't gone long!"

"'Tis my fault," Mrs. Tippet admitted, shame-faced. "I dozed off over my mending. Still, I don't know how I didn't hear the child leave!"

Natalie knew from experience how quiet he could be. In the last rosy rays of sunset, she saw the abandoned coach with its tiny horses on the floor. The pot of cocoa and a cup sat on one of the small tables, while a cheery blaze burned in the hearth. She felt a twist of alarm, for there was no telling where the inquisitive boy might have gone.

"I presume you've checked every nook and cranny here in the nursery?"

Flora vigorously nodded her head. "Even under the beds, miss! And in the cupboards, too. My littlest brother likes to hide in cubbyholes."

Taking a calming breath, Natalie organized her thoughts. "Flora, go to the stables to see if he might have slipped out to visit his new pony. Tippy, please search the other rooms on this floor and then stay nearby in case he returns. As for myself, I shall go down and check the bedchambers. It's possible he went looking for me and became lost."

"It's growing dark, so best to take a lamp," Tippy said, her brown eyes worried in her careworn face. "Oh, I do hope our sweet boy isn't frightened!"

Natalie thought him too inquisitive to be easily frightened. He had to be close, for he liked living at Clayton House and wouldn't have run away.

Accepting the glass-enclosed candle, she hastened out the door and headed for the stairs. If only she hadn't been delayed, this would never have happened. She should have been in the nursery with Leo at this hour. Blast that fancy ball and those endless invitations!

Having come straight from the duchess's suite in the other wing of the house, she had taken a different staircase and so wouldn't have passed Leo on the one closest to her bedchamber. She went down to her room first and found Hetty turning back the bedcovers. But the maid hadn't seen him and promised to march him straight up to the nursery should he appear.

Going back out into the shadowy corridor with its ornate moldings and landscape paintings, Natalie eyed the many closed doors on either side. She would take a peek into every bedroom. Starting with the one opposite her own, she knocked first before entering, holding up her lamp. The furniture appeared ghostly, draped in dust covers, and although the room looked too gloomy to interest a little boy, she called out, "Leo! Are you in here?"

Silence answered her, so she proceeded to the next chamber, methodically repeating the process again and again without success. Upon reaching the last door at the end of the passageway, she rapped hard on the panel, then turned the knob and stepped inside.

Instantly, she froze. This bedchamber was much larger and grander than the others. And it was clearly occupied. A branch of candles flickered on a table and a fire blazed in the marble hearth. An enormous bed draped in royal-blue-and-gold hangings dominated one wall.

Before she had even a moment to collect her thoughts, a sour-faced elderly man garbed in funereal black emerged from a doorway to her right. Chumley, the duke's valet.

"Miss Fanshawe!" he exclaimed, advancing on her. "What do you think you're about, walking into His Grace's suite? Manners might be lax in the colonies, but here in England, we wait for our knock to be answered!"

Natalie was too aghast to take offense at his tone. Dear God, this was Hadrian's bedchamber! She had presumed it to be located in the same wing as his mother's rooms.

She started to back out. "I'm terribly sorry . . ."

A movement behind him caught her eye as Hadrian strolled out of the same doorway. Her heart thumped so hard that it squeezed the air from her lungs. It was obvious she had caught him in the midst of dressing.

He wore only an unbuttoned waistcoat over a white shirt that was tucked into a pair of dark trousers. His throat was bare so that she could see a glimpse of broad chest. He was fastening a silver sleeve link at his wrist when his eyes met hers.

Surprise flashed in those dark gray depths, then a glimmer of heat that sparked an answering flare inside her. "Natalie? Did you need me?"

Yes, she needed him. She needed him to sweep her into his arms, carry her to the bed, and show her that exquisite pleasure again.

Fighting the rise of a blush, she babbled, "Actually, I'm looking for Leo and came in here by mistake. I had no idea . . . I thought there were only guest bedchambers on this floor."

Chumley harrumphed. "The rascal isn't here, so you'd best run along."

"Yes. Yes, I'll go now. At once."

"Wait," Hadrian commanded, stopping her retreat, before turning to the manservant. "Fetch my coat, will you?"

As the valet went grumbling into the dressing room, the duke came forward while buttoning his silver-striped waistcoat. "So the brat has disappeared from the nursery, has he? I could have sworn we'd cured him of that bad habit."

The slight smile on his lips warmed her heart, as did his use of the word *we*. He made it sound as if they were a married couple discussing the antics of their son. She banished the errant thought and tried not to stare at the wedge of skin revealed by the open collar of his shirt.

"Apparently not, and now he's been gone for perhaps half an hour." She gave him a brief overview of the circumstances and where the nursemaids were searching. "You know Leo. He could be anywhere."

"Hm. When we first met, he was homesick, so he tried to walk back to the ship at Southampton. Then at Oak Knoll, he was playing with his toy cavalry horse, which prompted him to visit the stables without permission. Did Tippy say what he was doing right before he vanished?"

"Playing with the mail coach your mother gave him—though I can't imagine him leaving the house to look for a real one." Frowning, she recalled the exact conversation. "There's something else. The maids, I gathered, were also discussing a problem with the bell rope. They thought it might not have rung in the kitchen, so Flora went down to check."

At that moment, Chumley appeared with a bluish-gray coat, helping the duke shrug into it. Natalie's throat went dry, her fingers tightening around the base of the lamp. It felt unbearably intimate to watch him dress. The tailored garment hugged his broad shoulders, the deep color enhancing his eyes and transforming him into a dangerously attractive nobleman.

He placed his hand at the base of Natalie's spine. "Come. We'll look for the scamp in the kitchen."

"But . . . you clearly have an engagement tonight."

"I'm meeting friends at my club. They can wait."

"Your Grace!" Chumley said, his voice vibrating with indignation. "Pray permit me to tie your cravat."

"I can manage it later," Hadrian replied. "Now, don't look so cross. I'll make sure to tell everyone that I unwisely refused your artistry this once."

With that, he guided Natalie out into the corridor. "Don't mind the old fussbudget," he said as they walked briskly toward a staircase. "He's been watching over me since I was five. Sometimes he forgets that I'm capable of doing things for myself."

The undercurrent of fondness in his voice touched her

heart. "He was with you at Lord Godwin's house while you were growing up?"

"Not at first, but he always came to fetch me whenever it was time to visit my mother. He joined me permanently when I was of an age to attend Eton. Beneath all his bluster, he's staunchly loyal to the family. And like my mother he was very much against my courtship of Lady Ellen."

He flicked a keen glance at Natalie, but in the wavering light of the candle, she didn't know quite what to make of it. What did he mean by *was*?

Corralling her curiosity, she changed the subject. "Well, speaking of Leo, I don't know how he could have managed to slip down to the kitchen without Flora seeing him."

"There are half a dozen staircases in this house. Flora likely took the one for the servants, while Leo used another. I suspect he was curious about that bell rope, as I would have been at his age."

Natalie hoped he was right. She held up the candle to light their way as Hadrian led her down a series of stairs and into the cellars. Here, the delectable scents of roasting meat and pungent spices drew them into a spacious kitchen, where pots steamed atop a large modern stove, presided over by a stout French chef who barked orders at the maidservants. Although the duke was going to his club and the duchess was dining out with friends, Natalie surmised that the staff must soon be eating their own supper.

Her attention went to a small cluster of servants near the far wall. To her relief, Leo was being boosted up by a footman so the boy could get a better look at the two rows of bells that ran the length of the upper wall. They were conversing and laughing, but as she and Hadrian approached, the chatter ended abruptly.

The footman set Leo back down on his feet and then bowed to the duke. "Your Grace!"

The others followed suit, the maidservants bobbing curtsies. They all appeared nervous at being caught in the dereliction of their duties. But Hadrian merely said, "I see you've found our little fugitive."

Leo's blue eyes shone like saucers. "Mr. Duke! Did you know that when you pull the cord in the schoolroom, it rings right here?" He pointed up at the bell marked *Nursery.*

"It's quite the handy system for summoning help, isn't it?"

"But how does it work?"

As the servants melted away to return to their tasks, Hadrian explained, "There are wires inside the walls, and a spring mechanism that activates them when you give a tug on the rope. My grandfather, the sixth duke, had the bells installed quite a long time ago."

"Flora and Tippy said that our bell might be broken. But I think Flora didn't pull the cord hard enough."

"That may be, but it wasn't your place to check. They had no idea where you'd gone. You know very well that a young gentleman doesn't wander off on his own and cause worry for everyone."

At his stern tone, Leo hung his head, kicking the flagstone floor with the toe of his shoe. "Sorry."

"It's Miss Fanshawe who deserves your apology. She's been hunting all over the house for you."

The boy threw his arms around Natalie's waist. "Don't be angry. It won't happen again, I *promise.*"

Trying not to melt, she smoothed his tousled sandy hair. "I won't be angry so long as you keep your vow in the future."

As Leo slipped his hand into the duke's, Hadrian

looked startled, though not displeased. They proceeded upstairs to the nursery, where Leo had a joyous reunion with the maids. They scolded and fussed over him, agreeing with Natalie that he must go straight to bed without his cocoa.

Leo bore his punishment stoically. "You may kiss me good night now, Miss Fanshawe, for I oughtn't have a story read to me, either."

She bent down to press her lips to his brow. "Sweet dreams, darling."

He looked up at Hadrian. "I want to be a duke someday. Then *I* can have a house with bells, too." With that, he went trotting off to bed.

Natalie caught Hadrian's twinkling gaze and felt an answering bubble of mirth inside her. As they left the nursery, she said, "I expect he'll learn soon enough that the aristocracy doesn't work that way."

"Never fear, by tomorrow, he'll want to be a groom or a butler."

Hadrian's hand came to rest lightly against her back as they went down the stairs. His warmth penetrated the thin saffron silk of her gown, feeding the fizz of desire she always felt in his presence. In the shadowy darkness lit by her lamp, they might have been the only two people in the world.

To distract herself, she said, "None of this would have happened if it hadn't been for that irksome ball. I was writing invitations in your mother's suite all afternoon, when I ought to have been with Leo."

"Lizzy didn't help you?"

"She and the duchess decided that I have neater penmanship, so the task fell to me. But truly, I believe they both just preferred to plan all the many details. And seeing their enthusiasm as they wrote out long lists of things to purchase only made me think . . ."

They had reached her bedchamber door, and he pushed it open to allow her to enter. "Think what?"

"Your mother needs a purpose in her life, Hadrian. Something useful that will also satisfy her love of shopping and extravagant spending." Natalie spoke over her shoulder before turning to face him. "By the way, I should warn you that she intends to order five hundred beeswax candles. It will cost you a fortune!"

"We can hardly entertain our guests in the dark." Looking amused, he took the lamp from her and set it on a table. "And I hope you don't suggest substituting cheap tallow candles, for they can cause a dreadful stink."

Natalie ruefully acknowledged making that very recommendation to Her Grace, only to be regarded in horror. "They intend to procure a champagne fountain, too. Whoever heard of such a thing? And dozens of ells of white silk and masses of hothouse flowers to create an indoor garden. I told them it was far too wasteful, but they wouldn't listen."

He chuckled. "If you expect me to reason with them, I gave up on that years ago. But what did you mean about giving my mother a purpose?"

"The duchess loves nothing better than to buy things, yet she already owns everything she could ever need. If spending gives her such pleasure, why not direct her generous nature toward helping others? There must be any number of schools and orphanages in London that need a patroness."

"You want her to be a philanthropist."

"But not simply as a donor dispensing funds. Her Grace is such a kindhearted woman, Hadrian. I believe she would enjoy visiting the children, distributing food and clothing and toys, making the little ones happy."

"That seems an undertaking you would enjoy, as well."

He was standing across from her, lounging against

the wall with one hand on his hip, his coat pushed back to reveal his lean waist. His indulgent smile set off a tremor of longing deep within her. It occurred to her that she'd unthinkingly led him into her bedchamber, as if he belonged here. With the covers turned down invitingly and a fire burning low on the hearth, it was a scene made for seduction.

Her throat felt dry as she dragged her mind back to the conversation. "I'd be happy to find an appropriate project for the duchess. Subject to your approval, of course. I realize it isn't my place to meddle in your family affairs."

"Darling, you may meddle to your heart's content."

The warmth in his eyes was so meltingly affectionate that she wanted to sink into his arms. That besotted look made her long for the ecstasy he'd shown her the last time he'd been in her bedchamber. It would be wise to banish him at once.

Instead, she paced the floor in an effort to work off her untimely yearnings. "Well, the project gave me something to think about as I penned all those invitations. There were hundreds of them, by the way. My hand aches from writing, and I've a permanent ink stain on my finger."

"Do you? Let me see."

He came closer to take hold of her right hand, turning it to the candlelight. Brushing his thumb over the dark blot on her middle finger, he brought it to his mouth for a soft kiss. "Poor girl, and you didn't even want this ball to be given in your honor. Rest assured, all the fuss will be worthwhile in the end. You'll have a chance to see that we aristocrats are not all ogres as you've been led to believe."

Her heart quaked as they stared at each other. Heat leaped between them, almost palpable in the dim-lit room, as his nearness eroded her ability to think. It was clear that if she gave him the least encouragement, he'd be more than willing to make love to her. Her blood throbbed with such longing that she had difficulty keeping her own desires firmly in check.

Whirling around, she stepped away from him. "I lost count of the number of titles I had to inscribe on the invitations. Lord this and Lady that, earls and marquesses and dukes and viscounts and honorables. To be candid, Hadrian, I don't see how a common American woman can possibly fit in with such exalted company."

"Are you truly so much opposed to the ball?"

He looked genuinely concerned, so she answered him honestly. "Part of me would like to step into your world for one night, if only out of curiosity. And I do very much enjoy dancing and conversing. But if I'm expected to simper and curtsy to snooty people who are no better than any other person on God's earth, well, it may be difficult for me not to disgrace you and your mother."

"You needn't simper and curtsy. Just be your usual lovely self. No one will dare to criticize you in my house, or they'll hear from me." He closed the distance between them, his warm hands coming to rest on her shoulders. "To be perfectly clear, Natalie, I want you there with me in the receiving line. At my side, as my honored guest."

His nearness, along with his declaration, set her mind in a turmoil. She tried to fathom the strange intensity that seemed to vibrate in him. Surely it wasn't acceptable even for a duke to flaunt a potential paramour in front of polite society. Especially when the girl he was courting would be in attendance.

Swallowing hard, she found the courage to address the issue directly. "What about Lady Ellen? Wouldn't you prefer to have *her* beside you?"

"No, I most certainly would not."

"Your mother and sister questioned me today about your intentions toward her. I gave nothing away, but told them that they must ask you."

His fingers gently rubbed at the tension in her shoulders, making her want to purr like a kitten being petted. That small smile was playing at the corners of his mouth again. "I'll admit I've been remiss in telling them the truth."

"The truth?"

"That I've no intention of marrying her."

Startled, she could only stare at him. Ever since the previous day when Lord Godwin and his family had come calling, she had been plagued by the memory of Hadrian bending his head to kiss Lady Ellen's hand. A fierce knot of envy had twisted inside Natalie. "But . . . you said that you would be paying your addresses to her here in London."

"I said nothing of the sort. Though I *was* guilty of allowing you to assume that—only because I didn't think the time was right to speak of *us*." He lowered his head to feather his lips over hers in a butterfly kiss. "For such an astute woman, you ought to have noticed that my interests have undergone a fundamental shift."

Her heart leaped into her throat. Feeling breathless and befuddled, she tried to make sense of his words. Certainly, she knew he had a strong interest in her. But he wanted her only as his mistress . . . didn't he?

My intentions toward you are honorable.

His declaration in the park had been firm, his gaze as unwavering as it was now. At the time, she had presumed his words to be flirtatious nonsense. Noblemen like him surely spoke all manner of drivel in order to charm a woman into bed.

Unless she was mistaken. Unless he had something else in mind.

Trembling, she took a step back. She shook her head, unable to believe the notion that had just dawned on her. "Hadrian, you can't mean . . . are you intending to *court* me?"

Chapter 23

He watched her intently, his mouth curled into a slight smile. "I've already been doing so. It's you who have deemed me to be up to no good."

Her mind in a whirl, she crossed her arms. His dark gray eyes held a compelling sincerity that both gratified and unnerved her. Dear God, she'd been right to think he had a secret purpose in bringing her to London, yet so very wrong at the same time. She had never imagined that an English duke could have respectable intentions toward a woman not of his class.

She drew a breath before being able to speak. "You can't honestly be thinking of me in terms of . . . marriage."

"Yes, I most certainly can be." Betraying a hint of anxiety, he combed his fingers through his hair. "Admittedly, I never meant to bring up the matter in so slapdash a fashion. My intention was to wait until after the ball, to give you a chance to see my world first. But lately I've felt it was wrong of me not to be truthful with you about my intentions."

"I—I don't know what to say."

"Say that you'll at least consider my suit." When she

didn't answer, he continued in a softer tone, "I've admired you from the moment we met at that inn during the ice storm, Natalie. I was haughty and arrogant and sorely in need of being knocked off my pedestal. You inspired me to change, and that makes you quite the remarkable woman."

His words moved her, even as she tried to wrap her mind around his revelation. "But I'm not a lady."

"Bosh. You most certainly *are* a lady. Perhaps not in the narrow-minded opinions of some, but I'm finding that I care less and less for convention."

Reaching out to clasp her hand, he led her to a long pier glass mounted on the wall beside the door to her dressing room. She went unresisting, still in a state of stunned confusion. He placed her in front of him, nestling her back against his chest while his arms held her in a snug embrace.

His breath stirring the delicate skin at the nape of her neck, he murmured, "You're a woman of character and warmth and charm, not to mention great beauty. There isn't a lady in society who is your match. You've only to look in the mirror to know that."

She studied her shadowy reflection. The stylish gown of saffron sarcenet lent distinction to her figure in a way that would please even the most critical eye. But more than that, Natalie was deeply aware of the attractive couple that she and Hadrian made. Handsome and enticing, he stood directly behind her. She was tall, but he was that much taller, the ideal height for kissing. And she craved his kiss with an intensity that threatened to sweep away all reason.

She drew a shaky breath. "Outward appearances cannot change the fact that I'm not bred to your world."

"Perhaps those differences are part of the reason why we're attracted to one another. It's a way for both of us to break out of the dullness of norms." He tucked a wisp of her hair behind her ear, her skin tingling from his touch. "I was raised with the fixed belief that the perfect wife was a docile young lady with impeccable bloodlines. That it was my duty to wed a wellborn debutante. Then I met you, Natalie. And all of that went out the window. Simply put, you're everything I never knew that I needed."

His declaration melted her heart. There could be nothing more romantic than to be chosen by a powerful man who made her feel alive, body and soul. A duke who could have any woman he wanted. Yet logic whispered that it would never work. She could list a hundred reasons why he was all wrong for her, not the least of which was the life she had planned back in America. Still, the fire that heated her blood could not be denied.

Turning in his arms, she stroked her fingers over his smooth-shaven jaw. "I have to be honest, Hadrian. I don't know if I can ever marry you. It's impossible for me to think straight right now. Yet I *do* know that I need you. I crave you with an urgency I've never felt for any other man."

His eyes darkened. "Then allow me to convince you."

He brought his mouth down onto hers in a crushing kiss that surpassed all of her starry-eyed dreams. She gave back as much as she took, reveling in his potency, savoring the taste of him. With her bosom pressed to his hard chest, she felt his heart beating with a wild rhythm that matched her own.

A rising excitement made her dizzy with desire. Nothing had ever seemed so right as being clasped in his arms. Their clothing formed a frustrating barrier as she slipped her hands inside his coat in an effort to learn the solid contours of his body. She could think only of experiencing again the amazing rapture he had shown her. And this time she wanted him to share it with her.

They were both gasping after the long, luscious bout of kissing. He nuzzled her cheek and hair, his damp lips sending delightful ripples down to her core. His hands followed the curve of her waist and hips, caressing in a way that bespoke intense passion.

His breath warm on her face, he murmured, "There's a bond between us, Natalie. I felt it from the very moment we met. Tell me you felt it, too."

"Yes, I did. As I do now, too." A reckless fever swept her with the irresistible urge to become one with him, to discover if intimacy might clear up her doubts about a future with him. "Hadrian, come to bed with me. Show me what we never finished the last time we were here."

His fingers tightened around her waist, and he drew a ragged breath as he kissed her brow. "My God, I want that, you can't imagine how much. But your virtue belongs to your husband." He paused, a hint of deviltry lifting one corner of his mouth. "Unless, of course, you'll accept my offer of marriage."

The wicked glint in his eyes challenged her. So he thought to bribe her with the promise of pleasure?

Natalie decided that two could play that game. "If you hope to win my favor, denying me my dearest wish is hardly the way to do so."

To entice him, she rubbed her hips against his, to spectacular effect. A groan tore from deep in his chest. He lifted her more firmly against him so that she could feel his rigid length, as his lips sought hers in another fierce, openmouthed kiss. Her arms around his waist, she clung tightly to him, returning his ardor with her own.

"Saucy wench," he muttered against her hair, his voice

vibrating with amused passion. "You're making it damnably difficult for me to be honorable. I don't want you to regret this later."

"I'll suffer regrets if you walk out on me. So I suggest we dwell no more on the future and simply enjoy the here and now."

Giving him a smile of wicked provocation, Natalie traced his lips with her fingertip. His teeth caught her finger in a tender love bite, his tongue laving her skin so that her insides contracted with a pulse of desire.

Then he drew her palm to his cheek and held it there a moment while he looked deeply into her eyes. "It shall be as you wish, my lady."

Releasing her, he went to the door and turned the key with a metallic click. The sound sent a shiver of excitement over her skin. Their need for privacy underscored what was about to happen in this darkish bedchamber lit only by a single candle and the glow of the fire.

Watching as Hadrian stripped off his coat and dropped it onto a chair, she felt on fire with nervous anticipation. He removed his waistcoat, too, leaving him clad in only a white cambric shirt tucked into dark trousers. Her heart beat faster at the sight of his strong, muscled form.

Natalie realized this wouldn't be like the other time when he'd simply reached beneath her skirts. Instead of gawking, she, too, ought to be undressing. Taking her cue from him, she stepped out of her shoes, turning away to place them neatly by the wall before stretching her arms to reach the buttons at the back of her gown.

She sensed his presence behind her in the instant before he spoke. "Allow me."

He undid the row of tiny gold buttons, pausing now and then to kiss her exposed skin. Wanton yearning swept away all trace of misgivings in her. When the gown lay open to her waist, he untied her stays and then worked his hands inside the loosened garments. He cupped her bare breasts and feathered his thumbs over the tips. As ribbons of heat unfurled downward to feed the fire in her depths, Natalie sighed in pure delight.

Her knees wobbly, she leaned back against his chest, tilting her head to tuck it into the crook of his neck. "Mm, *Hadrian*."

His lips nuzzled her cheek, his fingers continuing their skillful stroking. "So many times I've imagined doing this," he murmured. "Undressing you, holding you, learning every inch of your beautiful body."

"I confess to harboring such thoughts about you, too. Though perhaps a lady shouldn't speak of such matters."

From behind, Hadrian divested her of gown and corset, leaving her clad in only scanty lingerie. "There is only one rule in the bedchamber. That we are to give each other pleasure."

He turned her to face him, his hands on her shoulders. His gaze lowered to the filmy chemise that allowed him a titillating glimpse of her breasts and hips. The hot gleam of appreciation in his eyes awakened Natalie to an awareness of her own sensual powers. If she had enjoyed watching him remove his coat and waistcoat, perhaps the tables could be turned.

When he reached for the undergarment, she batted his hands away. "Not yet, Your Grace."

She sauntered to the bed, braced her foot on the edge of the mattress, and drew the hem of her chemise to mid-thigh. To her gratification, he paced after her with all the keen interest of a stallion following a mare in heat. Folding his arms, he leaned against the bedpost to watch. She took her time untying her garters and then rolling down her stocking. As she tossed the scrap of white silk in his direction, he reflexively caught it in his fist.

Natalie felt a little anxious that he might find her

behavior too bold. But his face wore a look of stunned hunger, encouraging her to perform the same ritual on her other leg. She sent that stocking fluttering at him as well.

He made a growl deep in his chest and dropped the hosiery to the floor. As he started forward, she wordlessly held up her hand to stop him. Clearly intrigued, he stood waiting for her next move.

Did she dare do it? The total absorption on Hadrian's face made her feel recklessly naughty, so she slipped the straps of her chemise off her shoulders. A flick to help it clear her breasts, then a little shimmy of her hips, and the garment slithered to the floor, leaving her stark naked.

He scanned her in a sort of concentrated daze, and Natalie held her breath, wondering again if she'd gone too far. Never in her life had she allowed any man to view her unclothed body. A sense of vulnerability caused the warmth of a blush to creep upward from her neck and into her cheeks. She crossed her arms to shield her bare bosom, murmuring, "Have I . . . done something wrong?"

He snapped out of his stupor. "What? No." In two steps, he closed the distance between them and pulled her against him, directing that dazed smile at her. His questing hands glided over the smooth skin of her back and hips. "You're adorable. How did you know I'd love that?"

"You inspired me when you undressed." Placated, she fingered the open collar of his shirt. "Although I'm very sorry that you stopped halfway."

"A situation that can be easily rectified."

She was beset by a sudden, swooning dip as he tilted her backward, guiding her down onto the bed. Her head landed on a cloud of feather pillow, the linen sheets cool and sensual beneath the rest of her body. It felt wickedly decadent to lie here in all her fleshly glory, gazing up at the handsomest, most intriguing man she'd ever known. Hadrian, with his granite eyes and the chiseled features that other people found haughty.

But they didn't know him as she did.

Her arms still looped around his neck, she smiled up at him, feeling bubbly with happiness, as if she'd drunk too much champagne. "Have I thanked you for providing me with this wonderful bed, Your Grace?"

"What happens in it can be even more wonderful."

His mouth sought hers in another deep, drowning kiss that stirred a wild hunger in her soul. She felt his hands on her breasts again, kneading the heavy globes in a way that made her burn with longing. When he tried to draw away, she moaned a protest.

He soothed her with a soft finger over her lips. "One moment."

As Hadrian arose, she pushed up on her elbow to watch him. He stood beside the bed and yanked his shirt free of his waistband, pulling the garment over his head in one swift move. Enthralled, she stared at the ripple of muscles in his chest and arms, the breadth of his powerful shoulders. How differently a man was built, the perfect complement to feminine softness.

When he unbuttoned his trousers and pushed them down over his lean hips, she experienced a deep throb of desire. Never had she imagined that a man in full arousal could look so magnificent. She glanced away, blushing, not wanting to be caught staring.

The mattress dipped beneath his weight as he sat down beside her. His fingers touched her chin to draw her face back to his searching gaze. His muscles were taut, his jaw clenched, his eyes fierce with passion. "Having second thoughts? Tell me."

Lifting her arms, she drew the pins from her hair and dropped them on the bedside table. Then she shook her head and combed her fingers through the heavy sable mass, the curls cascading over her shoulders and bosom. She curved her lips into a come-hither smile. "Does that answer your question?"

He muttered her name with lusty reverence as he came down over her, a mutual hunger drawing them together. As they kissed and caressed and whispered sweet nothings to each other, she reveled in the weight and strength of him. It was a joy to finally have the freedom to learn the hard contours of his body, to run her hands over his chest and waist and backside. He truly had a superb form, and tonight he belonged to her alone.

In a haze she realized it somehow made all the difference to learn that Hadrian was ready to commit his life to her. The knowledge filled her with a tangle of radiant emotion that took too much effort to examine at a time when she wanted only to rejoice in the pleasure of being in his arms.

When he bent his head and suckled her breasts, she whimpered from the rush of liquid heat that poured through her body. His seduction of her was relentless and intense, sensual and spellbinding. He knew precisely how to touch her, finding places she'd never known to be erotic, from the hollow of her throat to the backs of her knees. His warm palms glided over every inch of her skin until Natalie thought she might expire from need. At last, he slid his fingers in between her legs for the most intimate caress of all.

With breathy cries of pleasure, she moved restlessly beneath him. Her head tilted back on the pillow, she dug her fingers into his shoulders and abandoned herself to the scorching sensations aroused by his touch. The irresistible blaze increased its torment until a white-hot flare of euphoria convulsed her body.

As the fire subsided into glowing embers, she strove to catch her breath. The tension in Hadrian's jaw and the sheen of perspiration on his brow indicated his relentless control of himself. He had given her ecstatic release, and she longed to return the favor. If only she knew how.

Drawn by temptation, she shifted position slightly and slid her hand down to touch the hard length that lay against her thigh. It felt hot and heavy in her palm and she experimentally rubbed it. "Do you mind if I do this?"

He sucked in a breath, his male member leaping with urgency. "Mind?" he said on a choked laugh. "Certainly not."

He groaned as she lightly squeezed him, moving her fingers up and down his silken heat, intrigued to discover a dab of moisture at the tip. Gasping, he managed to add, "But there's a better way."

He shifted slightly, parting her legs and positioning himself so that his shaft probed against her privates. A pulse of that earlier excitement assailed her again, and she intuitively tilted her hips to him. He kissed her deeply until she was half delirious before penetrating her with slow, inexorable pressure.

She had heard enough whispers among married ladies to expect a stab of pain, but it was not so dreadful as she'd been led to expect. Any discomfort swiftly melted away beneath a stunning sense of fullness. Hadrian whispered her name, skating his lips over hers in a tender kiss. As he moved inside her, leisurely at first and then faster, she yielded to the instinctive urgings of her body, rocking her hips in rhythm with his. That blissful inner friction reignited the wild passion that she'd naïvely believed already sated.

Panting, she tucked her face into the lee of his shoulder, her tongue tasting his salty skin. Their intimate joining transcended anything she could ever have imagined in her sheltered innocence, for she felt connected to him not only in body but in soul as well. They were two parts of a whole, male and female, designed for each other as perfect mates.

As the sensual storm broke again, she clung to him as her anchor in the waves of pleasure. She was still blissfully adrift when he gave one final thrust, his body shuddering from the force of his culmination. Against her hair, he breathed her name in a hoarse groan, *"Natalie."*

Utterly spent, she welcomed the weight of his body settling over her. It felt perfectly right to be entwined with him as their heartbeats slowed and their breathing returned to normal. But as passion ebbed and sanity returned, so did her awareness of their impossible dilemma.

Hadrian sensed the subtle change in her even before he opened his eyes. He couldn't say exactly how he knew she was withdrawing into herself, the feeling was just there, twisting his gut. He wanted desperately to ignore it.

Lying in her arms, he inhaled the subtle fragrance of her hair and exulted in the womanly curves beneath him. The shattering intensity of their coupling still resonated in his cooling blood. When he'd come here to her chamber, he'd thought only to hone her desire to a fever pitch, not to consummate their relationship. But he was fiercely glad they had made love. It had been perfect in every way.

Except one. Natalie had not committed herself to him.

That knowledge made his chest tighten. She'd teased him, traded wits with him, craved him with such fervor that she'd given him the gift of her virginity. Yet it might not be enough to overturn her reluctance to wed him.

There had to be a way to convince her.

Disengaging their bodies, he rolled to the side to gaze into her face. She looked charmingly tousled, her dark hair tangled, her lips reddened from his kisses. Ah, those emerald eyes. Always candid, they held a combination of warmth, wonder . . . and distress.

Hiding an inner rawness, he brushed a curl from her cheek. He ought to say something romantic and charming, something that would capture her heart, but all that came out of his mouth was the unvarnished truth. "I suspect I haven't yet won your favor."

A naked goddess, she sat up against the pillows. "Oh, but this was marvelous, Hadrian. I haven't any regrets."

"That isn't what I meant. You still don't want to share my bed for the rest of our lives."

Natalie parted her lips so swiftly, with such a look of yearning, that he had a searing flash of hope she would prove him wrong. Then her eyebrows drew together in a look of tender remorse and she shook her head. "I'm sorry," she murmured. "I—I just don't see how a marriage between us can work. We come from different worlds. Your life is in England, and mine is in America."

"Don't make a final decision just yet," he urged, cupping her face. "Give me a chance to court you properly, to convince you to be my wife—and a mother to Leo. We can have children of our own, a nursery full of them."

Her eyes softened with longing, even as her lips firmed with denial. "But I'd have to become an English duchess. Please try to understand. I love the country of my birth. I love that America was founded on freedom and equality. I don't know if I could ever fit into your class system."

He set his jaw. "Society will accept you. I'll make certain they do."

Smiling wistfully, she shook her head in gentle exasperation. "You have it all wrong, Hadrian. It isn't whether English society will accept me. It's whether *I* will accept English society."

Chapter 24

Two weeks later, on the evening of the ball, Natalie sat at the mirrored table in her dressing room while Hetty pinned up her dark brown locks into a collection of lustrous curls. On the duchess's urging, Natalie had spent the afternoon primping, starting with a decadently hot bath in a large copper tub, then drying her hair by the fire, applying scented lotions, and having her nails trimmed and buffed. She had thoroughly enjoyed all the pampering.

This could be her life forever, she thought with a pang. She distracted herself with the stern reminder that it was unfair for a few lucky women to live in the lap of luxury while others had to labor for a living.

She studied the maid's placid features, guessing her to be in her mid-thirties. "Do you mind having to do all this work on my behalf?"

"Mind?" Hetty looked astonished at the question. "Why, never, miss! It's a pleasure to serve a lady so lovely as yourself."

"But surely you've wished that you could go to such a ball as this."

The maid chortled. "Me dad's a cobbler, and he'd hoot

at such a notion! Nay, I'm blessed to be an upstairs maid in this grand house after starting as a lowly tweeny. Now, it's time to don your gown."

As Hetty helped her into the elegant creation, Natalie reflected that the maid seemed content with her life. Perhaps English commoners weren't necessarily unhappy with the class system here. Though they'd never become nobles, they could still improve their situation through hard work as Hetty had done. In that sense, they were no different from the less fortunate in America.

"Lud, you'll be the prettiest lady tonight. Come and see, miss. Won't His Grace be pleased?"

Walking toward the mirror, Natalie bit her lip to stop a denial that the duke would have any particular interest in her appearance. It would be useless to prevaricate when the truth must be obvious to the entire household. Although no one knew of the intimate night that she and Hadrian had shared, he had appointed himself her devoted companion, escorting her and Leo to Astley's Circus to see the performing horses, to the Tower to view the menagerie of wild animals, to the Thames for a boat ride. They had gone riding in Hyde Park, sometimes with Leo, though often just the two of them, early in the morning when they could enjoy an exhilarating gallop. Hadrian also had convinced her on several occasions to join his mother and a small party of guests for dinner in order for Natalie to meet select members of the ton so that she wouldn't face a vast sea of strangers tonight.

He was courting her, she knew with a certainty that touched her heart. She had let herself be persuaded to put off a final decision about the marriage until after the ball. And he had made it clear that it was too risky for them to share a bed again without a betrothal. Pregnancy would compel her into wedlock, for neither would he abandon his child to bastardy.

Nevertheless, three days after their tryst, she'd mourned the onset of her courses. It made no sense, for she ought to have been thankful. Instead of making matters clearer, their assignation had only caused a bigger tangle of her thoughts and emotions. He had never spoken of love, and at times, she wondered if he kept the deepest part of himself hidden from her. There seemed to be an elusive missing piece in their relationship, something that made her hesitate to commit herself.

Yet there could be no doubt that he *cared* for her. Or that she craved him more than ever. Hadrian was everything a woman could want in a husband: considerate, witty, sincere, protective, exciting.

Alas, he was also an English duke.

How different things would be if he were a commoner. Then she could coax him to emigrate to America, where they could live happily ever after as husband and wife. But that was a foolish dream, for he would not be the same man. His high rank had created the circumstances that had shaped his character—inheriting the dukedom at age five, growing up under Lord Godwin's harsh tutelage, being denied his mother's love and companionship . . .

"Do you not approve, miss?"

She snapped out of her reverie to realize that Hetty stood waiting, looking a trifle anxious at her mistress's lack of enthusiasm. Natalie quickly examined her reflection in the long pier glass.

She saw a fine lady arrayed in rich bronze silk with a gossamer netting overskirt and a low-cut bodice that revealed a shocking expanse of bosom. A gold band cinched the high waist, with matching ribbons on the cap sleeves. From her softly styled hair down to the toes of her gold slippers, she looked like a member of Hadrian's world.

A quiver beset her. Tonight she would dance with him at her first London ball. Then tomorrow, he would press her for an answer to his offer of marriage. What would she say? There could be no denying that her attachment to him had deepened over the past weeks. The mere thought of parting from him forever wrenched her heart.

So she wouldn't think about it just yet. She would set aside her decision until the morning and wring every drop of happiness out of the present.

Giddy with anticipation, she twirled around, her skirt shimmering in the candlelight. "You've done exceptionally well, Hetty. Thank you!"

The maid beamed with pride just as a knock sounded on the door. Two ladies swept into the bedchamber. Lizzy wore a deep indigo gown that brought out the blue in her eyes and helped to camouflage her pregnancy. Beside her, the Duchess of Clayton was stately in lilac satin, her throat adorned with pearls, a majestic pearl-and-diamond tiara nestled in her graying blond hair.

A smile beamed across her aging features. "What a vision of loveliness you are! My dear girl, you shall be the belle of the ball."

"All eyes will be upon her," Lizzy said. "The ball *is* in her honor, after all."

Natalie shook her head in mock exasperation. "Pray don't make me any more jittery than I already am."

"I've just the thing to lend you confidence," the duchess said. She was carrying a black enameled box and opened it to reveal several pieces of diamond jewelry lying in the blue velvet interior. "These were a bride gift to me from my father."

Natalie gasped at the treasure trove. "Your Grace!" she exclaimed. "I couldn't possibly borrow something so expensive!"

"Why ever not? These gems are meant for someone younger and prettier than an old matron like me. I haven't worn them in years."

"Do try them on," Lizzy urged. "Besides, Hadrian suggested the jewels."

Of course it was his idea, Natalie thought wryly as Hetty fastened the necklace. He wanted her to experience the life of a duchess. In short order, she also wore diamond earrings and a tiara that glimmered richly against her sable curls. Charmed, she reached up with kid-gloved fingers to touch the spiderweb of diamonds set in gold above her bosom. The pieces were delicate and elegant, providing the perfect complement to her bronze gown.

Lizzy clapped her hands. "You look positively gorgeous. Shall we go down now? I can't wait to see the stunned look on my brother's face."

There it was again, the inference that Hadrian was besotted. Over the past few days, Lizzy and the duchess had dropped numerous hints that they'd be pleased by a match between Natalie and the duke. If only they knew, the mere thought of him stirred a bevy of butterflies within her.

The three of them left the bedchamber, and upon arriving at the grand staircase, Lizzy stopped Natalie. "Mama and I shall go down first," she said, her chinablue eyes bright. "It's proper precedent, you see."

The duchess patted Natalie's arm. "You may follow in a moment."

She watched as the two ladies descended side by side. They had spent the past fortnight stuffing her head with countless archaic dictums of society. But it seemed a silly rule for her to be obliged to wait. After all, the guests had not yet arrived. Peeking over the balcony railing, she saw that the vast entrance hall stood empty except for a few footmen stationed by the front door. It was a letdown to realize that not even Hadrian was here.

Then he stepped into sight.

Her mouth went dry as he came forward to greet his mother and sister at the base of the stairs. Feeling a rush of untimely desire, Natalie pressed her palm to her racing heart. He looked every inch the sinfully handsome duke in formal black tailcoat and knee breeches, a diamond stickpin glinting in his snowy cravat. In the brilliance of the candles in the crystal chandelier, his brown hair gleamed with the richness of caramel.

Lizzy murmured something to him. Instantly, he shifted his gaze upward, straight at Natalie.

She curled her fingers around the gilded balustrade. His sister and mother had arranged this moment, she realized with a touch of wry humor. No wonder they had wanted to go down first. But she didn't afford them even a glance. No one else mattered but Hadrian.

Drawn by his magnetic stare, she descended the curved staircase. She felt as if she were floating, buoyed by the admiration in his smoky-gray eyes. The slight smile that lifted one corner of his mouth made her think of lying in bed with him, bare flesh to bare flesh. The banked passion on his chiseled features hinted at his own wicked thoughts, especially when his gaze dipped to her close-fitting bodice.

When she reached the bottom step, the duke lifted her hand to his lips for a kiss. "You look ravishing, Natalie."

So ravish me. Her arched eyebrow and sensual smile conveyed those silent words, while she said very properly, "You're too kind, Your Grace."

He bent to whisper in her ear, "Minx. Now is not the time to tempt me."

His laughing undertone lent a sparkle to the evening as they gazed at each other. His fingers firm around hers, she felt bound to him by mutual desire and something else, something deep and vibrant that she had never felt with any other man.

As if similarly affected, Hadrian released a breath before looking at his mother. "It's time. The carriages are already lined up on the square."

The duchess came to join them, and at a signal from Hadrian, the footman opened the front door. A steady stream of guests began to flow into house, ladies in fine gowns and jewels escorted by gentlemen in well-tailored formal garb. Since she was not part of the receiving line, Lizzy disappeared into the crowd with her husband, the Marquess of Wrenbury, a quiet, fair-haired man who obviously adored his wife. Some people lingered in the entrance hall, while others headed upstairs toward the discordant sounds of the orchestra tuning their instruments in the ballroom.

Natalie's flutter of nerves swiftly dissipated as she concentrated on matching faces with the names spoken by the duchess and Hadrian. Everyone, it seemed, was curious about their American guest, and the reactions were generally friendly, especially from the gentlemen. Since Hadrian and the duchess had quietly spread word prior to the ball, no one seemed offended that she offered her hand instead of curtsying to the peers and peeresses. Only a few ladies wore snooty stares, notably Lady Birdsall and her blond daughters, Lady Eugenie and Lady Cora, who had called on the day that Natalie had brought her grandfather here for the first time.

Despite her earlier apprehension, she felt remarkably relaxed amid the buzz of conversation and the pleasure of greeting new faces. The situation brought a nostalgic reminder of the parties she'd hosted with her father back when he'd served in the Senate. This ball might be much larger and grander, but it filled her with the same effervescence of excitement.

She smiled warmly on seeing her grandfather and cousin Giles. Sir Basil planted a kiss on the duchess's cheek, much to her girlish delight, and then shook the duke's hand. "I trust you've been treating my grand-daughter with the respect she deserves, Clayton."

"Always, sir." Though his manner was perfectly respectful, Hadrian flicked a heated glance at Natalie that held the memory of their secret tryst.

She gave her grandfather a fond peck on his lined cheek. They'd become much better acquainted since he was in the habit of calling frequently at Clayton House. "I'm thrilled that you and Giles could be here."

"Doris wasn't happy to be left at home," Giles admitted, mentioning his sister. "But sixteen is too young to fend off gentlemen, and I told her she'll have to wait until at least next year . . . er, that is, if you're still here and, er, haven't gone back to America."

Her cousin stammered to a stop. With a pang, she knew her family still hoped she'd marry Hadrian and provide them a path back into society. She squeezed Giles's hand. "Please tell Doris I shall come to call on her soon."

As her relatives moved on, the crowds began to thin. Among the last to arrive were Lord and Lady Godwin, Lord Wymark, and Lady Ellen. The earl and countess offered stiff smiles and cool greetings. Lady Godwin scarcely acknowledged Natalie, seeming to look straight through her, unlike her livelier daughter, who appeared angelic in a blush-pink gown.

"How pretty you look, Miss Fanshawe!" Lady Ellen burbled. "Do you know, four gentlemen called today, begging to reserve the first dance with me? But I have promised it to Mr. Runyon, for he wrote me the loveliest poem!"

Her sapphire eyes bright, she appeared about to confide more, but Lady Godwin drew her away with a sharp word. Nevertheless, Natalie found it a pleasure to see the girl enjoying her first season and suffering no belated regrets over losing the duke as a suitor.

Bringing up the rear, Wymark bowed over Natalie's hand. He looked the quintessential English gentleman with his wheat-gold hair and finely tailored garb. "I see you've escaped the schoolroom again, Miss Fanshawe. I hope you haven't left my little orphaned nephew all alone."

"Leo has a nursemaid to watch over him, of course."

"Ah, I see."

As he gave her another veiled stare and then strolled off, Natalie felt her skin prickle. Wymark seemed to exude an edgy tension tonight that left her with a vague uneasiness. She shook off the sensation. Perhaps as a gambler, he was merely eager to join the card players in the drawing room.

After a few more stragglers were admitted, the duke offered one arm to his mother and the other to Natalie. "Thank God that ordeal is over at last," he said, chuckling. "Shall we go and join the festivities?"

With her hand tucked into the crook of his elbow and the lilt of music in the air, Natalie felt giddy with happiness. Once upstairs, they strolled along a wide corridor and through an arched doorway. The majordomo announced their entry, but she scarcely noticed the eyes that turned her way. She was too busy admiring the fairytale décor of the ballroom.

Although she'd peeked in earlier while the workers were setting up, the finished scene stole her breath away. Three immense chandeliers blazed with beeswax candles, casting golden light upon the shifting sea of elegant guests. Along the walls, swags of white silk provided a backdrop for masses of daffodils and irises and pink roses, creating the illusion of a spring garden. At one end, an elevated gallery held the string quartet of musicians, while at the other, a wall of glass doors opened onto a spacious balcony.

Hadrian snagged three flutes from one of the footmen circulating with silver trays, handing one to his mother and one to Natalie. "Champagne, ladies. If you'll excuse me now, there are some people I must see, but I'll return to claim you for the first dance, Natalie."

His eyes caressed her before he disappeared into the crowd, and the duchess patted her hand. "The first dance? That's a high honor, my dear. Tonight will establish you quite firmly in society."

Natalie smiled, though pleasure warred with caution. Did she want to be a part of this glittering life forever? There was no time to ponder as a stately couple approached the duchess. Natalie soon found herself surrounded by gentlemen and ladies who were curious about life in America, in particular, the frontier. Determining their interest was genuine, she related amusing stories of her encounters with beavers and porcupines, leaving out the massacre that had necessitated her journey to England with Leo.

Hadrian soon plucked her from the crowd of admirers and led her onto the dance floor where two long lines were forming, gentlemen on one side and ladies on the other. Natalie was glad for the dancing master the duchess had engaged this past week, for there were slight differences in the steps she'd known in America, where techniques were not quite so strict.

As the music began, the formal movements provided little opportunity for conversation. But as Hadrian gazed at her, the slight smile on his lips made her heartbeat accelerate. As well, her insides melted at the intensity in his eyes, and by the time the dance ended, she had to concentrate in order not to wobble on molten knees.

He placed his hand at the small of her back. "I dislike having to give you off to other partners, but I must do my duty to half the women present. I hope you'll reserve the waltz for me just before supper."

"*Two* dances, Your Grace? I hear that's scandalous behavior for London society."

His expression showed a stirring possessiveness. "If people wish to interpret it as a declaration of my interest in you, then so be it. Now, allow me to introduce you to a good friend of mine who's been anxious to meet you."

He escorted her to a rangy man with a calm smile, who secured her hand for the next dance. Mr. Gerald Remington was a member of the House of Commons, and on learning her father had been a senator, engaged her in an animated discussion of the workings of the United States government.

As the quadrille drew to a close, she said, "I'm surprised that people here are friendly to me when our two nations were so recently at war."

Remington grinned. "The war may have been of vital importance to the Americans, but to us Brits it was a minor skirmish. We've bigger conflicts going on, most notably with the French."

With that, he introduced her to another of Hadrian's friends. It was soon apparent the duke had arranged for her not to be left standing awkwardly alone in a sea of strangers. She had no lack of partners during the evening, including her grandfather and Lizzy's husband. She also danced with her cousin Giles, who blushed when he trod on her foot. Despite his lack of fortune, he seemed a decent young man, so she agreed to his request to make

him known to Lady Ellen, who was much taken with his
dark Romany looks.

Now and then, Natalie caught a glimpse of Hadrian
squiring a succession of dewy-eyed debutantes and elegant grande dames. She knew him well enough to detect
a hint of jaded ennui in his polite expression, a fact that
perversely pleased her. Then, after one dance, she spied
Lady Godwin sitting with a gaggle of equally sour-faced
matrons. They were glowering in her direction in a way
that cast a pall over her blithe spirits.

"She may be my kin," a familiar voice murmured,
"but I never did like that woman."

Natalie turned to smile at Lizzy. "Lady Godwin? I fear
she may be spreading gossip about me."

"Bah, what can she say? Everyone already knows
you're an American."

Natalie hesitated, then admitted, "Back at Oak Knoll,
she accused me of being a swindler trying to pass off my
own son as the earl's grandson."

Lizzy pursed her lips. "What a nasty woman! Pray be
assured, no one will heed her but a handful of her cro-
nies. What matters to society is that Hadrian and Mama
and I have given you our seal of approval."

"Perhaps you're right."

"There's no perhaps about it." Glancing into the
crowded ballroom, Lizzy absently rubbed her pregnant
belly. "Ah, there's Wrenbury. I suppose I must go and pla-
cate him. He fears I'm overtaxing myself, but *I* have no
intention of leaving early and missing the lobster patties
at supper." She squeezed Natalie's hand. "By the way, the
best revenge on those chinwags is to be happy and enjoy
yourself. Let people see that you don't care what they
think."

As Lizzy vanished into the throng, Natalie felt cheered
to have the support of a friend. She reminded herself there

were good and bad people everywhere in the world, not just in an English ballroom. It was liberating not to care what a few naysayers might think of her.

During a break in the sets, she joined the duchess and Sir Basil, who were seated near one of the lush garden displays. As she quenched her thirst with champagne and rested her feet for a few minutes, a buzz swept through the multitude. The disturbance seemed centered on the doorway.

"Can you look, my dear?" the duchess asked, lounging in her gilded chair while waving a dainty ivory fan at her face. "Oh, it is a plague to be so short."

Natalie arose to peer through the crowd. "There's a party of newcomers. One of them is quite corpulent, and he's wearing a blue cape with epaulets."

Sir Basil stood up to look, too. "Why, Millie. I didn't know you'd invited Prinny."

The duchess's eyes widened as she pushed to her feet, dropping the fan in her haste. "Oh no! I *didn't* invite him. This is dreadful!"

"Who is Prinny?" Natalie asked in confusion.

"The Prince Regent. He was left off the guest list on purpose. I thought it wise to do so, for your sake." Her manner agitated, she clutched Natalie's arm. "My dear, I realize it goes against your principles, but I *implore* you to make an exception this once. You simply *must* curtsy to the prince."

Chapter 25

Before Natalie could do more than blink, Hadrian joined them. "Forgive me, but I must disagree."

The duchess gazed beseechingly at him. "But you *know* His Highness sets great store on obeisance. If he takes it into his mind to cause trouble, it will create an unpleasant scene and ruin the ball. Natalie may be ostracized."

He listened gravely to his mother, then turned his attention to Natalie. As he lifted her hand and brought it to his lips, his keen eyes seemed to penetrate her very soul. "Never mind all that," he said softly. "You may do as you wish. I'll protect your good name."

His staunch willingness to defend her, even against a royal prince, held Natalie captivated. Under his unwavering gaze, she felt a rush of deep emotion that warmed her from head to toe. The truth came to her, not in a blinding flash, but with soft, steadfast certainty.

She loved him. She loved Hadrian.

Her heart overflowed with the richness of fervor. How could she have been so blind? These past weeks, she had been so distracted by her fixed views about the aristocracy that she had failed to heed what was most important. She had focused on his rank instead of on his character, his integrity, his honor.

But did *he* love *her*? He'd never said so, not even when he'd astonished her with his stated wish for them to become husband and wife. In the past weeks, she'd had the sense that he kept a part of himself closed off.

Was he drawn to her as a novelty because the ladies of society bored him? If she were to wed Hadrian, would he find the marriage less than exciting once the newness wore off? Would he turn to other women, then, as noblemen were wont to do?

Her heart urged her to trust in him. Yet her long-held beliefs made her cautious. Infidelity was the one sin she could never abide.

A sudden stir behind him interrupted her musings. Hadrian turned, keeping her at his side, as the throngs of people parted. Gentlemen bowed and ladies curtsied as the prince's party strolled toward the duke and duchess.

Despite her antipathy toward the monarchy, Natalie watched Prinny's advance with a sort of awed fascination. Though she had not known his nickname, tales of his lavish expenditures and many love affairs had reached even the shores of America. Parliament, she knew, had made him regent in his father's place ever since old King George III had been declared incurably mad.

The prince's features had a distinction that suggested he must have been a handsome man in his youth, though now his skin had a puffy, florid look. His dark locks must surely be dyed since he appeared to be past fifty. As a further sop to vanity, the feathery strands were brushed forward as if to conceal a receding hairline. His fancy blue cape revealed an overfed form in a black coat and white knee breeches, his cravat tied so absurdly high it surely must choke him. She suspected the style was meant to conceal multiple chins.

The duchess sank into a deep curtsy. "Your Royal Highness! My son and I are honored by your attendance."

Prinny regarded her rather dolefully. "That is a relief, Duchess, as I'd greatly feared you might not welcome the royal presence at your ball. One does so dislike presuming to go where one has not been invited."

"I understood you to be in Brighton this week," Hadrian said with a respectful bow. "It would have been presumptuous to make you feel obliged to return early to London. Dare we hope your health is much improved?"

The prince appeared mollified by the smooth explanation and eager to expound on his illness. "It's these horrid bouts of dyspepsia, they'll be the death of me! The doctor thought a bit of sea air might be refreshing. But it was so frightfully cold that I was in constant alarm of contracting a lung fever, so here I am. Besides, there was an intriguing rumor that you've a houseguest from the wilds of America. Might I presume her to be this lovely young lady?"

"Indeed," Hadrian said. "Your Royal Highness, if I may present Miss Fanshawe, lately of Philadelphia, and granddaughter to Sir Basil Fanshawe."

Natalie found herself the subject of that royal stare, his eyes gray like Hadrian's but far more fishlike. In the few short minutes since he'd come into her orbit, she had measured the Prince Regent to be a vain man coddled and flattered by his subjects, a blue blood who had been raised to believe himself superior to all others. But strangely, she found herself pitying him, for without the fine garb and the high position, he would be just a middle-aged man preoccupied with his own mortality.

The duchess watched them with an anxious expression. *His Highness sets great store on obeisance,* she'd said. Though Hadrian looked unperturbed, ready to shield her from any trouble, Natalie felt loath to ruin the ball, especially for his mother who had put her heart and soul into planning it. One exception could not be too much to ask after all they had done for her and Leo.

She sank into the first curtsy of her life and hoped it was adequately graceful. "It's a pleasure to make your acquaintance, Your Highness. May I add that I've been much impressed by the welcoming nature of the British people, yourself in particular."

The prince's expression warmed to a look of flirtatious charm that surely hearkened back to his glory days. "I daresay my father should have fought harder to quash the rebellion in the colonies and keep such beauty as yours within our empire. Clayton, you must bring Miss Fanshawe to Carleton House very soon."

"We'll look forward to it, sir," Hadrian said, with a formalness that made Natalie think he didn't really mean it.

Prinny and his companions took their leave and strolled through the ballroom so that he might accept more adulations from the hordes. There was a noticeable sense of relief in the air, emanating largely from the duchess.

She hastened to Natalie. "My dear, how brilliantly you charmed him!"

"Naturally," Sir Basil said. "She *is* a Fanshawe, after all."

Hadrian chuckled. "But now we're doomed to sit through a twenty-course dinner in tropical heat, for Prinny is known for his dislike of the cold."

"He won't really invite me, will he?" Natalie asked dubiously. "Surely he was just being polite."

"I wouldn't be so certain. The prince has an eye for pretty ladies, so I had best stake my claim on you before it's too late."

With that, Hadrian whisked her off to the dance floor, where the first lilting notes of a waltz had begun. He took her hand in his, placing his other at the back of her waist. As they joined the couples whirling around the floor, she felt a heady rush of exhilaration at being in his arms again. The dance steps might be relatively new to her, learned and practiced only this week, but they were the perfect expression for her soaring happiness.

When she tilted up her chin to smile dazzlingly at Hadrian, she found him gazing at her with mystified warmth. "Why did you do it?" he asked. "I'd have staved off any unpleasantness."

"Are you sorry you lost your chance to play knight-errant?"

Cocking an eyebrow, he guided her in a perfect twirl. "You mustn't feel compelled to act against your principles, Natalie. Failing to curtsy wouldn't have been a tragedy. It's just that my mother still remembers a time when *she* was snubbed as a young debutante for being a commoner."

That did explain the duchess's anxiety. Still, tonight something had changed in Natalie, something liberating and intoxicating. The issue of what society thought of her, or what she thought of society, no longer seemed so very important. Only Hadrian mattered.

"No one compelled me," she assured him. "One can stay true to one's ideals while occasionally doing what best suits the occasion. *When in Rome*, you once told me."

An ironic smile tilted one corner of his mouth. "We were on our way to Oak Knoll. I'd offered you and Leo a ride without realizing that my cool hauteur was about to undergo a momentous shake-up."

He sounded perfectly content with that, and Natalie marveled that she could have such a positive effect on this strong, powerful man. Hadrian wanted her as his wife, and she burned to tell him that she wanted that, too.

If only she could be certain of his love. If only she

could rid herself of a niggling impression that he had not opened all of himself to her.

As the music ended, he maneuvered her toward the open doors and out onto the large balcony. A full moon cast a silvery mantle over the couples who were strolling here to escape the warmth of the ballroom—or perhaps a chaperone's watchful eyes. Lighted lanterns were placed at regular intervals on the stone balustrade that overlooked the garden below.

Hadrian took advantage of the near-darkness to trail his fingers down her back and across her arm, causing a shiver in her that had nothing to do with the coolness of the night air. "It's nearly time for supper," he murmured. "But I confess to having a different sort of appetite."

Passion radiated from him, the same desire that pulsed hotly in her blood. A pity they had an audience, for she yearned desperately to be alone with him. "Will you come upstairs with me for a moment?" she asked. "I promised Leo that I'd leave him a slice of cake on his bedside table."

His hand stilled on her back, his eyes gleaming in the darkness. "Wait here. I'll fetch him a plate."

She smiled to see the swiftness of his steps as he headed back into the ballroom. They couldn't disappear for long, or people would talk. Nevertheless, anticipation fired her veins at the notion of having Hadrian all to herself, if only for a short while.

He returned bearing two glasses of champagne and a plate piled with tarts and cake. "It's best we're not seen," he said in low tone. "Follow me."

Hadrian led her toward an outside staircase that descended to the darkened garden. No one appeared to notice them since the other guests were heading inside for supper. With the steps in semidarkness, lit only by a few scattered lanterns, she was glad he'd gone first.

They had just reached the bottom when a man came hurrying out of the gloomy depths of the garden. He spied them and stopped dead, glancing furtively behind him. The moonlight made a pale cap of his wheat-gold hair and washed out his stark, startled features.

"Wymark," Hadrian said. "Why the devil are you prowling out here in the dark?"

"I—I wanted a breath of fresh air. No different from you and Miss Fanshawe. Excuse me."

Seeming anxious to avoid further questions, the viscount brushed past them and bounded up the stairs to rejoin the ball.

"His cravat looked disheveled," she said as Hadrian guided her to a door on the ground floor. "Do you suppose he was meeting a woman?"

"Well, the fool did look behind him. Perhaps he told her to wait so they weren't seen returning together." Deftly balancing the two flutes and the plate in one hand, he opened the door. "A true gentleman would have sent *her* back to the ball first."

He waved Natalie ahead of him, and she stepped into a corridor lit by candles in sconces set at intervals along the walls. "You don't see your cousin as a gentleman?"

"Richard is a weak-willed libertine who was spoiled by his mother."

"How odd that you were both raised by the same man, yet turned out so very differently."

"The first Lady Godwin set great store on proper behavior. By the time the earl married the present countess, I was away at school. Richard used to brag that she always intervened whenever Godwin tried to discipline him."

He ushered Natalie into a study lit only by an ethereal glow from the bank of windows that overlooked the moonlit garden. A rich leather scent came from the bound ledgers that lined the shelves behind the large desk. Despite its spaciousness, the shadowy room had a cozy aura with several seating areas and framed paintings on the walls.

Hadrian set down the plate and handed her one of the flutes. "But I didn't bring you here to talk about my kinfolk."

She took a sip of champagne, the bubbles tickling her tongue and filling her with an effervescence of spirit. The glint of his eyes in the semidarkness made her blood surge. "Oh?" she said flirtatiously. "What other possible reason could you have for luring me into your den, sir?"

His low chuckle sounded deliciously dangerous. "Saucy wench. You know perfectly well."

Without taking his gaze from her, he put down his glass, did the same with her flute, and then gathered her into his arms. Their mouths joined in a deep kiss that flared like wildfire through her veins. The magic of the moment surpassed the entirety of the ball, thrilling her far more than dancing, drinking champagne, and even meeting a prince.

Her arms wreathed around his neck, she arched to Hadrian, craving the pressure of his hard body against her softness. The urgent caress of his hands on her face and back suffused her with intense joy. She was exactly where she belonged, in the embrace of the man she loved. How strange to think that little more than a month ago, she hadn't even known he existed. Now it had become difficult to imagine her life without him.

He broke the contact to glide his lips over her cheek. "My God. I've been wanting to do this all night."

"Mm. I've been wanting to do it for the past two weeks. Especially this." She swirled her hips against him.

His chest vibrated in a choked laugh. "You know why we mustn't . . . unless you've changed your mind about us." Just like that, the ambience grew serious as he cupped her face in his hands. "Have you, Natalie? Have I convinced you to accept my offer of marriage?"

Aware of his watchful gaze in the shadows, she ached to say yes. They could spend the rest of their lives together, raise a family, enjoy that rapturous intimacy again and again. After tonight, she felt confident that she could fit into his world without having to relinquish her core beliefs. Even her attachment to America held far less sway over her heart than he did. Yet she could not commit herself without laying to rest one niggling doubt.

"Do you love me, Hadrian?"

His fingers tensed around her cheeks; then he dropped his hands to her shoulders. Much to her dismay, he seemed uncomfortable with the question. "Of course I care for you. I wouldn't want you as my wife otherwise."

Care seemed a pale shadow of true, abiding love. "There can be many reasons why you find me appealing that have little to do with love," she said, forcing herself to enumerate them. "Perhaps conquering me is a challenge, or perhaps I'm an antidote to the shallow ladies of society. Perhaps what you feel for me is merely an intense passion. But that isn't enough. Without love as the bedrock in our marriage, you may tire of me eventually and turn your eyes to other women."

"That's absurd. You must know I'm not so dishonorable."

A part of her desperately wanted to believe that. Yet how could she be sure? "It's the way of the aristocracy. My father was a bastard. Sir Basil may have sent him to the best schools, but the fact remains that my grandfather was a notorious libertine in his younger days. So, tell me honestly that you don't know any married noblemen who keep a mistress on the side."

Hadrian drew a breath as if to speak, but remained silent. Of course he couldn't deny it. The dissolute foibles of the British upper class were something she'd grown up hearing about. Hadrian was warm, attentive, kind, witty, and wonderful in so many ways. But if he lacked a deep, abiding love for her, then it simply wasn't enough.

Though her heart felt torn in two, Natalie held her head high as she stepped away and picked up the plate of sweets. She couldn't stay a moment longer for fear he'd see the tears that stung her eyes. "I'd better deliver this to Leo before people notice we've both disappeared from the ball."

She turned on her heel and walked out into the corridor, leaving Hadrian standing in the study. But not for long. The sharp scrape of his footsteps echoed against the marble walls.

A harried expression on his face, he caught up to her at the back staircase. "Don't judge me by the actions of other men."

"Rather, I'm merely trying to be realistic about the mores of the ton." She grasped her skirt and ascended the steps, and when he kept to her side, she went on, "Consider my situation if I were to marry you. Instead of returning to America and opening a school, I'd be embracing a new life here in England. I'd be a fool to give up my plans and everything that's familiar to me without being certain of your steadfast love."

"I *am* steadfast, dammit. A regular stick-in-the-mud, remember?"

As they reached a landing and proceeded up another flight of stairs, she steeled herself to say, "You've had mistresses, I presume."

He appeared discomfited by the blunt statement. "Whatever I've done as a bachelor would have no bearing on my behavior as a husband." Placing his hand at the small of her back, he looked at her with a penetrating gaze. "I believe in marital fidelity, I swear it to you, Natalie. I would never betray my vows to you. Would that I could convince you of my sincerity."

Then tell me that you love me.

Her throat taut, she continued up the steps until they reached the top floor, where the nursery was located. She didn't doubt Hadrian was smitten with her; he had displayed his interest in many ways over the past few weeks. But she still sensed there was a part of him she didn't know. Just how deep was his attachment to her? Was it more than mere passion? Could he love her and comfort her, in sickness and in health, forsaking all others, and remain faithful for the rest of their lives?

That was the nagging question.

As they entered the shadowed schoolroom, moonlight guided her path through the maze of miniature tables and chairs. She had a poignant vision of Hadrian here as a little boy, allowed to visit Clayton House for only two weeks out of each year. He would have been a well-behaved child, obedient to adult authority. That meant enduring many tearful good-byes from his mother when he had to return to Oak Knoll and Lord Godwin's cold guardianship.

A revelation struck her. It wasn't any lack in their relationship that kept him from acknowledging that he loved her; it was his past. Hadrian must have walled off his heart at a young age. Perhaps, due to the frequent separations from his mother, he had come to associate love with pain. It would explain quite a lot. With his upbringing, it made sense that he was not a man who could easily give voice to his deepest emotions.

Natalie also realized that she'd expected him to bare his soul when she herself had not done the same. If the prospect made *her* feel vulnerable, only imagine what it would do to a strong man who had been conditioned to bury his feelings.

She stopped near the corridor that led to the nursery bedchambers and turned to face him. The faint lilt of music carried from downstairs, but the crowded ballroom seemed worlds away from the two of them, cocooned in silken darkness.

Lifting her hand, she stroked his cheek, relishing the slightly raspy feel of his smooth-shaven skin. "I'm afraid I haven't been entirely fair to you. There's something I ought to have told you down in your study a little while ago. I love you, Hadrian. I love you with all my heart and soul."

He went very still, and Natalie wished she could read his expression through the gloom. She felt terribly in need of his arms around her. What was he thinking? Would it be the catalyst for him to finally lower his guard? Or would he back away from such a blatant declaration of sentiment?

His hands tightened almost painfully on her shoulders. "My darling," he murmured in a low, husky tone, "I can't begin to tell you what that means to me—"

Just then, a muffled thump sounded behind her. The noise seemed to have emanated from one of the bedchambers. Despite the intensely charged moment, her motherly instincts sprang to full alert.

She twisted around. "Did you hear that?"

"Perhaps Leo fell out of bed. Let's see."

His door stood wide open, when he usually slept with it closed. Too alarmed to wonder why, she hastened inside the dim-lit room. A candle enclosed in a glass chimney flickered atop the chest of drawers and illuminated the portrait of Audrey that they'd brought from Oak Knoll, for the boy found the image of his mother to be comforting.

But Leo wasn't lying on the floor.

Mystified, Natalie tiptoed toward the shadowed cot and set down the plate of sweets on the bedside table. His covers lay in a tumbled heap, but when she leaned over to check on him, a gasp paralyzed her throat.

The bed was empty.

Chapter 26

"Hadrian! Leo is gone."

Striding forward, the duke threw back the blankets. "Then what the devil was that noise?"

"Who knows? I'm more concerned about where he is."

He placed a comforting arm around her shoulders. "There's no need to panic, darling. He likely slipped downstairs to peek at the ball. It's just what the little brat would do."

His reassuring tone calmed Natalie. Of course. The distant sound of music might have lured Leo out of bed. Then her gaze sharpened on a piece of folded paper that lay on his pillow, and she snatched it up, hastening to examine it by the light of the candle.

The message printed in black ink sent an arctic chill down her spine. She uttered a cry, spinning toward Hadrian. "Dear God! Leo's been abducted!"

Grim disbelief on his face, the duke read the note aloud. "'*If you wish to see the boy alive again, Miss Fanshawe must come alone with five thousand in banknotes to the dam in Hyde Park by eleven tomorrow. Leave the sack underneath the mulberry bush at the east end. If anyone should attempt to accompany her, the boy dies.*'"

His stark gaze met Natalie's as he flung the paper back down onto the bed. "What blasted foolery is this? How the devil could a villain have broken into my house? Where were the nursemaids?"

"Flora was needed in the kitchen tonight. But Tippy should be here."

Natalie darted out to the next bedroom and rapped hard on the door before opening it and hurrying inside. Hadrian had seized the candle before following her, and the feeble light fell upon Mrs. Tippet lying on the floor beside her bed. Clad in a gray flannel nightgown, she was bound and gagged, her brown eyes wide as she made muffled noises of distress.

Hadrian sprang to remove the strip of cloth from the servant's mouth, and Natalie gave the gasping woman a drink from the water glass on the bedside table. "Are you all right?"

"Aye . . . though I fell from the bed just now . . . whilst trying to wiggle out of these bonds."

"Who did this to you?" Hadrian demanded, untying the ropes that secured her wrists and ankles. "Did you see him?"

"'Twas two men . . . dressed in black . . . wearing masks."

"Were they tall, short, stout? Anything you can re-member will help."

Rubbing her wrists, Mrs. Tippet managed to sit up with Natalie's aid. "It happened so fast, Your Grace. Heard a noise that woke me out of a dead sleep. Soon as I opened my door, they grabbed me. One was big, hulking, foulmouthed. The other was slighter and . . . he talked like a gentleman."

"How long ago was this?" Natalie asked.

"Mayhap half an hour." The woman clutched at the duke's hands. "Where is Master Leo? Is he safe?"

"He's been abducted."

She crumpled in horror. "Oh, my darling boy! I feared they meant him ill. Pray find him, Your Grace!"

Hadrian's face was carved in stone. "I shall. But I must ask you to remain here, lock your door, and don't speak a word of this to anyone. One of the men may still be in the house and I won't have him warned."

As he pivoted on his heel and strode out of the room, Natalie dashed after him. They passed swiftly through the schoolroom and headed toward the stairs. "It's Wymark," she hissed, with sickening certainty. "That must be why he was out in the garden. He seemed nervous, glancing over his shoulder."

"My thoughts precisely. The bastard needs that ransom money. He's deeply in debt from gambling. When we saw him, his accomplice must have just spirited Leo away through the garden gate, probably to a waiting carriage."

Her heart pounding in dread, she imagined the little boy bound and gagged and frightened. She fought off a bone-deep shudder as they raced down two flights of stairs. Heading toward the ballroom, Hadrian stalked along an ornate corridor, and she hastened to keep up with his long strides. "What are we going to do?"

"I intend to find that weasel and choke the truth out of him."

Eyes narrowed, he frowned as he strode straight ahead, his fingers gripped into fists. Wymark had returned to the party, she remembered, likely in an attempt to deflect any suspicion once Leo's absence was discovered. No doubt the viscount would pretend that he'd been in the ballroom all night, so he couldn't possibly be the perpetrator. Then tomorrow he would collect the ransom from the appointed spot in Hyde Park and no one would be the wiser.

Except that things wouldn't go according to his diabolical plan, Natalie thought fiercely. She had been right to distrust him, and she had no intention of staying out of the fray. They would corner him and if Hadrian couldn't make the villain talk, then she would.

The music grew louder as they approached the arched doorway. The large open area outside the ballroom teemed with elegant guests, drinking and chatting. Others strolled in and out of the drawing room that had been set up with tables for cardplaying. The scene had an otherworldly quality to Natalie. How strange that people could be laughing and dancing when Leo had just been snatched from his bed!

She stayed close to Hadrian as he skirted the edge of the throng. Like him, she kept her eyes sharp for a glimpse of Wymark's wheat-gold hair and narrow features. Since he was nowhere in the reception area, they entered the ballroom. The long, spacious chamber wasn't nearly as crowded as earlier, for many guests had repaired to the adjoining parlor to partake of the buffet supper. But there were still a fair amount of people milling around, and Hadrian paused near the wall to scan the horde.

As the masses shifted, she spotted their quarry and leaned closer to murmur in Hadrian's ear, "There, by the balcony doors!"

No sooner had the sentence left her lips than the duke stalked in that direction. Wymark stood with a group of young gentlemen who looked as dissolute as himself. One of them swayed, stumbling into a fern and nearly knocking it over, which made all of them hoot with laughter.

It was then that Wymark looked up and his eyes widened on Hadrian. He stood frozen, apparently noting the grim fury on the duke's face. Abruptly, he spun around and vanished out the open door.

Hadrian muttered a curse and sprang after him, weaving through the clusters of guests, ignoring those who attempted to speak to him. Natalie did likewise, until disaster struck just shy of the exit. Their path was suddenly blocked by none other than the Prince Regent himself, with his retinue of courtiers, several ladies and gentlemen.

"Ah, there you are, Clayton. Do compliment that French chef of yours on the excellent crab fingers, though he might add a little less cream next time. I've the merest touch of dyspepsia, but I find that it improves if I take a little promenade before finishing my meal."

"Pray stroll to your heart's content, sire," Hadrian said smoothly. "Now, if I may beg your pardon, Miss Fanshawe is feeling faint. I must escort her outside at once for a breath of fresh air."

Natalie clutched Hadrian's arm and strove for a weak, swooning look. "Too much excitement, I fear. We're not used to such grand balls in America."

The prince granted permission with a royal wave of his sausage fingers, and she and Hadrian made their escape onto the deserted balcony without further ado. But the delay had cost them. He dashed to the railing to peer down into the large garden. "Bloody hell! He's making for the gate!"

He raced down the stone steps with Natalie close behind him, hampered somewhat by her skirts. She spied a shifting movement in the shadows ahead before the creak of hinges disturbed the night air. "Stay here," the duke ordered over his shoulder before sprinting after the fugitive.

Natalie ignored the directive, lifting her hem to dart down the path. She reached the darkened mews behind the house in time to hear the rattle of wheels and the swift clopping of hooves.

Hadrian came jogging back and passed by her without stopping to speak. She was forced to run alongside him. "Is he gone, then?"

"He's in his phaeton, the one with the yellow wheels. By God, I'll find the bastard if it's the last thing I do."

Twin lanterns marked the wide door of the brick stables, and the duke vaulted ahead of her to vanish into the building. She entered to the familiar smell of hay and horses, to find Hadrian already leading his bay gelding from a stall as a groom scrambled out of the tack room, lugging a saddle. The duke arranged the bridle, slipping the bit into the horse's mouth.

Natalie dashed down the row of stalls to find her chestnut mare. As she reached for the half-door, Hadrian stopped her with a glare. "No! You're staying here. You aren't dressed for riding and it's far too dangerous."

She parted her lips in a retort, then clamped her teeth, recognizing that a quarrel would only slow him down when time was of the essence. While the servant completed the saddling and tightened the cinch, Hadrian disappeared through another door and returned a moment later with a small pistol, which he tucked into his coat. He swung into the saddle, looking incongruously like a pirate in elegant evening clothes.

His fierce gaze bored into her. "I'll find him, Natalie."

Then he flicked the reins and rode out, vanishing into the darkness.

The instant he was gone, she opened the stall door and led out the mare. Blast the man, she would not sit idly while Leo was in grave danger. She could ride as well as Hadrian, and if she'd survived a bloody massacre in the wilderness, then she could face down a weakling like Wymark.

"Nay, miss! His Grace forbade ye!"

She sent her most quelling stare at the young groom. "Fetch a bridle. And be quick about it."

He blinked before vanishing into the tack room to bring the requested halter, which she swiftly placed on the mare. Then she led the horse to the mounting block.

"Yer saddle, miss!"

"There's no time. Have you a knife?"

The groom dug in his pocket and produced a small one in a battered leather sheath. Handing it over with obvious reluctance, he eyed her as if she were a madwoman. And she *was* mad, Natalie knew as she tucked the knife into the bodice of her ballgown. She was mad with fear and fury that anyone would dare to threaten Leo.

Ignoring the gawking groom, she stepped onto the mounting block, hiked up her skirts, and threw her leg over the horse. She'd ridden bareback often as a girl, though only on her father's horse farm and never in the city. If any of the society snoots could see her now, with her silk stockings exposed to mid-thigh, they'd condemn her as an irredeemable hoyden.

They could choke on their rules.

Hadrian could be no more than two minutes ahead of her. She prayed he'd picked up Wymark's trail and they could find Leo. With a determined kick of her gold dancing slippers, she urged the mare into the gloom of the mews and out onto the street.

Richard parked his phaeton in the narrow alley and hoped it wouldn't be stolen. There was no stable behind the derelict house and he hadn't dared to bring one of his father's grooms for fear of having another witness to his crime.

He tied the reins to a broken fence post, his fingers

clumsy from the fright he'd endured. The moment he'd spied Clayton's face, dark with fury, across the ballroom, he'd known with sick certainty that the gig was up. By horrid mischance, the duke had already discovered the boy's abduction.

And he suspected his cousin of the deed.

Richard cursed his rotten luck for having run into the duke and Miss Fanshawe in the garden, right after he and Bert had bundled the squirmy little devil into the coach. At the time, he'd only been relieved that they hadn't noticed the red mark on his forefinger where the bugger had bit him. If all had gone according to plan, Richard would've had an iron-tight alibi simply by staying at the party all night.

But Clayton and Miss Fanshawe had put two and two together with terrifying speed. The fact that the duke had chased after Richard confirmed the awful truth. His only stroke of luck had been making a clean getaway in the phaeton that Bert had left for him in the mews just in case such a quick exit was needed.

Now, he grabbed the mask that he'd tossed under the seat after the abduction. It was merely a precaution, for his nephew ought to be asleep in the upstairs bedchamber.

Then he stepped hastily through the rubbish-strewn back yard. Cutthroats and criminals roamed this district. Hearing a scrabbling noise, he nearly leaped out of his skin. But it was only a rat scuttling through the shadows.

Maybe he oughtn't have run from the ball. Maybe he should've brazened it out. But it was futile to imagine he could withstand Clayton's interrogation. Richard's bowels turned watery at the very thought of his cousin's wrath.

All was not lost, he reminded himself. If the duke

wanted the boy back, he'd have to comply with the directives in the ransom note. Richard had intended to use the ransom to pay back the moneylender, but all that had changed now. With his pockets flush with banknotes, he would hightail it out of town, perhaps hide out in Scotland or Portugal or some other godforsaken place where Clayton couldn't track him. He'd stay away until the heat died down and his mother could smooth things over for him.

The back door opened at a push of his hand. Entering a murky passage that stank of cabbage and other foul odors, he headed toward the glow of light at the front of the house. There, he suffered another shock.

The hulking groom sat at the table playing cards with the boy. Leo's midsection was bound to the chair, leaving his hands free. Bert tilted back his curly black-haired head as he took a long pull on a blue gin bottle, which explained why he hadn't even heard the approach of an intruder.

Richard slapped the black mask over his face and tied it behind his head. "What the devil's going on here?"

Spewing a mouthful of gin, Bert sprang up. He wiped his sleeve across his wet lips. "Wasn't expecting ye till the mornin', milord! Do they already know the lad's gone? Did ye get the blunt early?"

"Don't call me that." *Milord*, for pity's sake! Richard saw no need to have his identity irrefutably confirmed in front of the *enfant terrible*. "And yes, his absence has been noted. But the banks aren't open at this hour."

"Bah," the groom said, sitting back down, his rough features etched with discontent. "The duke must have a heap o' gold in his safe to pay the ransom."

"What's a ransom?" Leo asked.

"Be silent," Richard snapped, tilting his head down to

view his nephew's inquisitive face through the eyeholes of the mask. "It's no concern of yours."

"You look like a robber in that mask, Uncle Wymark. I 'member you almost ran over me with your horse, but Mr. Duke saved me."

Ice shot down Richard's spine. There went his last slim hope of escaping recognition and spinning a tall tale to explain his abrupt departure from the ball. In the unlikely event he was caught, of course.

He tore off the useless mask and flung it away before scowling at the groom. "Why didn't you keep him locked in the bedchamber as I told you?"

Bert shrugged. "The tyke said he weren't sleepy. Don't see how it matters if he's upstairs or down, so long as he's tied up. Besides, it's mighty dull sittin' here alone."

"I was bored, too," Leo piped up. "So Bert is teaching me to play loo."

"Good God!" Richard growled, ignoring the boy. "I'm not paying you to play card games."

"Ain't paid me naught yet, and ye best not cheat me o' my fair share." Bert narrowed his eyes. "Even if the duke refuses to hand over the blunt."

"He won't dare," Richard said, pacing restlessly. "I made it very clear in the note that the boy's life hangs in the balance."

"Mr. Duke will catch you. He'll punch your face." Leo swung a miniature fist in Richard's direction. "Pow!"

Clayton would relish doing that, Richard thought with a lurch. Blister it, he mustn't panic. He just needed a distraction to settle his nerves until he could collect his five thousand. Pulling up a chair, he snapped, "Deal me in."

He reached for the gin bottle, fussily wiping it with his handkerchief before taking a swig. The rotgut burned down his throat and almost made him gag. Despite the liquid courage, however, the memory of his cousin's furious expression continued to plague him.

As a precaution, Richard took out the small pistol from inside his coat and placed it on the table within easy reach. It paid to be careful, though there was really no cause for alarm. None at all.

Clayton couldn't possibly find him here.

Chapter 27

Keeping an eye on Wymark as he parked his vehicle in an alley across the street, Hadrian swung off his mount and kept to the dense shadows beneath a tree. His instincts as to where the viscount would go had proven correct. Not home, where he could be easily caught, but straight to his ticket out of debt. Leo would have been stashed someplace cheap and reasonably close, in a neighborhood where the locals wouldn't blink an eye at strange doings or even kidnapped boys. Since traffic had been relatively light at this late hour, it had taken only a few minutes before Hadrian had spotted the distinctive phaeton with its yellow wheels barreling east along Oxford Street, heading toward the slums of Seven Dials.

He quietly secured the reins to the spindly tree trunk and waited for Natalie to join him. The viscount might be fool enough not to realize when someone was tailing him, but not Hadrian. He'd glimpsed her behind him halfway here. It was hard to miss a lady riding *ventre à terre* with her filmy skirts fluttering in the breeze.

She dismounted a short distance away and walked the horse so as not to alert Wymark. His chest tightened to see her gliding like a slender wraith through moonlight and shadow, her elegant ballgown, elbow-length white gloves, and diamond jewelry looking incongruous against the decrepit brick tenements. As she tied her horse near his, he noted the lack of a saddle.

Despite his tension, he felt a twist of humor. "Bareback?"

"It's how I rode as a girl," she whispered. "Look, Wymark has gone into that house."

"I don't suppose it would do any good to tell you to wait here."

Natalie huffed at that. "Come, we must hurry."

She laced her fingers with his and tugged him across the street. They moved in unison, with stealth and haste, aiming toward the one downstairs window where a light shone through a slit in the curtains. As it turned out, there was more than one slit, the dark fabric being tattered in several places and allowing them both to peek inside at the same time.

Her hand tightened on his. "Leo is tied to a chair," she said in an anguished whisper. "And there's that groom, the one who attacked me in the kitchen at Oak Knoll."

Inside the parlor, Bert and the viscount appeared to be exchanging heated words. "Indeed," Hadrian said tersely.

Shivering, Natalie rubbed her bare upper arms. "They won't hurt Leo, will they?"

"No. Wymark needs that ransom money too badly."

At least he hoped so, Hadrian thought grimly. He shrugged out of his coat and placed it around her shoulders to ward off the chill of the night air. He took up a stance behind her and folded her into his arms, bringing her back firmly against his chest. She settled naturally into his embrace, her gaze still riveted inside the shabby parlor. His attention was, too, though he couldn't deny a peripheral awareness of her shapely form.

They watched as the two men continued to quarrel, Wymark pacing back and forth in an agitated manner before sitting down to play cards with them.

She sucked in a breath. "He has a pistol."

"He's merely placed it on the table," Hadrian said to calm her. "He isn't going to shoot anyone."

"But we have to rescue Leo!"

He soothed her by stroking his fingertips over her silken cheek. "Patience, my dear. The scamp doesn't look frightened, so it would be better to wait for the right opportunity. Let those two buffoons get a little foxed first. It will hamper their ability to fight back." With effort, he forced himself to release her. "While they're busy playing cards, I'll take a quick look around back to find the best way inside. Stay right here, promise me?"

Natalie nodded, her gaze flashing briefly at him in the gloom, reminding him of that riveting moment in the darkness of the nursery and the sound of her soft voice. *I love you, Hadrian. I love you with all my heart and soul.*

The memory made his chest ache. He'd never had the chance to respond to her because a moment later, they'd discovered Leo's abduction. His gut still felt twisted in knots over her stunning declaration. But now was not the time to sort out the tangle of emotions inside him.

Taking an unsteady breath, he left to reconnoiter the perimeter of the house. It proved a somewhat treacherous business not to make any noise since the yard was a glorified rubbish heap. He made his way around back to quietly test the rear door, then returned to do the same to the front.

It was a relief to see Natalie still at her post. He'd been half afraid she would act impetuously, without a care for her own safety. She looked so appealing with his coat draped around her shoulders that he took up his original position behind her, sliding his arms around her again.

"We're in luck," he muttered in her ear, breathing the fragrance of her hair. "The locks on both doors are broken, so entry won't be a problem. The wisest course of action is to separate the two men, so I can take them down one at a time."

"We'll have to create a distraction."

"Precisely. When the time is right, you'll knock on the back door. Bert will go to answer it, but you'll have ducked around the side of the house by then and hidden yourself. Meanwhile, I'll slip through the front, grab Wymark's gun, and subdue him. Then I'll deal with Bert when he returns."

"I'm coming in with you."

"*No,*" he said in a sharp whisper. The very thought shook him to the core. "I don't want you in harm's way."

"Someone will have to free Leo. He could be hurt during a fight."

She had a point about that, but it wrenched him to think of her risking injury. "I'll move him and his chair to the corner of the room."

"You may not have an opportunity. I'm not helpless, Hadrian. Have you forgotten that I killed a man during that massacre?"

His arms tightened on her. For as long as he lived, he would never forget her wild bout of weeping in the kitchen at Oak Knoll, or later in the library, when she'd trembled while relating the violent experience to him. Gruffly, he said, "That's precisely why I don't want you endangering yourself again."

"I can protect myself." She reached into her bodice and withdrew a metallic blade that glittered in the moonlight. "Besides, the least I can do is to cut Leo's bonds."

The sight jolted him. "Where the devil did you get that knife?"

"From your groom," she said, tucking it back into its sheath. "So I'll hear no more about me hiding while our little boy is threatened."

Hadrian was torn between railing at her and admiring her pluck. He settled for rubbing his cheek against her hair while he held her close. He especially liked the way she referred to Leo as theirs, as if they were a family. "All right, then, but take care. I couldn't bear to lose you."

He felt her quiver slightly, but didn't think it had anything to do with the cold night air. She tilted back her head and brushed a tender kiss to his jaw. "Nor I, you."

I love you with all my heart and soul.

How he ached to hear her speak those words again. But he mustn't expect her to repeat them. Not when earlier in his study, he'd been flummoxed by her question. *Do you love me?*

In that moment, he had felt utterly stupefied as if a wall barricaded his emotions even from himself. Everything in him had resisted examining the question. He'd always dismissed love as a soppy sentiment out of the pages of the gothic novels his mother liked to read. In his youth, he'd had only Lord and Lady Godwin's cold union as a model. Love was never anything he'd believed to be important in a marriage.

But now he wondered.

His passion for Natalie burned like an eternal flame. She had the candor, wit, and warmth he'd never known he needed in a wife. She stirred in him a profound yearning that absorbed his dreams both day and night. Without her, his future would be stark, for she possessed him, heart and soul.

He dragged in a shaky breath. By God, he *did* love Natalie. There could be no other explanation for this fierce devotion he felt. The unique nature of his feelings was not mawkish, but rather, a deep sense of certainty that she was his other half, that he could never be complete without her in his life. She deserved to know that. He *wanted* her to know.

Would it be enough to convince her to marry him, though? To give up her life in America? To overcome her distaste for the aristocracy? There was only one way to find out.

Beset by tenderness, he bent closer. "Natalie, I must tell you—"

"Oh no, look! Leo has the pistol!"

For the first time in his misbegotten life, Richard found himself staring down the circular barrel of a gun. He'd never had a taste for the danger and duels that attracted other gentlemen. Now, he sat frozen in his chair, still clutching his cards, while the *enfant terrible* pointed the pistol at him.

How the devil had the boy grabbed it so quickly?

He slid a panicked glance at Bert, who looked bleary-eyed from drink. "Don't just sit there," he hissed, "*do* something. Controlling him is supposed to be *your* job."

"Now, little fella, that ain't a toy." The groom slowly reached out a meaty paw. "Give it over to yer uncle Bertie."

"*He's* my uncle, not you." Leo pointed the loaded pistol from one man to the other. "I want to go home to Miss Fanshawe and Mr. Duke. Right *now*."

"Stop waving that thing around," Richard said, trying to inject command into his voice while ignoring his clenched innards. "You don't know how to use a gun. It could go off by accident!"

"My papa taught me how to shoot when we lived in the woods. I even killed a squirrel once." Leo cocked the pistol. "Bang!"

Gulping, Richard slid down in his chair. At this close range, the boy couldn't miss. The thought made him dizzy, or perhaps that was the effects of the gin. "Rush him, Bert. He's only six. What else am I paying you for?"

"Six or sixty, don't matter. It's still a bullet. Besides, I ain't got even a ha'penny from ye."

"You'll get your blasted money tomorrow—"

A voice spoke from the doorway. "No he won't. Nor will you, Wymark."

Richard leaped up so fast he nearly jumped out of his skin. His cards went flying, and his chair crashed to the floor. He stared in sick disbelief at the Duke of Clayton, who stood eyeing him with a menacing scowl.

He held a pistol that was pointed straight at Richard's heart.

His knees actually knocked together. Unlike that six-year-old demon, Clayton had a reputation as a crack shot. "D-don't shoot!"

"Then don't tempt me, either of you two felons. If, that is, you wish to live long enough to stand before the magistrate."

The magistrate. It struck Richard that he was ruined. Not even his mother could fix this mess, and without her help, he'd never be able to count on his father. Clayton would see to it that Richard was punished for his crime. And if he somehow managed to escape being tossed in a dank prison cell, he'd be shunned from society, barred from all the clubs, abandoned by his friends. Worse, he couldn't repay the moneylender now. Which meant that if he remained in London, he'd be beaten to within an inch of his life.

All bright eyes and smiles, Leo shouted, "Mr. Duke! I knew you'd come!"

"You've been very brave, brat," Clayton said, his face softening briefly. "Now, give the gun to Miss Fanshawe."

Richard had been so focused on the duke that he hadn't even noticed the American. She walked forward, cool as a queen, affording Richard a look of utter contempt. All of his dread and fear and despair coalesced into an intense resentment. How dare she act superior to him. She, the daughter of a bastard! None of this would have happened if she hadn't brought Audrey's whelp here to England.

To add insult to injury, Clayton had hosted a ball tonight to honor Miss Fanshawe, courting *her* instead of Richard's own sister, thereby cheating him out of having a wealthy brother-in-law who might have bailed him out of debt.

Bert lumbered to his feet. "'Twas milord's plan, Yer Grace. I took fine care o' the lad. We just been playin' cards."

When the duke's stern gaze flicked to the traitorous groom, Richard saw his chance. He lunged at Miss Fanshawe just as she approached the boy. He seized the pistol with one hand and her with the other, spinning her around so that her back slammed into his chest.

She uttered a choked gasp and squirmed against his hold. But Richard had a death grip around her middle. Panting, he pressed the barrel of the gun to her throat. "Be still!"

Luckily, she obeyed, only her bosom heaving. His heart was thudding so fast he felt faint. Desperation threatened to cloud his thinking. He reminded himself he had no other choice, and only this one chance to escape.

The duke took a step toward him and stopped. Horror widened his eyes before those gray orbs turned to granite. When he spoke, his voice had a hard, mocking edge. "Using a woman as a shield, Wymark? How brave of you."

"Don't come closer or she's dead."

"And then *you're* dead. I'll break your neck."

At that ferocious vow, Richard imagined the crack of his bones and felt the prickle of cold sweat. For an instant, he considered using the single bullet on himself rather than face his cousin's wrath. His death would be quicker and less painful. But there'd be no need for bloodshed if everyone cooperated.

"Don't hurt Miss Fanshawe," Leo yelled, wiggling against his bonds.

"Hush, darling," she said with surprising calm. "Everything will be fine."

Her composure irked Richard. She'd always acted high-and-mighty, as if she were the equal of him and his family. It also annoyed him that she stood an inch or two taller than himself, an unnatural Amazon of a female. But at least she was slack, making no move to fight him.

If he could just reach his carriage, spring his horse, head for the coast . . .

He backed toward the door, dragging her along with him, his gaze fixed on his cousin's murderous expression. "You're to stay right here, Clayton, while she and I go to my phaeton. Bert, get his pistol."

The groom started around the table. It was then that it happened.

Miss Fanshawe shifted one arm slightly. Richard yelped as something sharp pierced the tender flesh of his groin. *A knife.*

"No," she stated. "*You* give your pistol to Hadrian. Unless, of course, you prefer to be gelded."

Her threat wrested a whimper from him. God only knew what tricks she'd learned from living in the wilds of America. He slowly lowered the gun and then stood paralyzed, his attention fixated on the proximity of the blade to his privates. "Do have a care!" he choked out.

The next moment happened in a blur. As Clayton took a step forward to collect the weapon, Bert made a dive for the duke. Clayton spun toward him. A gunshot split the air, and the groom crashed to the floor with a loud thump. He lay there, moaning, clutching his leg, blood staining his thigh.

Horror-struck, Richard surrendered his own pistol to Clayton. His limp fingers had lost the strength to grasp it, anyway. "The knife, Miss Fanshawe! Do remove it at once!"

The duke removed Richard instead, pulling him away from her with an ungentle yank. The brutal fury on his face curdled Richard's blood. "I wouldn't have hurt her—or the boy, I swear it! It was my blasted debts . . . I'm sorry!"

"Sometimes being sorry just isn't enough."

Clayton's fist flashed out and struck Richard's jaw. The force of the blow jerked his head back and propelled him into the wall. Fiery pain splintered his skull, a torment so excruciating that he lost the ability to hold himself upright. He crumpled into a groaning heap on the floor, his mind dazed to all but the throbbing agony in his head.

He lay there in a half-faint, sensing movement around him but unable to comprehend what was happening until he felt someone staring at him. He cracked open his watery eyes and struggled to focus.

The *enfant terrible* stood gazing down at him with unholy interest. "Miss Fanshawe, what does *gelded* mean?"

The memory of that singular horror sent Richard into a full swoon, and he sank into oblivion without even hearing her reply.

Chapter 28

She was dreaming of Hadrian.

His tantalizing caress stirred tingles over the bare skin of her arm and up to her neck, traced the shape of her ear and then lightly stroked her face. Purring, she snuggled her cheek into his palm, her hips moving restlessly as heat began to pulse in her depths. A tender fingertip outlined her lips, then the brush of his mouth against hers took on a curious note of reality.

Enticed from the mists of slumber, Natalie lifted her lashes to see the duke gazing down at her with the crooked half-smile that always melted her heart. She watched him in happy bemusement, too absorbed by his beloved features to question his presence in her bedchamber. Then she blinked up at the blue-and-gold bed hangings and the events of the night came rushing back.

This was not her chamber, but his.

After putting Leo to bed, she had come here to wait for Hadrian. He had been closeted in his study with Lord Godwin and Wymark, and she had been anxious to hear the outcome of that meeting.

She sat up, attempting to straighten the wrinkled bronze silk of her ballgown. Her diamond jewelry lay in a heap on the bedside table beside a guttering candle. "Heavens, I just put my head on the pillow for a moment. I didn't intend to fall asleep. I hope I didn't startle you."

"Not in the least. Chumley warned me there was a hoyden in my bedchamber who'd had the cheek to banish him from the room."

The twinkle in his eyes made Natalie blush. "Well, it was three in the morning and he was snoozing on a stool in the dressing room, awaiting your return. So I sent him off to bed."

"Hm. I found him snoozing on a bench outside my study. Amazingly, he didn't even grumble once he saw how pleased I was to learn you were here. I do believe the crusty old fellow is beginning to like you."

But it was only Hadrian's feelings that mattered to her at the moment. In particular, his reaction to her confession of love the previous evening. *My darling, I can't begin to tell you what that means to me . . .*

His husky response had been cut short by their discovery of the kidnapping. What had he intended to say? Would he now try to coax her into marriage without opening his own heart and soul? Would she allow him?

As if sensing her emotional muddle, he stepped back to allow her space. She scooted off the bed and stood up, feeling unsettled by the heat of his gaze. He had discarded his cravat and coat, and his hair was attractively tousled. She ached with the need for him to sweep her into his arms. But though he radiated a banked desire, he seemed disinclined to act on it.

"It's nearly dawn," he said. "I thought you might appreciate a small repast since we missed supper last night, so I raided the kitchen. Come and eat and I'll tell you how things went with Godwin."

With gentlemanly courtesy, he took her arm and led her to the hearth, settling her into one of the overstuffed chairs. On a nearby table sat a silver tray heaped with pastries and other leftovers from the ball. As he poured her a steaming cup of tea, adding the perfect trickle of cream, Natalie had a lovely vision of them as an old married couple, sitting down for a cozy chat.

The fantasy vanished under the realization of just how ravenous she was. She filled a plate with goodies, tucked her stocking feet underneath her, and nibbled to her heart's content while Hadrian took the fire iron and stirred the glowing coals into a blaze.

Watching him, she marveled at his strength and fortitude. If not for his quick action, they wouldn't have found Leo. She shuddered to think the little boy might still be in Wymark's clutches, perhaps punished for having dared to pick up that pistol.

While she'd cut Leo loose from his bonds, Hadrian had warned Bert that the watch would be dispatched to arrest him. Then he had loaded the unconscious viscount in the back of his phaeton, tied his own horse behind it, and driven back to Clayton House, while she had ridden alongside.

Leo had been excited to sit with Mr. Duke, but began to yawn hugely as they'd reached Mayfair. Since music drifted from the ballroom, they had entered through a back door, she to take Leo upstairs to the nursery, and Hadrian to summon Lord and Lady Godwin to his study.

That was the last she'd seen of him until a few moments ago.

As he sat down opposite her with his own plate of food, she said, "After that awful event, it seemed strange that there were still guests in the ballroom when we returned. I'm glad the duchess had the prescience to concoct a story about me having suffered a sprained ankle and you refusing to leave my side."

"That'll cause a little stir in itself, but not so great a

scandal as what she presumed we were busy doing." He flashed a wicked smile over his cup of tea. It almost made Natalie forget about the delicious peach compote on her spoon. He went on, "Did the brat fuss about going to bed?"

"Leo was asleep before his head hit the pillow, though he did give me a very tight hug first. He also told me that he does *not* wish to be a criminal when he grows up."

Hadrian chuckled. "Proving the old adage that experience is the best teacher."

"A pity Wymark never learned that lesson." Troubled, she put her plate on the table. "What will happen to him?"

All humor vanished from the duke's face. "Godwin was furious, of course. He blames himself for being too soft on his son. Lady Godwin tried to make excuses, but even she was shocked into silence when Wymark confessed everything. To cover his gambling debts, he'd borrowed a large sum from an unscrupulous moneylender, and with the repayment looming, he plotted Leo's abduction as a means to extort the funds from me. I made it clear that I was prepared to hand him over to the magistrate at Bow Street."

"But you didn't?"

"Godwin and I agreed that it will be sufficient punishment to banish Wymark to Canada for the next ten years, to oversee the earl's timber and mining properties."

"Canada! That hardly seems much of a punishment."

"Perhaps not to a fellow inhabitant of North America, but he'll be separated from the temptations of London, and who knows? Perhaps this time, it will be the making of him." Hadrian's gaze intensified on her. "Besides, I don't care to be involved in the scandal of a lurid court case at this particular time."

Her heart lurched at that steady stare. She saw the heat

of passion, of course, but something else as well, something profound and spellbinding. Yet despite her penchant to face life head-on, she felt nervous to hear what he might say about their future. If he didn't love her, then she must leave England—forever.

How strange to think that just a few weeks ago, she had been eager to return to America. Now, it seemed a bleak and colorless prospect to live her life without him.

Setting aside his plate, Hadrian leaned forward in his chair. His lips firmed with a hint of discomfiture. "I owe you an apology, Natalie. It was my fault that Wymark held that gun to you. I oughtn't have taken my eyes off him, not even for a second."

"You couldn't have guessed what he would do. Besides, all's well that ends well."

"Thanks to your quick skill with a knife." He gave a cringing chuckle. "I must say, what you did is every man's worst nightmare."

"What I *threatened* to do," she corrected. "One can only imagine Lord Godwin's fury had I actually gelded his heir and denied him a future grandson to continue the male lineage. The nobility cherishes bloodlines and dynasties."

Hadrian eyed her pensively for a moment before arising from his chair to come down on one knee in front of her. Taking her hand in his, he held on tightly. "I know you dislike our class system, Natalie, and the dukedom I inherited as my birthright. But I hope you can come to appreciate that it's a valuable component of England's social order. Hundreds of workers depend on me, servants and tenant farmers and shepherds—even all citizens, considering my lawmaking duties in the House of Lords." He brought her hand to his lips and tenderly kissed the back. "I can't change that. Yet, if it were possible, I would abdicate my position for you."

Stunned, she could only gaze at him in wondering silence. His unwavering stare attested to the sincerity of his words. He would give up everything, his wealth and status, his very uniqueness—for *her*?

She hardly dared to hope what it might reveal about his feelings for her. He still clasped her fingers, and she put her hand over his. "I would never expect you to do such a thing, Hadrian. The dukedom is an essential part of who you are. Your rank and your background have shaped you into a fine, admirable man."

His mouth twisted wryly as he glanced away. "Yes, the rigid upbringing that taught me to hide my emotions behind a wall of cool hauteur. At least *that* is something I can change."

When he returned his gaze to her, she was touched by the vulnerability on his strong features. Out of necessity, he had learned at a young age to steel himself against the pain of affection after he'd been torn from the arms of his mother and placed under the tutelage of a cold guardian.

Now, he looked hesitant and uncomfortable, but she was pleased to provide a little gentle prodding. "And?"

He drew a ragged breath. "And . . . I love you, Natalie. With all my heart and soul. And with everything that I am."

Her heartbeat quickened as she absorbed the words she'd so yearned to hear. In his warm gray eyes, she saw a naked love and longing that matched her own. Could it really be true? *Yes.*

"Oh, Hadrian, I love you, too. With everything that *I* am."

Joy propelled her up from the chair and into his arms. Their mouths merged in a kiss of fire and fervor, as a wild hunger consumed them both. His touch, his ardor, made her feel as if she were drowning in a sea of happiness.

Mutual passion brought them down onto the plush carpet in front of the hearth, where she lay draped over him, reveling in the strength of his hard, muscled body. It seemed a lifetime that she had craved him like this, needing to know that he belonged to her alone, and she to him.

In a frenzy of lost buttons and torn fabric, their clothing vanished until they lay tangled together, skin to skin. Despite her glowing memory of the one time they had made love, she quickly realized that the bond between them had created a vast capacity for pleasure beyond her wildest dreams. Fire and tenderness and exultation transported them upward, and in the glorious heat of the moment, it seemed they were one flesh, one body.

Yet nothing brought her greater bliss than his whispered words of love.

In the aftermath, as they lay sated in each other's arms beside the fire, Natalie smiled to remember how much she had resisted the notion of falling for an English duke. It seemed they both had needed to learn that love was the most precious gift of all—and that all else in life paled by comparison.

Rubbing her cheek against his raspy jaw, she murmured, "Now, it wasn't so terribly difficult to admit your feelings, was it?"

"Had I known this to be the reward, I'd have analyzed my heart much sooner." His eyes gleaming, he let his hands glide appreciatively down her silken curves to cup her bottom. "To be honest, I fell hard for you from the very start, but I was so scornful of love that I failed to recognize it in myself."

"Perhaps saying *I love you* is a bit like curtsying. It's difficult the first time, but if you can manage to do it once, then it becomes easier."

"No curtsying," he said, his grip tightening on her.

"You are the equal of any noble. I won't have you acting against your principles."

Meekly, she said, "Yes, Your Grace."

"Minx." He leaned over to drop kisses on her face, culminating in a long, deep, tender one on her lips that stirred flames from the embers of passion. In a husky whisper, he added, "Why are we lolling on the floor when there's a perfectly comfortable bed over there?"

She laughed from sheer exuberance. "Perhaps because you're far more rakish than the haughty stick-in-the-mud duke that people believe you to be."

Hadrian waggled a dark eyebrow. "I intend for you to be the only woman who is privy to that secret."

He stood up in all his naked, powerful splendor and scooped her into his arms. She clung to his neck, her mouth nuzzling his throat and tasting his salty skin, as he gently placed her against the pillows. It was the love-liest notion to think that she was his one and only, for-saking all others.

Sliding beneath the covers, he gathered her close and pressed a kiss to her tumbled hair. "I want you to be happy here in England, Natalie. You may open a school, care for as many orphans and urchins as you like. Only think how much more you can do with the proper funding."

She gave him a droll look. "Between your mother and me, you'll end up beggared."

"Then so be it. And perhaps we can spend our hon-eymoon in America so that you can show me the coun-try that you love." He drew back to look deeply into her eyes. "But I'm getting ahead of myself again, aren't I? You *will* marry me, won't you?"

His unguarded look held an anxiety that plumbed the depths of her tender heart, and from those depths arose a smile of pure happiness. "Yes! Of course I will. But are *you* sure, Hadrian? I'll be the most unlikely duchess in all of England."

His handsome face eased into an expression of warm satisfaction and wicked promise. "You'll be the perfect duchess. *My* duchess. And I intend to show you how very much I love you every day for the rest of our lives."

As he made good on his promise, his hands exploring her body with breathtaking skill, she arched against him, deciding that nothing in all the world could be better than forever with a duke.

Don't miss the next book in the
Unlikely Duchesses series
by **Olivia Drake**

WHEN A DUKE LOVES A GOVERNESS

Coming in Winter 2021